Celebrate the legend that is

PENNY JORDAN

Phenomenally successful author of more than 200 books with sales of over 100 million copies!

Penny Jordan's novels are read and loved by millions of readers all around the word in many different languages. This beautiful collection of six volumes offers a chance to recapture the pleasure of a special selection of her fabulous stories.

As a special treat, each volume also includes an introductory letter by a different author. Some of the most popular names in romantic fiction share their personal thoughts and memories, which we hope you will enjoy.

Desert nights

This sizzling collection of Penny Jordan favourites features the renowned author's first book for Mills & Boon and showcases the intense, passionate heroes she loved to create.

D1081495

Mills & Boon® proudly presents
a very special tribute

PENNY
JORDAN
COLLECTION

DESERT NIGHTS
Available in August 2012

WEDDING NIGHTS
Available in September 2012

MEDITERRANEAN NIGHTS
Available in October 2012

CHRISTMAS NIGHTS
Available in November 2012

PASSIONATE NIGHTS
Available in December 2012

SINFUL NIGHTS
Available in January 2013

PENNY JORDAN
COLLECTION

Desert nights

Published in Great Britain 2012
Mills & Boon, an imprint of Harlequin (UK) Limited,
Eton House, 18-24 Paradise Road, Richmond, Surrey TW9 1SR

DESERT NIGHTS © Harlequin Enterprises II B.V./S.à.r.l. 2012

Falcon's Prey © Penny Jordan 1981
The Sheikh's Virgin Bride © Penny Jordan 2003
One Night with the Sheikh © Penny Jordan 2003

ISBN: 978 0 263 90208 2

027-0812

Printed and bound
by CPI Group (UK) Ltd, Croydon, CR0 4YY

Dear Reader,

Falcon's Prey was Penny's first novel published by Mills & Boon and she was always rather proud of it. It's easy to see why. The story contains all the essential elements which were to become trademark Jordan. The ordinary heroine in the shabby coat. The powerful male who intimidates everyone around him until he falls hopelessly in love with that very ordinary girl.

Picking up the book today, it's astonishing to find that it's just as fresh as when it first came out in 1981. Immediately, the reader is swept up in the story and carried away by it. Penny had that knack of portraying emotion so openly and so honestly that it's easy to feel instant identification with the heroine. And, of course—to fall in love with the hero! She went on to create this incredible alchemy with every single one of her books—two more of which are also included in this sizzling volume.

So many things have been written since Penny's untimely death. Words like "legendary" and "glamorous" have peppered her eulogies—both true (and how she might have smiled to hear them!). Many people have pointed out what a fantastic mentor she became to new writers, and what a consummate professional she was. Again, true.

But I shall remember Penny as an animal-mad friend who lived for her writing. Who was as passionate about her hundredth-plus novel as she was about her first. Who poured everything she had into her current story and then found that extra something to pour in a little bit more. That's the 'secret' behind a really great writer.

I hope you enjoy reading this as much as millions of others have done.

With warmest wishes,

Sharon Kendrick

Penny Jordan is one of Mills & Boon's most popular authors. Sadly Penny died from cancer on 31st December 2011, aged sixty-five. She leaves an outstanding legacy, having sold over a hundred million books around the world. She wrote a total of a hundred and eighty-seven novels for Mills & Boon, including the phenomenally successful *A Perfect Family*, *To Love, Honour & Betray*, *The Perfect Sinner* and *Power Play*, which hit the *Sunday Times* and *New York Times* bestseller lists. Loved for her distinctive voice, her success was in part because she continually broke boundaries and evolved her writing to keep up with readers' changing tastes. *Publishers Weekly* said about Jordan: 'Women everywhere will find pieces of themselves in Jordan's characters' and this perhaps explains her enduring appeal.

Although Penny was born in Preston, Lancashire, and spent her childhood there, she moved to Cheshire as a teenager and continued to live there for the rest of her life. Following the death of her husband she moved to the small traditional Cheshire market town on which she based her much-loved Crighton books.

Penny was a member and supporter of the Romantic Novelists' Association and the Romance Writers of America—two organisations dedicated to providing support for both published and yet-to-be published authors. Her significant contribution to women's fiction was recognised in 2011, when the Romantic Novelists' Association presented Penny with a Lifetime Achievement Award.

Falcon's Prey

PENNY JORDAN

CHAPTER ONE

THE restaurant was well known and expensive, and Felicia had to pretend to be unaware of the waiter's contemptuous appraisal of her shabby coat as she hurriedly surveyed the occupants of the tables.

Her spirits lifted when she saw Faisal, and the waiter, plainly reviewing his opinion of her when he saw with whom she was to dine, cleared a path for her with an alacrity which she secretly found amusing. It spoke volumes for the power of money, she reflected, as Faisal pushed back his chair and stood up, an appreciative smile lighting his handsome features.

'I'm sorry I'm so late,' she apologised as they sat down. 'I was late leaving the office.'

'The office! Zut! Have I not told you before to give up this worthless job?' Faisal demanded with an arrogance that slightly dismayed her.

An attractive girl, with auburn hair that curled on to her shoulders and sombre green eyes that hinted at a natural reserve, Felicia was unaware of the assessing glances of some of the other diners. Although her neat ribbed sweater and toning tweed skirt instantly placed her apart from the elegant creatures in silks and furs who sat at the other tables, she had a lissom grace which automatically drew the male eye.

That Faisal was aware of this was obvious from the jealous looks he gave these other men who dared to look upon his Felicia; but Felicia herself was completely unaware of the slight stir caused by her entrance.

She had known the young Kuwaiti for just six breathless weeks. A mutual interest in photography had led to their initial meeting at night school classes and one or two casual dates had grown into regular thrice weekly meetings, and more latterly dates most nights of the week as Faisal grew increasingly possessive.

With Faisal's insistence that he take her out to lunch most days of the week, and dates nearly every night as well, it had proved impossible to keep their romance a secret from the other girls in her office. At first they had teased her unmercifully, until they realised that the affair was becoming serious. Then their lighthearted teasing had turned to warnings of a more serious nature as they repeated direful tales of what could happen to European girls foolish enough to take the promises of rich males too seriously. Felicia kept her own counsel. She was sure that Faisal respected her too much to hurt her in the way that they were suggesting, but even so, she had been surprised and then flattered when he began to talk about marriage.

During these talks he had told her a good deal about his family, just as she had told him about her parents, dying so young and so tragically when she was little more than a baby, and leaving her to be brought up by Aunt Ellen and Uncle George in their bleak granite house on the Lancashire moors.

Her childhood had not been a happy one. Uncle George had been a strict and unbending guardian, whose constant rejection had built up in her a lack of self-confidence coupled with the feeling that in failing to gain his love she had somehow failed as a human being. Consequently, in the warmth of Faisal's readily expressed adoration she had begun to bloom like a plant brought out of the frost into a tropical conservatory.

Faisal's stories of his own childhood enchanted her, and she often reflected upon how fortunate he had been to be brought up surrounded by the love of his mother and sisters. If only she too might have been part of such a happy family!

She readily admitted that Faisal had swept her off her feet. They had not known one another nearly long enough, she protested when he talked beguilingly of marriage, but Faisal swept aside her protests. They were made for one another. How could she deny it? How could she, when he wrapped her in the protective warmth of his love? She had said nothing of this to the girls at work. Faisal merely wanted her as a playmate to while away his time in London before returning home to make a 'good' marriage, arranged by his family, they warned her, but Felicia knew that this was not so.

She and Faisal were not lovers. He had been at first reproachful, and then approving of her refusal to give in to his pleas that she spend her nights with him as well as her days.

Her refusal had nothing to do with being prudish, or a calculated holding out for something more permanent than an affair. The truth was that Felicia was half frightened of such as yet unknown intimacies. In her teenage years Uncle

George had been far too strict to permit her to indulge in the usual sexual experimentation of her peers, and as she had grown older she had developed a fastidious hesitancy about committing herself to any purely physical relationship. The first time Faisal had kissed her, he had been gentle, and almost reverent. But more lately, as his desire for her increased, Felicia had to confess to a feeling of nervous, spiralling alarm. And yet what was there to be afraid of? she chided herself. Faisal loved her. He had said so on many, many occasions, and she had agreed to be his wife. At first she had been anxious in case her inexperience made him turn to another, more willing girl, but to her surprise he seemed to approve of her hesitancy, even while he railed against it.

'It will be different once we are married,' he had soothed one evening when his emotions had threatened to get out of control, and Felicia had moaned a small protest at the passion of his kiss, but she had been comforted by his words. Even now she could hardly believe that someone actually loved *her*. After all, she reflected humbly, there was nothing special about her; thousands of girls had creamy skin and red-gold hair; and thousands more had slender, elegant bodies; she was nothing out of the ordinary.

Faisal told her that she was far too modest. He told her that her eyes were as green as an oasis after rain, and her hair the colour of molten sand as the dying rays of the sun scorched it. He likened her body to the movement of a falcon in flight, and told her that with her milk-white skin and soft, vulnerable mouth she was his heart's delight.

Already, despite her protests, he had bought her a ring—

a flashing emerald to match her eyes, and so patently valuable that when she saw it Felicia had caught her breath in dismay.

Ten days ago Faisal had written to his family in Kuwait telling them of his intentions. Over the weeks Felicia had heard a good deal about Faisal's family—his mother and two sisters, the life they led, but most of all Faisal had talked about his uncle, who, upon the death of Faisal's father, had become the head of their household. Although it was never said directly, Felicia sensed that there existed a certain amount of constraint between Faisal and his uncle, and guessed that the older man did not always approve of the actions of the younger.

Felicia already knew that through his mother and uncle, Faisal was related to the ruling family of Kuwait and that this uncle had done much for the bereaved family, even to the extent of taking them into his own home and undertaking all the responsibility for the education of Faisal and his sisters.

The tribe to which Faisal belonged had come originally from the desert; fierce, proud warriors with a long history of tribal warfare and bloodshed. As recently as the lifetime of Faisal's great-grandfather the tribes had waged war upon one another, and Faisal had confided to Felicia that his uncle's grandmother had been an English girl, plucked from the desert by a hawk-eyed chieftain whose prompt action had probably saved her life. She was the daughter of an explorer, Faisal went on to explain, and as a reward for his timely rescue the desert chieftain had claimed the hand of his pale-skinned hostage in marriage.

Privately Felicia thought the story unbelievably romantic. She had longed to ask Faisal more about the couple, and found it vaguely comforting to know that there was already English blood running through the veins of the family into which she would be marrying.

Nowadays Faisal's family no longer roamed the desert, for Faisal's maternal grandfather had founded a merchant bank at the time that oil was first discovered in Kuwait, and now that bank had offices in New York and London, ruling a financial empire so vast and complex that Felicia's head spun whenever Faisal tried to explain its workings to her. As he had also told her, and not without a hint of annoyance, this empire was directly controlled by his uncle, who was the majority shareholder, and who, therefore, had the power to manipulate Faisal, as an employee, very much like a pawn on a chessboard.

That Faisal should find this irksome, Felicia could well understand. She too had suffered from the dictatorial attitude of an unkind guardian. However, some of Faisal's sulky observances concerning his uncle she was inclined to take with a pinch of salt. Faisal was an extremely wealthy young man, by anyone's standards, kept short of nothing that would make his life more comfortable, and if his uncle was insisting that he learn the ropes of their business from the bottom upwards, so to speak, wasn't this, in the long run, a sensible method of preparing him for the responsibility which would one day be his?

However, today Faisal seemed more inclined than usual to complain about his uncle, and sudden uneasy intuition made Felicia ask anxiously:

'Have you heard something from Kuwait, Faisal?'

His dark eyes flashed angrily, reminding her for a moment how very young he was—barely twelve months older than her.

'My uncle thinks we should wait before announcing our engagement,' he admitted at last. 'He is doing this deliberately. He does not want me to be happy.'

'But we have only known one another a short time,' Felicia soothed. 'And it's not as though your family know me at all. Naturally they must be anxious.' She broke off to stare at Faisal, wondering what had changed his anger suddenly to excitement. 'What have I said?' she asked in bewilderment.

'It is nothing—just that you voiced Uncle Raschid's own doubts. You have never met my family and because of this he would have us delay our engagement, but I have thought of a way to outwit him, my Felicia, and force him to admit that he is wrong when he says that East and West cannot live in harmony. In his letter my uncle suggests that you might go to Kuwait to see for yourself how we live. Oh, I know what is behind his invitation,' he added, before Felicia could speak. 'He thinks that you will refuse—that you are as those other girls who flock around rich men like vultures to meat—but we shall prove him wrong, you and I. Once we are married there will be no need for us to spend much time in Kuwait, and Raschid knows this. Still he insists that you must accustom yourself to our ways. I know what is behind his thinking, but it will not work. Tell me you will go to Kuwait, Felicia, and prove him wrong in his assessment of you.'

Felicia was taken completely off guard. Whatever reaction she had expected from Faisal's family it was not this! It was becoming increasingly plain that Faisal's uncle did not want him to marry her. But why not? Didn't he consider her as worthy of Faisal as a Kuwaiti girl? The thought sparked off instant anger and her chin lifted proudly. If Faisal wanted her to go to Kuwait with him to prove to this uncle just how wrong he was, then she would.

'When are we to go?' she asked determinedly, dismayed when Faisal flushed slightly.

'I cannot go, Felicia,' he muttered. 'Uncle Raschid has given orders that I am to start work at the New York office in a week's time.'

Felicia could barely take it in. 'A week? But....'

'Raschid is determined to part us,' Faisal announced bitterly. 'He knows I cannot ignore his command. Despite the fact that he is my uncle, I am only an employee until I get my shares—but that is not until I am twenty-five, another three years.'

'I could come to New York with you,' Felicia said eagerly, trying to find a way round Raschid's edict. 'I could get a job, I....'

Faisal shook his head regretfully.

'It is not that simple, my lovely one. To get a job you would need a visa, which would not be easily forthcoming. Of course you could simply accompany me, but then Raschid will claim that you are my mistress, and my mother and sisters could then never acknowledge you. No...' he said bleakly, 'the only way is for you to convince Raschid that he is wrong, that you are not what he thinks you.' He grasped her hands, his eyes pleading, and Felicia felt her anger melting. 'Promise me you will go...for the sake of our future together. My mother will make you truly welcome, and Raschid will be forced to acknowledge his error.'

Unable to deny how pleasurable this prospect was, Felicia still frowned a little. Kuwait—a civilisation away.

And yet if she refused... She would go! She would show Faisal's uncle that English girls could be just as chaste as those of his own race. She would show him just how worthy of Faisal's love she was! He was Uncle George all over again, she thought resentfully, rejecting her, casting her aside as though she were some sort of inferior being. Well, she would show him!

The rest of the meal passed in a daze for Felicia. A thousand questions clamoured for answers.

Not for one moment did she believe that Faisal's uncle cared about her accustoming herself to their ways—no, he merely wanted to prove to her how unsuitable she was to be Faisal's bride. Faisal himself had practically admitted as much. 'Raschid will never expect you to accept his invitation,' he said with a good deal of satisfaction, when Felicia conveyed her decision to him.

Invitation! Command, more like, Felicia thought wrathfully. A command to present herself for inspection and rejection. Well, for Faisal's sake she would 'present' herself, but not for one moment was Faisal's lordly uncle going to be allowed to think that he could pass judgement on her!

'Come back with me to my apartment,' Faisal begged her when they had finished eating. 'There is much I must tell you about my family and our ways....'

Normally Felicia avoided being too much alone with Faisal, but tonight she did not demur, and in the taxi she plagued him with questions about his country.

'Shall I have to wear a veil or go into purdah?' she asked him anxiously.

Faisal shook his head.

'Of course not. The older generation still adhere to those

ways, but nowadays our girls are well educated, part of the equalization that has swept our country. Your will love Kuwait, Felicia, as I do myself. Although I must confess that I also love London, for different reasons….'

The sudden passion she saw flaring in his eyes made Felicia glad that the taxi had stopped. Faisal had an apartment in an expensive and exclusive Mayfair block, furnished with a modern décor of stark white walls and carpets, with plushy hide chesterfields in dark leather and a quantity of glass coffee tables and matching display shelves. She admired the apartment, but found it too palatial and immaculate; too impersonal in its stark elegance.

Faisal's manservant greeted them, offering Felicia coffee which she refused, watching Faisal while he put on some music. The haunting and evocative sound of Felicia's favorite song swept the room; Faisal pressed a button, instantly dimming the lights, the heavy off-white curtains shutting out their aerial view of London.

As he took her in his arms, Felicia felt herself stiffen slightly. Why couldn't she relax? she chided herself. Faisal meant her no harm. He was, after all, the man she was going to marry. What was the matter with her? Why could she not abandon herself to the passion she had heard other girls discussing so frankly?

'What is wrong?' Faisal whispered, unconsciously reiterating her own thoughts. 'You stiffen and tremble at my touch like a dove in the talons of a hawk,' he told her indulgently. 'When we are parted, I shall dream of the moment when I lift the gold necklace from your bridal caftan and unfasten the one hundred and one buttons, to discover the one thousand and one beauties of your body.

Do not worry,' he assured her confidently, 'your reluctance is as it should be. You are as chaste as the milk-white doves my mother keeps in her courtyard, and soon my uncle shall know that for himself.'

There was a certain element of satisfaction in his words, but Felicia could not help trembling a little with fear. Faisal seemed so confident that once they were married she would respond with passion to his lovemaking, but what if this should not be so? What if she was incapable of passion? Although her heart thrilled to his words of love, her body felt only nervous fear. Faisal's desire for her was increased by his knowledge that she had had no other lover, she knew that. But what if this had not been so? Did he love her, or her chastity? She banished the thought as unworthy. This was undoubtedly an after-effect of Faisal's disclosure concerning his uncle. It was only natural that Faisal should place greater importance on purity in his bride than her own countrymen, it was part and parcel of his upbringing. And yet this admission served only to stir fresh doubts.

'It is just as well that I am not rich enough to support more than one wife,' Faisal murmured with a small smile in his voice, 'for with you in my arms I could want no other, Felicia.'

It was this knowledge to which she must cling in the weeks ahead, Felicia reminded herself—not her own lack of reaction to Faisal's lovemaking. It was only her inexperience that made her doubt her capacity for response. However, his remark about the four wives permitted to men of the Moslem faith had also disturbed her. It came as a shock to remember that he came from a vastly different culture from her own; a culture that permitted a man more than one wife as long as he was able to maintain them all in equal comfort; a culture that made no pretence of being anything other than male-orientated, and yet the Arab women she had seen were always so serene, Felicia acknowledged, so candidly appealing; so protected from all the unpleasantness of life by their male relatives. There was the other side to the coin, though; harsh punishments for those women who went against the rulings of the Koran, or so Felicia had read, and she could not in all honesty picture herself as merely a dutiful plaything, living only through her husband.

All at once the task ahead loomed ominously. If only Faisal could accompany her to Kuwait, to ease those first uncomfortable and uncertain days when she was still a stranger to his family. How subtle his uncle had been, suggesting this visit; more subtle than she had at first realised. Although Faisal was a comparatively wealthy young man, as he had told her, the bulk of his inheritance was tied up in the family merchant banking empire, held in trust for Faisal by his uncle until his twenty-fifth birthday. Until that time Faisal was virtually dependent upon his uncle both for employment and finance. Discarding the disloyal thought that Faisal could have got round his uncle's edict simply by finding a job in England as totally impractical, Felicia acknowledged uneasily that at present it appeared that Faisal's uncle had the upper hand.

Here she was, virtually committed to journeying alone to a strange country, forced to court the approval of a man who, she was sure, was deliberately trying to force her to show herself in a bad light, and would probably never approve of their marriage.

'Are you sure your mother will like me, Faisal?' she asked in a small uncertain voice.

'She will love you as I do,' he promised 'It will not be so bad, you will see. I am to spend two months in New York, and then we shall be together again. Then we shall make plans for our wedding. Perhaps it is as well that you will be with my family. That way no other man can cast covetous eyes upon you. You are mine, Felicia,' he told her arrogantly, unobservant of the faint shadows lingering in her eyes.

Faisal drove her back to her flat himself in the car he kept parked in the underground car-park provided for the use of the apartment tenants. It was an opulent Mercedes with cream leather upholstery and every refinement known to technological man, from a hidden cocktail cabinet to a GPS system.

Privately Felicia considered that Faisal drove too fast, but on the one occasion she had mentioned this to him he had looked so angry that she had not done so again.

'As you are a guest of my family, it is only right that we should pay all your expenses,' he told her when he stopped the car outside the small and rather shabby bedsit that had been her home since she first came to London.

Felicia protested, unwilling for Faisal's family to think of her as being financially grasping and reminding him that the knowledge that she had not paid for her own ticket would surely influence his uncle against her.

'He will not know,' he assured her carelessly, 'and besides, you will need some new clothes, more suitable for our climate.'

It struck Felicia that perhaps he feared that she would shame him with her small wardrobe, for she was aware of the importance his family placed upon outward show, and so, unwillingly, she allowed him to persuade her to accept the gift of her ticket and save her money for what he termed 'necessary expenditure'.

The days flew past, with her seeing Faisal every evening. She wanted to learn as much about the country she was going to as she could, and often by the time Faisal took her home her brain was a confused jumble of facts and figures.

Even so, she could not help but admire the tireless energy of the Kuwait Government when she learned just how much had been achieved in such a very short span of time.

Even allowing for the fact that the country's vast oil revenues had made many types of technological advancement possible, the swift rebuilding after the war left her breathless.

Naturally Faisal was proud of his country's progress, the more so because his own family had had a large part in it. It was with great sincerity that he told Felicia of their democratic form of government, with the Head of State chosen from amongst the descendants of Sheikh Mubarak al Sabah, who had ruled the country from 1896 to 1915, and was, even now, referred to simply as 'Al Kebir'—The Great.

Although Faisal deliberately played the relationship down, Felicia was a little dismayed to learn that his family were distantly connected to the ruling house. Faisal assured her that she must not let this overwhelm her, but she was beginning to see why his uncle Raschid might not approve of Faisal's choice of bride.

Naturally, she was fascinated by this glimpse into another world—albeit a very rich and exotic one; however, whenever she tried to voice her doubts as to her ability to cope with so many changes, Faisal merely laughed, telling her that his family would adore her.

'Even Raschid will be impressed by your beauty. You have the colouring of his grandmother,' he told her, eyeing her speculatively. 'You will surprise him with your innocence and modesty.'

Felicia could only pray that this was indeed so, pressing Faisal to tell her a little more about his own background.

Nothing loath, he described to her the modern town of Kuwait, which had now taken the place of the old mud-brick port. His family had extensive financial interests in the city—their bank had helped finance the erection of a modern hotel in which they held a controlling interest, and there were other buildings, office blocks, apartments, shipping interests; all of which made Felicia uneasily aware of the vast gap that lay between them.

Kuwait had one of the best social service systems in the world, Faisal boasted proudly, with excellent schooling, a hospital system that would have made a Harley Street surgeon pea-green with envy and very much more. Felicia was properly impressed, but Faisal shrugged it all aside. 'Much is made possible by money,' he told her. 'But there is still the huge vastness of the desert, which Uncle Raschid claims will never be tamed. For myself I prefer London or New York, and it is in one of these cities that we shall make our home.'

Felicia was surprised that this should make her faintly sorry.

She noticed also that Faisal was at pains to assure her that although most Kuwaitis were adherents to the Moslem faith, there was no bias against people of other faiths; nor would she be expected to change her own religion when they married.

'That at least is something Uncle Raschid cannot hold against you,' he surprised her by saying, 'for although all of us are of the Moslem faith, because of the great love Raschid's grandfather bore his English wife, her descendants are of your faith, thus Uncle Raschid himself is a Christian.'

Christian or not, Felicia was not looking forward to making his acquaintance—especially without Faisal's comforting support. The eventual confrontation loomed unpleasantly on the horizon, but not wanting to burden Faisal with her own worries, she kept her fears to herself, trying to ensure that their last few days together were as carefree as possible.

For Faisal's sake she would do all she could to make a good impression on his uncle, but her pride would not let her adopt a fawning attitude to an older male relative—no matter how he might disapprove of her independence!

With her seat booked, she handed in her notice at work, and carefully scoured the shops for suitable clothes. Fortunately the early summer fashions were already on display and she had no trouble at all in buying half a dozen pretty cotton dresses and pastel-toned separates.

She hesitated over the purchase of beach clothes, but as Faisal had told her that the beaches off Failaka Island and the surrounding coast were particularly beautiful, she succumbed to the lure of the matching apple-green set of shorts, bikini and jacket. Egged on by the assistant, she added another bikini in swirling blues and greens which complemented her eyes, and a plain black swimsuit for good

measure, unaware that its skilful cut emphasised the slender
length of her legs and the unexpectedly full curve of her
breasts. One evening dress in palest Nile green silk completed her new wardrobe, and although she could barely
afford it, Felicia could not deny that the slender slip of fabric
was infinitely becoming, tiny diamanté straps supporting the
swathed bodice, the skirt falling in folds to whisper seductively round slender legs. Her purchases complete, she
allowed herself the luxury of a taxi back to her small bedsit.
Faisal was taking her out to dinner and as it would be their
last evening together, she wanted to look her best.

As she put away her new clothes, her eyes alighted on
the jewellers' box which contained the emerald he had
bought her. Only the previous evening they had quarrelled
because she refused to wear it until their engagement had
the sanction of his family. He had teased her about being
old-fashioned, but she sensed that to flaunt the opulent
stone before his uncle would immediately set his back up.
She suspected that the older man would hold rigid and old-
fashioned views on such subjects, and while she intended
in no way to kow-tow to him, she had no wish to deliberately offend against his opinions.

Even so, it was hard not to feel bitter about his obvious
contempt of her—contempt he had expressed overtly in his
letter to Faisal, and this without knowing the first thing
about her! Perhaps it was this bitterness that made her
more reckless than usual, choosing to wear a dress which
had hung unworn in her wardrobe ever since she had
bought it, deeming it too sophisticated and eye-catching.

She had purchased it at the insistence of the colleague
with whom she had gone shopping, and afterwards had re-

gretted the impulsive buy, deeming it more suitable for the baby blue eyes and blonde curls of her friend than herself. Not that she had anything against the colour as such. The dress was black, which she knew suited her creamy skin, but it was low-cut, with a pencil-slim skirt, slit up one side to reveal slim thighs, its design emphasising her curves to a degree which made her feel acutely self-conscious. It was just the sort of dress Faisal's uncle would expect a gold-digging girl to choose, she acknowledged wryly as she zipped it up, and she was in two minds whether or not to change it when she heard Faisal's knock on the door.

His eyes smouldered with desire when she went to let him in, and she was glad of the long-sleeved jacket which went with the dress, although she could not help noticing how the matt black fabric made her auburn hair seem much more vivid than usual, darkening her eyes to a slumbrous, mysterious jade.

Faisal himself looked extremely smart, dressed in a plum velvet dinner suit—affected on anyone else, but somehow on him exactly right—his complexion somehow more olive and Eastern so that she was immediately reminded of the vast gulf in their cultures.

'I wish we were eating in my apartment—alone—and not in a restaurant where I must share your beauty with others,' Faisal murmured huskily, capturing her hands.

She tensed as he kissed her, telling herself that with their parting so very imminent it was no wonder that she felt so nervous. Even so, she was glad when he released her, bending to help her into her fake fur jacket.

'Why will you not let me buy you a proper fur?' he grumbled as he led the way to his car. 'You are very stubborn and foolish. Remember that once you are my wife I shall have the power to compel you to accept whatever gifts I choose to bestow upon you.'

'Then you may buy me as many fur coats as you please,' Felicia retorted lightly, wishing she could throw off the childhood training which prevented her from responding to him as lovingly as she would have wished.

Faisal, however, seemed to notice nothing amiss in her response. Felicia knew that he would have bought her the sun, the moon and all the stars if she let him, but she had no intention of accepting expensive gifts from him before their marriage. She knew from listening to his friends' conversation what they thought of girls who gave their favours so freely in return for a diamond bracelet or a fur, and she wondered if those same girls had the slightest idea of the contempt in which they were held by their erstwhile escorts. Soberly she admitted that Faisal's uncle might have grounds for doubting her suitability as a wife; but surely Faisal was capable of using his own judgment in these matters? He was not, after all, a child, and her anger at his uncle's casual dismissal of her burned afresh, bringing a sparkle to her eyes and a faint flush of colour to her cheeks.

Faisal had booked a table at one of the newer Mayfair clubs. The club had a gaming room, which was full of expensively jewelled women and their wealthy companions, but when they had eaten, it was to the dim privacy of the dance floor that Faisal led Felicia, taking her in his arms and holding her closely against him as they swayed to the strains of the latest poignant ballad.

It was stuffy on the dance floor, cigar smoke mingling

with the rich perfumes of the women, and Felicia had left her jacket behind at their table. She wished Faisal would not hold her so tightly, nor so closely, but every time she tried to move slightly away, his grip tightened, a look in his eyes that warned her of the effect she was having upon him.

As they danced, she became uncomfortably aware of speculative eyes upon them as an Arab who had been at the gaming tables wandered across to watch the dancers.

She was just about to ask Faisal if he knew the onlooker, when he swore suddenly, releasing her, frowning, as he acknowledged the other man's presence.

'What's the matter?' Felicia protested, as he attempted to usher her off the floor.

'Do you know that man? He seems to be trying to attract your attention.'

'He is an acquaintance of my uncle's,' Faisal replied tersely. 'And he is bound to tell him that he saw us here together.'

'Does it matter?' Felicia protested in some bewilderment, unable to understand the reason for Faisal's annoyance.

'He is not a man of honourable reputation,' Faisal explained. 'I do not wish to introduce you to him, but if I do not, and he tells Raschid, Raschid will think I have not done so because I am ashamed of you. He will also think it not fitting that I bring you to such a place.'

'But that's ridiculous!' Felicia started to protest, falling silent as the Arab suddenly stepped out of the crowd in front of them.

'By the Prophet! Faisal al-Najar!' he exclaimed genially, but Felicia was aware of the speculation in his eyes, and flushed with embarrassment at the way they roved her body.

That Faisal was furious she could tell, and despite all the other man's attempts to draw him into conversation, Faisal stubbornly insisted that they were on the point of leaving and could not delay.

At first amused by his refusal to acknowledge *her* presence, Felicia's amusement gave way to annoyance when he persisted in engaging Faisal in further conversation. Listening rather half-heartedly to his description of events which in no way included her, she learned that he had been at the gaming tables when he saw them dancing and that he had lost several thousand pounds. Even without Faisal's remarks to colour her judgment Felicia knew that she would not have liked him. He was shorter than Faisal and rather squat, with small, narrow eyes which flicked lasciviously over her person to return knowingly to Faisal's angry face.

'What's all this I hear about you going to New York?' he exclaimed as they were on the point of leaving. 'Plenty of obliging women there, my friend!'

He gave Faisal a look that made Felicia freeze with resentment, longing to tell him that she was not Faisal's mistress, but Faisal himself cut him short, exclaiming angrily,

'I have no interest in the charms of other women. My uncle may have told you that I hope to be married shortly.'

LATER, WHEN they were on their way home, Felicia asked Faisal if he thought it was wise to mention marriage, especially when his uncle had not yet approved it, but Faisal seemed to have lapsed into a brooding silence.

'That he should dare to look at you so!' he exclaimed violently, as he swung the car into the road where she lived. His hands were clenched over the steering wheel, and Felicia wondered if he was perhaps thinking that had she been an Arab girl the confrontation would never have been allowed to occur.

'Our last evening together, and it is quite spoiled!' In that moment, with his handsome face marred by a scowl, Felicia was hard put not to laugh. He reminded her so much of a small boy, thwarted in some desire.

'There will be other evenings,' she consoled him. 'And I'm coming to Heathrow with you tomorrow. I suppose you're travelling first-class?'

'Is there any other way?' he asked with a touch of hauteur that reminded her once again of the wide gulf that lay between them. He stopped the car, taking her in his arms, and kissing her with a fierce passion that previously he had always held in control. The violence of his emotions unnerved Felicia. She tried not to shrink under the pressure of his kiss, but he sensed her withdrawal, releasing her with a murmured apology.

'I forget how truly innocent you are. But soon we shall be man and wife, and then I shall teach you to respond to me, my cool white dove. I shall write to you, and you must write to me. You will soon be able to persuade my uncle to relent.'

He sounded so sure, so confident; but Felicia could not share his confidence. She was full of misgivings. Faisal's uncle would never accept her, and yet somehow she had to find a way of proving to him that she would make Faisal as good a wife as any Moslem girl.

Pride sparkled in her eyes. She would do it. She *would* find a way. She would show Faisal's uncle the stuff of which English girls were made!

CHAPTER TWO

BRAVE words! But she was feeling far from brave now, Felicia acknowledged as she stared out of the plane window and down on to the banked clouds below. Unbelievably, she had never flown before, Continental holidays being disapproved of by Uncle George, and outside her slender budget in any case.

The other passengers were obviously well seasoned travellers; businessmen with tired faces and bulging brief-cases; Arabs in traditional white robes wearing headdresses held in place by cords she had learned from Faisal were called *igals*.

Some of the male passengers were displaying a keen interest in the stewardesses, and watching the neatly uniformed girls going about their business. Felicia lost any envy she had ever had of their supposedly glamorous lives; the girls seemed to be little more than glorified waitresses! One of them had made a special point of putting her at her ease, showing her how to use the earphones that tuned into eight different channels of music, or permitted one to listen to the in-flight film.

It was a long flight—six hours, although with the time

difference Felicia knew that she would lose another three hours as Kuwait was three hours in front of Greenwich Mean Time, and many of the more seasoned travellers were apparently asleep. Felicia had started to watch the film, but the tight knot of tension that had been steadily taking possession of her insides from the moment the plane took off refused to let her relax, and after a very short time she abandoned the film, devoting her attention instead to her fellow travellers. Faisal had insisted that she travel first-class, and she was grateful for his insistence when she saw the cramped quarters of the economy cabin, full of what looked like entire Arab families, complete with crying babies and restless toddlers.

In the plane's hold was her shiny new luggage, all neatly labelled, and the small gifts she had purchased for Faisal's mother and sisters.

She had not bought anything for Faisal's uncle, quite deliberately so. They would not meet as friends and she was not going to give him the opportunity to hand her gift back to her with sneered accusations of bribery, or of trying to flatter him into acceptance of her.

And yet wasn't that exactly what Faisal wanted her to do? she asked herself uneasily; use her charm to try and sway his judgment? Her thoughts gave her no peace, jostling this way and that until her head ached with the effort of trying to reconcile her heart with her head. In the end she abandoned her efforts to put herself in the right frame of mind to meet Faisal's 'wicked uncle' and concentrated her thoughts instead on the other members of Faisal's family.

For his mother, who quite obviously worshipped him, she had bought perfume, and for his younger sister, soon to be married, a luxurious make-up kit with all the latest eye-shadows and lipsticks. His elder sister had been a little more difficult. Felicia knew that Nadia was married with a small child and that her husband was in charge of the Saudi Arabian branch of the family bank, so she had bought her an exquisite glass paperweight which had caught her eye in an expensive London store.

Indeed the paperweight was so beautiful that for an instant Felicia had been tempted to keep it for herself, but her present-buying had already stretched her slender budget to its limits and regretfully she admitted that she could not afford two such luxurious items; not when she had bought herself what amounted to a complete new wardrobe for this trip. Even now the extent of her spending spree dismayed her, but she wanted Faisal to be proud of her, so she had dipped quite deeply into the small nest egg she had been saving ever since she had started work.

When the skies opened out beneath them, and the businessmen began to ruffle their papers, Felicia guessed that they were nearing journey's end.

In the small washroom she inspected her make-up, hoping anxiously that the heat would not make her nose shine. Her skin was very fair and burned easily. She had deliberately used even less make-up than usual, not wanting to offend against Moslem tradition, and inspected her reflection anxiously in the mirror, hoping that she would not look too pale and washed out in comparison to the dusky Arabian beauties of Kuwait. Faisal had told her that in the Arab world, Kuwaiti women had the reputation of being the most beautiful, and she was dreading letting him down by comparing unfavourably with his countrywomen.

Strained green eyes stared nervously back at her, the length and thickness of her eyelashes startling against her pale skin. A faint flush of natural colour highlighted her high cheekbones, her mouth curving vulnerably beneath its covering of lip-gloss. She was wearing her hair loose, and it curled luxuriantly on to her shoulders, shimmering like raw silk whenever she moved. Should she wear it up in a discreet knot? she agonised, lifting it off her shoulders. It would look much tidier. Outside she heard the metallic request for seat belts to be fastened and realising that there was no time, she let it drop back on to her shoulders, running cold water over her wrists and dabbing on her favourite perfume, before hurrying back to her seat.

'Chanel Number Five—my favourite,' the stewardess commented with a smile, as Felicia sat down. 'Soon be down now.'

Felicia's stomach clenched as the big jet descended on to the runway. The engines screamed protestingly as the captain applied reverse thrust, then they were taxiing gently down the runway.

AS SHE EMERGED from the aircraft, the heat and noisy bustle of the airport almost threatened to overwhelm her, and then she was anxiously following the other disembarking passengers to have her visa and passport inspected.

The official who took her passport flashed her a warm, appreciative smile, as he glanced from her photograph to her face. There was a tiny scar high on her arm from the mandatory typhoid injection and tucked away in her handbag were the salt tablets Faisal had warned her that she would need as the temperature started to climb into the eighties and nineties.

Everyone apart from herself seemed to know exactly where they were going and what to do. An incomprehensible flood of Arabic washed all round her, punctuated here and there by heavily accented English from the taxi drivers and porters.

Felicia looked round in despair. Faisal had told her that she would be met at the airport, but by whom? Could one of these immaculately uniformed chauffeurs be waiting for her?

She was just debating the wisdom of making enquiries at the Tourist Information Desk, when a tall figure strode towards her, effortlessly parting the milling crowds.

'Miss Gordon?'

He was tall; taller than Faisal by several inches, and his voice held the certainty of a man who makes a statement rather than asks a question. She probably did stand out like a sore thumb, Felicia acknowledged wryly, but need he make her feel like an unwanted package he had come to collect?

She gave him a faltering smile, instantly quenched as she felt his cool scrutiny. Now, when it was too late, she wished that she had found time to put her hair up. It would have given her some badly needed sophistication. She darted her companion a surreptitious glance. Was he a relative of Faisal's, or just an employee sent to collect her?

'My luggage,' she murmured hesitantly, noticing the impatient manner in which he shot back the cuff of an immaculate pale grey silk suit to glance at the heavy gold Rolex watch strapped to his wrist. The gesture, so completely and arrogantly male, disturbed her, although she could not have said why.

'Ali is collecting your luggage,' she was told. 'Come.' He took her arm, propelling her through the crowd.

Even Felicia, inexperienced in these matters, was aware of his aura of command. His clothes looked expensive, his manner cool and decisive, and she decided that whoever he was, he was obviously a man of some importance, used to giving orders rather than taking them.

Dazzled by the colour and light, she hurried wearily after him to a waiting Mercedes, humiliatingly forced to drop behind him when his pace increased.

There was nothing welcoming in his manner. In fact he seemed to derive considerable mocking amusement from her hot and bothered state.

In the sunshine his hair had the blue-black gleam of a raven's wing, thick, and long enough to cover the collar of his suit. He wasn't wearing sunglasses, and Felicia was surprised to see that his eyes were grey and not brown, a cold, hard grey like the North Sea in winter. She shivered suddenly, and a chill ran over her despite the heat.

When she hesitated by the car he raised his eyebrows in silent mockery.

'A plane leaves for England in three hours, if you have changed your mind,' he told her.

Changed her mind? Felicia shot him a suspicious glance. Was that what he had been expecting? Was that why he had been so offhand with her? Obviously Faisal's uncle had confided in him, and her soft lips tightened at the thought of the two of them discussing her disparagingly. No doubt for all his outward Westernised appearance this man was as much a traditionalist as Faisal's uncle. He had looked her over and found her wanting. She tilted her chin and looked up at him bravely, quelling her fear. Already the sun was dropping over the horizon with a

speed that surprised her, used as she was to the more leisurely sunsets of more northerly climes.

'I am not going back,' she told him firmly.

In the silence that prickled between them she could
almost feel his antagonism and then he was holding open
the car door, his expression unfathomable.

'Please get in, Miss Gordon,' he requested curtly. 'It is
an hour's drive to the villa.'

Did he have to make her feel like a stupid child? she
asked herself crossly, as she got into the Mercedes. After
all, despite his air of authority he could scarcely be much
more than thirty-two or -three—a little more than ten years
older than she was herself.

The chauffeur—who she guessed must be 'Ali'—
appeared with her luggage, which was stowed away in the
trunk, and then they were driving out of the airport and
down a wide tarmac road in the direction of Kuwait itself.

Felicia stole a glance at her companion's impassive
face. He must know how strange and nervous she felt, and
yet he made no attempt to put her at her ease—very well,
she decided mutinously, *she* was not going to be the one
to end the smothering silence. He moved slightly, thick
black lashes veiling his eyes as he turned his head suddenly
to look at her. Colour flooded her cheeks. Now he would
think she had been staring at him! Hateful man!

'No doubt Faisal has prepared you for the kind of life
we live here in Kuwait,' he drawled coolly in perfect ac-
centless English, which Felicia suspected was the product
of an exclusive public school.

'He has spoken to me of his family, yes,' she replied
equally disdainfully. She paused deliberately, then added,

as though it were an afterthought, 'And of his uncle, of course. You know him?'

'To judge from the exceedingly challenging note in your voice, you have already come to your own conclusions,' her companion replied very dryly. 'But I shall answer your question anyway. Yes, I know him.'

'And you know that he does not approve of our engagement as well, I suppose?' Felicia said bitterly.

'Engagement?'

Did she imagine the faint hardening of those cruel lips as they looked down at her ringless hand?

'Faisal wanted us to be engaged,' she flashed back, thoroughly enraged, 'but I prefer to wait until we can have the sanction of his family.'

'How very wise!' he mocked sardonically. 'But then of course any marriage without Raschid's approval would result in a discontinuation of Faisal's extremely generous allowance, as I am sure you already know.'

His words shocked Felicia into momentary silence, and then colour stormed her pale face as she contemplated their significance. Her fingers clenched into small, impotent fists. How dared he insinuate that she had deliberately and calculatedly persuaded Faisal to wait because she was motivated by greed? If Faisal's uncle thought like this man she would have no hope of persuading him to accept her. The thought made her reckless.

'I would have married Faisal without his uncle's sanction,' she stormed, 'but he didn't want to cause a rift in his family. His money means nothing to me. It's him that I love!'

'And that is why he has sent you to persuade Raschid? You with your red-gold hair and sea-green eyes? Did he tell you that you bear an unmistakable resemblance to Raschid's grandmother?'

Felicia's colour betrayed her, and he surveyed her in silent contempt, his eyes cold.

'You have come on a fool's errand, Miss Gordon. Faisal knows that Raschid will not give his consent to any betrothal. Indeed I suspect this is merely another of his attempts to persuade Raschid to release to him the control of his inheritance. How much is he paying you to come here and....'

'It's not like that!' Felicia stormed. 'I love Faisal and he loves me....'

'How very touching!' he mocked, ignoring her distress. 'But Raschid will never give his consent.'

His arrogance infuriated her.

'How do you know?' she demanded incautiously. 'Who are you to speak for him?'

'Who am I?' he repeated softly, his eyes narrowed and watching. 'Why, Miss Gordon, I thought you must have guessed. I *am* Faisal's uncle, Sheikh Raschid al Hamid Al Sabah.' Mocking irony informed the words, and Felicia was glad of the encroaching dusk to mask her confusion. She supposed she ought to have guessed, she thought tiredly, but somehow she had it firmly fixed in her mind that Raschid would be a much older man. He had deliberately deceived her, she thought angrily, aware of the merciless scrutiny of cold grey eyes that told her how much he was enjoying her embarrassment.

You can't be Raschid, she wanted to protest. She had expected a man of middle age, with a greying beard and the traditional flowing white robes; this man with his expensive European clothes and elegantly groomed appearance bore no resemblance at all to the Raschid of her imaginings.

He had tricked her into a trap, and she had foolishly helped him, but there was one point at least that she could make clear.

'I *do* love Faisal,' she told him shakily. 'And I loved him before I knew he was your nephew.'

Green eyes clashed with grey, but it was Felicia's that dropped first.

'And what, I wonder, is that supposed to mean?'

At his side Felicia fumed silently. He had already trapped her into enough indiscretion; she was not going to compound her folly by admitting that she suspected he believed her interest in Faisal stemmed from avarice.

They were driving through the heart of the city and she roused herself sufficiently to stare interestedly out of the car window, ignoring the silent disparagement of the man at her side. Faisal had told her that his family lived on the coast between Kuwait and the town of Al Jahrah, although apparently his uncle had a villa at the oasis which had been the original home of their tribe.

'This is Arabian Gulf Street,' Raschid informed her dryly. 'It runs along the coast. If you look carefully you will see the Sief Palace.'

Mutinously Felicia ignored him, staring resolutely through the window. As the car swept down the road a shattering wail broke the silence, jerking her upright to stare wide-eyed out of the car.

'The muezzin,' her companion said sardonically. 'This is the hour of sunset when the faithful must face Mecca and pray, but if you expect to see them do so in the streets as they once did, you will be disappointed, Miss Gordon. Nowadays our lives are ruled by more mundane needs than prayer.'

'But you're a Christian,' Felicia began impulsively, remembering what Faisal had told her, and falling silent when she saw the anger tightening his face.

'By baptism, yes,' he agreed curtly. 'But make no mistake, I live my life according to the laws of my family, laws which Faisal's wife will have to obey as implicitly as he does himself. Make no mistake, Miss Gordon, my English blood will not incline me to look favourably upon you, no matter what Faisal might have told you.'

Felicia snatched a look at the forbidding line of his mouth, and knew that he meant what he said. Despair filled her. She had promised Faisal that she would do her best to impress his uncle, and yet already she had aroused his anger and, worse, his contempt. Crossly she bit her lip, fuming in silence until they were clear of the town, the powerful car carrying them swiftly through the suburbs, where houses of all shapes and designs jostled one another, the scent of lime trees heavy on the evening air, when Raschid pressed the button to wind down his window and throw out the stub of the thin cigar he had been smoking.

'Still sulking?' he drawled when Felicia remained silent. 'And yet I am sure Faisal impressed upon you the importance of gaining my goodwill.'

'Which we both know will never be forthcoming,' Felicia shot back unwisely. 'I know why you suggested this visit. You wanted to part us, to prove to Faisal that I will not make him a good wife, to make him have second thoughts....' To her horror her voice wavered and weak tears blurred her vision. 'Well, you won't succeed!' she stormed at him. 'We love each other, and I would still love him even if he were a beggar!'

Her companion's mouth twisted sardonically.

'Woman's eternal cry when she knows there is little chance of it coming to pass. Faisal could no more live in poverty than you could yourself.' He looked at the expensive linen suit she had bought for travelling, his eyes mocking. 'Look at yourself, Miss Gordon. From the top of your undeniably lovely head to the tips of your feet, you evidence expensive grooming. Do you honestly expect me to believe that you would live in poverty with my nephew—a boy who has never wanted for anything in his life?'

But I have wanted, Felicia wanted to throw at him. And I've wanted the most important thing of all—love! But she knew better than to expect the man seated opposite her to understand her deep-seated need for that. Money was all he understood, she thought bitterly. Money and power.

'I know what you're trying to do,' she said eventually, 'but you won't succeed. You're a cruel, hard man, Sheikh, and I know you for my enemy!'

In the darkness she saw the white flash of his smile.

'Enemies?' His voice was like velvet. 'Is that what you think? In our country there is no enmity between man and woman.'

'There is between the hawk and the dove, though,' Felicia retorted, 'and that's what you are—a cruel predator, determined to destroy our love.'

'And you are the dove?'

He was sneering openly, his eyes contemptuous as they rested on her slender form beneath its linen covering.

'Vulture would be a more appropriate description, don't you agree?'

There was nothing to be gained by arguing with him, Felicia thought, blinking away weak tears. The uncle of her imaginings had been bad enough, but the reality was far worse. She, who had never hated anyone in her life, disliked him so acutely that the emotion was almost tangible, filling the silence between them with crackling hostility as the car swept past the oil tank farm, the glare from the oilfields illuminating the distant horizon, a sombre reminder that she changed her world for Faisal's.

They were travelling parallel to the coast, the sky like a dark blue velvet cloak sewn with diamonds. If only Faisal was with her, Felicia thought unhappily. At this moment she needed the warm protection of his love as she had never needed it before.

'Don't bother to assume an air of mock modesty for my benefit, Miss Gordon,' Raschid advised her coldly. 'I have already learned how you comport yourself, from a friend who observed your antics on the dance floor with my nephew.'

The words were icy with a disdain that drove the colour from Felicia's face. Her hands gripped together in her lap to stop them from trembling.

'Apparently Faisal all but stripped you where you stood,' the bored voice continued sardonically, 'and you apparently made no protest at all. Do you honestly believe that is the sort of behaviour I would tolerate in a niece, or is it that having already granted Faisal the privileges of a husband, you feel confident enough to behave exactly as you wish?'

Felicia all but choked in her fury. Hot colour stained her cheeks. How dared he imply…. 'Your friend!' she managed to grit at him. 'I suppose you mean that horrid man who looked at me as though I were a piece of merchandise he was contemplating buying?'

'Perhaps he was,' came the uncaring retort. 'It is a long time since I was last in London, but my friends are amused by the low price your women put upon themselves. The British were once greatly respected, but who can respect a race that allows its women to sell themselves for so little?'

She was going to be sick, Felicia thought wretchedly. She could not listen to any more of this.

'Faisal and I were *dancing*—nothing more.'

'Do you always *dance* so close to your partner that you could be making love?' was the biting response.

Felicia suppressed an urge to demand him to stop the car so that she could get out. He was deliberately and relentlessly destroying the fabric of her dreams, but she could not let him see it.

'It was nothing like that,' she told Raschid coolly. 'Faisal respects me.'

Just for a second she thought she saw shock mingled with anger, in his eyes, and then he had himself under control.

'Does he indeed?' he drawled speculatively. 'Then he is even more of a fool that I had imagined.'

The dulcet words held a subtle threat. She had handed him a weapon, Felicia acknowledged unhappily, and one that he would not hesitate to use against her if he ever got the opportunity.

'If you were so convinced of my moral laxness, why did you invite me here?' she challenged. 'Aren't you afraid that I might contaminate Faisal's sister with my wanton behaviour?'

Raschid ignored her wild outburst, studying one elegant gold cufflink with apparent absorption for so long that she almost wanted to scream.

'I have sufficient faith in my niece to know she would not be influenced by you,' he announced at last. 'And as to my reasons for asking you here…. You are an intelligent woman, Miss Gordon, what do you think?'

'I don't think you wanted me here at all,' Felicia accused slowly. 'You never really wanted to get to know me, did you?'

'Most astute,' Raschid acknowledged dryly. 'But now that you are here, let me make one thing quite clear. You are here strictly on sufferance. My sister knows only that you are a friend of Faisal's—nothing more, and that is all she will know…'

'Until I can prove that I'm fit to marry her son,' Felicia interrupted angrily. 'Well, I don't care what you think of me, but if it makes Faisal happy I'm quite willing to go through this farce of trying to get your approval. After all, in three years' time he'll be free to marry without it in any case.'

His expression warned her that she had angered him deeply. His voice harsh, he said coldly, 'You are more determined than I realised, but then with good cause. After all, you do not have much to look forward to in England, do you? A very run-of-the-mill job; an aunt in the North of England who may or may not leave her home to you, and very little else….'

'Must you reduce everything to terms of money?' Felicia protested bitterly. 'If I'd merely wanted financial security I could have married before now.'

'But instead you chose to wait until a more attractive proposition presented itself to you,' the hateful voice drawled smoothly. 'How wise of you!'

Wearily Felicia sank back into the leather seat. What was the use of trying to convince him? She was wasting her time. He was determined to believe the worst of her. For a moment she contemplated demanding that he turn the car round and take her back to the airport, but to do so would be to acknowledge him the victor, and that was something she would never do. After all, she knew that she was none of the things he believed, and surely, in time, by just being herself, she would prove to him beyond any shadow of a doubt just how lacking his judgment had been.

This thought was enough to quell her desire to return home. Faisal loved her, and this was the raft to which she would cling throughout the stormy seas of Raschid's displeasure.

Some hidden well of courage she had not hitherto plumbed enabled her to face Raschid with a composure to match his own, her voice controlled as she said calmly:

'If you have so little faith in Faisal's ability to choose a wife for himself, I'm surprised that you didn't do it for him—an arranged marriage with the bride carefully selected to match up to his uncle's very exacting standards.'

She had meant the words as a taunt, but something in Raschid's face warned her that unsuspectingly she had stumbled upon the truth. Pressing a hand to her aching temple, she whispered,

'Was there a girl? No, I don't believe it. Faisal would never....'

'You'd be surprised what folly young men will perpetrate in the name of love, Miss Gordon.' Raschid's hard voice cut through her protests. 'But in this case there was no actual betrothal. I did not consider Faisal mature enough to take on the responsibilities of a wife. You are not the first young woman with whom he has considered himself "in love", but you are certainly the first with whom he has actually contemplated marriage. The others were content with a more tenuous relationship.'

Felicia refused to believe it. And yet hadn't she already guessed that Faisal was nowhere near as inexperienced as she was herself? At the time she had smothered the thought, but now it was resurrected, and she was forced to acknowledge that there were parts of Faisal's life of which he had told her nothing. But what really hurt was that Raschid should so casually condemn her to the ranks of those girls with whom Faisal had enjoyed a brief affair. Surely his own knowledge of his nephew told him that Faisal would never have contemplated marriage unless he was sure of his feelings?

'Faisal is young, and impetuous,' Raschid drawled, as though he had read her mind, 'and the two do not make for good judgment. You have known one another a matter of weeks only, what basis is that for a lifetime together!'

A moment was all it took to fall in love, Felicia wanted to protest, but dismay kept her silent. She was seeing a side to Faisal that she had not known existed. In her eyes he was a protective, although sometimes, admittedly, impatient man. In Raschid's he was an impulsive boy, falling in and out of love on the whim of the moment. Which of them was right? She gave herself a mental shake. She was, of course. How could she doubt it?

The car swerved off the main road and at her side she felt Raschid move slightly to adjust to the slight sway of the car.

'Not much farther now,' he told her coolly. 'Faisal's mother and sister have delayed the evening meal to

coincide with your arrival. I hope you like traditional
Kuwaiti food, Miss Gordon?'

As he stretched lithely, she wondered at the glint of
humour in his eyes. Was his amusement at her expense? If
so he would be disappointed. Faisal had already assured
her that while his mother preferred to stick to the old ways,
his sisters had insisted that they eat in the European fashion
instead of seated cross-legged on the floor, and that she
need have no fears about being offered some choice morsel
such as sheep's eyes, or something equally unpalatable. In
fact he had once taken her to a small restaurant in London
where they had eaten delicious saffron rice and kebabs,
followed by almond pastry and small cups of coffee, and
she had thoroughly enjoyed it.

She was well and truly caught between the devil and the
deep, Felicia acknowledged as the powerful car purred along.
On the one hand, if she flouted Raschid and informed Faisal's
mother of their engagement, she would incur his immediate
displeasure, and yet if she said nothing he would take her acquiescence as a sign that she was deliberately trying to court
his approval. If only Faisal were not dependent upon his
goodwill—but she knew it was useless to dwell on this.
Naturally Faisal would want to take his rightful place in the
family business, which meant that they would probably not
be able to marry until he was twenty-five—aeons away to
someone with such a volatile nature as Raschid claimed Faisal
possessed. There was no doubt at all in her own mind that
Raschid hoped that during their enforced separation Faisal
would find himself someone else, and helpless with impotent
anger, she stared bleakly out into the darkness, wishing she
had never been foolish enough to accept Raschid's invitation.

They were travelling through empty countryside, with the sea on one side of them, and what Felicia took to be the open desert on the other. Even though Faisal had prepared her for Kuwait's modern outlook, her first glimpse of the family villa still caught her off guard. She did not know quite what she had expected, but it was not this large, two-storey building, with its painted shutters and white walls, vaguely reminiscent of the Moorish houses of Andalucia; not at least until she remembered the origins of those same Moors.

Without checking, the Mercedes slid through an arched gateway and across a flagged courtyard, decorated with urns of tumbling flowers. Lights shone from several windows illuminating the courtyard and others beyond it, where she could just see the outline of trees, and hear the musical tinkle of fountains.

Raschid opened the car door for her, and she drew in a shaky breath of fresh air spiced with unfamiliar scents.

'This way, Miss Gordon.'

It was a command, and she responded unthinkingly, wondering at his ability to cloak his dislike of her in such formal politeness.

Her earlier attack of nerves was nothing to what she was experiencing now. What was she going to do if the rest of Faisal's family were as hostile towards her as his uncle? She tried not to dwell on the thought as the wooden door was flung open and she stood in a rectangle of light.

'Fatima, this is Miss Gordon,' Raschid said to the small, plump woman who stood there. 'Miss Gordon—my sister, Faisal's mother.'

Felicia's sharp ears caught the warning beneath the

coolly drawled words, as she extended her hand slowly to the woman watching her.

It was taken between two soft, beringed hands, while Faisal's mother beamed at her, chattering incomprehensibly to the tall man at her side.

'In English, Fatima,' Raschid told her. 'Miss Gordon does not have any Arabic.'

Another black mark against her, Felicia reflected bitterly, but Raschid was wrong. She did know how to say 'good evening', thanks to Faisal, although it was difficult to get her tongue round the unfamiliar Arabic words.

'*Massa'a al-Khayr,*' Faisal's mother responded delightedly, darting a mischievous look at her brother.

'There you are, Raschid!' she exclaimed in heavily accented English. 'She does speak Arabic.'

'Only a few phrases,' Felicia protested apologetically. 'And Faisal laughs at my pronunciation.'

'Poor Miss Gordon!' another female voice chimed in prettily. 'Let her get into the house before you start cross-questioning her about Faisal, Mother.'

'Zahra, what will Miss Gordon think of you?' her mother chided. 'Young people today have no manners.' She turned to Felicia. 'Please ignore this foolish child. She teases me because I am anxious about Faisal, but when she has a son of her own, then she will feel differently…'

So this was Faisal's younger sister, Zahra. Felicia studied her covertly. She was small, plump like her mother, with sparkling dark eyes, and a warm smile that held none of Raschid's cold reserve. Faisal had neglected to tell her how pretty his sister was, Felicia reflected, relieved to see that Zahra at least seemed to harbour no dislike for her.

'You will sleep in the room next to mine,' Zahra explained as she led her upstairs. 'Mother would stick to the old ways of keeping to the women's quarters, if she could, but although we use our own sitting room whenever Faisal or Uncle Raschid entertain business colleagues, Raschid does not believe in women being strictly segregated.' She pulled a wry face. 'Mother is dreadfully old-fashioned. She hated it when I first started at university, but Uncle Raschid was insistent, thank goodness. I hope you are hungry? Mother has had a feast prepared for you, although I warned her that you might not be hungry, having travelled so far.'

Mentally blessing Zahra for her tactful warning of what to expect, Felicia shook her head. In point of fact she felt exhausted and longed only for a hot bath and a comfortable bed, but it would be bad manners to show anything less than immense pleasure in her hostess's preparations—she knew enough about Arab protocol to be aware of that!

'Faisal has written to me about you,' Zahra confided, eyeing Felicia speculatively. 'You are to become betrothed...'

'Perhaps,' Felicia tempered, remembering Raschid's warning. 'Provided your uncle approves of me.'

Her room overlooked the gardens and was quite Western in concept, with a comfortable single bed and modern fitted bedroom furniture along one wall, with hanging space for far more clothes than Felicia had brought. There was a bathroom off it, tiled in deep pink to match the sanitary fittings which all boasted gold taps and wastes, and were quite obviously all of the very most luxurious quality.

'I hope you weren't expecting sunken baths with marble pillars,' Zahra giggled. 'Uncle Raschid swore you would

expect us to live like something out of the Thousand and
One Nights.'

'Well, I did wonder how you managed those flimsy
trousers and curly-toed shoes,' Felicia agreed lightly,
earning an approving grin from Zahra.

'I knew that you would have a sense of humour, despite
what Uncle Raschid said!'

And what exactly had that been? Felicia wondered
grimly. Plainly Zahra knew about their plans, although she
suspected that Raschid had also warned the younger girl
not to mention them to her mother.

'If you *do* have a hankering to see the old Kuwait, you
must ask Uncle Raschid to take you to his villa at the
oasis,' Zahra surprised her by saying. 'It was built by his
grandfather, although he rarely used it. He preferred to
travel with his people and live in their black tents. He built
it for his English wife. Leave your unpacking,' she instructed, changing the subject. 'One of the maids will do
that for you. Are you ready to eat?'

Guessing that she had already delayed the family meal
long beyond its normal hour, Felicia assured her that she
was quite ready.

As they went downstairs, Zahra explained to her that the
house was built around the enclosed gardens she had
noticed on her arrival, and that it comprised the traditional
women's quarters, with two separate wings; one of which
was used by Raschid and the other being set aside for
Faisal's use when he was at home.

'Not that Raschid sticks rigidly to his quarters,' Zahra
explained. 'He normally eats with us unless business
prevents him. In my father's time the women never ate with

the men, but things are different now, and Uncle Raschid encouraged both Nadia and myself to take advantage of a modern education.'

'How kind of him,' Felicia murmured sarcastically. She was surprised to discover that Zahra evidently held her uncle in great affection, but wished she had not given vent to her own feelings for him when Zahra paused to eye her enquiringly.

'Don't you like Raschid?'

'I haven't known him long enough to form an opinion,' Felicia countered diplomatically, but Zahra was not deceived, and chuckled, explaining,

'When we heard you were coming, I think Mother was frightened that you would fall in love with him. All my friends think he's wonderful, and when he was at university in England he had many girl-friends.'

I'll bet he did, Felicia thought sourly, and she could just imagine his lordly reaction to them.

'He is very good-looking, isn't he?' Zahra murmured judiciously. 'Much more so than Faisal.'

'But not as gentle or kind,' Felicia responded before she could stop herself.

Zahra's brown eyes twinkled with amusement.

'Zut! Kindness! Is that what you look for in a man? I think Uncle Raschid is wrong when he says you are experienced in the ways of men, otherwise you would know that kindness is not necessary between a man and a woman, where there is love.'

She said it so seriously that Felicia could not contradict her, although her own love-starved childhood had taught her that kindness was a precious virtue. Perhaps the harsh-

ness of their desert climate bred the need for it out of these
people, she reflected. To her amusement Zahra was dressed
in jeans and a thin T-shirt, her long hair caught back off
her face with a ribbon, and as they entered what was obviously the family dining room, Felicia noticed the younger
girl's mother frowning rather despairingly as her eyes
alighted on her daughter.

'Raschid, you must speak to this child,' she protested.
'Look at her!'

'Mother, everyone at the university wears jeans,' Zahra
laughed, 'and Uncle Raschid will not forbid me, because he
wears them himself,' she said triumphantly. 'I have seen him.'

Faisal's mother looked at her brother, as though seeking
confirmation, and although his mouth twitched a little he
betrayed no embarrassment.

'Maybe so,' he allowed, 'but not at the dinner table.
Tonight we shall excuse you, but in future, unless you
come to dinner properly dressed you will eat alone in the
women's quarters.'

Zahra pulled a face, but subsided a little, obviously accepting that Raschid would put his threat into practice if
she defied him.

'Come, we must eat. Miss Gordon....'

'Oh, call her Felicia, Mother,' Zahra cried impetuously.
'And she must call you Umm Faisal.'

Felicia was about to demur, conscious of Raschid's cool
scrutiny, and her own tenuous position in the family, when
Faisal's mother looked anxiously at her, and said something in Arabic to her brother.

'My sister begs you not to take offence at Zahra's impetuosity, Miss Gordon,' he said sardonically. 'She had

intended to ask you herself to do her the favour of calling her "Umm Faisal", but Zahra has forestalled her. She also reminds me that as I am head of our family it is my duty to welcome you to our home, and beg you to treat our humble dwelling as your own for as long as it pleases you to remain with us.'

While there was no doubting the sincerity of Faisal's mother's welcome, Felicia stiffened, knowing that Raschid did not mean a word of what he was saying. His expression told her that much. However, before she could say anything, Zahra caused a minor disturbance by remarking teasingly,

'Miss Gordon! You cannot call her that, Uncle Raschid, not when she is to…not when she is such a close friend of Faisal's,' she amended hurriedly. 'You must call her Felicia—mustn't he?'

She turned to Felicia for corroboration, unaware of the cold antipathy in her uncle's eyes as they skimmed the slender figure of the girl standing in the shadows. Personally she did not care what Raschid called her, although she was sure he had adopted the formal 'Miss Gordon' to remind her that he wanted to keep her at a distance. Fortunately no one else seemed to be aware of the antagonism pulsating between them, and Felicia was invited to sit down and help herself to the food set before them. Despite the variety of dishes pressed upon her, she could barely touch a morsel. She did her best, glad of Zahra's distracting chatter, and answering her many questions as best she could. A curious dreamlike state seemed to have engulfed her, and it was all she could do to keep her eyes open. Her heart felt weighted with despair, and nausea churned her stomach—a legacy of her long flight, and the confrontation with Raschid, she acknowledged wearily.

Once or twice during the long meal she suffered the disturbing sensation of the room blurring and fading, although on each occasion she managed to jerk herself back to awareness.

'Are you feeling all right, Felicia?' Zahra asked in some concern, observing the other girl's increasing pallor, but Felicia shook her head, not wishing to draw the attention of cold grey eyes to her predicament.

Later she was to regret this foolish pride, but as she struggled to swallow another mouthful of almond pastry and drink a cup of coffee she was concentrating all her energy on merely quelling her growing nausea, from one moment to the next.

At long last the ordeal was over. Shakily Felicia got to her feet, swaying slightly as faintness swept her, and from a distance she heard Zahra cry anxiously,

'Quick, she's falling!'

And then there was nothing but the blessed peace of enveloping darkness and the strength of arms that gripped her, halting the upward rush of the beautiful crimson Persian carpet she had previously been admiring.

CHAPTER THREE

'WILL she be all right?'

The anxious question hovered somewhere on the outer periphery of her subconscious, registering in a dim and distant fashion even while its import eluded her. The voice was familiar, though, and Felicia struggled to recognise it. Mercifully, someone else took on the responsibility of replying, a male voice, deep, crisp, with faintly indolent overtones; a voice that sent small feather tendrils of fear curling insidiously down her spine, so that she was tempted to curl up into a small ball and hide away from it.

'Don't worry, Zahra. It's a combination of exhaustion and temperature change, I suspect, coupled with too much rich food on an empty stomach. Now you know why your mother forbids you to go on these ridiculous slimming diets.'

'Felicia doesn't need to slim,' Zahra objected. 'She looks so pale, Raschid. Don't you think we ought to send for a doctor?'

Raschid! Now she remembered! Felicia opened her eyes, wincing in the electric light, forcing away the darkness that reached out for her and struggling to sit up. She was in her bedroom—she recognised that much at least—and Umm Faisal was hovering anxiously in the doorway, while Zahra and Raschid stood by her bed.

'I don't need a doctor,' she croaked, disconcerted when all three pairs of eyes focused at once upon her.

'You've come round!' Zahra exclaimed thankfully. 'We were so worried about you. What could we have told Faisal if you had fallen ill?'

'I'm sure Faisal would have agreed with me that Miss Gordon should have told us she was feeling unwell,' Raschid interrupted unsympathetically. 'Zahra, find one of the maids and get some fresh fruit juice for our patient. After her long flight she is probably somewhat dehydrated, and perhaps a sleeping pill will help Miss Gordon to get a good night's sleep, Fatima?'

'Didn't anyone warn you that jet travel can be extremely dehydrating?' Raschid asked her severely as his sister and niece hurried to do his bidding. Felicia closed her eyes, turning her face to the wall, dismayed to hear him drawl mockingly,

'Still hating me, Miss Gordon? How wise of you not to try to deny it. Your eyes smoulder in a most disconcerting fashion when you are angry, but you had best not let my sister see them. She comes from a generation that believes implicitly in the absolute supremacy of the male.'

'Then you must be a throwback!' Felicia muttered unwisely under her breath, shocked when, without warning, Raschid's fingers grasped her chin, forcing her face round so that she was obliged to endure his cool scrutiny.

'What can have happened to all your good intentions?' he mocked unkindly. 'Were we not agreed that for Faisal's sake you must seek my approval or are you perhaps foolish enough to believe that this *is* the way to do so? Allow me to disillusion you. Do not continue this foolish and point-less defiance. I am not renowned for my patience, Miss Gordon, but neither am I the monster of your imaginings. Faisal is an extremely wealthy and spoilt young man. I am his guardian—for my sins—and although I cannot stop him marrying where he chooses, I do have the means to delay that marriage if I am not convinced that it is right for him. If you really seek his happiness you must see the sense of what I am saying.'

'Is it so difficult for you to accept that his happiness lies with me?' Felicia countered shakily, determined to withstand the fierce onslaught of his gaze. 'You talk to me of sense and reason, and yet you condemned me without knowing the first thing about me. Whether you admit it or not you don't want Faisal to marry me. And yet why? By what right do you take it upon yourself to choose for him? You know nothing about me. How can you say that we won't be happy?'

'Zut! Either you are an imbecile or a stubborn fool, Miss Gordon. Faisal is a Moslem—an Arab, with all that the word encompasses. You are British. Even today the two worlds lie far apart. Marriage to Faisal would make you his possession, every bit as much as his car or his home.'

'Perhaps I *want* to be,' Felicia retorted, refusing to be quelled.

Raschid's expression was sardonic. 'You may want him to possess your body, Miss Gordon,' he stated baldly, 'but, as you will discover if you do marry Faisal, he will own you body *and* soul.'

'I thought women weren't supposed to have souls,' Felicia commented rather unwisely. 'I thought they were

just men's playthings; bearers of children. You won't
frighten me by telling me these things. If you honestly
believe a woman to be an inferior being, why do you let
Zahra attend university?'

'We are not talking of my beliefs, Miss Gordon,' he
reminded her coolly, 'but those of my nephew. Do not
deceive yourself. For all his outward Westernised views,
Faisal is every bit as conservative as his father, and his
father before him. He may not expect you to go into purdah
or veil yourself, but he will not countenance a loss of face
because you, his wife—his possession—refuse to acknowledge his superiority.'

His ears, sharper than hers, caught the sound of feet on
the stairs, and he frowned warningly. A hectic flush stained
Felicia's previously pale face. She was so angry that she
trembled beneath his suave gaze.

'This is neither the time nor the place to discuss these
matters,' Raschid told her, 'We shall talk again when you
are rested, but I warn you now that nothing you have said
so far has done anything to convince me that you could
make Faisal happy. Marriage is a serious business, Miss
Gordon, not to be undertaken on a mere whim.'

'How would you know?' Felicia muttered bitterly, as
Zahra bustled in. 'You've never been married, have you?'

He turned on his heel, ignoring her taunt, and when he
had gone Zahra cast a nervous glance at the closed door.

'Felicia, you have been quarrelling with Raschid,
haven't you?' she whispered.

'I think you can guess why. He doesn't want me to
marry Faisal,' Felicia told her bleakly, driven by the need
to confide in someone.

'I know,' Zahra admitted. 'He has spoken of this to me. You must not get upset, Felicia, it is just that Faisal....' she coloured, patently embarrassed. 'Well, you are not the first girl he has believed himself in love with, and Uncle Raschid is merely anxious to protect my mother. She does not understand these things. To her a betrothal is as sacred as a marriage, and that is why Uncle Raschid will not allow you to become engaged until he is sure that your marriage will be a happy one.'

In other circumstances Felicia might have seen the wisdom behind these words, but Raschid's implied criticism of Faisal fuelled her anger, causing Zahra to eye her with growing concern as indignant colour burned her cheeks.

'You must have patience,' Zahra soothed. 'Raschid will come round in time, I am sure of it. You must have *siyasa*.'

'*Siyasa?* What is that?' Felicia enquired, intrigued in spite of herself.

Zahra laughed. 'It is what in England you would call tact, but more! It is the art of getting what you want without forcing the other man to lose face.'

'It is obvious that your uncle does not think me deserving of *siyasa*,' Felicia complained. 'I honestly believe he wants to humiliate me!'

Zahra made a shocked, tutting sound.

'Never would he be so impolite to a guest,' she averred firmly. 'He is merely anxious for my mother. He wishes to protect her, that is all. Marriage is a big step....'

'So your uncle was telling me,' Felicia agreed wryly. 'He seems to be quite an expert on the subject, although he isn't married himself.'

'That is because his betrothed died,' Zahra explained in

a low voice. 'It used to be the custom for a girl to be
engaged to her first cousin, and this practice was adopted
by Raschid's father, so that Raschid is my mother's brother,
but he was also my father's cousin.'

It was all rather difficult for Felicia to assimilate, with
an aching head, but she did her best.

'Raschid is, of course, my mother's stepbrother,' Zahra
continued. 'He was the child of my grandfather's second
wife. That is why he is of your religion and we are not.
Faisal will have told you something of this?'

'He told me that your uncle's grandmother was an
English girl—a Christian,' Felicia admitted, curious,
despite her averred dislike of Faisal's uncle.

'Yes, that is so,' Zahra agreed. 'Raschid's grandparents
met in the desert, when he rescued her from a sandstorm.
They fell deeply in love and since Raschid's grandfather
was the head of his family he was free to marry whomever
he chose. It was for her that he built the house at the oasis,
for despite their love, sometimes she yearned for her old
life amongst her own people. Raschid's mother was their
only child, and she was the second wife of my grandfather.
That is how Raschid comes to be Christian. It is a romantic
story, is it not?'

Felicia allowed that it was.

'I do not think Raschid will marry now,' Zahra mused.
'I think he enjoys his single state too much.' She dimpled
a smile at Felicia. 'Mother is constantly suggesting this girl
or that, for his approval, but he always has an excuse.'

'Another example of *siyasa*!' Felicia commented dryly,
wincing when Zahra clapped her hands and laughed.

'I am going to enjoy having you staying with us, Felicia.

Poor Uncle Raschid! He will not be able to stand out against you for long, especially when Faisal comes home. Mother has always spoiled him dreadfully, and I don't think she would object if he took *four* English wives!'

Umm Faisal might not, Felicia thought tiredly, but she certainly would. She closed her eyes, trying to relax and ease the tension from her muscles, but Raschid's darkly sardonic features would keep transposing themselves between her aching head and the peace she sought.

In the end she welcomed Umm Faisal's entrance, to bear her chattering daughter away and leave her guest a glass of chilled fruit juice and the promised sleeping tablet.

IT WAS THE unfamiliar figure of the maid tiptoeing past the window that eventually woke Felicia. She opened her eyes, disorientated, and wondering where she was, and then the events of the previous day came flooding back. Of course! She was in Kuwait faced with the seemingly impossible mission of trying to persuade Sheikh Raschid to accept her into his family.

The maid threw back the curtains with a shy smile, but in response to Felicia's questions, she only shook her head and left the room, reappearing several minutes later with Umm Faisal.

'So! You are feeling better?' the older woman exclaimed in her slow English, giving her guest a beaming smile. 'That is good. Zahra has gone to the university, but she left a message to say that she will meet you in Kuwait later in the day. Ali will take you in the car and wait for you.'

'Zahra has left?' Felicia sat up and stared disbelievingly at her watch. How on earth could it be eleven in the

morning? When she broke into an appalled apology Umm
Faisal shook her head, plainly undisturbed.

'It is the pill,' she assured Felicia, 'and you will feel
better for the long sleep. My brother has gone to the bank,
and so we are alone. Selina will bring you rolls and honey
or fresh fruit if you prefer and then we shall drink tea and
you will tell me all about my Faisal. Zahra laughs at me,
but a mother grows anxious for her only son, when he
lives amongst strangers.'

Felicia could only sympathise. She missed Faisal
already, and longed for his presence as a bulwark between
herself and Raschid.

'It is a bad time for him to go to New York, just when
you are visiting us,' Umm Faisal acknowledged, 'but
Raschid thought it necessary.'

And Raschid's decisions must never be questioned,
Felicia thought resentfully.

The fresh fruit and delicious warm rolls Selina brought
helped to revive her, and after a refreshing shower Felicia
dressed in a flattering ice blue linen skirt, attractively
pleated at the front, a toning striped blouse, completing an
outfit that was both cool and practical. The skirt had a
matching jacket, but the morning was so warm that Felicia
left it hanging in the wardrobe. Pale blue eyeshadow and
soft pink lip-gloss gave her a hint of sophistication,
building up her seriously depleted self-confidence.

With a good many nods and smiles Selina led her to
Umm Faisal's private sitting room on the ground floor.
The older woman was sitting cross-legged on the carpet,
and she rose gracefully when Felicia entered. The room
was cool and shadowy, a long divan beneath the iron grille

of a window, heaped with cushions covered in vivid silks, the rich crimsons and peacock blues picked out in the jewel-coloured Persian carpet, a vibrant note of colour against the black and white tiled floor. On a small low table stood a brass samovar, bubbling gently, the scent of mint tea wafting towards Felicia as she crossed the room. Above the faint whirring of the air-conditioning she could hear the sound of birds singing.

'Raschid had an aviary built when we moved to this house,' Umm Faisal explained. 'It is pleasant to walk in the gardens in the evening and listen to their song.'

'I thought I heard fountains playing when we arrived last night, and they sounded wonderful,' Felicia acknowledged.

'Ah yes. There is no sweeter sound to the Arab ear than that of water, and even now when we no longer need to fear the dry season I have to force myself not to waste a drop.' She shook her head. 'Old habits die hard, and Raschid is constantly chiding me for my folly. He bought this house for us when my husband died—Raschid really prefers the desert, but it is not safe to bring up children so far from medical care even in these days. He gave up much when Saud died—but then Faisal will have told you that.'

Had he? Felicia could remember well enough Faisal's complaints about his uncle. 'He must have been very young,' she murmured now involuntarily, referring to Raschid.

Umm Faisal smiled. 'Barely nineteen. He was the son of my father's second wife. My mother bore no sons to my father, so he took a second wife, but Yasmin was never truly happy. She was her parents' only child and had been educated in England according to her mother's wish. However, when it came to her marriage her father insisted that it must be in the old tradition. My father was her second cousin, but although she was a dutiful wife, she rarely smiled or laughed. She died when Raschid was three, and I have often wondered if she yearned for her mother's country. Raschid does not speak of it, but her death saddened him greatly. He has not had an easy life,' Umm Faisal continued quietly, 'and it is for this reason that I should like to see him settled with a family of his own.' She looked at Felicia with contemplative eyes. 'In Raschid, East and West meet, and I know that he is sometimes impatient of our ways. It was his wish that Zahra and Nadia attend the university—and I think the English part of him yearns for a closer companionship with his wife than Moslem girls are taught to expect. It is for this reason, I think, that he has never taken a bride.'

She pitied the woman who eventually took him on, Felicia thought grimly, but naturally she did not voice these thoughts to her companion.

Today Umm Faisal was dressed in Eastern costume, and Felicia suspected that the Western garb of the previous evening had been donned merely to put her at her ease. Her heart warmed towards this tiny, plump woman whose ways were so very different from her own, but who was plainly willing to welcome her son's friends into her home. Remembering the gifts she had bought in London—still unpacked—Felicia was tempted to run upstairs and get them, but decided to wait until Zahra returned.

She tried not to feel too dismayed when Ali brought the Mercedes to the door later that afternoon, wishing that Umm Faisal was going with her.

The arrangement was that Ali would drive to the uni-

versity to collect Zahra and then take both girls back to
Kuwait town so that they could look at the shops at their
leisure, but when they were driving through Kuwait, Felicia
remembered that she had no Kuwaiti money and she persuaded Ali to drop her outside a bank and go on to collect
Zahra without her.

'I shall wait for Zahra here,' she assured the puzzled
servant, gesturing to the large plate glass building behind her.

As she emerged from the interior of the car she was glad
that she had changed her striped blouse for a thinner,
sleeveless one, with a gently scooped neckline.

The bank cashier was politely helpful, patiently explaining the denominations of her Kuwaiti money and showing
her the rate of exchange. He spoke excellent English, and
although Felicia doubted that her few pounds would go
very far, it was reassuring to have money in her purse.

She emerged from the welcome coolness of the bank
into the harsh sunlight, fascinated by the panorama of life
passing by in front of her while she waited for Ali to return
with Zahra. Hawk-eyed, bronzed men in their white *dish-
dashes*; their robes immaculately clean, their headdresses
held in place by glinting gold *igals*.

A group of old men sat cross-legged on the pavement,
and to her amusement Felicia realised that they were
watching a television in a shop window.

Although men were undeniably in the majority, she
noticed several girls walking about unescorted, some
wearing jeans and blouses, but there were still plenty of
women who retained the traditional black *burga*, veils
covering their faces as they swayed gracefully in the wake
of their men. The men were fascinating, Felicia reflected.

Even in middle age they retained their upright carriage and good looks. Black eyes glittered curiously at her, hawk noses and thin lips a reminder of their heritage. It was impossible not to admire them in their strict adherence to their way of life, though she liked that Faisal was more gentle by nature, more malleable, ready to indulge and cosset her, the effect no doubt of his Western education, and a result of the close bond that evidently existed between him and his mother. Raschid was cast in a far different mould.

All too easy to imagine him staring down the length of his arrogant nose at some unfortunate female who had incurred his displeasure.

Ali was gone longer than she had anticipated, and she scoured the busy street looking for the familiar Mercedes. A group of youths were approaching her, their eyes bold and assessing, and Felicia was beginning to feel increasingly uncomfortable. So much so that she almost wished for the protection of the enveloping black garments of the other women to hide her from the openly lascivious glances she was attracting.

When she did see the Mercedes gliding to a halt several yards away, she started to hurry towards it, but it was not Ali who got out of the car. It was Raschid himself, his face dark and forbidding as he strode towards her, the thin silk of his shirt open at the neck to reveal the strong, tanned column of his throat. A tiny thread of awareness filtered through her dismay, coupled with the unwelcome admission that these olive-skinned men with their arrogant profiles and lean grace made their English counterparts seem pale and flabby in comparison. Her heart was beating uncomfortably fast, her pulses racing, her mouth dry with nervous fear.

Instead of going to meet Raschid, she hung back, frozen to the spot like some poor little mouse, petrified by the cruel grace of the falcon on his downward swoop.

Dark fingers, like talons, gripped her arm, swinging her into shocked contact with a hard male body, the scent of male skin filling her nostrils as, momentarily, she was pressed against Raschid's lean length.

'Miss Gordon!' There was exasperation as well as tightly controlled anger in the two words, and Felicia found herself stammering weakly, searching for some means to dispel his wrath:

'I was waiting for Zahra.'

'Having told Ali to leave you, completely alone, in the middle of a strange city—Yes, I know,' he agreed grimly. 'Fortunately Ali had the good sense to come and tell me.' His eyes slid over her body; the fragile hip bones revealed by her clinging skirt; the slender curve of her waist below the unexpected fullness of her breasts. Aware of his regard, Felicia went hot and cold all over, suppressing the instinctive desire to conceal herself from him.

'In this country, Miss Gordon,' he told her, 'a woman of good family does not walk the streets alone, with her body on display for the delectation of all and sundry, to be gossiped over and speculated about, as those boys were discussing you. I tell you this—Faisal would not be pleased were he to learn of this escapade.'

Shocked into silence by the censorious words, Felicia bit hard on her lip.

'I just wanted to get some money,' she choked, nearly in tears, humiliated by the thought that Raschid was witnessing her distress.

'You could have applied to me,' Raschid's cold voice continued inexorably. 'Or does that much-flaunted liberation you European women are so fond of mean that you are unwilling even to do that!'

He made her sound so petty and childish that she could have wept. She had simply never thought of asking him to change her few travellers' cheques for her, but a corner of her mind acknowledged that he had some basis for his accusation, although stubbornly she resisted it.

'I'm sure it isn't a crime to walk alone—other women were doing so, and in European dress,' Felicia said defiantly.

Raschid snapped long fingers, ignoring the challenge in her eyes.

'Foreigners!' he announced contemptuously. 'Women whose families do not have a care for their reputation.'

'My reputation is my own,' Felicia snapped crossly. 'And I'm perfectly capable of taking care of it myself. After all, I've been living alone in London for the past five years.'

'In Kuwait, Miss Gordon, a woman's reputation is the concern of all her family, and a slur upon that reputation reflects upon all members of that family. Faisal may or may not have told you that Zahra is betrothed to a young man of exceptionally rigid family. The betrothal has only been settled after a good deal of very delicate negotiation. These are sensitive times where the Moslem religion is concerned. The information that a young woman attached to our family—in however nebulous a fashion—is disporting herself as you have been today could have very serious repercussions indeed where Zahra's future is concerned.'

If he expected her to be cowed and chastened then he had another think coming, Felicia fumed.

'An arranged marriage? How typical of you!' she stormed. 'If you had your way you would ruin Faisal's life in the same way, and then your life wouldn't be disturbed by an unwanted English girl whose morals and antecedents you so obviously suspect! I'm sorry to disappoint you, Sheikh Raschid, but I will marry Faisal, and there's nothing you can do to stop us, even if we do have to wait three years.'

She wondered if it was anger or disgust that made his mouth tighten so forbiddingly. No doubt he thought that girls of good family did not state their intentions so openly, but waited with dutifully downcast eyes for their fathers and brothers to tell them whom they would marry. Poor Zahra! How did she feel about her arranged marriage?

The cruel fingers were still holding her prisoner, while relentless grey eyes swept her from head to foot and back again, so that she was reduced to trembling fury.

'Let me go!' she muttered. 'People are staring at us!'

'And that offends you?' His mouth thinned cruelly and for the first time she was aware of its full lower curve, indicating a passion she would have thought foreign to his nature.

'Do you realise that were you married to Faisal you would have just given him cause to divorce you twice over; firstly by disporting yourself as you did in the street for all to see, and secondly for allowing me to address you so intimately and in full view of anyone who cares to see? Faisal would not like that, Miss Gordon.'

She knew that it was true. There was a certain inflection in the younger man's voice whenever he mentioned his uncle that hinted at the beginnings of a jealousy which could easily be fanned from a small spark to a blazing conflagration.

'And *I* don't like being stared at as though I were on sale in the market-place!' Felicia replied tartly, tearing her gaze away from the hypnotic effect of his cool stare.

'You surprise me. In one respect at least I cannot fault Faisal's judgment. You are an extremely beautiful woman, but it takes more than a desirable body and a pretty face to make a good wife.'

'Although they are admirable traits in a mistress? Is that what you mean?'

Raschid's eyebrows rose quellingly, adding to his formidable air of hauteur.

'I did not say so,' he replied positively. 'Was that your intention when you agreed to come out here? To sell yourself to the highest bidder, knowing that a wealthy Arab would pay well for that lissom white body you conceal so inadequately?'

She would have struck him there and then in the middle of the crowded thoroughfare if he had not transferred his grip from her arm to her wrist, pain stabbing through her tender flesh like a shock from red-hot wires at the ferocity of the fingers clamped round her frail bones.

'Why do you ask?' she cried bitterly. 'Are you thinking of putting in an offer yourself?'

She knew instantly that she had gone too far. His mouth tightened ominously, his eyes condemning as they swept her with thinly veiled contempt.

'No way,' he said cruelly, shaking his head. 'I don't buy soiled merchandise, Miss Gordon, desirable though it may be superficially. A chipped jade figurine, a flawed carpet, a second-hand woman, they are all worthless!'

His words left her gasping with mingled shock and rage.

She tried to pull herself free and suffered the added indignity of being jerked against the hard length of his body, shock driving the breath out of her lungs as she bunched her muscles against the impact. The contact lasted only a second, but as she pulled away and stalked across the pavement to the car, where Zahra was staring curiously from the window, she felt as though the imprint of Raschid's flesh was burned against her own, and she, who had been held far closer to Faisal, wondered why she should have found that momentary contact with Raschid so intensely disturbing. Long strides brought the object of her tumultuous thoughts alongside her, lean fingers descending over hers, clinical eyes studying the way she flinched away as he grasped the car door, holding it open for her.

The entire episode could have lasted no longer than the space of a few minutes, but Felicia felt for some reason as though it were one that she would never forget. Tense and defensive, she tried to calm her jangled nerves as Raschid closed the door and walked round to the front passenger seat.

Just for a second she had glimpsed the emotions Raschid concealed behind his cool façade, and what she had seen had frightened her. He was as different from Faisal as chalk from cheese, she reflected shakily. He had none of Faisal's gentle compassion; none of his boyish charm, so why should he linger in her thoughts when she badly needed to cling to the memory of Faisal's love?

CHAPTER FOUR

THERE was no opportunity for conversation on the return journey to the villa, although once or twice Felicia caught Zahra's sympathetic eyes on her in a way that made a mockery of her own hopes that the latter had not noticed her uncle's anger.

When the car stopped in the outer courtyard, she whispered gently to Felicia,

'Don't be too upset, I always hate it when Raschid is annoyed with me. That dreadful cold anger of his is far worse than if he actually lost his temper.'

Felicia was feeling far too ruffled to be soothed by the placatory words and only exclaimed shortly,

'Your uncle may take it upon himself to order your life, Zahra, but he will never order mine. If I want to walk the streets of Kuwait alone, then I shall do so!'

With that she stalked into the house, head held high, Zahra following hurriedly behind.

'He has made you very angry, hasn't he?' she sympathised.

'Angry?' Felicia almost choked in her indignation. 'He practically humiliated me! Treating me like...' She broke off. There was no point in trying to make Zahra understand her feelings. 'Oh, what's the use?' she said wearily. 'I'm only glad that once we're married, Faisal and I can go our own way. I would hate to live here under your uncle's roof!'

She sounded so bitter that Zahra frowned unhappily, touching her arm.

'Perhaps it is that Raschid does not understand, Felicia. If I were to tell him that you were upset…. Faisal would not have approved either, you know,' she added gently. 'I shall speak with Raschid…!'

'No! No, Zahra, don't do that.' In her mind Felicia was thinking how badly she was failing in the mission Faisal had set her, but Zahra misinterpreted her words, and her face broke into a relieved smile.

'You are beginning to forgive Raschid already,' she breathed. 'I *know* he didn't mean to upset you, Felicia. He forgets sometimes how formidable he is!'

Like a falcon forgets its prey, Felicia thought bitterly. Zahra saw her relative through rose-tinted glasses. Forgive him indeed! That was something she would never do! When she remembered what he had said about her, and the look in his eyes….

HER MOTHER normally rested during the afternoon, Zahra explained to Felicia as they went inside. It was a practice she herself would probably want to adopt as the days grew hotter, she added, and because of this it was the custom that the family did not gather for their meal until early evening.

After she had showered and slipped into a refreshingly cool dress, Felicia inspected her reflection in the mirror. Was her appearance 'chaste' enough to pass Raschid's

rigid specifications? she asked herself wryly. Her dress
had a gently rounded neckline and small puffed sleeves, the
neck and hem piped in crisp white scalloping in contrast
to the lemon-gold cotton. She had washed her hair and it
curled attractively on to her shoulders, more red than gold
in the fading light. A thin gold necklace drew attention to
the slender column of her throat, a matching bracelet round
one delicate wrist, high-heeled, strappy sandals completing her outfit.

For dinner they were served with roast lamb, deliciously
flavoured with herbs, pastries stuffed with exotic vegetables, and spicy rice dishes, and Felicia groaned a little
to think of the effect of all this rich food on her figure.

When the first course had been cleared away, the maids
reappeared with an immense tray of fresh fruit, and more
of the frighteningly fattening almond and marzipan tartlets
they had had the night before.

Felicia accepted a slice of melon and some fresh, sweet
dates, noting that Raschid had the same, although his sister
and Zahra tucked into the almond tarts with a cheerful dis-
regard for the consequences.

After the meal a manservant came in with coffee cups
and an elegant silver coffee pot, pouring the thick, steaming
liquid into the fragile cups and handing them round.

Felicia had brought her gifts downstairs and hidden
them under her chair. She had intended to distribute them
after the meal when, she hoped, Raschid would retire to his
own quarters, but to her annoyance he seemed determined
to linger, leaning back in his chair, with a tigerish grace she
had never seen in a European, his hair blue-black under the
light of the chandelier. She wondered if he had ever sat

cross-legged in the tents of his tribe, eating from the communal dish and drinking from the communal cup as Arabian hospitality demanded. In his expensive hand-made silk suit he looked every inch the sophisticated business- man, but she sensed that under the suave façade lurked a man as elemental as the desert which was his natural home.

While Umm Faisal and Zahra chatted, Felicia's eyes strayed again and again to the shuttered face of the man seated opposite her. The betrayingly passionate curve of his lower lip caught her attention, as it had done before, and she shivered involuntarily, imagining what it would be like to feel that hard mouth against her own; that warm golden skin next to the creamy paleness of her own.

A shudder racked her. What on earth was she thinking? In vain she tried to conjure up the protective image of Faisal's softer features, as though they were a talisman to ward off the potent effect of Raschid's masculinity. What was wrong with her? she wondered despairingly; Raschid stood for ev- erything she most despised, and yet here she was comparing him to Faisal, and finding the harsh features had somehow insinuated themselves into her memory, superimposed over Faisal's more gentle image. It was not to be tolerated. In vain she tried to recall Faisal's warm smile and liquid eyes, but as though he had worked a spell upon her, all she got back was a mirror image of Raschid's cold grey eyes and derisory smile. Like one in a trance she tried to shake off her torment- ing thoughts, dismayed by her momentary awareness of the man seated across from her. Hurriedly she bent down to retrieve her gaily wrapped packages, her colour high.

'I've brought you both a little something from England— a small token of my gratitude for your hospitality.'

Umm Faisal inclined her head graciously, but Zahra was far less inhibited.

'A present?' she exclaimed with shining eyes. 'Oh, Felicia, how lovely—but you shouldn't have.'

'Nothing very exciting, I'm afraid,' Felicia warned her, remembering the deprecatory words Faisal always used before giving her some shockingly extravagant treat. It was an Arab trait to deprecate their possessions, stemming from the days when to boast of one's achievements could call down the 'evil eye' upon the bragger, and she knew it was still the custom for an Arab to welcome a visitor to his 'humble' home, even if that home were a palace.

A little apprehensively she watched Zahra open her present, but the younger girl's gasp of pleasure obliterated her fears that it would not be well received. Even Raschid was commanded to admire the contents of the make-up box, although he did so with typical male indulgence for so purely a female delight.

Umm Faisal's pleasure was a little more restrained, but genuine none the less, and Felicia was pleased that she had taken the trouble to ask Faisal what sort of perfume his mother preferred.

'It's gorgeous!' Zahra exclaimed, sniffing the bottle. 'It reminds me of the one al-Azir mixed for you the last time we were in Jeddah, Mother—do you remember?'

'I certainly do,' Raschid interrupted drily. 'It was extremely expensive.'

Felicia smiled politely at his little joke, and looked up to find Zahra watching her expectantly.

'Where is Raschid's present, Felicia? Or are you

keeping it from him until he apologises for this afternoon?' she teased with a smile.

Felicia felt her colour come and go. How could she say that she had not brought a present for Raschid? She bit her lip and then remembered the paperweight she had bought for Nadia, Faisal's elder sister.

'It's upstairs,' she improvised hurriedly, hating the guilty blush that mantled her cheeks. 'I wasn't sure that Raschid would be eating with us.'

'You have forgiven him, then. I knew you would. Do go and get it,' Zahra urged Felicia, before turning to her mother, her eyes twinkling. 'Uncle Raschid was unkind to Felicia this afternoon, Mother. She didn't realise she could have asked him to cash her travellers' cheques and she had gone into the bank *alone*!'

The shocked expression on Umm Faisal's face told Felicia that Raschid had spoken no less than the truth when he warned her about her behaviour, and she used the diversion created by Zahra's announcement to excuse herself and slip upstairs to collect the paperweight.

Fortunately it had been wrapped in a silvery striped paper suitable for either sex, and hating herself for the deceit, she hurried downstairs with the small package. When she had decided against bringing a gift for Faisal's uncle, she had not bargained for being faced with a situation such as this evening's!

As she handed Raschid the small square box her fingers trembled, accidentally brushing his, the brief contact sending alarm bells jangling along her nervous system, her eyes wide and dismayed in her small heart-shaped face. She knew that it was too much to hope that the man thanking her so urbanely for her thoughtfulness had not noticed the small, betraying gesture.

Nothing escaped those smoky-grey eyes, now sardonic with comprehensive amusement, and Felicia slipped hurriedly back into her chair, wishing that she had waited for a more propitious moment for her present giving.

'Go on, then, open it!' Zahra commanded her uncle, her eyes on the package. 'I'm dying to see what it is!'

'Then I had better unwrap it quickly, before Miss Gordon accuses me of further cruelty to my family,' was Raschid's cool comment as lean fingers made nonsense of the sealing.

When the paper fell away to reveal the dark blue leather box, Zahra expelled an impatient sigh.

'Raschid, do hurry—it looks very exciting!'

In the growing darkness of the Oriental room with its plain white walls and luxurious, richly coloured Persian carpets; its priceless antique furniture with its glowing patina, the pure beauty of the blue-green glass was a poignant reminder for Felicia of the country she had left behind. The glass was Caithness, from Scotland, where craftsmen took a pride in fashioning the heavy paperweights, imprisoning within the depths of the molten glass, small flowers; petals; sea anemones so that their beauty would live for ever. The one Felicia had chosen held a blue-green sea anemone, and it had been one of a limited range and consequently frighteningly expensive, but she had fallen in love with its cool, remote beauty.

As she watched, her breath caught in her throat, Raschid lifted it out of its white satin bed, balancing it on his open palm. The silence that followed was a tribute to the craftsmen who had conceived and made it.

'It's beautiful,' Zahra whispered, touching it with a delicate forefinger. 'So cool and fresh—like you, Felicia.'

'It is a gift any Arab would treasure, Miss Gordon,' Raschid's deep voice agreed. 'The glassblower has captured the quality and colour of the sea in our gulf, and nothing is more precious to our race than water.'

'It can be used as an ink-holder, or just a paperweight,' Felicia told them, dismayed by the faint huskiness in her voice. For some subtle reason which she could not define, the gift had taken on an intensely personal aura she had never intended it to have. When she bought it, the sales-girl told her that it was designed to be used as an ink-holder or perfume bottle, and it was for the latter reason that she had deemed it suitable for Nadia, apart from its obvious beauty. Thank goodness she had not bought her perfume, she decided, quelling a nervous giggle; then she would have been placed in an embarrassing position. If she had not been so stubbornly against buying anything for Raschid in the first place, she would not now be in this un-pleasant situation, she reminded herself, trying not to notice Raschid's cool scrutiny both of her and the gift.

'You are very generous,' he said at last, silvery-grey eyes holding anxious green ones. 'More generous than I deserve.' He placed the paperweight back in its box, snapped the lid down and got up. 'If you will excuse me, there are certain business matters I have to attend to.'

Felicia had wanted to enquire whether there were any letters for her. She had learned from Zahra that all the mail, irrespective of its eventual recipient, was passed to Raschid, and she was hoping that there might be a letter for her from Faisal. Although she had only been in Kuwait a very short

time, Faisal had not written to her since his departure for
New York, and she had half expected to find a letter
awaiting her arrival. A letter from him would help banish
the memory of those tension-fraught seconds when awareness of Raschid had threatened to swamp her, and she badly
needed the reassurance that hearing from him would bring.

'How clever of you to choose such marvellous presents,'
Zahra murmured admiringly later. 'Especially Raschid's.
Did Faisal tell you that he collected rare glass?'

Felicia shook her head. There seemed to be rather a lot
of things Faisal had neglected to tell her about his uncle,
and she guessed intuitively that these omissions had been
deliberate.

'You are showing *siyasa* after all, Felicia,' Zahra dimpled
up at her. 'Your generosity will surely melt Raschid's heart.'

That was the last thing it was likely to do, Felicia
thought despairingly. If Raschid thought that she was deliberately trying to soften his hostility he would be less
likely than ever to view her in a favourable light.

'It is my name day soon,' Zahra confided. 'Raschid has
promised that we may go to the oasis for a few days. You
will like it. I don't expect I will be able to spend much time
there once I am married, as it is really Raschid's house, so
this is by way of being a special treat.'

It was the first time Zahra had mentioned her marriage
and Felicia did not like to pry. However, they were alone,
Umm Faisal having excused herself, and Zahra seemed to
be in the mood for confidences. 'They brought the material
for my wedding gown this afternoon,' she told Felicia,
wrinkling her nose slightly. 'Of course, I am not supposed
to know anything about it.'

'Don't you mind marrying a stranger?' Felicia asked curiously, hoping that she wasn't treading on dangerous ground, for she had no wish to upset the younger girl.

Zahra looked shocked and indignant.

'Saud is not a stranger! Whatever gave you that idea?' She shook her head.

Feeling rather perplexed, Felicia ventured hesitantly, 'But when your uncle mentioned to me the negotiations I thought your marriage must be an arranged one.'

Zahra laughed. 'Well, yes, in a way I suppose it is. Saud and I met at the university, but his family is a very important one and very old-fashioned. Saud was to have married his first cousin, as is customary, but fortunately Raschid was able to discover that the girl wanted to marry elsewhere, and so he was able to persuade Saud's family to accept me as Saud's wife. It could have been very difficult, for it would have been an unforgivable insult were Saud to refuse to marry his cousin, and conversely, had the girl objected to him, it would have caused her father to lose face. Our wedding is to take place quite soon, but first must come the formal visits.' She pulled a face. 'It is all so silly really, both of us having to pretend that we don't know one another. I would be quite happy to get married in your English fashion, but Raschid says that sometimes the more roundabout route is actually the shorter.'

Felicia did not know what to say. She had imagined that Zahra was being forced into the marriage for reasons of policy and had even suspected that somehow or other Raschid would benefit financially from the marriage. Now she was being compelled to review her suspicions.

'Of course Saud's family demanded a very large dowry,'

Zahra continued matter-of-factly, startling her still further. 'But Raschid has been very generous. You must ask Mother to show you my bridal chest. It will hold Saud's gifts to me on our marriage, and it has been passed down through our family for ten generations.'

Felicia was still digesting this unwelcome insight into Raschid's actions when Zahra excused herself, saying that she had some studying to do. When she had gone Felicia stared out into the darkness of the gardens. It seemed that she had completely misunderstood Raschid's motives—at least as far as Zahra was concerned, for there could be no mistaking his attitude towards her. Was inviting her here a roundabout way to destroying Faisal's love for her? With considerable misgivings, she wandered restlessly from the window to the door leading out into the courtyard, tempted by its inviting solitude and fresh air. It was cooler outside than she had expected and she shivered in her thin dress, but the music of the fountains was particularly haunting by night, suiting her mood, and she found herself drawn to where the clean, cool water splashed down into its marble pool. She passed the birds in their aviary and sighed faintly. She was as much a prisoner as they, although there were no walls to her cage other than custom and hostility.

'Miss Gordon!'

She froze as the dark shadow loomed over her, the sound of her name on those cruel lips sending shivers of apprehension running over her skin. All at once the velvet darkness seemed to press down on her, every instinct warning her to flee as Raschid emerged from the shadows, crossing the courtyard with silent stealth.

She had thought that she had the courtyard to herself,

Raschid the last person she had expected to materialise at her side, and she choked back her dismay, forcing herself to say coolly, 'Sheikh—I didn't see you, Zahra told me you'd gone out.'

'So I had,' he agreed. 'But now I have returned, and like you I was tempted into the garden to enjoy its solitude.'

Felicia turned, intending to return to the protection of the house, but his fingers grasped her shoulder, forcing her to stand mute under his considering scrutiny. His eyes seemed to strip away her fragile defences, leaving her exposed and vulnerable, her eyes wide and uncertain as she tried to hold his gaze.

'This meeting is most opportune,' he drawled at length. 'I am glad of the chance to speak privately with you.'

'I thought my presence was yours to command,' Felicia retorted bitterly. 'Or are you no longer master in this house?'

He ignored her taunt, his eyes mocking as they pierced the darkness. 'I was thinking of your embarrassment and my sister's curiosity were I to send for you privately; not my own ability to command you if I so wished. Fatima tells me that Zahra was to have shown you the town this afternoon, and apparently my appearance on the scene deprived you of this treat.'

When Felicia refused to reply he continued coolly,

'That being the case, I shall put myself at your disposal later in the week. You know, of course, that Friday is our holy day, but if you will name another, I shall make sure that it is free.'

Munificence indeed, Felicia thought wryly, but being escorted around Kuwait by a disapproving Raschid was the last thing she wanted.

'There's no need for you to go to such trouble,' she assured him quickly—too quickly, she realised, when she saw him curse under his breath, his fingers tightening painfully.

'It seems that you are determined to quarrel with me,' he accused. 'You British have a saying that is particularly relevant, and I suggest that you accept the olive branch I extend. We are extremely dependent upon the olive in our harsh climate, and we never take its name in vain. It is plain that Zahra has taken you to her heart—perhaps the fault for this is mine in not warning her more thoroughly about the type of woman you are— However, the damage is now done, and it will hurt her if she sees that we are enemies. She is to leave us soon, and I will not have her last days with her family spoiled and marred by ill-feeling between us.'

'A pity you didn't think of that before you insulted me so grossly this afternoon,' Felicia reminded him bleakly, dismayed by the bitterness that swept over her.

'So!' He seemed to consider her for a moment, his eyes probing the darkness until she shrank under their assessing gleam. 'Very well. If I cannot gain your co-operation through goodwill, I shall have to gain it in some other fashion.'

A frisson of fear ran over her skin. In the dark the fountain played, but the sound suddenly seemed heightened to her overstrung nerves, emphasising the solitude of the garden.

'If you're thinking of bribery,' she said distastefully, 'I suggest you think again. There's nothing you could offer me that would change my love for Faisal.'

'Nothing?' Raschid taunted softly, coming towards her like a jungle cat, all feline grace and terrifying danger. Although it was dark she could see the faint sheen of his skin, marred by the dark shadow of his beard along his jawline. It was unfair that any man should possess such arrogant certainty of his own power to compel others to do his bidding, she thought nervously, her tongue wetting her dry lips, as long lashes flicked down over his eyes, hiding his thoughts from her. His touch had become less brutal, his fingers gently massaging the fragile bones of her shoulders, sending a warning screaming through her veins. This man is dangerous, it seemed to say, and with trembling certainty she knew that she had pulled the tiger's tail and must surely suffer the consequences.

Without her being able to do a thing about it, Raschid slid his hands from her shoulders to her waist, propelling her towards him, his voice a mocking imitation of tenderness, as he murmured softly against her hair, 'You leave me with very little choice, Miss Gordon. You have continually defied me, and must pay the price. You cannot expect me to believe you are naïve enough not to know how a man will retaliate when you challenge his most basic instincts?

'Very well then,' he said harshly, when she refused to answer, 'let this be your punishment.'

Cruel hands imprisoned her against the hard warmth of his body, his voice cold as he commanded her to abandon her vain struggles to be free, as his mouth descended on hers with a punishing ferocity.

If she had once read passion into that full underlip, there was none now. It was a kiss of bitter anger; a contemptuous punishment of her defiance, breaking through the fragile cobweb dreams she had spun of a moment like this; alone in an Eastern dusk, in the arms of a man who could trace his origins back to the fierce tribesmen who called the whole desert home. But then, of course, she had been thinking of Faisal—not this man who crushed her against the steel wall of his chest, without a thought for the fragility of her own soft curves; who destroyed her dreams as easily as he might tear the wings from a foolish moth.

Furiously resentful, she withstood the harsh pressure of his mouth; rigidly refusing to admit defeat, her lips clamped shut against the demand of his. He might be able to physically restrain her, but nothing could make her respond to him in the way he had obviously intended.

This kiss could only have lasted seconds, but it seemed an eternity before she was released, feeling mangled like some poor creature set free from the talons of the falcons that sheikhs flew from their wrists.

She beat at his chest with ineffectual hands, but he grasped her wrists, smiling down tauntingly.

'Well, do you still say that you can defy me?'

'I'll tell Faisal what you've done!' Felicia all but wept, trembling with humiliation, but Raschid only laughed.

'You would never dare,' he told her softly. 'We have a saying in our country, that it takes two to commit adultery. Mud sticks, Miss Gordon. By all means tell Faisal. I wish you would…!'

Leaving her to digest that remark, he released her so suddenly that she almost fell. Her fingers went instinctively to her throbbing lips, tears blurring her vision.

'Oh, by the way,' Raschid added casually, slipping a hand into his jacket and withdrawing the blue leather box that held the paperweight, 'I suggest you give this to the person for whom it was originally intended.' And he threw the box towards her. 'I think we both of us know that you would never have bought such a gift for me, and you insult my intelligence by expecting me to believe that you did. Keep it for Faisal. I am sure he will be far more appreciative—and show it in a more acceptable way!'

He had gone before Felicia could admit that the paperweight had been purchased for Nadia, his anger leaving an almost tangible atmosphere in the cool garden.

He had shamed and humiliated her; mocked her love for Faisal and his for her, and treated her in a way that no man should ever treat a female member of his family, and yet try as she might she could not conjure up the comforting memory of how it felt to be in Faisal's arms, and it came to her, with shock, that although he had driven her to fury and bitter despair she had not shrunk under Raschid's embrace as she did when with Faisal. Because she had been too angry, she assured herself, staring down at the box in her hand.

Suddenly she hated the paperweight more than she had ever hated anything in her life. Before she could change her mind she hurled the box as far as she could, barely aware of the small, distant thud as it fell amongst some roses, then she turned her back on the courtyard and sought the sanctuary of her bedroom.

Under the electric light she saw the faint beginnings of what would eventually be bruises from Raschid's tight grip.

Removing her clothes, she showered, soaping her flesh until it glowed, as though by doing so she could remove for all time the memory of Raschid's kiss. She hated him! Hated him, she told her flushed reflection defiantly. So why was she crying, silly, weak tears, that would only afford her self-confessed enemy the greatest satisfaction?

She touched a tear-damp cheek with shaking fingers. In the space of a few earth-shaking minutes Raschid had destroyed her illusions and ripped away the veils of innocence which had hitherto protected her, and all because she had dared to flout his authority and walk unattended in the streets of Kuwait.

But as she waited for sleep to claim her, Felicia admitted that it went deeper than that. For the first time in her life she had experienced true fear, and as her eyes closed she fought desperately to remember what it had felt like to be held in Faisal's arms, investing her memories with a passion they had never possessed in an endeavour to obliterate every last trace of Raschid's touch.

CHAPTER FIVE

FEMALE voices rose and fell, punctuated with laughter and the rattle of coffee cups. Umm Faisal had invited her friends round to meet Felicia, and judging by the number of women crowded into the room, Felicia suspected that her hostess numbered the entire town amongst her acquaintances.

Most of the visitors were of Umm Faisal's generation, and from an upstairs window Felicia had seen them hurrying from opulent cars, their bodies draped in heavy black cloaks, glancing neither to the left nor the right. Once inside, though, the cloaks were discarded like so many unwanted chrysalises to reveal Paris couture fashions and jewellery to rival the contents of the Tower of London.

From her cross-legged position on a damask cushion Felicia listened to her neighbour describing a recent visit to America. All the women spoke English, although sometimes with accents which made it almost impossible for her to recognise her native tongue.

This was the first time she had observed the formal ritual of receiving guests, Arab fashion; the gracious welcome and lavish hospitality; and above all the enthusiasm with which the visitors greeted her. Most of them had visited London at one time or another, and they all displayed an almost childlike curiosity about her life there.

The maid, Selina, came round with fresh coffee, and Felicia sighed. Her stomach was awash with the bitter liquid, but since no one else seemed to be refusing, she felt she could hardly do so herself. Umm Faisal caught her eye, smiling understandingly. She whispered something to Selina and to Felicia's relief the dusky serving girl passed by without filling her delicate porcelain cup.

Marble floors, and damask cushions; they were a far cry from her small bedsit with its second-hand furniture. Felicia found that she no longer thought of the austerity of plain white walls as a strange contrast to the luxurious silks and satins the Arabs used for furnishings. She had grown used to seeing Umm Faisal sitting cross-legged on a cushion on the floor, although most of the rooms were furnished in a more Western style, but she doubted if she could ever come to terms with the segregation of male and female; the absolute and all-embracing dominance of the male. However, Zahra told her that even this was less strictly adhered to than had once been the case, and she was forced to admit that where his family were concerned, Raschid was a very forward-thinking man indeed. A pity that his enlightened views did not extend to include her!

Someone knocked on the door, and instantly women were reaching for their veils, without haste or pretension, slipping them into place, as Selina opened the door. Servants, Zahra had told Felicia, did not need to veil.

'It is the Master, *sitti*,' the girl told Umm Faisal.

'Ah, yes, he has come to collect you, Felicia. Raschid

is going to show Felicia Kuwait,' she explained for the
benefit of her guests, adding something in Arabic that
brought a twinkle to more than one pair of dark eyes.

'She says that it is as well that Raschid is a man of im-
peccable honour,' Felicia's companion whispered. 'In our
day such a thing would not have been allowed, but times
change.' She shrugged as though to say who was to tell
whether or not such changes were for the better, laughing
when Felicia got unsteadily to her feet. No wonder these
women were so graceful and fluid; their limbs would be
trained from childhood to accept such a pose, while hers
protested agonisingly, pins and needles stabbing painfully
through both feet.

After their confrontation in the garden, Felicia had never
expected that Raschid would pursue his promise to take her
sightseeing—if indeed a 'promise' it had been—but pride
would not let her back down and refuse to go with him.

She had dressed for Umm Faisal's guests with special
care, but as she opened the door, the horrible thought struck
her that Raschid might think that she had donned her attractive outfit for his benefit.

She was wearing a peach linen suit, perfect with her
warm colouring, a simple cream silk blouse underneath the
neatly fitting jacket. Cream shoes and a slim clutch bag
toned perfectly with subtle peach linen, and thin gold
bangles chimed musically as she moved. They had been a
gift from Faisal, and one which she had tried to refuse until
he told her that unless she accepted them the bracelets
would be thrown away. She thought of the emerald ring he
had bought her—now with him in New York—and his
anger when she had refused to wear it until his family

accepted their engagement. Now, when it was too late, she wished she had brought the ring with her. Perhaps the sight of it might help to restore some of the high hopes with which she had come to Kuwait.

In Eastern garments she knew that she could never hope to rival the grace of girls who had been wearing them from babyhood, but as she glanced in the full-length mirror set into the wall, she reflected that she had every reason to feel pleased with her appearance, and knowing that she looked her best lent an air of confidence that bloomed in the soft colour of her cheeks and the warm glow of her eyes.

Today she had overcome an important hurdle. Umm Faisal's friends had accepted her, despite the differences in their cultures—East and West could blend happily, no matter what Raschid said. With the light of battle in her eyes, Felicia went to meet the man waiting for her in the paved courtyard.

Dim light filtered in through the tall narrow windows of the entrance hall, and at first she could not see him. Then he moved and she caught the white flash of his shirt, the cuffs immaculate as he shot one back to glance at his watch. The gesture, so typically male, made her smile, and that was when he turned and saw her, poised in the doorway, the dark wood a perfect foil for her translucent beauty, laughter trembling the generous curve of her mouth, her eyes calm and composed.

He came towards her, his expression unreadable. This time Felicia was determined to retain the upper hand.

'I'm sorry if I kept you waiting,' she apologised formally, 'but your sister's friends....'

'You have no need to explain the female of the species

to me, Miss Gordon. I'm perfectly conversant with its addiction to senseless chatter.'

His arrogance all but took her breath away.

'If it's senseless, it's because men like you refuse to give them the opportunity to be anything else,' she retorted, the serenity dying out of her eyes to be replaced by anger, but Raschid merely looked amused.

'Is that what you have been doing? Lecturing Fatima's guests on the rights of the liberated woman? You will not be very popular with their husbands, Miss Gordon.'

'I don't care whether I am or not,' Felicia announced recklessly.

'Foolish of you,' was Raschid's only comment. 'For those same husbands have the power to forbid their wives to have anything to do with you, if they wish, and Faisal would not approve of that. He may appear Westernised to you, Miss Gordon, but he will expect his wife to adhere to the rules of his own society, I assure you.'

Ignoring the warning, Felicia tossed her head, walking past Raschid to where the car was parked. Where once she had wanted to gain his approval for Faisal's sake, now she seemed to derive intense satisfaction from deliberately needling him—a trait so alien to her personality that she wondered a little bitterly why it had to be Faisal's guardian of all people who should arouse it within her.

'Faisal and I will not be living in Kuwait,' she told Raschid, remembering what Faisal had said.

'No?' His sideways glance was mocking. 'Aren't you forgetting something, Miss Gordon?'

She refused to look at him, preceding him across the

courtyard, where the scent of early roses already hung intoxicatingly on the warm air.

'If I am I'm sure you'll remind me of it.'

'Exactly so,' Raschid agreed urbanely. 'As an employee of the bank—and make no mistake, Faisal *is* an employee—he has a duty to go where the Board decides he will be of most use.'

'The Board?' Felicia queried bitterly. 'Don't you mean yourself?'

'In these circumstances I think I can agree that the two are synonymous.'

His suave satisfaction jarred, like a nerve in an aching tooth probed by an unwary tongue. Felicia hesitated, on the point of refusing to accompany him, but then she remembered Zahra's approaching birthday, and accepted that there would probably be no other suitable opportunity to buy her a present. Swallowing the words, with her pride, she contented herself with a cold glare in Raschid's direction.

For the last few days the household had gone busily frantic over the arrangements for transporting Umm Faisal, Raschid, Zahra and herself, as well as the staff and everything that they would require, to the oasis for the duration of the birthday celebrations. Only that morning Zahra had laughingly confided that without Raschid to master-mind the move she doubted if they would get any farther than Kuwait City. Felicia had suggested rather hesitantly that perhaps she ought to return home, in case her presence at such a time proved to be a nuisance, but Zahra's swift dismay soon reassured her. In point of fact, she and Zahra had become very close, and it was only her growing affection for the younger girl that prevented Felicia from giving full rein to her growing antipathy towards Raschid. As he had so rightly said, it would hurt Zahra if she thought they were quarrelling, and Felicia had as little desire to cast a blight over the birthday festivities as Raschid. For that reason an uneasy—on her part at least—truce had developed between them.

'A wise decision,' Raschid drawled suddenly, startling her. She glared at him suspiciously, caught off guard when he said smoothly, 'Don't bother denying that you were contemplating refusing my company. I dislike liars almost as much as I despise fortune-hunters.'

The sheer rage engendered by his dismissive tones rendered her speechless, totally unable to retaliate, and it wasn't until he walked round to the opposite side of the parked car and opened the driver's door that Felicia realised that Ali would not be accompanying them. Raschid leaned across the passenger seat, unlocking the door and pushing it open.

'I think I would prefer to sit in the back,' she said stiffly. 'Isn't that what you think good women should do—dutifully take a back seat and leave the driving to their lords and masters?'

'On this occasion I think we will opt for the Western custom,' Raschid replied drily. 'Otherwise I shall be endangering both our lives by constantly having to look over my shoulder to converse with you— Or do you perhaps read a more sinister purpose into my request? Your imagination runs away with you, Miss Gordon.'

If anything his voice had become even more cuttingly unkind, and Felicia flushed painfully, knowing he was deliberately taunting her.

'Even if such was my desire,' he continued, 'which most assuredly it is not, I never, but never make love on the open carriageway between my home and the city. Kuwaiti drivers are not the most polite in the world, nor the most tolerant of dawdlers, as you will soon discover. I am sorry if I don't match up to the prowess of your previous escorts in this regard, but in the East we prefer to suit the activity to our surroundings.'

Felicia stood by the car, longing to slam the door shut, wishing she could think of a suitably cutting retort to burst for once and for all the complacent arrogance with which Raschid surrounded himself. She had forgotten that even though she was standing by the side of the Mercedes, Raschid could still read her expression quite accurately in the driving mirror, and she jumped when he drawled mockingly, 'I can almost feel the knife entering my heart, Miss Gordon. Be careful. In this country we believe in taking a life for a life.'

'Heart? What heart?' she retorted, too furious to pay much attention to the rest of the sentence. 'You don't possess such a thing, Sheikh Raschid!'

'Get in the car, Miss Gordon, and save your anger to fuel something more profitable than pitting your wits against mine.'

The arrogance of it! Felicia seethed as she slid into the seat, ignoring his smile as he leaned across her to close the door. At such close quarters an aura of taut masculinity emanated from him. She was pulsatingly aware of the warm sheen of his skin, drawn tightly over the narrow bones of his face; the way his eyelashes lay, long and dark against the sculptured bone; silk against satin, she thought irrelevantly, shiveringly aware of him in a way that she had never been aware of Faisal, but underneath lay a core of pure steel.

'Do I pass muster?'

She flushed as vividly as the roses blooming in the inner courtyard, hating to be caught out paying him any attention, no matter what the reason—and in this case, pure curiosity had drawn her eyes to his face, unwilling admiration keeping them there to wonder at the perfect symmetry of the bone structure underlying the smooth skin, even while the arrogant profile made her anger rise like a river in a flash flood, coming out of nowhere to appal her with its ferocity. How strange it was that a mingling of East and West should have produced this lordly, sensual man, while Faisal's pure Arab blood had produced a man in a much softer mould.

While she battled with her anger, she told herself that for Faisal's sake she must learn to tame it, to sit meek and docile under the razor-sharp tongue and probing glance. She had once read that a falcon could focus on its prey from many thousands of feet above it in the sky; so it was with Raschid. Those grey eyes held all the latent power of a modern laser beam.

They took the coast road. The day was deliciously warm, the merest breath of fresh air from the air-conditioning fanning her hair as they sped towards the city. The leather seats reclined to contour the body, and the radio emitted soothing music, but Felicia could not relax. She was as tense as a coiled spring, unwittingly betraying her anxiety in her tightly clenched fists.

'Relax,' Raschid surprised her by saying. 'Or is it

merely the fact that you are a passenger rather than the
driver which makes you so tense? How you European
women rob yourselves of your very femininity by insisting on doing everything for yourselves!'

'Perhaps because our experience of your sex has taught
us how unwise it is for us to rely on them for anything,'
Felicia retorted unwisely, thinking of Uncle George, and
how selfishly he had refused to allow either her aunt or
herself the slightest little pleasure, begrudging every small
thing he had done for them.

'Is that why you want to marry Faisal?' Raschid asked
astutely. 'Because you see in him a shoulder on which to
lean? Strange—I had not thought of you as a clinging vine;
I see I shall have to revise my strategy. Clinging vines are
notoriously difficult to remove, but Faisal is weak, Miss
Gordon; whoever marries him will need to be mother,
lover, and even jailer at times. Are you sure you are able
to fulfil all those roles?'

'It's easy to list his failings when he's not here to defend
himself,' Felicia retorted hotly, trying not to acknowledge
the truth of what Raschid had said. Hadn't she sometimes
noticed an inclination to adopt the role of helpless little boy
by Faisal, when all was not going his way?

'You are loyal at least,' Raschid responded in clipped
accents, as though the admission displeased him, then
changed the subject to draw her attention to the British
Embassy. Because he hoped that she would soon be
entering that building, asking to be sent home, all her
dreams of marriage to Faisal turned to so much dust.

Not for the first time Felicia wondered at her own
foolish impetuosity in allowing Faisal to persuade her to

come to Kuwait. He had paid for her air ticket; her own slender savings had gone on her new wardrobe, but Faisal had glibly assured her that it would not be long before he was able to join her in Kuwait, taking it for granted that she would remain with his family until their marriage. If that was not to take place until he was twenty-five she would have to return to England. Which meant that she would have to write and ask Faisal for the money for her ticket, for she was convinced that Raschid would never allow him to return to Kuwait while she was there.

As soon as Zahra's birthday was over she would write to him, she promised herself, comforted by this gesture of independence.

They drove past the Sief Palace, where guards stood stiffly to attention. A flag flew from the tall, square clock tower.

'His Highness the Emir is holding his *majlis*,' Raschid told her.

'And I'm sure I'm safe in assuming the Emir's government is overwhelmingly male,' Felicia could not resist retorting.

'You seem to have an outsize chip on your shoulder regarding my sex, Miss Gordon—or is it that having gained your independence, you find you no longer want it?'

Felicia turned away from the malice-spiked glance. She had never been an advocate of Women's Lib, being quite happy to play the role for which nature had intended her; a role which she did not in any way consider to be subservient, however, so she now found herself saying quite heatedly, 'You do not deny that in your country women often still have to fight for equal status?'

'And that arouses your crusading instinct? Would it

surprise you to know that women do have rights here; that
they can vote or run for office?'

'But they didn't have those rights until very recently,'
Felicia responded briefly, looking away, suddenly conscious of the insolent appraisal of narrowed grey eyes.

Raschid swung the car over, throwing her heavily
against him, his arm brushing against her breasts and
leaving her tingling with an awareness she had never experienced in Faisal's arms. What was this tension that
seemed to vibrate in the air whenever she was near him?
Whatever it was she did not like it.

'We are now entering the main *souk* and banking area,
Miss Gordon,' Raschid informed her. 'I suggest that I park
the car so that we can do the rest of our tour at a more leisurely pace.'

They left the car in a huge underground car-park
beneath a towering plate glass and chrome office block.

'This is where we have our head office,' Raschid explained. 'In fact this building was one of our first ventures
into the construction industry.'

'But not your last,' Felicia commented, remembering
Faisal saying that the Bank had helped to finance the
building of a hotel, amongst other things.

Raschid's hand was under her arm, a courtesy she had
not expected, and she stumbled slightly as they emerged
into the bright sunlight, his hard body taking the full
impact of her tensed slenderness as they collided. Even that
brief contact was enough to disturb her; the grey eyes
cynically amused as they took in her flushed cheeks and
angry eyes.

'No, not our last,' he agreed. 'Although this particular

venture was extremely profitable. As I am sure you already
know, construction finance accounts for some forty per
cent of our profits.' He looked at her averted profile, and
gave her another thin-lipped smile.

'Am I boring you? Surely not. It is my experience that
most women find the making of money almost as absorbing as the spending of it.'

'Well, I'm not most women,' Felicia replied shortly,
pulling up with a start as they rounded a corner.

The wide street in front of them was laid out with trees
and flower beds, greenery and tropical colour rioting everywhere. Where once there had been barren desert, fountains
played, and instead of walking beneath the scorching glare
of the sun, cool shady trees spread their green cloak invitingly over the strolling shoppers.

'Kuwait's Bond Street,' Raschid offered sardonically, as
Felicia stared at the bewilderingly exotic display of
precious stones in a jeweller's window.

'I have no doubt that you would far rather tour this area
in Faisal's company than mine,' he drawled coolly, intimat-
ing that Faisal could have been persuaded to do more than
merely glance disparagingly at the glittering diamond
display that commanded the front of the window.

'I *would* have preferred to. But not for the reasons you
suppose,' Felicia stressed pointedly, peering a little closer
into the plate glass in the hope of finding something a little
more modestly priced that she could buy for Zahra.
Already she had learned of the younger girl's love of jewellery, and she smiled a little as she contemplated her
reaction to the display of gems in front of her. She gave a
faint sigh. There was nothing here to suit her slender

pocket, and the shops, although luxuriously expensive, were disappointingly Westernised.

'What did you expect?' Raschid asked in thinly veiled amusement when she ventured to say as much. '*Souks* in the traditional manner, complete with beggars with alms bowls? At one time the blind men of the city were employed to call the muezzin from the minarets, lest strange male eyes perceived an unveiled woman—such are the wonders of modern science that nowadays the minaret towers are fitted with loudspeakers which do the job far more effectively, and our poor are supported by the State.'

'Blind men were deliberately employed for such a purpose?'

Intrigued despite her hostility, Felicia hesitated, to turn an enquiring face up to the saturnine dark one above her.

'You find such safeguarding of the modesty of our women amusing, I am sure. But not so long ago for a man to look upon the face of another's wife was a gross insult to them both—in your country a worse crime than sleeping with one's best friend's wife—although I learn that nowadays such occurrences are commonplace.'

Felicia's face flushed.

'Not in the circles in which I move,' she denied energetically.

Raschid's eyebrows rose and he shrugged dismissively. 'It matters little to me one way or the other, so you may save your protestations for other ears. Now, if you have seen enough, I suggest we return to the car.'

'But I haven't bought Zahra a present,' Felicia began in dismay, faltering into silence as Raschid turned to stare at her.

'*That* was why you agreed to come? What did you have in mind?'

He looked so bored and remote that Felicia almost stamped her foot.

'It isn't what I have in mind, but what I can afford,' she said bluntly, gesturing towards the jeweller's window. 'Certainly nothing in there.'

For a moment she thought she saw his mouth curl in faint, amused condescension.

'No,' he agreed. 'Sadeer's is probably the most expensive jeweller's in Kuwait, and anyway, you could not hope to rival the gifts Zahra will receive from Saud and her family.'

'It isn't a question of "rivalling",' Felicia stormed, furious at his lack of understanding. 'It would be embarrassing and impolite if I had no present for her.'

'Are you asking for my help?'

Was she? She fought against a desire to tell him to go to hell and instead nodded her head mutely.

Was that satisfaction she read in his smile? Seething, she stared across the road, not really seeing the constant stream of opulent cars flashing past.

'Very well, Miss Gordon.' He took her arm, guiding her across the road towards a narrow alley, but before they could enter it a young woman hailed them, her eyes heavily kohled and her jeans and thin cotton blouse a replica of the uniform worn by her Western sisters. Felicia judged her to be around her own age, perhaps a little younger. She had the impression that Raschid would have preferred not to acknowledge her, and yet his smile was polite enough, and he listened attentively enough while she talked in rapid Arabic.

'Yasmin is the daughter of a friend of mine,' he explained

for her benefit, commanding the other girl to speak in English. 'She was at university in England for a while. Miss Gordon is a friend of Faisal's, Yasmin, and is staying with us for a while.'

'While Faisal is in New York?' She tossed her long, dark hair and eyed Felicia assessingly. 'I wonder if he knows how friendly you are with his "friend" Raschid, or perhaps he no longer minds sharing.'

She was gone before Felicia could say anything, and Raschid watched her depart in grim silence.

'If you found Yasmin's hostility strange, perhaps I should explain that she is one of the casualties of Faisal's ability to fall in and out of love. They became very close when she was in England, and I suspect she read more meaning into my description of you as Faisal's "friend" than I would have wished. No matter.... She is hardly likely to broadcast the true nature of your relationship. Not in view of her own feelings for Faisal.'

Yasmin and Faisal! Strange that the thought of them together caused her no jealousy, Felicia reflected. Indeed what she actually felt for the other girl was a vague pity, despite her insinuating remarks concerning herself and Raschid. 'Sharing' indeed! If only she knew! A bitter smile curved her mouth. She was the last woman Raschid would want in his life.

Raschid directed her down the narrow alleyway, shadowed and almost secret in the blank face it showed to the world.

Plainly he knew where he was going. He guided her through a labyrinth of narrow streets, some built from the original mud bricks from which the earlier town had been constructed.

'Where are you taking me?' she asked him at one point, alarmed by the sudden transformation from West to East, as cloaked figures shuffled silently past them, and exotic, unrecognisable fragrances filled the air.

Raschid chuckled.

'Not to the slave market, if that's what you think. Oh yes, they still have them in the more remote oases, where captured tribes are sold as slaves. It is illegal, of course,' he shrugged, 'but by the time the crime is discovered it is often too late to prevent it. All that one can do is to make sure that the unfortunate victims are set free.'

Felicia shuddered, suddenly glad of his tall presence at her side. They were walking through an old-fashioned covered *souk*, where merchants called to passers-by from their open doorways. Above one hung jewelled Eastern rugs so beautiful that Felicia stopped to stare.

'They are made by Badu from Iran,' Raschid told her. 'They use patterns passed down from generation to generation.'

The merchant called out a greeting, sensing a possible sale, but although Raschid acknowledged his presence, he did not stop.

Eventually he touched Felicia lightly on the arm, directing her footsteps towards an open doorway.

When her eyes had accustomed themselves to the darkness within the small shop Felicia saw that the shelves were stacked with bottles and boxes, the air redolent with cedarwood, ambergris, sandalwood, and other scents too unfamiliar for her to recognise. With dawning delight she realised that Raschid had brought her to the shop of a maker of perfumes.

While she stared round her surroundings in an absorbed trance the two men talked in low undertones. The owner of the shop was as wizened as a walnut, his face dried and seamed by time, but the dark eyes that glanced at Felicia were shrewdly assessing. He said something to Raschid and Felicia saw him shake his head, his expression cold.

'Will he be able to mix something for Zahra without seeing her?' Felicia whispered anxiously, wondering what they had been saying.

'The perfume is for Sitt Zahra?' the old man asked, betraying a knowledge of English Felicia would not have expected. Under her fascinated gaze the old man ran his eyes along the shelves, at last removing one small bottle. 'I have here the perfume I made for her the last time she came. If the Sitt cares to purchase some?'

It was dark in the interior of the shop, but Felicia saw Raschid nod his head, as she glanced at him for guidance.

'Yes, please,' she murmured.

A wide grin split the merchant's face.

'May Allah curse me, I had almost forgotten that the Sitt is to be married shortly. We must add something for fertility, and something else to enhance the womanhood that will shortly be hers.'

While they waited he measured and poured, sniffing occasionally, and then he was transferring the mixture to a small crystal jar.

'May I smell it?' Felicia asked eagerly.

To her disappointment he shook his head.

'This perfume is not harmonious to the Sitt's beauty.' He turned to Raschid and said something in Arabic, before saying to Felicia, 'Your beauty is that of the rose before it opens fully; a bud which has not yet blossomed, and so it must be with your perfume.'

Felicia was glad of the darkness to hide her blushes, as he handed the small package to her. She dared not look at Raschid, fearful of what she might see in his face. And yet the old man had been uncannily correct; she was still a 'bud', the petals of innocence furled tightly about her, awaiting the warmth of a man's lovemaking, before she could blossom into full flower.

In silence she followed Raschid from the shop, dazzled by the bright glare of the sun. It was the hour when the shops closed for the afternoon and everywhere shutters were being placed over windows, and doors closed against the heat. They were just emerging into the street when the perfume blender called something after them, and Raschid turned, glancing back into the scented darkness they had just left.

'One moment,' he said curtly, and disappeared back inside.

Felicia hesitated, unsure whether or not she ought to follow him. The two men were deep in a low-toned conversation, and unwilling to appear curious, she hovered in the doorway.

The old Arab was busily searching his shelves, moving jars and bottles. She caught the elusive scent of English lavender, instantly evocative of home, and then a more subtle, spicy scent. The old man pounded something in a wooden bowl with a small pestle and the fragrance of wild violets drenched the air. Fascinated, Felicia watched. Raschid was buying more perfume? For his sister? Then why the low-toned conversation? Some other woman, perhaps? A sophisticated creature with the chameleon ability to make the transition from East to West? A woman who would guard her beauty from curious eyes in public but who had the self-confidence to reveal it without shyness to the man she loved—in private?

'Miss Gordon?'

How many more times would she have to endure hearing her name called in those bitingly imperious tones?

Her errant footsteps had taken her beyond the confines of the shop and cool exasperation laced Raschid's voice as he strode towards her.

'Has all that my sister and I have said to you been as so many grains of sand dispersed by the winds, or is it merely wilful caprice that prompts you into such constant disobedience?'

Disobedience! Felicia spun round, her eyes darkened to jade green with anger. Dear God, she did not want to quarrel with this man, but neither would she let him walk roughshod over her pride, trampling it beneath the fiery scorn of his contempt.

'I walked away because I didn't want to intrude,' she flung at him. 'Your business was plainly private.' Anger made her reckless. 'A gift for some woman who is permitted to share your bed, but forbidden any other part in your life….'

'You have described the *type* of person for whom the perfume was intended to a nicety,' Raschid gritted at her. 'But the perfume maker does not share my view of you, Miss Gordon. Oh yes!' He laughed scornfully at her shocked expression. 'Did you not guess? The old man was making the perfume for you—his own idea, not mine, I hasten to add. Here, take it,' he commanded, thrusting a small package into her hand. 'He insists that it incorporates the innocence which he claims is an integral part of your nature. I did not want to tell him that his eyesight must be failing if that is what he thinks. I know my nephew, Miss Gordon,' he concluded grimly, 'and I know the type of women who share his life.'

Felicia turned, intent only on escaping from his cruel words, but his hands reached out and stayed her, his expression cautionary.

'Do not be foolish,' he advised her. 'Even nowadays the *souks* are not entirely free from danger for the unwary. Your careless footsteps might have led you down any one of a hundred alleys and before too long you would have been hopelessly lost—an experience I am sure neither of us wishes to endure.'

She pictured herself, lost and frightened, dependent on this cold, autocratic man for succour, and her chin lifted proudly.

'You need not worry, Sheikh Raschid,' she told him. 'If I were lost, *you* would be the last man I would want to rescue me.'

She pulled away from him as she spoke and a piece of flint half buried in the sun-baked earth caught her unprotected ankle, lacerating the soft skin. She winced as pain shot through her and blood welled from the cut.

Raschid tensed, frowning as he heard her involuntary protest, then dropped on to his haunches, a muttered curse falling softly into the golden silence of the afternoon when he saw what had happened.

'It's nothing,' Felicia protested unsteadily as lean fingers probed the wound with surprising gentleness.

'It's bleeding. It must be washed and cleaned,' Raschid replied curtly.

There were some moistened tissues in her bag which she

used to keep her hands and face fresh and she opened it, removing them.

'I'll do that.'

The authoritative tone could not be ignored, and in silence she handed Raschid the moistened pad, flinching a little at its coolness against her throbbing flesh.

'How one admires the British in adversity,' Raschid mocked as he straightened up. 'So cool, so controlled...so prepared for every contingency.'

The light in his eyes reminded her that a few nights ago there had been a contingency for which she had not been prepared, but Felicia ignored it, murmuring lightly, 'One tries....'

'Indeed one does. But sometimes we must fail, for the good of our souls.'

Was he warning her that she would fail to convince him to allow her marriage to Faisal? She moved away, wincing afresh as she put her full weight on her ankle. Raschid's hand on her wrist steadied her; a momentary contact—no more— but in that moment the air between them seemed fraught with some intangible emotion and then she was free, the clean male scent of him fading from her nostrils as quickly as the imprint of his fingers was fading from her wrist.

'What's the matter?'

Her eyelashes flicked down, but not in time to prevent him from reading the expression in her eyes. He laughed softly.

'Ah yes, I see! You thought perhaps I might repeat our romantic scene of the other night. I'm afraid I must disappoint you, Miss Gordon.'

'Romantic? Is that what you call it?' Felicia retorted bitterly. 'Then you have very strange ideas of romance,

Sheikh.' She turned away, anger and resentment flaring simultaneously to heated life, possessed by an urge to escape from this man and his tormenting mockery; a desire to put as much distance between them as possible, heedless of the dangers.

In the empty *souk* her heartbeat thundered in her ears, steadily increasing as she hurried past shuttered shop fronts, like so many unseeing eyes, disdainful of the folly of the pale foreigner who ran unveiled along the shadowed alley. Pain throbbed through her ankle, but she disregarded it. The thudding of her heart drowned out every other sound bar one—the relentless footsteps behind her, firm and tireless, driving her like a terrified gazelle before the beaters.

He caught her, as she had known he must, his fingers biting into her waist as he swung her back against him, shaking her until she thought her neck must break.

'You little fool! Don't you know any better than to run in this heat? Do you really want me to give you a reason to run from me?'

Felicia looked up at the thin line of his mouth, harshly forbidding, and a tremor of something so alien and unwanted shot through her that at first she did not recognise it. When she did the shock was so great that she could barely comprehend that *she*, a girl who had never deliberately set out to arouse any man, and indeed shrank from physical contact, had felt a thrill of surging satisfaction at the blazing anger in Raschid's eyes, and a desire to push him over the limits of his control, her own fury fuelled by his.

Common sense warned her that the ensuing conflagration could destroy her totally, but she no longer cared. She wanted Raschid to experience anger as consuming as her own; to endure the lash of her contempt against his pride, as she had been forced to endure his.

'Well, Miss Gordon?'

'You have already given me sufficient reason, but in your arrogance you will not admit it.'

His fingers curled round the soft flesh of her upper arms, frightening in their intensity. He smiled without pity when she winced at their crushing pressure.

'This is the East,' he reminded her. 'I could punish you here and now for what you have just said and no man would raise his hand against me, not even if I beat you publicly in the streets. Beware! In every man there lurks the falcon; a streak of ruthlessness and thirst for power.'

His fingers lifted to her throat, trapping the wildly beating pulse she could no longer control. All at once the fight had gone out of her, and where there had been momentary elation there now was dread. He laughed mirthlessly when she shivered under his touch, nervous as the silky-maned Arab mares of the Badu.

'You see?' he taunted. 'At last you realise that a man is not an equal, but an alien force, bent on destruction when he is aroused to anger.'

'Stop it! Stop it at once,' Felicia begged him. 'I won't listen to you!' Her voice trembled, caught somewhere between indignation and fear. 'You don't deceive me at all. You're hoping to drive me away; to frighten me into giving up Faisal. You think I'll be overpowered by that potent masculinity you're so proud of, like a timid, shrinking Victorian heroine, caught in the trap of her own senses. Well, you're going to be disappointed! I'm well aware of the difference between my senses and my heart.'

'Are you indeed?' he challenged softly, the sensuous movement of his thumb against the silkiness of her neck making her aware too late of her danger. She trembled under the deliberate provocation of the caress and he laughed, deep in his throat.

'And what do your senses tell you now, Miss Gordon?'

It was too late to pretend that his touch left her unaffected, too late by far to wish she had never allowed fury to betray her into this hopelessly untenable position. She closed her eyes and gritted bitterly:

'They tell me that sex without love is like the desert without water—an arid wasteland where nothing can flourish.'

'But that arid wasteland, as you call it, possesses a magic of its own.'

His thumb was stroking along her jaw now, the steel fingers forcing her chin to tilt upwards no matter how much she fought against their pressure. She opened her eyes. His were barely inches away, darkly grey, the sensuously curving mouth smiling thinly.

He bent his head towards her, and she was like the falcon's prey, transfixed, accepting her fate. His faint breath stirred her hair.

'Have you experienced the potency of the desert, Miss Gordon?'

Dear God, what was happening to her? With an anguished cry she tore herself free. What was he trying to do to her? Seduce her away from Faisal? Faisal! Why had she not thought of him before now? Why had the memory of his lovemaking not protected her from responding to Raschid?

Gathering the tattered remnants of her pride about her, she stared coldly at the man towering over her.

'The desert holds no attraction for me, Sheikh Raschid—and neither do you.'

CHAPTER SIX

TALK about the best laid plans of mice and men! Felicia thought ruefully as she dressed for dinner. A cowardly corner of her heart prayed that Raschid would be absent from the meal. She stared critically in the mirror at her too-pale face. She had known from the start that her self-imposed task was hopeless, but after this afternoon she could never hope to convince Raschid that she would make Faisal a good wife. She shrugged bravely. What did it matter, after all? He could hardly swear on the Bible that there had been no provocation! Provocation! Colour washed over her skin as she remembered the sensuous movement of his thumb against her flesh, and the peculiar weakness that had made her legs feel as though they had turned to an unset jelly.

All sheer magnetism, of course. She wielded her hair-brush fiercely for a few seconds until the auburn curls framed her small face in a silky cloud. Raschid had done it deliberately—there could be no doubt about that! Playing on her fears and uncertainties, unleashing the powerful aura of his masculinity. And how near she had come to succumbing!

Slowly she put the brush down, staring at her trembling

mouth and wary eyes. There was the crux of the matter. She had been dangerously affected by Raschid's caresses; so much so that shame scorched her as she made herself relive those seconds in her arms. She had deliberately encouraged him to unleash his anger against her, but she had never dreamed it would take such a damagingly sensuous course, or that she herself would be swept away in its fierce tide. In vain she told herself that it was merely an automatically feminine reaction, trying desperately to drive away the tormenting image of Raschid's taunting smile by replacing it with Faisal's loving smile. But for some reason she found it impossible to reconstruct his boyish features; the memory eluded her, as though overpowered by Raschid's stronger personality. The harder she tried to cling to the memory of Faisal, the more difficult she found it to superimpose his features over Raschid's. Honesty had always been one of her strong points, and now she was forced to question the strength of her feelings.

Could there be a grain of truth in Raschid's accusation that her love for Faisal was founded on what he could give her—Oh, not wealth, that mattered little—but security, warmth, the affection and companionship of a family. The more she contemplated this point, the more plausible it became. Faisal had surrounded her in warmth and love, and she had sunk into its security without deeply questioning her own feelings. It had been enough merely to be loved. But would it always be enough? And wasn't she cheating Faisal as surely as though she had merely wanted him for his money?

She was glad when the dinner gong put an end to these useless speculations. She was bound to have doubts, second thoughts, but once she and Faisal were together again.....

Not even in the tiniest corner of her heart was she willing to admit that her real doubts sprang from the untenable discovery that while Faisal's lovemaking affected her hardly at all physically, Raschid had merely to touch her to send her pulses racing, her body flooded with sexual awareness.

Dislike could be as powerful an emotion as love, she reminded herself, as she zipped up her dress and added a quick touch of lipstick to the soft curves of her mouth. It toned with the pink in her dress, swirls of pink and pale green chiffon, an unusual combination for a redhead, but one that brought an indefinable touch of the exotic to her appearance, darkening the colour of her eyes and highlighting the richness of her hair. A lacy white stole covered her shoulders, although the dress had small cap sleeves and a neckline that was discretion itself. Untouched on the dressing table was the perfume Raschid had given her. She refused to open it; for a moment tempted to dispose of it in the same way as she had disposed of the glass paperweight, but acknowledging that the perfume had come from the perfume-maker and not Raschid. Even so she was reluctant to discover what sort of woman he had thought her, and she pushed the small package to the back of her drawer, unwilling for Zahra's curious eyes to alight on it.

She was the first downstairs, and on impulse she hurried into the gardens, to where she had thrown the blue leather box. It had been stupid to try to destroy a thing of so much beauty out of momentary pique, but although she searched diligently among the rose bushes she could find no trace of the package and surmised that the gardener must have disposed of it.

Tonight the delicious spicy aromas coming from the

dining room did nothing to tempt her appetite. Her stomach muscles knotting with tension at the thought of having to face Raschid, she felt as though the merest morsel of food would choke her.

Zahra greeted her in her normal ebullient fashion, smiling approvingly at the cool picture Felicia made; the fresh green colours of an English spring flowering in the desert.

'Uncle Raschid will not be joining us tonight—he is entertaining business acquaintances,' Zahra explained as they sat down.

Felicia relaxed with relief. So at least one of her wishes had been granted. Now all she needed was for her good fairy to wave her wand twice more—once to bring Faisal home and a second time to dissipate Raschid's dislike—but such wishes were hardly likely to be granted, not if Raschid had anything to do with it.

'Did your sightseeing tire you?' Zahra asked solicitously. 'You look very pale.'

'A little.' But it wasn't her tour of the shops and town that had left her feeling so drained, it was her clash with Raschid and the disturbing thoughts it had aroused. Now wasn't the time to question the strength of her feelings for Faisal, but for some reason she was finding it increasingly difficult not to compare Faisal to his uncle. Raschid would never allow anyone to dictate his way of life! She was being unfair, she reminded herself. Faisal had very little choice in the matter. Raschid had the whip hand!

'Has Zahra told you that my elder daughter and her family are to pay us a visit shortly?' Umm Faisal asked, as Selina heaped Felicia's plate with savoury saffron rice.

Felicia shook her head and looked enquiringly at Zahra.

'Yes, it is true,' the younger girl acknowledged. 'Nadia is to join us at the oasis. You will like her, Felicia, she looks very much like Faisal.' She smiled understandingly when Felicia flushed; which only increased her own feelings of guilt, for it had been of Raschid's darkly sardonic features of which she had been thinking and not Faisal's.

She toyed listlessly with her food while Umm Faisal and Zahra discussed the arrangements which had to be made for the trip to the oasis. Was the memory of this afternoon's unpleasantness destroying Raschid's appetite? Did a mental image of her face torment him? Somehow she doubted it.

Refusing coffee, Felicia excused herself. Her small white lie that she had a headache was not entirely untrue. The beginnings of tension in the back of her neck had spread to her temples and she was glad to lie down on her bed and let her mind wander at will, relaxing under the hypnotic hum of the air-conditioning and the perfumed velvet of the Eastern night.

A tap on the door roused her, and she sat up and smiled reassuringly at Selina when she poked her head round the door.

'The Sitt is wanted downstairs in Sheikh Raschid's study.'

At first Felicia thought the girl had made a mistake, and knowing that her English could not always be relied upon, she shook her head kindly. 'Sheikh Raschid is entertaining some friends, Selina, I do not think he would want me to join him.'

'Friends all gone,' Selina replied firmly. 'Sheikh alone now. Everything quite proper. If the Sitt will come.'

It was obvious that she intended to wait and escort her

downstairs, Felicia realised in exasperation. Her dress was slightly creased where she had been lying on it, but there was no time to worry about that now, nor to drag a comb through her unruly curls and wish that tiredness did not give her face such a look of soft vulnerability.

What could Raschid want? A further reiteration of his disapproval? She hesitated, and Selina paused enquiringly at the bottom of the stairs. Giving herself a mental shake, Felicia followed. After all, what could Raschid do? Eat her?

Raschid's apartments were reached by a corridor linking them with the harem quarters of the house. They had their own private entrance and a large square hall furnished with soft Persian carpets and an intricately carved brassbound chest, plainly of great antiquity. Old-fashioned oil lamps threw a soft glow across the well polished floor.

There was richness here, and simplicity too, the one harmoniously blending with the other to give a feeling of timeless serenity which had the immediate effect of soothing her ragged nerves. The tall, narrow windows were open to the night, and the sharp scent of the lime trees stole in with the dusk.

'This is the Sheikh's study, *sitt*,' Selina said respectfully, motioning her towards an iron-studded wooden door. Felicia gave her a wan smile, uncertain as to whether she should go straight in or knock. The decision was made for her when the door opened abruptly.

In the half light Raschid seemed to tower above her, and Felicia bit back a gasp. She would never have recognised him. He was wearing a *dishdasha*—the traditional white flowing robe of the Kuwaitis—his headdress hiding the night-black hair, a dark cloak lavishly embroidered with gold thread worn casually across his broad shoulders.

'What is the matter, Miss Gordon?' he asked urbanely as he ushered her into the room.

'N-nothing,' Felicia stammered, but her eyes remained glued to the undeniably impressive figure he made, outlined against the starkness of the white walls.

'When dealing with my compatriots I find it better to wear the traditional garb of our country. In point of fact the *dish-dasha* is more comfortable by far than Western-style suits.'

'And far more impressive.' She could have bitten her tongue out, when he turned and stared coolly at her. A frisson of awareness tingled across her skin, and she shivered slightly, despite the warmth of the night.

'And what, I wonder, does *that* remark imply? That you think me a posturing fool, practising for a part in *The Desert Song*?'

Anger underwrote the cold words. Horrified, Felicia stammered a denial. No European could ever have worn the flowing garment with the grace of his Arab counterpart, and her surprise had sprung merely from the fact that this was the first time she had seen Raschid dressed in the traditional manner. Although she would not have admitted it to a soul, when he opened the door to her, for a moment he had embodied every single one of her romantic teenage dreams.

And now to crown all her other follies she had offended Raschid's pride, touching the most sensitive spot of his personality. She bit her lip, wishing they were on good enough terms for her to explain that he had misunderstood.

'What? Nothing to say for yourself?' he asked harshly, surprising her with the raw anger she sensed beneath the words. He moved with the stealth of the desert fox and the sureness of an Arab stallion, coming to stand at her side and spinning her round to face him.

Felicia moistened her lips, wetting them with a nervous tongue, the movement instantly stilled as Raschid's gaze pounced on the betraying gesture.

'Why did you send for me?'

He released her, and she could feel her nerve ends quivering with relief as the tension eased.

'Merely to give you this,' he replied, handing her an envelope bearing an airmail stamp.

Her heart lurched. It was from Faisal; it must be! With eager fingers she reached for the envelope, and her hand brushed against Raschid's as she did so. It was like receiving an electric shock. She shrank back, recoiling from the contact, her face pale as she gripped her letter.

'You may cease the charade, Miss Gordon,' Raschid mocked. 'The ordeal is over. You have your letter, which you can take to your lonely bed to read and perhaps remember the nights you have spent in my nephew's arms. Faisal is no stranger to the delights of the flesh, but then I have no need to remind you of that, have I?'

'No, you have not,' Felicia agreed, suppressing her instinctive denial of his accusations. For some reason allowing Raschid to believe that she and Faisal were lovers made her feel safer, although why she could not have said.

She saw his face darken, tightening with anger and contempt. No doubt she had just confirmed his initial impression of her, but she no longer cared. Secretly in the hidden recesses of her heart she was beginning to doubt her own ability to make Faisal happy, but her pride would not

allow her to admit her discovery to Raschid. Time enough
to know that he had been right when she was safely back
in England, away from those mocking grey eyes.

By the time she reached her room she was trembling
with a mixture of anger and pain. Feverishly she ripped
open Faisal's envelope, withdrawing the letter with a fast-
beating heart. Surely here she would find the reassurance
that she so badly needed? Surely the written words of
Faisal's love for her would banish all her doubts?

The letter was depressingly short, barely more than a
few scrawled lines, with none of the tender reassurances
she had hoped for. Indeed, it struck Felicia, as she read the
letter for a second time, that Faisal too might be having
second thoughts. He had written more as though to a friend
than a lover; the phrases stilted and cautious; one betraying sentence almost leaping off the paper.

'….New York is much more fun than I had imagined….'

With a sinking heart Felicia remembered what Raschid
had told her about Faisal's propensity for falling in and out
of love. At the time she had thought he was merely trying
to upset her, but now she was not so sure. Faisal's letter was
not that of a man deeply in love and committed to that love.
Now, when it was too late, Felicia wished passionately
that she had not allowed him to persuade her to come to
Kuwait, and worse still, to spend her hard-earned savings.
With a feeling of sick despair she acknowledged that had
it been possible she would have gone straight to the airport
first thing in the morning and booked her flight home.

She even toyed with the idea of contacting her aunt and
requesting her help with the fare, but she knew she could
not. It seemed ironical that the one person who would have

been more than glad to finance her return to England was the one man in the world she would never ask.

No, distasteful though it was, she would have to write to Faisal and sort things out. Once he knew that she was no longer expecting to become his wife, he would probably be delighted to pay for her ticket, she thought wryly.

As she switched off the lamp and slid down between the cool sheets, she wondered morosely why the discovery that Faisal no longer loved her should affect her so little. Less than a week ago he had formed her entire world; now all she wanted was to return home. And yet she would miss this land, she admitted. Despite its alienness it had touched her heart, and she felt that she could have adapted had her love for Faisal been strong enough.

Her last thought before sleep claimed her was that at least she was having a small measure of revenge against Raschid. While she slept in the knowledge that she and Faisal would never marry, Raschid was probably lying awake thinking of ways to part them. Strangely enough the thought brought her precious little comfort.

ALTHOUGH SHE FELT no guilt at deceiving Raschid, it was far harder having to pretend with Zahra. She would have liked to have the younger girl as a sister-in-law, she acknowledged, as Zahra waylaid her on the way to breakfast, bouncing up and down in excitement.

'Look what Raschid has given me as a pre-birthday present!' she exclaimed, waving a cheque in front of Felicia's bemused eyes, and gloating gleefully over its size, enlarging enthusiastically on how she intended to spend it.

'There's a shop in Kuwait that sells the most dreamy

lingerie!' She rolled her eyes dramatically. 'How about coming with me this afternoon?'

Felicia hadn't the heart to refuse her, and Zahra's grateful hug when she nodded her head was more than reward enough.

Ali drove them into Kuwait, dropping them in the area of Fahd Salim Street, where Raschid had taken her the day before.

As Felicia had half expected, Zahra tended to linger over the glittering displays of jewellery.

'Those pearls come from the gulf,' she told an interested Felicia. 'Until oil was discovered, pearls were Kuwait's richest source of income.'

Ali hovered protectively behind them, reminding them that they had not come to window-gaze. As before, Felicia was impressed by the graceful boulevard with its trees and flowers.

'Our government is spending a great deal of money on irrigation schemes and desalination plants,' Zahra told her. 'In the fruit markets you will find all manner of fruits and vegetables grown on specially developed farms. The sun, once our greatest enemy, is being harnessed to provide the energy to grow perpetual crops. Saud is studying agriculture at the university,' she added by way of an explanation for all her knowledge. 'His family own lands near to our own at the oasis and he and Raschid are hoping to develop a fruit farm there eventually.' She pulled a wry face. 'I'm not sure what he loves best—me, or his precious greenhouses.' She touched Felicia's arm, motioning towards one of the shops. 'In here. Ali will wait outside for us.'

The shop was small—no more than a boutique really—

the walls hung with pale green silk panels, tiny gilt chairs covered in the same fabric, standing on an off-white deep-pile carpet. No pretensions to Eastern origins here; the boutique was blatantly Bond Street, or Fifth Avenue.

A mouthwatering selection of satin and lace underwear was produced for Zahra's inspection, and as she fingered a peach satin nightdress lavishly trimmed with coffee lace, Felicia reflected rather enviously on the advantages of possessing a wealthy and generous uncle. Not that she would want Raschid to pay for her trousseau. The thought made her go hot and cold, and the peach satin dropped from her fingers as though it had burned.

'Something wrong?'

'What? Oh no—nothing. I think you should have the peach, Zahra, and the pale blue nightdress and negligee set.'

'What about this one?'

Felicia examined the nightdress she was holding up for her inspection. It was a filmy mist of sea-green shifting to jade, in a silken shimmer of the finest gossamer chiffon.

'It's lovely,' Felicia admitted.

'And most suitable for a bride,' the sales assistant pressed.

'Would you not like something like this for your own marriage?' Zahra asked, much to Felicia's embarrassment. She closed her mind to a vision of herself clad only in the whispering chiffon, held in the arms of… Not Faisal, that was for sure, she told herself, shaking her head and handing the nightgown back to Zahra.

Ali was still waiting patiently outside, and something about the set of his shoulders suggested that they had been gone rather a long time.

'Anything else you want?' she asked Zahra, and the other girl shook her head.

They were crossing the wide pavement when Felicia saw the familiar figure striding towards them, and her heart gave a double somersault before hammering urgently against her ribs.

'Isn't that Raschid?' she asked Zahra, surprised when the younger girl compressed her lips and immediately turned in the opposite direction.

'What's the matter?'

'Didn't you see that woman with him?' Zahra hissed.

Felicia had. The woman was tall and dark, dressed with an understated elegance, wrapped in an aura of wealth. Felicia had guessed her age to be somewhere in her late twenties.

'She must be his mistress,' Zahra decided. 'She cannot be a woman of good family, otherwise she would never walk openly in the street with him.'

So Raschid had a mistress! Why should Felicia feel so surprised? She already knew how potently male he was; surely it should not be surprising that there were other women in his life besides his sister and niece. So why had her legs suddenly turned to quivering jelly; the muscles in her stomach cramping in agonised protest? The hypocritical pig! Resentment fanned the flames of her anger. How dared he insult and revile *her*, when she was quite innocent of all his accusations, and yet openly flaunt his mistress through the streets!

Suddenly she longed to confront him; to sneer contemptuously at him as he had done at her, and when she hesitated, Zahra grabbed her hand, shaking her head.

'It would embarrass Raschid if he saw us. He could not acknowledge us, while he is with *her*!'

Embarrassed? Raschid?

Zahra, correctly interpreting her expression, added seriously, 'He *would* be embarrassed, as I would myself. Naturally a single man has certain…needs, but….' She shrugged comprehensively, trying to convey the impossibility of introducing the women who served those 'needs' to the sheltered females of his own family. Felicia stared unseeingly ahead. Was that how Raschid thought of her? As the woman who served the 'needs' of his nephew? Shame and rage scorched her, and her fingers balled into two small fists.

'What's wrong?' Zahra asked. 'You look so fierce.'

'Oh, it's nothing.' But she knew she was lying. A queer little pain had lodged somewhere in the region of her heart, but she steadfastly ignored it. Why should she care if Raschid chose to walk side by side with some dusky beauty, his dark head inclined towards her in a gesture of attentive protection? She had no need of his protection, nor his attention. How could she, when all that existed between them was open dislike?

NATURALLY ON THEIR return to the villa Zahra had to inspect her purchases all over again, although Felicia was surprised when she did not unwrap the sea-green chiffon. Perhaps she was frightened of soiling it, she decided. Together they enthused over the peach satin, as Felicia held it against Zahra's skin.

'I doubt your Saud will have eyes to spare for anything but you,' she teased. 'Which one will you wear on your wedding night?'

'Neither,' Zahra replied seriously. 'Our wedding will be completely traditional. It is my wish and Saud's. I shall be dressed in my bridal caftan with its one hundred and one buttons down the front, and round my neck will be the gold necklaces given to me by my family and Saud's.' When Felicia still looked puzzled, she explained, 'It is our custom for the bridegroom to remove the necklaces one by one while the bride keeps a modest silence. Then he unfastens the buttons, starting at the hem,' she blushed a little. 'You find it strange, perhaps, that I should want to be married in this way, but...'

'No stranger than the wearing of a white dress in the West,' Felicia assured her. In point of fact a small lump had lodged in her throat, but the image shimmering in her mind was neither that of Zahra nor Faisal, but another dark, masculine head bent painstakingly over the tiny buttons, lean fingers making nonsense of their many fastenings. A deep shudder trembled through her, and her stomach churned with disturbing sensations. Dear God, what was she thinking? Imagining Raschid of all people kneeling tenderly at his bride's feet, his normally sardonic expression replaced by one of intimate desire. What was happening to her? She felt sick and dizzy, and had to sink down into a chair to try and gather her composure. If only she could go home. If only she had discovered that gratitude was not and never could be love, before she had come to Kuwait. If she had not left England she would never have discovered that it was possible to respond to the potent maleness of a man without even liking him; that one could be aware of everything about him, and yet still know nothing. Her mouth had gone dry, the strange ache in her heart seemed to grow with every breath she took.

'Did Faisal tell you when he would be coming home?' Zahra asked innocently. 'Last year he flew back from London just to give me my birthday present. Raschid arranged it.' Her face brightened. 'Perhaps he will do the same thing this year.'

Felicia shook her head. There was no point in raising the younger girl's hopes.

'I don't think so.'

'Raschid might do something if you went to him and told him how much you are missing Faisal. Why don't you, Felicia? You must be longing to see him.'

She was. But not for the reasons that Zahra supposed. If Faisal were to return she could ask him to help her get home, but of course she could not say this to Zahra. Thank goodness she had not allowed him to persuade her into wearing the ring he had bought her.

'I'm sure you could coax Raschid round,' Zahra continued. 'He isn't a complete monster, you know.'

'That wasn't the impression I got this afternoon,' Felicia reminded her drily, remembering the younger girl's desire not to be seen.

'That was different,' Zahra replied promptly. 'Mother worries because Raschid does not marry. The responsibility of caring for her and us has aged him, I think, although he never lets us see it. Perhaps when I am married he will look for a wife, although it will not be easy. Mother fears that his English blood makes him impatient of our own girls.' She glanced speculatively at Felicia. 'Faisal must have told you how like Raschid's grandmother you are. I wouldn't have put it past him to have deliberately sent you out here to tease Raschid. When we were little I remember our father saying that Raschid, as a child, had been fascinated by the portrait of his grandmother. I think he has a softness for you, Felicia, even though he hides it.'

A softness for her! Felicia nearly told her how wrong she was, and why. So Zahra thought that Faisal's motives in sending her to Kuwait might not have been entirely altruistic. Felicia suspected that she might be right. It was obvious to her that there had been differences of opinion between Faisal and Raschid in the past, and she wondered if Faisal had announced their 'engagement' to Raschid, in a deliberate attempt to annoy him. It was not pleasant to realise that she might have been used in this fashion, and she was coming to accept that Faisal was not the charming young man he had seemed on the surface.

ONCE AGAIN Raschid did not join them for dinner, and when Umm Faisal explained that he was dining with friends, Felicia smiled rather mirthlessly to herself. Friends, or friend, in the singular? She was tired, and excused herself, going to her room.

Each day the temperature seemed to rise a little more and Felicia had grown quite used to rising each morning to a cloudless blue sky; the muezzin no longer a weirdly unfamiliar sound, but part and parcel of everyday life. She was coming to love this country of stark contrasts, she admitted, and would miss it when she left. She had still not written to Faisal, and she knew that it was a task she must complete, but her pride shrank from having to beg his aid. Sensitive to the opinions of others, she was reluctant to have him think that she expected him to pay her fare home. And yet what alternative did she have?

The scent of the roses reached her from her bedroom window. Throwing a crocheted shawl round her shoulders, she went downstairs, through the silent hall and into the welcome coolness of the garden. They were particularly attractive, these enclosed courtyards with their fountains and shady trees. The sharp, acid scent of the limes mingled with the fragrance of the roses. Doves cooed softly from the dovecote by the fountain. She trailed her fingers in the water, watching the fish slide quickly away. With the moon full the garden was almost as bright as day, the landscape etched in stark silver and black.

She sighed and froze as feet crunched on the gravel.

'Wishing there was someone to share the enchantment of our evenings with you, Miss Gordon?'

Raschid! Her hand crept to her throat to still the small pulse beating frantically there. He was dressed Arab-fashion once more, one leather-booted foot resting arrogantly on the rim of the pool as he surveyed her. She bit back a sharp retort, swallowing her dismay.

'As a matter of fact I was,' she lied lightly, her hands clenching impotently at her sides, as his cool glance slid over her small, flushed face, resting momentarily on the rise and fall of her breasts beneath their thin covering, before lingering thoughtfully on her neat waist and the narrow tautness of her hips. For some reason it had become desperately important to conceal from Raschid the truth about her feelings for Faisal.

His eyebrows rose, and again she bit back the burning anger clamouring for utterance. All her senses were urging her to escape, but she would not let him see her fear.

'I believe you wish me to arrange for Faisal to come

home? Zahra has been soliciting my forbearance on your behalf. Her tender heart aches for what she imagines to be the tragic parting of two star-crossed lovers. Naturally I have had to disabuse her of what is merely romantic fantasy.'

Forgetting her own doubts about her feelings for Faisal, she stared at him, her eyes blazing.

'By doing what? Giving her your interpretation of our relationship?'

'Oh, come,' he mocked mildly, 'why all the maidenly indignation? You made no demur the other night when I implied that you and Faisal had already shared the delights which Zahra only merely anticipates. You forget that I have lived in your country. I know in what scant regard your women hold their modesty and innocence.'

'Which, of course, a woman of your race would never do!'

'And what is that supposed to mean? Or can I guess? If you are referring to my companion of this afternoon—oh yes, I know you saw me, that hair of yours is instantly recognisable—she makes no pretence to being anything she is not.'

Felicia's lip curled in a fair imitation of his own sneer. 'Unlike you! I must admit that you surprised me. You don't look the type of man who needs to buy a woman's favours, but I suppose when all you can offer is physical gratification, the pill has to be sweetened somehow.'

His incredulous, 'Why, you little…' told her that she had managed to slip under his guard, but allied to trembling satisfaction was the certainty that she would be made to pay for that moment of victory.

Retribution came sooner than she had imagined.

'I sought you out because Zahra was concerned for you. She tells me that you grow pale and do not eat, and she attributes this to the fact that you are missing Faisal. I know otherwise, but I will not be deceived by your playacting. I shall not allow Faisal to return now to be ensnared by you all over again. However, we cannot have you pining for lack of his lovemaking,' he told her silkily. 'It is fortunate that Zahra's window does not overlook this courtyard—she may not approve of the methods I employ to assuage your need of him.'

Zahra wasn't the only one who did not approve, Felicia thought numbly as her flaying hands were captured and pinned to her sides, as hard masculine lips plundered the trembling softness of her own, parted to voice her fury. She was forced backwards, imprisoned against Raschid's arm, her throat and the swelling softness of her breasts exposed to his merciless scrutiny. His eyes glittered over the answering fury in her own, fastening on the erratic pulse beating frantically in her creamy throat before lingering on the pale blur of flesh revealed by the V neckline of her cotton dress.

'Let me go!' she muttered furiously, her mouth throbbing. 'Save your kisses for the women who are obliged to endure them in return for some worthless trinket!'

She heard the angry hiss of his escaping breath, hard fingers tightened on her wrists, and her flesh burned from the contact with his.

'Never worthless, Miss Gordon. I can assure you of that.'

But despite the lazy drawl she knew that his anger was no longer held in check. She had unleashed it with her hasty words. She closed her eyes, against a sudden weak rush of tears, as his hands moulded her hip bones, forcing her against him. She would not cry now! She bit her lip.

She could feel the warmth of his breath against her face, and stiffened, willing him to release her.

'Oh no, Miss Gordon, you will not escape so lightly this time!'

She could feel the tensile strength of his chest muscles against her breasts; the faintly harsh rasp of the dark hairs exposed by the open neck of his robe, so compellingly masculine that reaction flooded through her on a shock wave, making her painfully aware of just how inexperienced she actually was. The contact—which obviously meant nothing to him—suffocated her with its implied intimacy of flesh against flesh, and she struggled to get away, panicking as his lips took their fill of the exposed column of her throat, lingering appreciatively against her skin. If she had once doubted his skill and experience she could do so no longer. The deliberately arousing caresses would have melted ice; but she struggled not to give in; not to admit the drugging sensation of rising desire as his assault of her senses was subtly increased.

There was no affection or tenderness in his touch—she knew that; she knew that all he offered was the hollow sham of sexual need, and that even that was probably counterfeit, but she could do nothing when his free hand slid downward from her shoulder, cupping her breast, and stroking the soft curves.

Fear and indignation shot through her. Not even Faisal had touched her so intimately—nor so insultingly as though her body held no secrets, no pleasures, but merely the familiarity of the oft-known. She shuddered as his fingers found her nipple, coaxing it into hardening desire without exhibiting either haste or urgency; the pain and shock of her body's betrayal there for him to see in the widening of her eyes and tensed muscles.

Satisfaction gleamed in the night-dark eyes, as they raked her pale, shocked face.

'Well, now you can join the ranks of those who have known my objectionable touch, Miss Gordon. Although unlike them your reward was not well earned,' he taunted.

She reeled as he released her, hating the grim comprehension in his voice. There was a parcel in his hand, wrapped in tissue paper, and tied with green ribbon.

'It seems that Zahra purchased a gift for you on my behalf this afternoon. I only trust you will think of me when you wear it.'

The package was flung at her feet. Speech would have been a complete impossibility, as she stared up at him with hate-filled eyes.

'Pick it up,' he commanded inexorably. 'Otherwise I shall be obliged to deliver it again—in person, and since the gift has been given twice, it will have to be paid for twice.'

'You're nothing but a barbarian!' Felicia choked. 'I was a fool to think you could ever understand what I feel for Faisal...or any other *human* emotion!'

She bent down, picked up the parcel, and fled before he could retaliate, clutching the tissue paper in trembling fingers. In her room she flung it against the wardrobe door, and the fragile paper tore on the sharp edge of the handle, releasing a froth of sea-green chiffon.

She paled, staring at the silky fabric. The nightgown! Zahra had bought it for her! With Raschid's money! She was shivering with reaction and despair. In the mirror she could see the redness on her lips from his kisses. Her neck and shoulder burned from the searing heat of Raschid's practised kisses and her breast was on fire from the arrogant sureness of his hard caress. Her body stiffened with rage.

How dared he treat her like a woman he had bought for the night! She suppressed a wild sob. He had tainted her— stamped on her pride and destroyed the protective shield she had thrown around herself. Never again could she assert that desire was nothing without love and that she could never experience the former without the latter, because for one fleeting moment she *had* known desire; and it was that more than anything else that caused the hot tears to roll down her cheeks as her fingers curled furiously into her palms and she found some slight surcease in contemplating Raschid's muscular body writhing in mortal agony.

As for the nightdress…. She stared disparagingly at the fragile silk she had coveted not so many hours ago. She would burn it before she allowed it to come anywhere near her body!

CHAPTER SEVEN

BEMUSED, Felicia asked herself how on earth order would ever result from such chaos. The household was preparing to move to the oasis, and Zahra, lifting yet another armful of dresses from her wardrobe, said impishly that it was no wonder that Raschid had absented himself from the house. His excuse had been that he would go on before them to make sure that everything was in readiness for their arrival, but Felicia believed that if he had the smallest spark of decency he would be as anxious to avoid her company as she was his.

Never, if she lived to be a hundred, would she forget the emotionless destruction of her flimsy barriers, the calculated assault on her senses, and the bitter lessons she had learned. When she slept at night she dreamed of him, of his cold, jeering face, and most of all of his knowledgeable, caressing hands, and she would wake, trembling with anguish, tears cascading down her cheeks.

It was no wonder that she was losing weight. Several times she had started to pen a letter to Faisal, telling him as gently as she could that their love had died, but every time she reached the part where she had to beg him to send her the money for her fare home, her pride stopped her. She was reaching the point where she was contemplating paying a visit to the British Embassy, but Zahra's delight that she would be with them for her birthday celebrations prevented her from making a move until they returned from the oasis. She could manage for a few more days, she told herself, trying to believe that it was true.

'It's a pity that Raschid cannot spare Faisal,' Zahra mourned. A pity indeed, Felicia agreed, although she knew that the supposed 'emergency' that kept Faisal in New York was no more than a figment of Raschid's Machiavellian imagination.

She was helping Zahra with her packing. She had not imagined that a girl could possess so many clothes at the same time, and said as much.

Zahra grinned. 'Raschid makes me a very generous allowance.' She indicated a filmy harem outfit comprising baggy trousers in flame chiffon and a matching sequinned top. 'What do you think of that? I bought it for a joke. Raschid would be furious if he knew.' Felicia's raised eyebrows prompted a defensive outburst. 'Saud said it was a pity that harem dancers no longer existed, outside the imagination of Hollywood producers, and I thought....'

'I can see what you thought,' Felicia murmured drily, amused and touched to see Zahra blushing a little. What business was it of Raschid's if the younger girl chose to play the harem dancer for her undoubtedly appreciative bridegroom? She folded the outfit briskly.

'It won't go in this box, it's full,' Zahra complained.

'Never mind, give it to me. I've plenty of room in my case.' Felicia looked rather quizzically at Zahra. 'Why do you want to take it? You won't be wearing it until you *are* married, I trust?'

'I daren't leave it here in case one of the maids sees it,' Zahra confessed. 'Mother wouldn't understand.'

'I can see why,' Felicia agreed, thinking of the transparent chiffon. It was obvious that Zahra was very much in love with her Saud, and Felicia wondered a little enviously what it was like to prepare for marriage basking in the warm approval of one's family. Had she ever anticipated Faisal's caresses with the enthusiasm with which Zahra looked forward to Saud's?—and not for the first time she questioned her ability to respond to a man's lovemaking. Had her uncle's cold rejection of her as a child destroyed her ability to give and receive love? And yet she *had* responded to Raschid. But she did not love him. She hated him. He was determined to destroy her, she thought bitterly, gathering up the small pile of garments which would not fit into Zahra's boxes and putting them in her own case. And he did not care what means he had to use to do so. She straightened up and her breast throbbed pulsatingly as it had done when he had touched her. Her face flaming, she squashed the impulse to place her own hand against her quickening flesh in an effort to eradicate the tingling memory.

IT WAS NOT a great distance to the oasis when measured in mere miles, but the journey would take them through empty desert and careful preparations had to be made, checked and re-checked by Ali, who had been left in charge of their safety. Water bottles had to be filled, tires checked, and spare gasoline cans placed in the trunks of cars. They were to travel in convoy, the Mercedes carrying Umm Faisal, Zahra and Felicia, going first, three other cars with the staff and the luggage following on behind

Felicia tended to be amused by the flurry of preparation, until Zahra pointed out the fate of other, less careful travellers. To die of thirst under a burning sun was no pleasant death, and could happen even to the most experienced desert traveller if a sandstorm blew up, obliterating the road, or a sharp stone pierced a gas tank, leaving them without transport.

It was just over a hundred miles to the oasis, but Felicia was ready to agree feelingly that it might have been a thousand, long before the green fringe of the palm trees warned her that journey's end was in sight. Even with the air-conditioning on full the heat inside the car was stifling, the sun dazzling as it bounced off the immaculate black hood of the Mercedes. The tires hissed wetly along the soft tarmac until they turned off on to a sandy track, throwing up clouds of fine dust to clog the throats and eyes of those driving behind.

'Now you see why we go first,' Zahra explained. 'The last vehicle is the most at risk. Even an expert driver can lose his way when the windscreen is covered in sand.'

Felicia repressed a small shudder at the thought of being lost in this vast wasteland. And yet for all its terrible emptiness the desert held a beauty all of its own. As far as the eye could see there was nothing but mile upon mile of never-ending sand, burning golden-red against the cobalt blue sky. The intensity of it hurt the eyes, and Felicia wondered anew at the tenacity of a people who had carved out their lives from this unyielding wilderness.

'Nearly there,' Zahra said cheerfully, as the fringe of palm trees on the horizon grew tantalisingly larger. 'You will love the oasis, Felicia. I believe Raschid considers it is our true home, although Faisal does not care for it in the same way, but in you I sense a sympathy for our ways. You do like our country, don't you?' she asked anxiously.

Felicia acknowledged that she had fallen under its spell, surprised to realise how true this was. Had circumstances been different, she would have been content to make her life in this magnificent, timeless land.

'Only one more day until Nadia arrives,' Zahra added. 'I'm longing to see her!'

Felicia hoped that Faisal's elder sister was as easy to get along with as his younger. Since the arrival of Faisal's letter she was conscious of being something of an impostor, in her own mind at least, and having Raschid as her enemy was more than enough to cope with.

It was dusk when they drove into the oasis, so Felicia could see very little of her surroundings apart from the clustering tops of palm trees, swaying lightly in the evening breeze, and the silky shine of moonlight on water as they drove past the silent oasis.

'Once the Badu camped here,' Zahra said softly, 'but now the tribesmen have retreated into the interior of the desert to pursue their chosen way of life unhindered.'

The house bore no resemblance to the villa outside Kuwait. Built of white stone, its narrow Moorish windows presented a blank face to the world. They drove through a fretted archway into a courtyard slightly similar to the one belonging to the villa, but whereas that was of modern construction combining the best of East and West, this one bore mute evidence of age. Behind them enormous iron-studded oak doors slammed shut, a reminder that once visitors to the oasis might not have been friendly. The soft footed Moslem servants added to the sensation of having stepped back in time, and Felicia would not have been surprised to see a couple of Zahra's harem dancers wandering in the garden, the bracelets on their ankles tinkling in time to their sinuous movements.

Instead, Ali ushered them into a large hallway, and then Felicia did gasp with amazed delight. Huge pillars of malachite supported an intricately patterned ceiling, painted in jewel-bright colours. She could hear the sound of water somewhere in the distance and the timeless enchantment of the East engulfed her.

Zahra laughed at her open-mouthed wonder.

'I knew you would like it!'

Ali and the other servants were bringing in their luggage, stacking it on the cool marble floor. Selina hurried away, promising that soon they would have a cup of coffee, and as the double doors at the other end of the hall opened, Felicia saw Raschid framed there, his flowing white robe in stark contrast to the rich bronze of his skin and the jewelled silks of the furnishings.

'Zahra will take you to the women's quarters, Miss Gordon. They overlook an inner courtyard. In the desert a wise man kept his rarest treasures under lock and key, and in my grandfather's day the women of the harem were never allowed outside the confines of this house. For my grandmother's pleasure he had a garden constructed inside the protective walls of his home so that she might enjoy the cool breeze that blows over the desert when dusk falls. She used to say that it reminded her of England.'

'You will love it, Felicia,' Zahra said softly, 'and the harem quarters. They are ridiculously exotic. Believe it or not, there is even a marble bath large enough to swim in.'

She laughed delightedly when Felicia flushed, exclaiming suddenly, 'Uncle Raschid, Felicia's eyes are exactly the same colour as these pillars!'

'The colour of malachite,' Raschid agreed, looking down at Felicia, and running his lean fingers caressingly down the pillar nearest to him. 'But I don't suppose Miss Gordon will be complimented to have her eyes compared with the cold hardness of marble—mm?'

As always his tone when he spoke to Zahra was teasingly indulgent, and Felicia was struck by the difference from when he addressed her.

Ali staggered in with more boxes, which he dropped by Felicia's cases. The top one fell on its side, bursting open to spill its contents in gay profusion across the floor. Felicia had been looking at Raschid and she saw his face change suddenly, from avuncular indulgence to grim disgust. He stepped forward, crossing the floor with a couple of lithe strides, bending to finger disdainfully the crimson chiffon billowing against the starkness of his robes.

Zahra trembled, casting Felicia a look of agonised appeal, and instantly she rose to the occasion. It didn't matter that Raschid's fingers were flicking the chiffon away with arrogant contempt, nor that his eyes were narrowing thoughtfully on her flushed face, his mouth curving downwards in contempt.

'Mine, I believe,' Felicia said bravely, with saccharine

sweetness as she made a dive for the chiffon. Raschid was
holding the fabric more firmly than she had realised and
as she tugged effectually at it, the harem pants were
revealed in their full glory. Almost she would have laughed
at his distasteful expression as he relinquished the sequinned waistband after one look of incredulous contempt.

'I bought them in the *souk* the other day. I thought they
might start a new fashion at home.' Some devil of mischief,
too long submerged, suddenly reasserted itself prompting
her to add flippantly, 'I hope Faisal likes them.' Demurely
she let her eyelashes drop to veil her cheeks in mock
modesty, even risking a coy giggle. 'They aren't the thing
for shopping in Sainsbury's, of course, but for a quiet
evening at home....' She deliberately let her voice trail
away, raising limpid eyes to the concentrated acidity in
Raschid's and allowing just the merest hint of suggestive-
ness to peep through her assumed modesty. Watching his
impassive features, she admitted that she was playing with
fire, but shrugged the thought aside—in for a penny, in for
a pound! When long seconds ticked by with Zahra frozen
like a sphinx and Raschid's expression remotely unreadable she wondered if she had gone too far.

A cold grey glance, informed with deliberate and exactly
calculated insult, roamed her body, oblivious to Zahra's
shocked protest, and at length he drawled carelessly:

'Not your colour, I would have thought, Miss Gordon,
with that hair.'

'No.' She was all smiling sweetness. 'You surprise me.
I should have thought you would consider it *exactly* right
for me, being scarlet.'

The way the heavy-lidded eyes narrowed told her that

he had not missed the point, but he did not deign to answer and it was left to Ali to bundle up the rest of the clothes cascading across the floor and carry them from the room.

It was just as well that Raschid's annoyance with her was occupying the best part of his thoughts, Felicia reflected as she followed a thoroughly shaken Zahra, otherwise he might have realised that the rest of the clothes littering the floor had belonged not to her but to his niece!

It was a very subdued young girl who came into Felicia's room an hour later, when she was completing the last of her unpacking. The bedroom was as different from the one in Kuwait as chalk from cheese. For a start it was devoid of modern furnishings, apart from the comfortable double bed. The floor was polished wood, scattered with soft Persian rugs, of great age and value. A long low couch stuffed with cushions was set against one wall beneath the arched windows, tempting the languorously inclined to relax and admire the cunning arrangement of trees and plants in the courtyard below. As in all Arab houses of any wealth, the sound of water was never far away, for in days gone by an Arab could measure his wealth in the amount of water he was able to waste.

A small dressing room had been fitted with wardrobes, but it was on the ornamental brassbound chest that Felicia had placed the carefully folded harem outfit.

Zahra pulled a face when she saw it.

'I've never seen Raschid so angry,' she said in a low voice, her eyes disturbed. 'Oh, Felicia, I'm so sorry—the way he looked at you—the things he said!'

'Well, now you know why I didn't enthuse over them

in the first place. But there's no harm done,' Felicia assured her lightly.

'No harm!' Zahra's eyes filled with indignant tears. 'You can't say that after the way Raschid treated you—and you Faisal's intended wife!'

Now was her opportunity to tell Zahra the truth, but before she could do so, Zahra continued impulsively, 'I shall tell Raschid how wrong he was, Felicia. I cannot allow you to take the blame for my folly, and Raschid shall apologise to you for what he said.'

Her lips trembled and Felicia felt moved to pity, guessing how much it had hurt the younger girl to see her adored uncle revealed in his true colours. In that moment she felt immeasurably older than the Felicia who had arrived in Kuwait such a short time ago. She comforted Zahra as best she could, promising that the now despised garments would be suitably disposed of and reminding her that she herself had added insult to injury by deliberately goading Raschid, but Zahra was not convinced. She shook her head sorrowfully.

'He wanted to shame you before us, Felicia. I could see it in his eyes, but instead he shamed me!' Her voice thickened on fresh tears. 'I thank Allah that I witnessed his contempt, for I could not bear it if Saud had looked upon me in the way Raschid did you.'

It saddened Felicia to hear the pain in her voice, but she could offer scant comfort, aside from pointing out that Raschid had his reasons for not liking her.

'Because he does not want Faisal to marry you? Felicia, promise me you will not let Raschid drive you from us. You have become very precious to me and already I think of you as a sister. Raschid will come round, I know it!'

THE NEXT DAY BROUGHT the noisy arrival of Nadia and her
husband with their small son. Several years older than
Felicia, she was a smaller, feminine version of Faisal,
complete with his white smile and soft brown eyes, and yet
the familiarity between brother and sister sparked off no
emotion in her, Felicia discovered.

Her little boy, however, captured her heart, and before
he had been in the house five minutes, Felicia was completely under his spell, listening delightedly to his important chatter as he followed her to her room. He exhibited
none of the shyness of his European contemporaries, his
large brown eyes frankly curious as he wandered around
her room. He found the tissue-wrapped parcel she had
stuffed in a corner of her empty suitcase and forgotten, and
insisted on seeing what was inside and was, in fact, engaged
on carefully removing the contents when Nadia walked in.

She raised her eyebrows and smiled, dropping carelessly on to the divan in the same cross-legged pose as
Umm Faisal. Far more Western in outlook than either her
mother or her sister, she had, nevertheless, the aura of a
sheltered Eastern woman. She ruffled little Zayad's dark
hair affectionately as he staggered towards her, relieving
him of the package.

'A present?'

'Something someone gave me in error,' Felicia heard
herself saying stiffly, changing the subject quickly. 'You
must be excited about Zahra's marriage.'

'Not as much as I was about my own.' Nadia chuckled
reminiscently. 'It seems strange to remember that there was
ever a time when I didn't want to marry Achmed.' She saw
Felicia's look of surprise and nodded her head. 'Oh yes, I

was a rebel when I was younger. Our marriage was arranged before my father's death, and I plagued Raschid to free me from it. I even threatened to starve myself if he refused.'

'What happened?' Felicia enquired, intrigued. She could not imagine any female getting the better of Raschid, but plainly Nadia was perfectly happy in her marriage, and she was curious to know how this had come about.

Nadia smiled ruefully.

'It was all Raschid's doing, bless him! You will have heard of the *siyasa* on which we pride ourselves? Well, when I refused point blank to marry Achmed—and you must bear in mind that this was at the start of the month of Ramadan with the wedding only weeks away, for it was to be celebrated at the same time as the feast of Eid al-Fitr which marks the end of our fast—Raschid did not attempt to argue or reason with me. Instead he told me that he had arranged for Achmed to visit the house and that if I positioned myself in his bedroom and looked out on to the courtyard I would see Achmed arrive. He begged me to wait until then before demanding to be freed of our betrothal.' She spread her hands, laughingly. 'What could I do? I agreed.'

'And?' pressed Felicia breathlessly.

Nadia laughed again.

'And when I saw this outstandingly handsome young man walk nervously into the courtyard I knew my protests had been those of a maid who fears the intimacies of marriage, but when I looked into Achmed's face and saw gentleness and understanding there, I knew there was nothing to fear. Raschid knew me better than I knew myself.' Her eyes softened into an expression of shining pleasure. 'I will say only this to you, Felicia. There are those of your race, and mine too, who anticipate their marriage vows, tossing away the kernel of the grain and keeping only the worthless husk, but there is no freedom, no equality that equals the pleasure of sharing the mysteries of one's body with the husband of one's heart, and knowing that those mysteries are revealed for him and him alone.'

The soft words almost moved Felicia to tears, expressing as they did sentiments she had always cherished but never been able to utter. In complete understanding they looked at one another, and Felicia knew that whatever Raschid might choose to believe of her, Nadia had guessed the truth.

As she got up to go, she pressed Felicia's hand lightly. 'Zahra tells me that Raschid has greatly wronged you. For her own sake she must tell him the truth, but he is a proud man, and apologising will not come easy. You will bear this in mind?'

And make it easy for him? Was that what Nadia was asking? Raschid was lucky in his family, Felicia thought enviously; they held him in high esteem.

'You are very like Raschid's grandmother,' Nadia sighed. 'But Zahra will already have told you this. My mother tells me that you and Faisal are friends.'

Sensing what was coming, Felicia said hurriedly, 'Can we talk of this at a later date—after Zahra's birthday? Nothing must be allowed to overshadow that.'

'Indeed not,' Nadia allowed, smiling, as she led her son away for his afternoon rest.

Felicia soon discovered that all the family shared Zahra's love of the oasis, and the luxurious home Raschid's grandfather had built there for his English wife. In the desert the family reverted to the ways of their ancestors, with the women gathering every morning to chat and drink coffee while Raschid and Achmed inspected the fruit farm on the other side of the oasis, and exercised the fiery Arab horses stabled in one of the outer courtyards. Zayad had attached himself to Felicia, following her wherever she went, much to the amusement of Nadia.

The day before Zahra's birthday, when the men were out riding, a messenger arrived from Saud's family inviting the ladies to drive over. Felicia was rather dubious as to whether or not the invitation was meant to include her, but Zahra and Nadia overruled her protests.

When the men returned, Zahra rushed to tell them the news. She exhibited no shyness in the presence of her brother-in-law, who in turn treated her with brotherly indulgence. Felicia liked Nadia's husband. He was all the things she had once thought Faisal—kind, gentle, tender to his wife and affectionate with his son. Against her will her eyes were drawn to Raschid's remote figure. How would he treat a wife? Never with tenderness!

He said something to Zahra and the younger girl shrugged and moved away. There was an air of constraint between them, and Felicia was sorry that Zahra had been disillusioned. From Nadia she knew that Zahra intended to confront Raschid with the truth, but she suspected that she was hoping for a more propitious moment. These seldom came, as Felicia knew from experience. She was still hoping to find a tactful way of breaking the news that she must soon return home. It was bound to cause speculation. Her original visit had had no time limit and it was generally accepted by Umm Faisal that she would stay with them until Faisal returned. That was no longer possible. Tonight she must write to him.

'And is Felicia looking forward to meeting Saud's family?' Achmed asked with a twinkle. 'You know, of course, how highly placed in Government circles they are?'

'Saud cares nothing for his family's prominence,' Zahra explained self-consciously, but Felicia could tell that the younger girl was deliberately playing down Saud's importance.

'Now you see why it is so important that our family observes the proprieties,' Raschid drawled. 'Already in certain religious quarters there is unrest because our government has brought in so many modern reforms. The greatest tact is needed in equating the needs of the flesh with those of the spirit, and if a member of a prominent family were seen to be flouting the unwritten rules of behaviour it could be interpreted in some quarters as a direct contravention of the Koran itself. Zahra is especially vulnerable through her connection with me. Have you forgotten that I am Christian?' he demanded.

Felicia had. She also saw much more than she had seen before.

'There is a letter for you, Miss Gordon,' Raschid added. 'From Faisal. If you will come to my study...'

'Raschid, if you have a moment there is something I should like to discuss with you,' Zahra interrupted hurriedly. 'I will come with you, Felicia, and then when Raschid has given you your letter he and I can talk.'

In vain Felicia tried to catch her eye to tell her that there was no need for her to confess her guilt to Raschid. As far as she was concerned the matter was over and done with, and besides, she doubted that anything would be gained by telling him the truth. Far better that Zahra put the episode completely behind her, but Zahra avoided her warning look and got to her feet, scattering silk-covered cushions.

'Overspent your allowance again?' Raschid commented humorously, opening the door for them.

'Will you see Saud tomorrow, when we visit his family?' Felicia asked Zahra as they walked behind Raschid.

She shook her head.

'That would not be permitted. In fact we should not see one another at all until he lifts the veil from my face during the wedding ceremony, but you will find our visit interesting. His family owns an old fortress about two hours' drive from the oasis, and his father still likes to spend at least a part of the year in the desert.' She hesitated as Raschid disappeared into his study.

'There's still time to change your mind, you know,' Felicia pointed out gently, but Zahra shook her head.

'No, I've made up my mind. Let's go in.'

In silence Felicia took her letter from Raschid's outstretched hand, her eyes telling Zahra that there was still time for her to back down if she wished, but the younger girl resolutely ignored her, placing herself in front of Raschid, hands clasped together, head bent.

As she closed the door gently behind her, Felicia heard him say indulgently,

'So, and what is this urgent matter you wish to discuss with me, little one?'

Little one! Just for a moment Felicia felt like a child herself—the child she had once been, deprived of love and affection, forced to see others more fortunate blessed with what was denied her. And then she shook the feeling off and retired to her room to read Faisal's letter.

The words seemed to leap angrily off the paper, a bitter jumble of accusations and demands, and even when she had read it twice Felicia could barely take it in. She supposed she had Raschid to thank for this, she thought bitterly, as she read it yet again, some of the more condemnatory phrases sticking in her mind.

'Your wanton behaviour…encouraging my uncle to behave in the most familiar fashion…making a laughing stock of my reputation….' These were but a few of Faisal's accusations, revealing how very thin his veneer of Westernisation actually had been. The letter finished quite abruptly, and Felicia read the last paragraph slowly.

'…and in view of your totally disgraceful behaviour I am forced to say that I can no longer countenance any marriage between us. I am writing to my uncle separately to inform him of my decision, and I am sure once it is known to him he will lose no time in sending you back to England, where you may parade yourself on the streets for the whole world to see without causing me to lose face.'

He had never really loved her, Felicia thought with a sigh, crumpling the letter into a small ball and throwing it into her wastepaper bin. She could not blame him entirely. She was as much at fault as he—and yet it hurt to read his letter, to know that Raschid had quite deliberately written to him showing her in a bad light—it must have been Raschid, it could be no one else. How would she have felt if she had in truth loved Faisal? What would her feelings have been at this moment? And yet she could not deny that it would be a relief not to have to pretend any longer. No

doubt as soon as Raschid heard from Faisal he would lose
no time in sending her home. Bitter pain shafted through
her. She did not want to leave this country. Strangely
enough, what hurt far more than Faisal's desertion was the
knowledge that Raschid had deliberately gone behind her
back and betrayed her. And yet why should he be so surprised? Hadn't he promised that he would find a way of
parting them? If only he had waited a little longer he need
not have put himself to the trouble. Time had achieved his
ends for him, without any help. The love she thought so
strong in the gentle climate of England had soon shrivelled
in the merciless heat of the desert.

She took a deep breath and then another. Outside her
bedroom window the swimming pool shimmered temptingly, blue as a turquoise stone set into the paved courtyard.
Raschid had had it installed, so Zahra had told her, and its
coolness drew her, as though somehow its silken caress
could wash away her pain and hurt. Like a wounded animal
she sought oblivion—not from Faisal's betrayal, which
had taken second place in her chaotic thoughts, but from
the new, dangerously hurtful knowledge that when she left
Kuwait, she would leave behind a part of herself—in the
hard uncaring hands of his uncle!

How it had happened she did not know. Nor why her
senses should be enslaved to the one man who had no
use or desire for her, but now the truth was inescapable.
She refused to use the word 'love' in conjunction with
her feelings for Raschid, but neither could she continue
to deny its existence. All her heart-searching, all her reluctance to leave Kuwait had their roots in the same
hidden depths of her being which had given birth to the

sensual excitement she had experienced at Raschid's touch. She was attracted to him, she told herself, nothing more. But it *was* more than attraction. That could not account for the driving need within her. The ache to touch and be touched; the burning, hurting desire that kept her awake at night.

She glanced in the mirror, barely recognising the white face staring back at her. She found her black swimsuit, deeming it more suitable than her bikini, unaware of how it accentuated her curves, flattering her slim shape, drawing attention to the valley between her breasts, the silky sheen of her skin. As she pulled it on she realised that in the move from Kuwait she had forgotten to buy herself a fresh supply of salt tablets. She shrugged. It hardly mattered now. She would not be here much longer—just as long as it took Raschid to read Faisal's letter. She did not think he would allow her to stay under his roof one moment more than necessary, birthday celebrations or no!

Although he might not know it, Raschid had won. How ironic that it should be Faisal who was responsible for his victory; the same Faisal who had sent her out here in the first place to win his uncle over. It seemed that Raschid had known Faisal far better than she had done.

It was hot outside, away from the protective shelter of the house. The pool shimmered under the bright sun. Felicia dived in, the water like cool silk against her heated skin. She swam a couple of lengths, then turned over to float luxuriously on her back, her hair a bright cloud of molten fire against the vivid blue of the water. She closed her eyes, letting her tense muscles relax. In the distance she could hear voices raised in angry protest, but they

faded and then there was only the benevolent heat of the
sun and the soothing slap of the water against the sides
of the pool.

As she lay there she wondered idly why neither Nadia
nor Zahra used the pool, and then dismissed the thought,
as she struck out for the far side in a lazy crawl.

She trod water for a few seconds, trying to find the energy
to haul herself out. Her eyes stung from the chlorine in the
water and she closed them, rubbing them with one hand.

Someone grasped her arms, hauling her unceremoniously out of the water, to stand at the side of the pool
dripping moisture on to soft leather boots.

Her eyes travelled upwards. Wide trousers were tucked
into the boots, a dark cloak flung back from broad shoulders.

'Miss Gordon!'

'Raschid!' Awareness shivered through her. Was this it?
Was he going to tell her that she was going home?

She forced herself to look up into his face. His expression was forbidding, his mouth tight, although whether
with distaste or anger she could not tell.

'I was on my way to the stables when I saw you here.'

Felicia gritted her teeth, willing him to get to the point.
Tears were not very far away, but she comforted herself with
the knowledge that after today she would probably never
need to endure his anger again. Oddly, it brought her no relief.

'What were you doing in the pool?'

She stared at him. 'Do I have to have your permission
before I can swim now?'

His glance impaled her, sending sharp splinters of apprehension through her trembling body. Her wrap was on
the other side of the pool, and she glanced helplessly at it,

wishing for its admittedly frail protection against the steely thrust of his eyes.

Even the doves seemed to have ceased their endless cooing and in the unnerving silence she felt sure he must hear the frightened thudding of her heart. His eyes searched her face, looking for she knew not what, and then, as though satisfied, he smiled coolly.

'I have been looking for you. I wish to speak to you.'

Of course he did. He wanted to gloat over Faisal's defection, no doubt.

Head held high, she refused to let him see how she felt. 'I'll go and get changed, and....'

He forestalled her, his touch on her deceptively light. 'I think not. What I wish to say to you requires privacy, and where better than here in the seclusion of this courtyard, where none will disturb us, since it is my own private domain.'

CHAPTER EIGHT

'YOURS?'

The word trembled between them, as Raschid inclined his head in sardonic acknowledgement.

'In my country, Miss Gordon, a woman does not flaunt herself unclad before male eyes—but I have already told you this. This pool and courtyard are part of my own private quarters—but then I'm sure you know that already.'

What on earth was he accusing her of now? Despite his suave manner Felicia had the distinct impression that he was battling with overpowering rage, and yet she could not understand why this should be so.

'I'm sorry if I intruded into your private domain,' she apologised stiffly, but he swept the words aside, his mouth twisting contemptuously.

'Oh, come, you can do better than that. It seems that I owe you an apology for the other night, and opportunist that you are, I'm sure you are aware that I would have to seek you out to tender it. Where better than here, where we could not be disturbed; where the enticement of your unclad body can tempt my instincts to overrule my common sense? I am a man as any other, Miss Gordon, and

no more immune than they to the charms you so provocatively display, in that apology for a swimsuit.'

A note of iron had entered his voice as his glance burned
over her, but it was lost on the girl standing at his side, filled
with a growing indignation and longing only to be free of
the smooth voice and its hateful insinuation. She forgot
about Faisal and his letter, and why she had assumed that
Raschid had sought her out, and demanded,

'Are you suggesting that I deliberately came down here
to entice you?' Incredulity sharpened her normally soft
voice, but Raschid seemed unaware of her heated cheeks
and flashing eyes. His mouth curled cynically.

'Are *you* suggesting that you did not?' He shook his head.
'There is no need for pretence between us, Miss Gordon.'
He lowered his head suddenly, grasping a handful of half
damp hair and twisting it round his hand, imprisoning her.

As she struggled his grip tightened inexorably, propelling
her towards him until there was nothing between them but
the flimsy barrier of her swimsuit, and not even that where
it plunged seductively to reveal the taut thrust of her breasts.

Her muffled protest was lost. She could feel the heat
coming off Raschid's skin. She arched desperately away
from him, but his strength was the greater and her tired
muscles were forced to concede victory and allow him to
draw her slender body against the hard length of his own.
Muscle for muscle he overpowered her, her body losing its
fight to reject the punishing familiarity of his. His shirt was
open, allowing him to hold her captive against his golden
skin, her senses swimming with the emotions she was
fighting to control.

Useless to protest that she had never been held so close

to any man before, or that the intimacy he was forcing upon her with the hard arrogance of his body was a violation of her innocence, because she knew he was beyond all reason.

As his hands slid the straps of her swimsuit from her shoulders she cried a protest, embarrassed colour flooding her cheeks as he stepped back to look down at her unprotected body. Her hands went instinctively to shield her breasts, but he grasped her wrists, looking his fill until her skin was on fire with rage and humiliation.

'Charming, but not necessary,' he drawled, plainly amused. 'Faisal may have been deceived by that air of mock modesty, but you waste it on me, Miss Gordon.'

'Miss Gordon!' Felicia swallowed mounting hysteria. Dear God, he had the audacity to treat her body as though it were just another of his possessions, and yet he still called her 'Miss Gordon'!

Stiff as a figure of marble in the circle of the arms Raschid clamped round her, she tilted her own head upwards to meet the sardonic mockery she knew would be written in his eyes.

'You have a strange way of apologising, Sheikh Raschid!' She was trembling with fury, but he barely spared her flushed face a glance; his eyes rested on the fragile bones of her shoulders, his mouth traced a downward path that spelled destruction to her self-control.

'You think so?' he murmured. 'Perhaps I consider that whatever reparation was necessary has been made.'

'You think I wanted *this*?' Furiously she tried to push him away, but his hands curled into her shoulders, hauling her against him to lie defeated against the hard wall of his chest, her heart pounding in terror as his mouth swooped, capturing her defenceless lips and subjecting them to merciless plundering as they closed stubbornly against him. Relentless pressure forced them to part. Above her his eyes glittered as harshly as the pitiless sun in the sky, reminding her that soon she would be gone; that soon he must receive Faisal's letter and then there would be no more moments such as these…. Then she would never know the harsh mastery of his embrace….

As though someone had murmured 'Open Sesame' her body yielded, melting against him, her fingers curling into the warm darkness of the hair matting his chest. He muttered something, the blood beating up under his skin, and then she was crushed against him, moulded to his body, her mouth parting willingly to allow him full licence to savour its inner sweetness.

She neither knew nor cared what she was betraying; all that mattered was this moment, this stolen sweetness, which she would cherish for the rest of her life, the feel of Raschid against her bitter-sweet as she acknowledged that only passion stirred him. It stopped her in her tracks. Appalled by her response, she tried to push him away, her fingers trembling against bruised lips.

'Let me go!' She backed away, unshed tears shimmering in her eyes as she slid her swimsuit straps back over her shoulders. While she was unable to deny the cathartic effect of Raschid's lovemaking, he seemed completely unmoved by the incident. He leaned his long length against a stone pillar, his smile cruel as he surveyed her distressed state.

'Why the charade?' he asked coolly. 'You invited, I accepted. Not to have done so would have been churlish, as I'm sure you will agree.'

She invited! She had done no such thing. She told him so, half stammering with anger.

'No? You weren't hoping I would succumb to your charms and agree to your betrothal to Faisal? Wasn't that the whole purpose of your visit?' His lip curled. 'I am not a complete fool, Miss Gordon. If that was not the reason for your momentary acquiescence, then what was? I doubt my nephew would be very pleased to learn of the methods you adopt to gain my approval. What was in his letter, I wonder, to force you to such desperate measures? He wouldn't be growing tired of you, would he?'

'If he had I'm sure you would be the first to know about it,' Felicia parried, her mouth dry. So he had not heard from Faisal, but she had no doubts that his behaviour was deliberately designed to humiliate and denigrate her into giving in and returning home. She was only surprised that he had not tried bribing her into giving Faisal up, but perhaps treating her in this way afforded him some sort of satisfaction. Punishment for daring to aspire to marriage to a member of his family.

'One more thing,' he cautioned as she turned away. 'You will not run crying to Zahra of this. I do not want her birthday spoiled.'

Had he so little opinion of her that he thought she would do that, knowing how much Zahra thought of him?

She let a little of her scorn show in her voice.

'We have a saying, evil be to him who thinks evil. I wouldn't dream of hurting Zahra. I've grown very fond of her.'

'An emotion which plainly does not extend to include me.'

His audacity took her breath away. What did he expect when he treated her like some amoral gold-digger?

'An emotion which could never extend to include you,' she retorted. Never, never must he be allowed to think her momentary surrender sprang from anything other than a calculated intention to win him round to her cause. She could only hope that before he discovered that that cause had been lost long before she responded to his kiss, she would be gone, and she would not have to endure his amused contempt when he finally realised the truth.

During supper Zahra was rather subdued. Raschid had been particularly scathing about her harem outfit, she told Felicia, adding that she found her uncle changed of late, less inclined to show humorous indulgence, his temper sharper.

'When I asked him why Faisal could not come home for my birthday, he really snapped my head off. He and Faisal have never got on,' she admitted. 'Raschid thinks Faisal should be more conscious of his duty.'

A duty which no doubt included marriage to a girl of his own kind, Felicia thought wryly.

DESPITE THE laughter at the breakfast table Felicia felt as though a lead weight were attached to her heart. She had barely slept, tossing and turning, almost at one point ready to go to Raschid and tell him that she wanted to leave, but always the thought of his contemptuous indifference held her back, making it impossible for her to confess that he had been right and she wrong.

Zahra had been thrilled with her perfume, and Felicia's thoughts turned automatically to the unopened bottle in her drawer. One day, when her heart was less tender, she would open it, and the scent would bring back memories of that dusty alley and the feel of Raschid's hands on her skin.

All night long she had battled with her pride, and at last in the soft pearly light of the false dawn had admitted the truth. She loved Raschid. Only he had the key to awaken her dormant emotions, to draw from her a response she had never thought herself capable of giving. To no other man had she reacted as she did to Raschid. For no other man had her body quivered with deep, aching need, which overcame all her fears of rejection, built up during her lonely childhood. Raschid had the power to make her forget every single consideration but the overpowering need to satisfy the throbbing hunger his touch awoke within her.

Now she could admit that what she had felt for Faisal was merely gratitude for his attention to her. She had accepted his kisses without being stirred by them, thinking her lack of response sprang from some coldness in her nature, but Raschid had proved once and for all that this was not true. With Faisal she had always been passive, content to follow his lead, but in Raschid's arms she knew a longing to be consumed by the fierce passion of which she knew instinctively he was capable. Those fires would never burn for her. She knew that now, and every instinct for self-preservation warned her to flee before Raschid discovered her vulnerability.

She closed her eyes, her face pale, startled when Nadia asked anxiously if she was all right.

All right! She smiled hollowly. She doubted if she would ever be 'all right' again, but since she could not say so she smiled weakly and brushed aside Nadia's kind concern.

The fortress owned by Saud's family was a huge pile of stone perched grimly on a rocky outcrop and command-

ing excellent views of the surrounding countryside—a
reminder of the days when his forebears would have lived
by preying off unwary travellers or other tribes daring or
desperate enough to cross their territory.

Here the old ways still held sway. They drove in under
a formidable stone gateway and the women were led to a
side entrance, barely discernible. Following Umm Faisal's
example, Felicia removed her slippers as they entered the
dark cavernous hallway.

Saud's mother came forward to greet them. The traditional Arabic welcome and prayers for a long and healthy
life were exchanged. The visitors were led to opulent
cushions spread about the room, Felicia's muscles protesting a little as she tried to imitate the grace of the others.

In addition to Saud's mother there were various aunts
and cousins, all of whom had to be introduced to the visitor
from England, although Felicia was aware that their real
interest was, quite naturally, in Zahra.

It was Nadia who whispered to her that to mention the
marriage before it was a fait accompli was to put the 'evil
eye' upon it, but there was no mistaking the value of the
expensive gifts they pressed upon a blushing Zahra.

One of the women, obviously very old, commanded
Felicia to come forward.

'That is Saud's grandmother,' Nadia whispered. 'She
has seen six sons die in defence of their country, and even
His Highness puts great store by her advice.'

Felicia could well understand why. Despite the simplicity of her clothes, the strangeness of her henna-pat-
terned hands and feet, Felicia knew she was in the presence
of great wisdom. Although she spoke very little English,

her eyes were shrewd as they assessed Felicia's slender beauty. She said something in Arabic to Umm Faisal, who responded:

'She said that you are very like the English girl who married her third cousin—she means Raschid's grandfather.'

The visit seemed to last for a long time. A maid came round a second time with fresh coffee. Felicia found the ceremony endlessly fascinating. Zahra told her now to shake her coffee cup to signify that she had had sufficient to drink, and she also added the warning that it was considered impolite not to drink at least three of the small cups of the beverage.

Arabs placed great store by hospitality and ritual, as Felicia was coming to learn, and to refuse what was given so graciously could be considered a grave insult.

The visit was obviously a formal one, but when the other ladies rose to leave, Umm Faisal and Zahra were invited to stay on. Nadia touched Felicia's arm, indicating that she leave with her.

'Raschid is discussing the final arrangements for Zahra's dowry; Saud's mother will want to talk about the wedding, so you and I will walk in the courtyard and let them get on with it.'

It was pleasantly cool in the garden, and Felicia felt her tensed nerves relax for the first time since the previous day.

'You do not like Raschid, do you?' Nadia asked shrewdly, out of the blue. 'I have seen the look in your eyes whenever he is mentioned. What is wrong? Can you not tell me?'

'He does not approve of my…my relationship with Faisal,' Felicia admitted, glad of the opportunity to unburden herself. 'He thinks me a woman of the very worst sort—avaricious, designing…. It is natural for him to want to protect your brother….'

'But not natural to be so blind,' Nadia interposed softly. 'Not Raschid, whose astuteness is fabled within our family. He treats you as he treats no other woman, Felicia. You must know of his English blood? He has learned to guard his heart well, so that it is like an inner courtyard, its beauties revealed only to a privileged few.'

Felicia's heart ached with the weight of a thousand unshed tears. The delights Nadia's words painted so vividly were not for her.

'Raschid has no interest in me, other than an overriding desire for me to return home,' Felicia told her quietly. 'And were it not for the fact that if I left now it would spoil some of Zahra's pleasure in her birthday, I assure you I would already be gone.'

'Zahra is fond of you,' Nadia agreed. 'But as to your presence here, that is as Allah wills it.'

No, it was as Raschid willed it, Felicia thought despairingly. He alone had the power to banish her at will! If only she dared confide in Nadia and beg her help. She still had some of her savings left. Perhaps if she could borrow her fare from Nadia she could repay it within a few months if she was really careful with her budget. She started to speak, but Nadia stopped her. 'Quickly!' she urged. 'We must return to the harem.'

She whisked Felicia inside so quickly that she barely had time to comprehend what was happening, before Nadia was pulling her veil across her face and hurrying her away.

In the distance she caught the sound of male voices,

footsteps ringing across the courtyard they had so recently vacated.

'That was a close call!' Nadia breathed. 'Living away from home I tend to be less strict with myself, but it would have shamed Raschid before Saud's father had we been discovered in the garden. Achmed would have been furious with me,' She made a small moue. 'Fortunately I heard them coming in time. I'm trying to persuade Raschid to take us all out hawking. It used to be his favourite pastime, and his falcons are a sight to behold. It will be the last time we are all together as a family before Zahra marries, and it seems fitting that we should revert to the freedom of our childhood years, if only for a few hours.'

'In that case you won't want me along,' Felicia began, but Nadia swept her protests aside.

'Of course we shall want you.' She bent forward and kissed Felicia's cheek. 'You are a delight to us all, Felicia, and far too unassuming, although I hope Zahra does not speak the truth when she says that you may marry Faisal. Although he is my brother, I have to admit that he is weak, too changeable in his ways to make a good husband. Not like my Achmed.' She glanced speculatively at Felicia. 'You know, in a way I am surprised that you do not get on well with Raschid. He has always been a great admirer of beauty, and you have much of that. Also your manner cannot help but please; you are of his religion.'

'Liking does not come from any of those things,' Felicia said shakily, trying to stem the flood of longing Nadia's words had aroused. 'It comes from the heart, and Raschid's heart is closed to me.' This was her chance to beg Nadia for her aid, but she was too shy to ask, and by the time they had returned to the others it was too late.

Later, she was to regret her weakness, but when they joined the rest of their party, her own worries subsided in the general excitement over Zahra's wedding.

It was late when they started back. Somehow or other Felicia found herself travelling with Raschid, sitting in the front seat while Umm Faisal and Zahra occupied the back.

He was concentrating on the road, a barren landscape in black and silver, and she stole a glance at his remote profile, swept by a wave of love. Where on earth Nadia had got the idea that he could feel anything but disdainful contempt for her, Felicia could not imagine. She sighed, letting weary eyelids drop over aching eyes.

The land had already cast its timeless spell over her, and the man.... She looked again at his shadowed profile. His head turned and their eyes met, pleasure and pain mingled as another fierce wave of longing swamped her.

At last she had given her feelings their rightful name—she loved Raschid, against all the odds, in spite of the un-bridgable gulfs of background and upbringing that yawned between them, she loved him.

She sighed as tiredness drained even the ability to think properly. She might as well love the sun or the moon. Her eyes closed and opened as she struggled against waves of exhaustion. At her side Raschid turned and frowned.

'It has been a long day for you, Miss Gordon. My sister and Zahra are both sleeping. Feel free to join them if you wish. We have a good hour's journey in front of us.'

They were following Achmed and Nadia, and as he spoke the powerful headlights of the Mercedes picked out the car in front quite clearly—and its occupants, Nadia's dark head cradled on Achmed's shoulder. An aching longing so intense that it was almost a physical pain hit her. She longed to cry out against it, stifling it, but the sound was trapped in her throat. She fought to subdue the urge to move closer to Raschid, to place her head on his shoulder and know she would not be rebuffed.

Pride alone kept her upright in her seat, her eyes sliding away from Nadia and Achmed, but it was Raschid who said curtly:

'You're practically falling asleep sitting up, Miss Gordon. If pride prevents you from using my shoulder as a pillow, try telling yourself that very soon I shall be your uncle and capable of commanding your obedience. I know you detest me, but this road is very uneven in parts. If you fall asleep as you are you could easily be thrown against a window or do yourself some other injury, so let common sense take the place of pride and accept my offer in the spirit in which it is given.'

What could she do? Even so, she had not expected his arm to curve round her, pulling her against the warmth of his body, and in response to her unvoiced question he said curtly:

'I am perfectly able to drive with one hand—this is not a busy road, and I am not a young fool intent on showing off. Try to relax, I do not intend to harm you.'

But he was, whether he intended it or not. Merely the pressure of his body as he changed gear, the warm male smell of his flesh, harmed her irreparably as her heart wept for the unattainability of its one desire. She drew a steady breath and instantly her nostrils were full of the masculine odour of his body. She closed her eyes, but with his hard shoulder beneath her cheek, it was impossible to banish the tormenting image of his mouth, its well cut lines as well known to her as the softer shape of her own.

She fought against sleep as long as she could, not wanting it to steal from her these precious moments when Raschid gave his strength unstintingly, but the warmth of his body made her drowsy and her tormented senses were not proof against the smothering waves of sleep. Her body relaxed, her head falling against his shoulder. His arm tightened, holding her steady, as they drove into the endless night of the desert.

Felicia had no clear recollection of their arrival. Sleepy and bemused, she stumbled from the car, and Raschid's strong arm caught her as she fell.

She thanked him, returning awareness making her desperate to avoid the sharpness of his eyes.

Sleepily Umm Faisal offered a cup of coffee, but Felicia refused. Like a greedy miser, she wanted to gloat over her precious hoard of happiness to fall asleep, dreaming of those sacred moments when Raschid's arms had held her without anger or punishment.

It was quiet in the courtyard. Zahra was with Umm Faisal. With the month of Ramadan fast approaching, the arrangements for the wedding had to be finalised. Only that morning Umm Faisal had shown Felicia the soft rose silk from which Zahra's bridal caftan would be fashioned. Shimmering threads of beaten silver flashed in the sunlight, and Felicia fingered the fabric in awe.

Later Zahra had shown her the gifts Saud had sent her— the silver and turquoise hand jewellery handed down through seven generations of his family, necklaces of beaten gold studded with rubies, rings and ankle bracelets, a whole treasure trove of precious and semi-precious stones guaranteed to excite the most prosaic female imagination.

Lastly Zahra produced an intricately worked girdle of beaten silver. This was the symbolic girdle used to fasten the bride's shift, she explained, and once it *was* fastened in place, none but her bridegroom had the right to remove it.

'Raschid still has the girdle made for his grandmother,' Zahra told her, 'and although he is Christian, he will marry according to the laws of our faith as well, for that was his grandfather's wish, thus the two religions will live side by side in harmony with one another.'

Every mention of Raschid brought nervous tension to Felicia's body. Every day she expected to be summoned to his study and told that he had heard from Faisal. Why did she torture herself like this? Why did she not go to him and ask to be sent home before he discovered the truth about why she had been content to linger long after she knew of Faisal's change of heart? Her own heart gave her the answer. She was sitting by the fishpond, staring lazily into space. A tortoise-shell carp jumped in the water, showering her with tiny droplets; in the distance doves cooed; even the perfect symmetry of the house echoed the same pervasive sense of peace. Her red-gold head bent over the pool, unaware that she was being observed by the man who stood in the shade of the lime trees, the fragile vulnerability of her lightly tanned skin exposed to his searching gaze. His expression unfathomable, he continued to watch, and then turned abruptly, his progress across the courtyard fluttering the doves into noisy protest. Felicia glanced up, her expression unguarded, unable to quench the fierce joy running through her veins.

'Sheikh Raschid!' There was even pleasure in saying his name.

He inclined his head in the manner which had become so familiar that it was engraved on her heart. A small pang shot through her, and a hesitant smile quivered on her lips, as she suppressed her alarm.

'Have you heard from Faisal?'

Now what had made her ask that? His brows drew together in blank disapproval.

'No,' he replied curtly. 'Are you missing him so much that you are willing to beg *me* for news of him? Perhaps I did you an injustice. Perhaps you do care for him after all.'

Now was her chance to tell him the truth. The words trembled on her lips, only to be silenced as he added cynically, 'However, as we both know, appearances can be deceptive. Our strong sun darkens the colour of your skin to the colour of ours, but it cannot change what lies underneath. There can be no happiness in a marriage between yourself and Faisal.'

'East and West can live in harmony,' Felicia protested. 'Your own grandparents....'

'They were an exception,' Raschid interrupted curtly. 'My grandmother willingly gave up everything to be with my grandfather. Can you honestly tell me that your love for Faisal possesses that strength? Would you willingly wander the desert with him, an outcast to your own people?'

Her eyes gave him the answer. Not for Faisal, but for him.... She would willingly walk barefoot to hell and back for him. She longed to reach out and touch him, to slide her fingers through the dark crispness of his hair, to kiss those firmly chiselled lips and to urge that lean body to take her and make her a part of him, her flesh yielding and melting into his as his hard hands possessed her. She closed her eyes and prayed as she had never prayed before, that she might banish these tormenting images.

When she opened them again Raschid was watching her dispassionately. 'It is not safe for you to walk alone out here, Miss Gordon,' he warned her.

'In case I might be carried off by some desert barbarian, do you mean? Surely *they* would scorn me as you do, as being worthless and of little account. An unwanted intruder in their lives; a female of no virtue whose life means no more than a few grains of sand.'

'Faisal did not scorn you,' Raschid pointed out. 'And it is after all, he who holds your heart, is it not?'

She watched him disappear into the shadows, her body aching as though she had been beaten; which metaphorically she felt as though it had. She herself had lashed it unmercifully with the reminder that Raschid cared nothing for her.

All her pleasure in the garden was gone. She went to her room, drawn to the drawer where she had concealed the small phial of perfume. Almost against her will she unstoppered it, and the fragrant, fresh smell of the English countryside stole through the room, coupled with a scent almost bitter-sweet, but faintly haunting, so in tune with her emotions that she could only marvel at the perfume blender's ability to correctly judge her mood and transform it into this perfume which would always bring home to her the senselessness of unwanted love.

CHAPTER NINE

PROMPTED by Achmed, Raschid had made arrangements to entertain his guest by taking him hawking, a trip which could take two or three days dependent on the game to be had.

Nadia had begged Achmed to intercede with Raschid on behalf of the female half of the household, declaring that it was unfair that they should be left behind while the men enjoyed themselves.

The plan was that the men would take Raschid's falcons, a couple of servants and two Land Rovers to hold all their gear and spend a couple of days relaxing in the desert.

Nadia explained to Felicia that in their younger days she and Zahra had often accompanied Raschid on these trips, revelling in the freedom from routine these outings provided.

'In the old days the men used tents, like the Badu, cooking over an open fire, but nowadays things are a bit more civilised. We use sleeping bags and camping Gaz,' Nadia laughed. 'Raschid does not really approve. He still prefers to follow the old ways of our people, but Mother used to worry that Faisal would burn himself or get indigestion from half cooked food and so, in the end, Raschid had to give in.'

Even so it sounded enviably exciting—the wide open spaces of the desert, men in long white robes, eating under a dark blue velvet sky studded with stars. Felicia gave a faint sigh. Uncle George had never approved of picnics, or indeed eating out of doors at all.

'Don't worry, Achmed will be able to persuade Raschid. He'll have to,' she added with a darkling look, 'otherwise I've told him he won't be going himself.'

Felicia burst out laughing. Nadia was so refreshingly modern in her outlook, and it was plain that Achmed adored her.

He came into the women's quarters while they were watching Zayad's antics, a beaming smile splitting his face.

'Raschid has agreed that you girls can come with us. Not without an awful lot of persuasion, I might add, and I'd better warn you, we mean to set off after first light tomorrow, and Raschid is in no mood to make allowances for you. He says if you are to come with us you must expect to be treated just like the men.'

'Isn't that just typical of him?' Nadia complained. 'I swear he thinks more of his falcons than he does of us.'

'Quite probably,' Achmed agreed cheerfully. He looked thoughtfully at Felicia, who was trying to play cat's cradles with Zayad. 'This will be your first trip into the interior of the desert, won't it? Nadia will tell you what to take along.' He frowned and seemed to hesitate.

Had Raschid expressed doubts about the wisdom of taking her along because *she* was to be a member of the party? A casual enquiry of Zahra had elicited the information that unless they sent someone to Kuwait to collect it they would receive no mail while they were in the desert, and so, thinking herself safe for at least a few days, Felicia had closed her mind to the heartache she was storing up for herself, determined to make of the precious time left to her enough memories to warm her through the long cold years ahead.

A little later in the day Nadia went with her to her room to sort out what she ought to take on the trip. 'Your jeans, I think,' she announced, pursing her lips, 'and a long-sleeved blouse. I think I have riding boots that will fit you. When the falcons are hunting the hubara we shall have to follow on foot, and boots protect the ankles and legs from snakes and scorpions.'

'Raschid didn't want us to go because of me, didn't he?' Felicia interrupted quietly, needing to know the answer, in spite of the pain it might cause.

Nadia looked uncomfortable, and Felicia knew she had guessed correctly. 'It is just that it is our custom for each girl to be accompanied by a man to watch over her safety,' Nadia explained, 'and in Faisal's absence Raschid is very conscious of his responsibility towards you. Zahra and I are accustomed to the desert. You are not.' Her smile softened the words. 'Don't worry, Felicia, we shall take care of you, but try to understand....'

'To understand what? That your uncle considers me an unwanted nuisance? I understand *that* already.'

Nadia bit her lip, her eyes clouded. 'Forgive me, Felicia, but this hostility you feel towards Raschid—could it be that you use it to mask other—very different emotions?'

One look at Nadia's face told her that the older girl had guessed the truth. Pride made her grasp at any straw, however frail, to conceal her feelings.

'If you mean love, I consider that any woman who fell in love with your uncle would need to be either a fool or a masochist!'

Felicia saw with relief that Nadia was staring at her in stunned surprise, but it was several seconds before she realised why. When Nadia continued to stare over her shoulder, the hairs at the back of her neck began to prickle warningly, and she swung round just in time to see Raschid's coldly furious expression as he strode past the door.

'Do you think he heard me?'

Nadia recovered her voice, nodding her head commiseratingly. 'I'm so sorry. I never heard him until it was too late.'

Felicia shrugged, trying to tell herself that it did not matter; another stone on the wall separating herself and Raschid was hardly likely to make much difference one way or the other.

'It doesn't matter,' she assured Nadia. 'After all, he's never made any pretence of liking me. In fact I'm sure he's feeling exceptionally pleased with the results of his eaves-dropping. He'll be more positive than ever now that I'm everything he thought, and worse!'

'Let me explain to him,' Nadia suggested, but Felicia shook her head decisively. What was there to explain? That Nadia had accused her of being in love with him, and in order to defend herself she had claimed that no woman could be? He would know she was lying.

'What's the point? Let him think what he likes.'

'It's all my fault,' Nadia admitted apologetically. 'I shouldn't have teased you in the first place. I am sorry.'

When Nadia had gone Felicia stared at her clothes hanging in the wardrobe. Soon it would be empty. They

would not be staying at the oasis much longer, and once
Faisal's letter reached Raschid, she would have to face the
day of reckoning. If only she did not have to apply to
Faisal's family in order to get home! She was not left with
even that shred of pride intact.

AS ACHMED HAD foretold, Raschid lost no time in announcing that if the girls were intent on accompanying
them, they would have to present themselves in the outer
courtyard at first light.

That had been last night, and now, pulling on her jeans
in the pearly light of the false dawn, Felicia rubbed the
sleep from her eyes. Below, in the courtyard, she could hear
sounds of activity. Tiredly she brushed her hair, securing
it with a ribbon. Following Nadia's advice she added a
thick, chunky sweater to the absolute necessities Raschid
had limited them to—a change of underwear, a clean
blouse, some soft woollen socks to wear inside Nadia's
boots, and a pair of sunglasses.

She could see a couple of menservants loading things
into the two Land Rovers parked below. Nadia had invited
her to travel with herself and Achmed, and Felicia had
accepted. It would be less wearing on her fragile nervous
system than riding with Raschid.

Breakfast had been set out for them in one of the salons,
although Felicia's stomach rebelled at the thought of
yoghurt and dates before the sun had crept over the horizon.

Zayad gave them all a sticky kiss as they prepared to
leave, then went docilely to his nurse.

'He's so good, isn't he?' Felicia marvelled.

'Kuwaiti children are accustomed to being obedient,

Miss Gordon,' Raschid said crisply from behind her. 'Unlike in the West.'

It was an unjust accusation, and hot words of rebuttal trembled on her lips, to be swallowed when she reflected that any ill-feeling between Raschid and herself was bound to spoil the enjoyment of the others. Heroically she merely gave him a polite little smile, and pushed back her chair intending to follow Nadia.

The first rays of the sun crept over the horizon, glinting on the large oval brass dish on a small table, and Felicia, her attention momentarily diverted, felt the blood freeze in her veins. In the dish lay half a dozen envelopes; the top one an airmail letter, very obviously addressed in Faisal's hand and bearing Raschid's name.

Her hand crept to her throat, she longed to reach out and pluck the letter away before it could ruin her last precious memories, but Nadia was urging her through the door and she had perforce to follow.

The morning air rang with the bustle of their departure, the strident cries of the falcons drawing Felicia's attention.

Until Nadia had mentioned it she had not realised that Raschid trained the falcons himself when he could spare the time. Even hooded, their cruel beaks and curving talons made her shudder, striking a chill right through her; the birds' scarlet jesses were blood-coloured in the early morning sun.

The bird nearest to her let out a shrill cry and flapped its wings. The servant holding it grinned.

'Very good falcon, this one. He is named Sahud.'

Felicia raised her hand to touch the bird's tawny feathers, and instantly her fingers were seized in a crushing grip. 'Don't touch him!'

Both Zahra and Nadia looked round to see whom Raschid was addressing with such controlled fury, and Felicia's face burned beneath the open amusement of the *saggar* holding the falcon.

'Those birds cost upwards of two thousand pounds apiece, Miss Gordon,' Raschid said crushingly. 'They are trained to attack and maim anything that moves—and that includes those pretty fingers you were fluttering about in front of him.'

There was a large lump in her throat. She wanted to make a furious retort, to tell him that she thought the *saggar* had been inviting her to stroke the bird, but pride prevented her.

'No harm has been done, Raschid,' Nadia said soothingly, coming to Felicia's rescue. 'Honestly, you treat those birds like children!'

'Because like children they have to be trained to obey, and rewarded when they do so.'

A servant was handing him a leather glove, heavily embroidered with silver and gold threads, the leather as soft and supple as silk. Raschid pulled it on, smoothing it over his hand before transferring the bird from the *saggar*'s wrist to his own.

Felicia watched as he proffered it a piece of raw meat. It took it, ripping the flesh with its talons and beak. Slightly nauseated, she turned away.

Nodding to the *saggar*, Raschid handed the bird back to him.

'This is life, Miss Gordon,' he told her drily, proving that he had observed her reaction. 'In the desert one has to fight to survive.'

'And kill?' she whispered, trying not to look at the bright splash of blood on the cobbles.

'When necessary,' Raschid agreed coolly 'Perhaps you would prefer to remain behind and keep my sister company?'

And miss the opportunity of those last remaining hours of *his* company? She shook her head, and their eyes clashed.

'Very well, on your own head be it. I warn you now, though, there will not be time to make allowances for your inexperience and ignorance of our ways.'

Nadia and Achmed were already in the Land Rover, Zahra chatting eagerly to her sister through the open window.

'Sorry, I didn't realise we were ready to leave,' Felicia apologised, hurrying towards them.

Raschid's voice halted her.

'You will be travelling with me, Miss Gordon,' he announced. 'Please get in the Land Rover. Zahra, will you go with Achmed and Nadia. Selim, Ali, one of you go with Achmed and the other come with me.'

Almost paralysed with dismay, Felicia glanced pleadingly at Nadia. 'Miss Gordon, you are keeping us waiting,' Raschid reminded her.

Nadia made a sympathetic grimace and gave her a little push.

'Go on, he won't eat you!'

There was nothing else for it. With dragging footsteps she walked across to the second Land Rover, her face resolutely averted from Raschid's masked features.

The door slammed behind her. Selim climbed into the back, reaching over to hand Raschid the pile of letters Felicia had seen in the hallway.

'Ali brought the mail when we went for the Land Rovers.'

Taking it from him, Raschid stuffed the letters on to the shelf in front of him, giving them only the most cursory glance. Faisal's letter was at the bottom, and holding her breath Felicia waited to see if he had noticed it. Apparently he had not. She opened her mouth to say that she had changed her mind and would not be going with them, but it was too late. The gates were open and as the sun finally burst over the horizon in a dazzle of molten gold they drove out into the unknown.

With every second she expected Raschid to reach for his mail, but he was concentrating on his driving, and gradually she allowed her clenched muscles to relax. They would have to stop sooner or later, and when they did…. She closed her eyes in despair. When they did he would read Faisal's letter and then…. She dragged her thoughts away, trying to concentrate on her surroundings. Even this early in the day she could feel the heat rising from the desert, and before too long her blouse was clinging stickily to her back. Only the odd remark in Arabic punctuated the silence as Selim pointed out various landmarks to Raschid.

Secretly Felicia considered that one sandhill looked very much like another, but obviously this could not be so, for several times during the course of the morning Raschid changed direction.

After a while she noticed that he always kept the sun on the left-hand side of the Land Rover, and feeling rather pleased with herself she deduced that he was using it to navigate. There was no compass in the Land Rover, but to a man used to the desert and its ways, the sun would be all the guide he needed.

This supposition was reinforced when Raschid brought

the Land Rover to a halt shortly before noon, his abrupt nod confirming that she should get out. Her eyes flew instinctively to the letters, her mouth dry with apprehension.

Her clothes and face were gritty from the sand thrown up by the tires, but it was tension that was responsible for the cramped state of her limbs. She almost fell out of the jeep, and it was Raschid who saw what was happening and thrust open his door, striding round to swing her unceremoniously to the ground. Beneath lowered lashes she watched him. Hard and impassive, his face had a quality of strength that would give one confidence in him. If one had to be lost in this vast wilderness, he would make a good companion, she thought irrelevantly. A woman could rely on his strength even when she could not hope for his tenderness.

He started to walk back to the Land Rover.

'Stiff?' Zahra teased.

'A little,' Felicia acknowledged, her eyes on Raschid. He was taking the letters from the shelf. 'Do we hunt now?' she asked Zahra absently. Was he going to open them now? Already she could hear his sardonic jeers.

'After we have eaten and had a drink. The men will put up the falcons and we will follow them in the Land Rover. Sometimes they fly several miles without spotting a single hubara. They are wily birds, because although they cannot fly great distances, they have learned how to remain immobile while the falcon flies over them, and they can also discharge a thick, slimy substance into the falcon's eyes and feathers which renders it defenceless, so you see the hunt is not all one-sided.'

Achmed's eyes twinkled.

'I can see that such a state of affairs appeals more to

your British sense of fair play, Miss Gordon. Like your fox, our hubara, although a much humbler species, nevertheless has its own native cunning, which allows it to outwit its much more intelligent foe.'

Raschid hadn't spoken during this interchange, but at this he raised his head, regarding Felicia with a sardonic smile.

'I doubt if Miss Gordon would be quite as impressed with the hubara's cunning if she had to rely on its meat to survive.'

'I am not the fool you would have everyone believe me, Sheikh Raschid,' Felicia said quietly, with dignity, 'but I thought the purpose of this outing was to enjoy ourselves, not catch our dinner.'

'Touché, Miss Gordon. I doubt if Raschid has ever eaten hubara meat in his life, have you, my friend?' Achmed asked gaily.

'Then you would be wrong,' Raschid replied, without elaborating.

If only those letters had remained in Kuwait! How long would it be before he opened them? After lunch?

The falcons started to screech, sensing freedom, and the subject of hubara meat and its desirability was dropped. Accepting a cup of fresh lime juice from Zahra, Felicia sat down next to her, letting her aching limbs relax. She lay back and closed her eyes, letting her body absorb the sensations of her surroundings—the coarseness of the sand under her fingers, the heat of the sun, the faint smell of petrol, the soft murmur of Arab voices.

'What do you think of the desert, Miss Gordon?'

Raschid's voice startled her and her eyes flew anxiously to his.

There was no sign of Faisal's letter. She started to tremble, wondering if he had devised some subtle form of torture, whereby he was going to say nothing until she herself raised the subject. Very well, two could play at that game!

'It's magnificent,' she said coolly, glancing round.

'Whenever I'm here I wonder how I can endure to shut myself in an office, like an animal in a cage, but even the freest among us is chained by something; the greater our responsibilities, the greater the chains that bind us. A woman who shares the life of a man such as I has to learn to share his love for places such as these.'

'Like your grandmother, you mean?'

'She was an exception,' Raschid said curtly. 'There can be few women who would give up so much merely for the love of a man. In those days my family had no wealth as we know it today, and life was hard. I cannot see you, with your pale skin and pampered existence, forsaking life's luxuries to cleave to one man, and one alone.'

'Because you don't want to see it,' Felicia said quietly. 'You see in me only what you want to see.'

'I would to God that were possible,' Raschid said harshly, his eyes suddenly intent. 'Now you are angry,' he told her softly, 'and your eyes glint green fire as though they would consume me in their depths.' His own glittered like jet between the fringe of his lashes. 'And yet when I kissed you the other day, they were pools of mysterious jade.'

'Raschid, Felicia, are you ready to eat?'

Felicia didn't know whether to bless Nadia or to curse her. 'Ready!' she called, jumping to her feet.

They had a snack lunch prepared by the servants at the villa, and as soon as it was over the men moved over to the falcons.

'This is where we become unwanted appendages,' Nadia warned her. 'Once the birds are put up, the Land Rovers will follow. If you take my advice you will get in the front and be prepared to hold on tight. It can be a pretty hair-raising experience. It is a matter of pride not to lose a falcon, and the men don't make any allowances for female passengers.'

Felicia was glad that Zahra had warned her.

As she climbed into the Land Rover her eyes went automatically to where Raschid had placed the letters. They were gone. Her heart started to thump heavily. He must have read Faisal's letter. It could only be a matter of time before he confronted her, unless of course he *was* deliberately prolonging her agony, playing a game of cat and mouse, enjoying her mental torture. If only she had had the courage to tell him before. If only she had not let her foolish heart sway her judgment. She felt the jeep rock as Raschid climbed in. He slammed the door and switched on the engine, and then she was hanging on for grim death as the vehicle bounced and swayed over the sandhills, lurching from left to right as they followed the falcon, soaring above them, a tiny speck in the deep blue sky.

Sand clung to her eyelashes and hair. Every time she inhaled she tasted it in her mouth, the fine particles getting everywhere as the wheels threw up cloud after cloud behind them.

They crossed deep gullies and sharp inclines, at frightening speeds, the engine racing as it battled to obey Raschid's commands. At times they doubled back on themselves, and Felicia felt bruised all over as she was flung against the door and dashboard.

Selim shouted something in excitement and Felicia felt the Land Rover buck like a temperamental horse. The tiny speck disappeared. Raschid cursed, his hands tensing on the wheel as he swung the Land Rover hard over. Felicia held her breath, her fingers clinging to the dashboard. The whole world seemed to turn upside down, sand and sky rushing past the window. She was flung against the door with a jolt that drove the breath from her body, and then they were speeding across a flat plateau, sand spraying across the windscreen.

'You all right?' Raschid asked tersely.

She could only nod her head. Painful, nerve-tensing—the chase was nevertheless exhilarating, and she wouldn't have missed it for the world, she realised to her surprise.

Even when the falcon hovered motionless against the cobalt sky, dropping to earth with the swiftness of a desert night, she could feel no revulsion, only relief that the end was mercifully quick, the unfortunate hubara despatched with one efficient twist of the falcon's talons.

The *saggar* whistled tunelessly and within seconds the Land Rovers were halting, the *saggars* climbing out to wait for the falcons' return.

Exhausted but thrilled, Felicia waited while the whole business began again. She had been told that the falcons could kill up to eight or nine times in one day, but as Nadia explained, Raschid thought it unfair to take so much game when they were merely hunting for pleasure, so he normally restricted his bag to two or three hubara per falcon.

She had been relieved to discover that they would not be expected to eat the results of their expedition. Although the hubara were not particularly lovable creatures, her tender heart would have found it difficult to contemplate eating their flesh, no matter how delicious it might be.

The dying sun was casting long shadows across the sand when Raschid finally called a halt. Weary but exalted, Felicia tried to relax as the Land Rover plunged through the brief Eastern dusk to a small oasis where they were going to make camp.

Raschid had suggested that they would make the return journey that night, but Nadia had demurred, and from the looks she was casting Achmed, Felicia suspected that the velvet darkness of the desert night held special memories for them that both were eager to renew.

Nadia confirmed this later when they made camp at the oasis, informing Felicia that they had spent their honeymoon in the desert, just the two of them with a tent and a Land Rover, full of equipment. 'And very romantic it was too,' Nadia confided reminiscently, rummaging for the sleeping bags. 'I'd better give these to Selim. Make the most of this trip,' she advised Felicia. 'It's the only time you will see the men making themselves useful.'

It was true. Even Raschid was pitching in, helping Ali to unload boxes of food and the camping stove. It was all vaguely reminiscent of her Girl Guide days, Felicia thought, only on a far more sophisticated level.

Someone had got a fire going, feeding it with material brought from the villa, and in its flickering flames Felicia saw Raschid's face, his expression for once unguarded as he smiled down at Zahra. Her heart caught in her throat, and unbearable pain swept her because he had never looked at her like that.

As though suddenly aware of her intense scrutiny he

lifted his head, his eyes blazing into hers, and she trembled on a convulsive shudder. Maybe it was as well that her self-inflicted torture would soon be brought to an end. She was beginning to appreciate the meaning of the phrase 'living on one's nerves'.

'Will the Sitt have some rice?'

It was Selim, soft-footed as a cat as he padded up to her. Felicia shook her head. Despite the fresh air and Faisal's letter. Out of the corner of her eye she saw Ali filling Raschid's plate. Here in the desert formality went by the board. Selim and Ali moving among them, silent and hawk-eyed, filling plates and coffee cups with no regard for the normal rule of male precedence, and Felicia even saw Achmed draw Nadia within the curve of his arm, feeding her tidbits from his own plate, his eyes tender as he looked down into her laughing face.

There was a huge lump in her throat.

'They are fortunate, those two,' Zahra whispered at her side. 'Tonight they will share each other's bed under the stars, at one with the universe and each other. It makes me long for my Saud.' She smiled ruefully. 'I should not say that, I know. Poor Mother would be shocked if she heard me.

'Do you ache for the one you love, Felicia?'

Silently she nodded her head, her eyes lifting instinctively to Raschid's broad shoulders. He was sitting barely a yard away, talking to Selim, obviously deep in conversation.

'Yes,' she admitted painfully, 'I do, Zahra.'

SHE AND ZAHRA were to share one of the tents, while Achmed and Nadia had the other. Raschid and the servants were sleeping out in the open and after a quick dip in the oasis, Felicia was glad to crawl into her fleecy bag.

She had heard about the intense cold of the desert night, but this was the first time she had experienced it first-hand. Sleep evaded her; Raschid's face kept coming between her and the oblivion she desired. Next to her the sound of Zahra's quick, even breathing filled the tent. Outside was all the glory of the Eastern night—the stark beauty of the desert, palm trees whispering their indolent message to the night breeze; above, the dark blue velvet canopy of the sky studded with stars brighter by far than any diamonds. No wonder the wandering Badu called no man master, counting themselves more endowed with riches than any city-dwelling king.

She rolled on to her side, punching her pillow and trying to blot out the image of Raschid. Half an hour later she crawled wearily out of her sleeping bag. Her body was tired, but her mind refused to let her sleep. A short walk might help ease her tension, might help her to prepare some sort of defence against the accusations the morning was bound to bring.

Outside it was bitterly cold and she was glad of the thick sweater she had put on top of her blouse. Disregarding the boots Nadia had loaned her, she padded across the sand, breathing in the pure crystal air, and filling her lungs with its sharp freshness.

'Miss Gordon!'

She spun round. Raschid was standing by one of the Land Rovers watching her. Her heart sank. If only she had stayed in the tent! What better time than now, when they were alone, for him to confront her with her duplicity?

What possible excuses could she offer for abusing their hospitality by remaining with them when she knew that Faisal no longer wanted her? Could she plead Zahra's birthday, or would he see through the protective sham and pluck the truth from her heart?

'What are you looking for, Miss Gordon? Money? Romance? Does even your mercenary little heart yearn for a man's hard arms to possess your slenderness and bind it to him, on a night like this? His lips against yours as the coldness of the desert gives way to the heat of mutual passion?'

Felicia gasped in pain, wondering if he knew how he was tormenting her. She sensed that here in the desert he was a different man from the cool, sardonic entrepreneur who ran their vast empire.

'I merely wanted to walk,' she stammered. 'I couldn't sleep....'

'Because you longed so much for my nephew?' he mocked savagely. 'Well, I have longings too, and am as able to assuage your needs as Faisal—also I have the advantage of being here, while he is many miles away.' He crossed the small space dividing them and took her in his arms.

If he had wanted to punish her he must have succeeded beyond his wildest imaginings, Felicia thought despairingly, looking pleadingly up into his face for some trace of pity. In the moonlight her skin was the colour of a waxen waterlily, only her eyes glowing darkly as they searched in vain for some sign of remorse. There was none—only the hardening demand of his arms, and the cold implacable purpose in his eyes, as he bent his head, obliterating the moonlight and filling her world with darkness, his face reflecting all the cruelty of the falcon's descent to its prey.

It was impossible to resist. Impossible and unthinkable. This was her one moment stolen from time, and she admitted that in the hidden recesses of her heart she had dreamed of something like this. She longed for his touch even when it was fuelled by rage, and out here in the darkness she could pretend for a while that the arms that held her were those of a lover, that Raschid strained her body against his in desire and not anger, that the hands possessing her body trembled against her skin in passion and not fury.

She closed her eyes so that she would not see the contempt in his eyes, and gave herself up to his kiss, letting his mouth mould and teach hers. She had been kissed before—but she had never known this complete subjugation of self—this complete need to be one with another person to the extent that she was pressing herself against Raschid as though she wanted to imprint the feel of his body against her very bones.

Somehow her sweater had been removed and the buttons of her blouse unfastened, leaving her pearly skin exposed to Raschid's impatient mouth. Her own hands mutely implored closer contact with his body, her murmured protest silenced under the pressure of his mouth as it taught her the meaning of desire.

His lips trailed lazily across her cheek, nibbling the lobe of her ear, descending to caress her neck and the fragile hollows of her shoulder blade, and then lower still to the shadowy cleft between her breasts.

Her heart was beating like a trapped bird. Stupid to feel so shy and so aroused. A lassitude enveloped her; she longed for his complete possession, and arched instinctively against him. He growled deep in his throat, his hands inside the waistband of her jeans, holding her so close to him that she could feel his impatient desire, her breasts swelling tautly in answering need. Through the thin barrier of their clothes she could feel the hard maleness of him, and fire licked along her veins as she sought to convey her growing desire. A small creature moved in the undergrowth, disturbing the heavy silence of the night. Realisation shuddered through her, breaking the spell that had enchanted her. Her flesh shrank under Raschid's touch, and she felt him probing the darkness, listening...waiting....

The moment was gone. They were no star-crossed lovers, impatient for the culmination of their urgent love-making, but two enemies using their bodies to wage a war of attrition—or at least that was what Raschid thought. What had he intended to do? Make love to her and then throw Faisal's desertion in her face? Perhaps he didn't realise that she already knew, and was deliberately leading her on, waiting until she was at her most vulnerable, to throw the truth at her.

He was not like the falcon after all, she thought; they at least killed quickly and cleanly.

'Obviously I was not a totally acceptable substitute after all,' he drawled at her side. 'A pity. You should have used your imagination a little more, or have you forgotten that I am far richer than Faisal, and far better equipped to pay for my pleasure?'

And then he was gone, melting into the darkness, leaving her to stumble back to her tent alone.

'SO, DID you enjoy your journey into the desert?' Umm Faisal asked Felicia.

They had arrived back just after lunch and Nadia and

Achmed had gone to their own quarters with Zayad. Zahra was with the dressmaker being measured for her wedding clothes and Felicia was alone with Umm Faisal.

'Very much,' she replied listlessly. Since their return from the desert, a curious inertia seemed to have enveloped her, coupled with a nervous dread that kept her continually on edge.

'Raschid has received a letter from Faisal,' she continued. 'Soon he will be returning home, I am sure.'

Felicia shuddered. So Raschid *had* read the letter. Dear God, how was she going to face him? She could not! Excusing herself to Umm Faisal, she went to her room. If only they were still in Kuwait and escape were just a relatively simple matter of presenting herself at the British Embassy. But they were not in Kuwait. They were in the desert. The desert.... She looked out across its golden emptiness; perhaps a breath of fresh air might help clear her thoughts.

She went downstairs. Outside Umm Faisal's sitting room she paused, hearing voices. Raschid's voice.

'Rest assured, she will not marry Faisal,' she heard him saying, and her face whitened with pain and despair.

Without knowing how she got there she found herself in the courtyard. The huge wooden gates stood open; the desert beckoned, offering solitude and escape from her agony. Like a sleepwalker Felicia walked through the gates to where the waters of the oasis glittered.

So many small wounds, so carelessly inflicted, all combined to make her heart and body one dreary mass of pain from which there was only one cure—Raschid's love.

CHAPTER TEN

ONE tear followed another down her pale cheeks. She walked on, head down, not comprehending where her unwary feet were taking her, wrapped in her thoughts.

The sun was hot on the back of her neck. Her legs ached and she seemed to have been walking for a long time, but strangely she had no desire to stop. Some instinct beyond her control urged her on. Her blouse was soaked with perspiration and her hair clung damply to her skin. She raised a listless hand to ward off a persistent fly droning angrily next to her ear. Her head felt muzzy, and she was very, very thirsty. She thought longingly of a glass of fresh lime-juice—then she halted suddenly in her tracks and stared back in the direction in which she had come.

She was lost! Completely and absolutely lost. She had broken the first law of the desert. She had wandered away from the sheltering protection of the oasis and no one knew where she had gone.

What was worse, Zahra and Umm Faisal were to visit Saud's mother during the afternoon, and probably no one would realise that she was missing until she didn't appear for dinner! The harsh reality of her plight dispersed the woolly misery clouding her brain. No matter how hard she searched the horizon there was no sign of the oasis—no sign of anything apart from the vast solitude of the desert itself.

She had to sit down because her legs suddenly refused to support her any more, and anyway, wasn't there something about staying put in one place because when you were lost you just wandered round and round in circles, exhausting the body's pitifully frail defences and making rescue harder? Felicia licked her lips and tasted the salt rimming her top lip. Closing her eyes in despair, she remembered the salt tablets she should have been taking. Sickness and giddiness swept her in alternate waves; her eyes ached from the fierce glare of the sun, everywhere she looked an unending vista of sand upon sand.

At length when it finally sank in that she was well and truly lost, she crept into the lee of one of the sandhills hoping the meagre shade it afforded would provide some protection from the sun's dehydrating heat.

Nothing moved. The only creature foolish enough to brave the elements was herself—a pale, singularly ill-equipped female.

Time passed. She slept and awoke, stiff and more thirsty than ever. The world was a molten brass bowl with nowhere for her to escape the burning rays of the sun.

She closed her eyes again and tried not to think of the tinkling fountains in the courtyards. Her tongue snaked over cracked lips. Her throat felt as though she had swallowed the entire Sahara. Had her absence been noticed yet? Without her watch she had no means of gauging time.

Slowly at first, and then with growing fear, she acknowledged that by the time anyone did realise she was missing it could be too late.

She would have cried, but she had no tears left. Sick and exhausted, she tried to crawl a little farther across the sand, but fresh waves of nausea racked her, the landscape swayed unsteadily beneath her feet as her eyes stubbornly refused to focus properly.

She gave a dry sob. She was going to die, alone in this harsh environment, her bones picked clean by scavengers and vultures.

Hysteria bubbled up inside her. Stop it! she commanded herself. Nothing would be achieved by giving way to her emotions. She had no one but herself to blame, and anyway, what pleasure did life hold for her now?

The lengthening afternoon sun threw long shadows across the desert. High above the inert figure on the sand, a bird wheeled and hung motionless, a tiny speck in the distance. Its acute hearing, more finely tuned than any human ear, picked up a sound carrying on the clear air and it circled the girl once or twice before winging westward.

Voices impinged upon her consciousness with the imperfect clarity of waves heard from a sea-shell.

Felicia struggled to make sense of what she could hear, but it was too much effort and she succumbed to the desire to close her eyes and keep them closed.

Someone was rolling her over on to her back, touching her skin with hard, sure fingers, and she pushed ineffectively at them, wanting to be left alone in her comfortable, pain-free cocoon of nothingness.

She wasn't allowed to, though. Those merciless fingers

touched and prodded until she was forced to acknowledge their presence.

'She's suffering from salt deficiency,' she heard someone say, 'and over-exposure. Fortunately she had the sense to keep her face covered. We'd better get her in the Land Rover....'

The Land Rover! She stiffened. The Land Rover was associated with pain, and she had had enough of that, but it was useless, she was being lifted and carried by someone—the same someone who had discussed her so dispassionately—a someone whose identity hovered lazily on the periphery of her awareness. She could feel the rise and fall of the chest against which she was held. It was very comforting to be held thus, and she had a childish desire to remain there, surrendering to the cotton-woolly sensation that made nonsense of her efforts to comprehend what was happening.

'I'll drive, Raschid.'

Raschid! Her contentment splintered into a thousand tiny fragments, and her eyelids flickered open as a small moaned protest escaped her cracked lips.

'It's all right, Felicia, you are quite safe now,' Achmed comforted her.

Safe! Weak relief spread through her. Gone was the intense heat, punishing her sensitive skin, but still her body trembled with convulsions of reaction she was powerless to control. Of all her senses only those of touch and smell remained unaffected, and through her trembling palms she felt muscles contracting in what she guessed to be tightly reined anger, the scent of male sweat pungently close to her nostrils as the arms holding her tightened fractionally.

Raschid offered her security and she took it gratefully

like a tired child too exhausted to reason, her head dropping like a dust-streaked flower too heavy for the slender stem supporting it.

She remembered now! She had wandered out of the oasis because Raschid had hurt her, but her muddled thoughts could not tell her why. She only knew in his arms were peace and safety, a haven for which she had longed all those weary hours in the blistering sun. She closed her eyes and let her senses dictate her actions. Her fingers curled instinctively into the soft cloth of the *dishdasha* beneath her cheek, her breath expelled on a soft sigh as she sought and found the opening which gave her access to the sun-warmed male chest. Unaffectedly she turned her face into it, breathing in the scent of male skin, unaware that above her Raschid's face tightened, a small muscle beating suddenly in his jaw, as he looked down at her passive body.

'Little fool! She could have died out there....'

'She gives you her trust, Raschid,' Achmed murmured, looking from his wife's uncle to the girl lying against him. 'It is a precious gift.'

'She is still unconscious. I doubt if she is aware of anything at all,' was the uncompromising response. His fingers clenched and emotion broke through the barrier of his reserve. 'What possessed her to wander out into the desert? If Nadia had not alerted us....'

'She will tell us when she recovers,' Achmed told him gently. 'Now is not the time for recriminations and lectures. Let us praise Allah that she is safe. Thank God Zahra and Umm Faisal are still at Saud's. They at least have been spared the anxiety. Look,' he added, his eyes on Felicia's face, 'she stirs. She is recovering consciousness.'

Awareness came and went in encroaching and receding waves. Water splashed down on to her face and she drank greedily from the flask that was proffered, but she had barely done more than wet her lips with the life-giving nectar when it was withdrawn.

'Gently!' a stern voice warned. 'Too much will make you sick.'

The effort drained her. She closed her eyes and the world swung away. When she opened them again they were approaching the oasis. She heard Achmed say something to Raschid, and then the Land Rover stopped.

Achmed opened the door. They were in the courtyard of the villa. Nadia came hurrying towards them, her face breaking into a relieved smile when she saw all three of them in the Land Rover.

'She is safe?'

'Quite safe,' Achmed reassured her. 'I'll take her up to her room, Raschid.'

'I'll do it,' was his terse reply.

Felicia felt the bed give under their combined weight.

'Shall I send for Doctor Hamid?' Nadia asked worriedly.

Raschid was bending over her, and something of her panic must have shown in her eyes, because he said over his shoulder, 'No need. It's merely salt deficiency, as I told Achmed, that and too much sun. I'll deal with it. You get back to Zayad—I heard him crying as we came in.'

'He caught our anxiety,' Nadia admitted, glancing at her husband. 'You must go for Mother and Zahra. They will wonder what has happened. Thank goodness we don't have to greet them with the news that Felicia is missing. It was a wonder that you found her, Raschid.'

'Without the falcons I doubt that I would. She had wandered miles from the oasis.'

There was silence, and then cool, detached hands were easing her aching body out of the sand-stained garments on to deliciously cool fresh sheets. From the bathroom she heard the sound of running water—a sound she had longed for during her ordeal. She opened her eyes and discovered that Raschid was standing by her bed. Awareness came back on a floodtide. She had gone out into the desert because she had overheard Raschid discussing her with his sister. Raschid had read Faisal's letter! She struggled to sit up and was pushed back against the pillows, Raschid's hands cool against her heated skin.

'You are badly burned,' he told her unemotionally. 'Your skin must be attended to. I would call Nadia to you, but she is too upset.'

'I can manage,' Felicia assured him, knowing that she could not.

For a moment his eyes seemed to darken and then he was walking to the door. Long minutes dragged by while she tried to summon the energy to walk to her suitcase. Surely she had brought with her some anti-sunburn cream! She had small hope of it completely easing the heated burning of her skin, but it might ease the pain a little.

She was halfway across the room when an incredulous oath stopped her in her tracks, as Raschid plucked her up and returned her unceremoniously to her bed.

'What the hell were you doing?'

Tears stung her eyes. She dashed them away, suddenly noticing the tube of cream he held in his hand.

'I was going to the bathroom,' she told him. 'I wanted to have a shower, to comb my hair….'

'You nearly perish in the desert and all you can think of is brushing your hair?' He strode to the dressing table and returned with her brush. 'If I wasn't sure it's too late by a considerable number of years to have any effect, I would be tempted to wield this implement on a part of your anatomy where it might produce better results!'

Her face burned.

'You wouldn't dare!'

'Don't tempt me,' Raschid advised her. 'You've pushed me to my very most limits, Miss Gordon. Believe me, it wouldn't take very much at all to push me over them! Now sit up.'

She did as he told her, conscious of the scantiness of her brief bra and pants, as he methodically stroked the brush through her hair.

The effect was nerve-tinglingly sensual, but he seemed impervious to it, brushing her hair until it fell round her shoulders in a soft bell.

'That is your hair disposed of,' he said grimly, 'but as far as your shower goes, I'm afraid you'll have to forgo that in favour of something a little less exhausting. Stay there.'

He disappeared into her bathroom, and came back with a sponge and towel.

'I want to put some of this cream on your burns, but I think we had better remove some of the dirt first,' he told her.

'I can do it myself.' So this was what he had meant by 'less exhausting.' Felicia shuddered at the thought of having to endure the clinical touch of his hands on her body, when she longed for them to caress her in fierce possession.

He didn't bother to reply, merely pushing her back on to the pillows and disposing of her protests by the simple expedient of ignoring them.

His touch was sure, and strangely relaxing, as he bathed the dust from her tired limbs. There must be something wrong with her, she thought achingly. She was actually enjoying this, even though she knew Raschid felt not a single jot of answering desire. Only when his fingers brushed the exposed curve of her breast did she move, trying to stop the colour rising betrayingly in her cheeks.

Raschid seemed unaware of her tension.

'Soon be finished,' he told her coolly   so coolly that she replied crossly, 'Yes, doctor!'

His eyebrows rose, as he reached for the tube of cream he had placed on the floor.

'I can manage the cream myself,' she began hurriedly, but the glint in his eyes warned her that she was treading dangerous ground.

'I think not,' he murmured silkily. 'Now turn over, please.'

She knew better than to defy him, so she presented him with a mutely protesting back, hunching her shoulders and burying her face in the softness of her pillow. Nothing happened and she relaxed her tensed muscles, raising her head to look at Raschid. He was regarding her with glinting anger, coupled with another emotion she could not name.

His fingers were cool against her overheated skin, massaging the cooling lotion into her shoulders with a circular movement at once intensely relaxing and yet somehow subtly seductive.

At first she told herself she was imagining the steely determination she had read in his eyes, but as the pressure of his fingers deepened, their subtle message increasing with each punishing stroke, her breathing became more and more erratic as she fought to control the desire pulsating through her. Her brain screamed at her to tell him to stop, but she lacked the willpower. His hands lifted the heavy weight of her hair off her shoulders, his fingers kneaded the bunched muscles at the base of her neck, until the tension eased.

'Turn over, Felicia.'

Her heart seemed to be beating in her throat. She couldn't breathe. She felt his hands slide down to unclip her bra, the weight of his body as he kneeled over her. She closed her eyes, trying to breathe evenly and slowly while she fought for self-control.

Hard fingers slid under her, turning her resisting body. She refused to look at him, glad of the protective darkness of her room. She would not let him see the desire she knew must be in her eyes.

His touch remote, he smoothed more lotion along her burning forearms and neck.

Perhaps she was going mad, she thought hazily. Perhaps she had only imagined the sensuality of those earlier caresses?

Tears welled in her eyes. She lifted her hand surreptitiously to brush them away, but it was pushed away, as Raschid's hands cupped her face, forcing her to meet his eyes.

'Tears?' he whispered mockingly. 'For whom do you shed them, Felicia Gordon?'

'Myself.' One sparkling tear accompanied her forlorn admission, trembling like a diamond against the darkness of Raschid's skin, and then unbelievably she heard him curse, his arms tightened urgently around her, the warmth of his skin a welcome panacea for her bruises, his mouth brushed her face in light, butterfly kisses, teasing and tantalising, his hands returned to cup her face, so that her lips were forbidden the contact they craved.

'Well, Felicia Gordon, am I a substitute for Faisal now?'

Faisal! The letter! But it was too late. Her tears flowed faster, her hands going up of their own accord to lock behind the dark head those tormenting few inches away, pulling him down towards her.

'Please, Raschid!'

Where was her pride? Her determination to keep her love a closely guarded secret? They were gone, swept away in the wild tide of longing that surged through her, destroying the barriers of years. In the darkness her eyes begged silently. His hands moulded the fragile bones of her face, tracing the curve of her mouth which parted involuntarily to press a kiss against their hard warmth.

'Please what?' he mocked, his lips a mere breath away from hers.

All her need of him was in her eyes, giving her the message her lips could not frame.

Triumph edged the glittering look that swept her from head to foot, but Felicia closed her mind to it, tormented by a yearning desire to know his full possession just this once.

Moonlight silvered her body as she arched closer to him. Her body felt weak with longing, her hands trembling as she reached feverishly towards him.

'Very well,' he murmured at last. 'But be sure you know who it is who possesses your body, Felicia Gordon,' he told her as his mouth feathered across hers. 'Do you know?'

Her mouth dry, Felicia answered his whispered demand with a small nod of her head.

All the promises she had made herself, all the warnings were forgotten. With an inarticulate murmur, she pressed herself against him, and was lost in the punishing ferocity of his kiss, as his lips ceased teasing, and instead swept her into a maelstrom of passion, that left her shaking and vulnerable to the fierce hawk eyes, as they surveyed her bruised mouth and pale face.

Every instinct for self-preservation was sublimated to the desire that swept through her, curling insidiously through her body until a strange lethargy possessed her, and her flesh and bones seemed to melt into the burning heat of Raschid's skin, until there was no part of her he did not know.

His mouth traced paths of fire along her body, drawing from her a response that would once have shocked her to the core. His hands seemed to know instinctively how to teach her pleasure, and his lips followed their erotic journey, until she was pressing feverish kisses against his shoulders and throat, her hands trembling uncertainly against him as she tried to imitate his own skill.

The speed with which he had turned from cool mockery to heated desire reduced her to a mass of quivering nerve-ends, each one receptive to his every breath. Her need to know his complete possession was like nothing she had ever experienced before; wave after wave of a longing so strong that she could barely contain it, surging through her body.

At one point he paused, and she felt a cool shaft of air, followed by the realisation that now nothing separated them apart from her tiny lace briefs. She caught her breath as she acknowledged the full potency of his desire. His knee parted her thighs, his hands sliding over the softness of her stomach and upwards to cup her breasts, before sliding beneath her and lifting her against the hardness of his own body, crushing her against him, as his mouth possessed hers with heated urgency.

Her fingers touched the smooth muscled back. His mouth left hers, descending to the taut fullness of her breast. He muttered something in Arabic, and all at once the wave of sexual excitement she had been cresting crashed downwards, leaving her floundering in painful reality. What was she *doing*? She might love Raschid, but he did not love her. Why was he doing this? Not because he wanted her.

Her anguished protest was ignored, her thrashing attempts to evade his embrace stilled, as hard hands gripped her body.

'Oh no, you don't!' he grated in her ear. 'I don't play games, Felicia Gordon. Did you really think you could lead me on and then not pay the price?' He laughed deep in his throat, a feral sound that turned her blood to ice. 'You may play those games with Faisal, but not with me. And don't tell me you don't want me,' he said softly. 'Your own body betrays you, and anyway it has gone too far now. Nadia is with Zayad; the others will not return for some time. We have all night to spend together, and whether you are willing or not I intend to stay here with you. When the sun rises tomorrow, Felicia, Faisal will never accept you as his wife.'

He turned her to him before she could speak, leaving her in no doubt as to his intentions. What sort of man was he, she wondered incredulously, that he could cold-bloodedly make love to her, just to prevent Faisal from marrying her, especially when all the time he must know that Faisal no longer wanted her?

Her mind might realise the cruelty of what he was intending, but her body still ached for him. Her skin stung in a thousand places from the sun and sand, and she cringed instinctively from the look she saw in his eyes, as he let her feel the full force of his impatient desire.

She could not plead for mercy. Nothing she could say would stop him from pursuing his reckless course. She turned her head, closing her eyes so that he would not see the betraying shimmer of tears filming their jade depths, tensing every muscle against what she knew now would be a bitter defilement of all her dreams. Raschid must know that Faisal did not want her, so why this?

He meant to humiliate her; she sensed it, and bit down hard on her trembling lip as she felt the determined pressure of his thighs, hurting, unyielding.

'Don't play the innocent with me!' he gritted above her, his fingers grasping her hair and forcing her head round. 'Or has my nephew got a fetish about virginity that you pander to?'

Her eyes gave her away, her face bone-white as she flinched back.

Tears streaming down her face, she screamed at him, 'Stop it! Stop it! You know Faisal no longer wants me—I saw the letter. He told me he was writing to you.'

'Faisal no longer wants you?' He had gone very still.

'You know he doesn't,' she accused bitterly. 'I heard you telling your sister that he would never marry me. Because you'd written telling him about my "wanton" behaviour.

Is that what this was all about? Another example of my un-suitability to be his wife? Why bother to put yourself out? You've already done enough. I would have been gone from here long ago if Faisal hadn't urged me to spend all my savings.' She faced him proudly with bitter eyes. 'Have I suffered enough to pay for my ticket home, or must you humiliate me further?'

Raschid got off the bed, his back to her as he pulled on his clothes.

'I don't rape virgins,' he told her harshly, turning round suddenly, his face suffused with angry colour. 'What were you thinking of? Has no one ever warned you about pushing a man too far? Think yourself lucky I stopped when I did.'

He turned on his heel, leaving her alone with the shattered fragments of her dreams.

Not until she was quite sure that he would not return did she allow herself to break down, crying until she could cry no more. He had come to her room with one purpose and one only—to deliberately humiliate and denigrate her. Even knowing that Faisal did not want her he had still felt the need to torment and torture her. How he must hate her!

DAWN BROUGHT her no surcease from pain. Her heart felt like a lump of lead. How *could* she have thought—even for a moment—that Raschid actually wanted her? How could she have been so stupid? She had allowed her own love to blind her to the truth. Bitterly disillusioned, she contemplated the cynicism with which he had made use of her emotions, playing on them until she was too bemused to know what she was doing. That last painful scene her mind shied away from. Perhaps in time she might be able to re-live it, but not now.

The bedroom door opened and Nadia walked in.

'How are you feeling? I looked in earlier, but you were still sleeping, and Raschid said you were not to be disturbed.'

'How thoughtful of him,' Felicia said tightly. 'But I'm fine. I think I'll get up.'

'Felicia….' Nadia said gently, 'what is wrong? You have been crying. Tell me what is the matter, or I shall go and bring Raschid. Are you not happy with us?'

She could not have hit upon a more effective threat. At the mention of Raschid's name Felicia went white and then red.

'Nadia, I must get away from here,' she burst out desperately. 'If you really do care anything for me, will you help me?'

'To do what?' Nadia asked shrewdly, coming to sit by the bed. 'Return home, or escape from Raschid?'

'Both,' Felicia admitted bravely. 'Raschid despises me, Nadia. Please help me,' she sobbed. 'I can't endure to stay here any longer….'

Weak tears flowed helplessly down her cheeks, as though from some bottomless well, and Nadia's own eyes moistened in sympathy.

'I will do everything I can. I shall go and find Achmed, and ask him to make the arrangements. I am sorry that my family has brought you so much pain, for I see from your eyes that it has.'

'And you will say nothing to Raschid, promise me?'

What fresh, subtle forms of torture might he not dream up, if he knew how she longed to get away? His behaviour last night had not been that of a man with human failings and feelings, but a cold emotionless machine bent on exacting the last measure of payment for the crimes of which he had convicted her. The relentless manner in which he had destroyed Faisal's love for her, the way he had tortured her—they both pointed to a man without pity or compassion, and she had to get away—now—before her pride deserted her completely and she begged him to allow her to stay.

She would have to find Umm Faisal and Zahra and bid them goodbye, Felicia thought wretchedly when Nadia had gone. And then there was small Zayad and helpful Selina, so many people who had touched her heart during her short stay in Kuwait, so much pain when she had to leave them.

She eyed her reflection with distaste. Her hair was all tumbled, her skin flushed from its exposure to the sun. Her body felt gritty with the small particles of sand which had clung to the lotion Raschid had applied. She needed a bath, she decided tiredly, collecting her towel and wrap. Perhaps when she felt clean and fresh she would feel more inclined to tackle her packing.

Although her bedroom possessed a shower, there was only one communal bathroom in the women's quarters, and her footsteps echoed across the tiled floor as she opened the door. The room really was huge, she thought, and the bath positively enormous. She turned on the taps, pouring essence of roses into the water and watching the oil turn the clear water into milky foam.

It felt good to immerse herself in its warm silkiness, and she soaped herself vigorously, as though by doing so she could wash away the memory of Raschid's hands on her body.

The warmth of the water induced her taut muscles to relax, tempting her to linger, soaking in its perfumed embrace.

She never heard the door open, only the decisive footsteps crossing the marble tiles. She glanced up curiously and froze.

Raschid! Wordlessly she clutched the sponge protectively against her breasts, trying to sink beneath the milky cover of the water.

'Why do you want to leave us?'

So Nadia had betrayed her!

'What possible reason is there for me to stay, in a house where I've been abused, reviled, made mock of, tormented....'

'Tormented?' His sharp eyes fastened on her trembling hands.

'Please go, Raschid,' Felicia begged. 'If Zahra or your sister were to....'

'Interrupt us? They won't. They decided to spend the night with Saud's family, and Nadia has been warned not to intrude upon us. To make sure that she does not, I have taken a small precaution.' He reached in his pocket and produced an intricately carved key. 'So you see, my dear Felicia, you are completely at my mercy. Divine justice, one might say. I want to talk to you,' he said suddenly, 'and I cannot do so while you wriggle about in there like a shy fish searching for a lily pad. Besides,' he added sardonically, his eyes resting on the soft curve of her breasts, luminously pale against the water, 'I am quite sure the water must be getting cold.'

It was, but her wrap was on a chair out of reach, and she had no intention of leaving the comparative protection of the bath while Raschid remained in the room.

'If you'll leave me to get dressed, I will come down to your study,' she suggested, avoiding his amused, comprehensive glance.

'Leave you?' Was it her imagination or had his voice suddenly become slightly husky? His glance impaled her, a curious melting sensation running through her bones. In that moment he swooped, lifting her out of the bath and holding her against him, uncaring of the water soaking through his silk shirt, or the shivers that coursed through her as she tried to hold aloof.

'Last night when you denied me I thought you either the shrewdest little bitch I had ever met, or appallingly innocent,' he said suddenly, making her tremble with the swiftness of his attack. 'Why do you want to leave us, Felicia?'

'You know why,' she answered tremulously. His touch was completely impersonal, but she was not going to let him trick her a second time, betrayed by her inexperience into mistaking retribution for desire.

'Do I?'

She trembled convulsively, tears spilling down her cheeks to lie damply against his throat.

His muffled imprecation reached her as his arms imprisoned her. 'By Allah, Felicia. I want you!' he groaned against her lips, stifling her protests. 'I have wanted you from the moment I saw you. Last night when I discovered that Faisal had not touched you I didn't know who I hated the most, you or myself.'

He broke off, as his body shuddered uncontrollably against her, cradling her against him, while he murmured something under his breath. She couldn't move. She was frozen with terror— What was he trying to do? Make her betray herself again? She looked at him, her eyes wild with pain, her expression that of a trapped, tormented animal.

'What do you want?' she whispered in anguish. 'Haven't I paid enough? Just let me go.'

His skin flushed darkly as he looked at her, and she tensed, waiting, dreading what he would say.

'Very well, I will let you go,' he said quietly, 'but only if you listen to me first.'

When she nodded her head slightly he swung her up in his arms, carrying her over to one of the low divans and sitting down with her still in his arms.

'You shame me, Felicia,' he said at last. 'You shame me as no other human being has ever done. When I left you last night I felt sick to my soul, not only for misjudging you, although that was bad enough, but for teaching you to think that I would actually go to such lengths to part you from Faisal.'

'But you said....'

He placed his fingers to her lips. 'No—no more misunderstandings. Let me tell you the truth. Initially it is true that I did want to destroy the love Faisal bore you, for Faisal's own sake,' he admitted wryly. 'He is fickle and too young to settle down, especially with a girl not used to our ways, sophisticated, and perhaps more in love with his wealth than with him. This would not have been the first time I have had to extricate him from such a situation, and shall we say that his track record to date has made me somewhat cynical.

'But it didn't work out like that. For one thing you were so beautiful, so proud and spirited, and I found myself less and less concerned with Faisal and increasingly determined to make you turn from him to me, at the same time despising myself for being attracted to a woman of the type I thought you to be.

'I told myself I was a fool, letting your beauty steal away my common sense. But it was my heart you took, driving me mad by coming to life in my arms like the desert after rain, and yet still insisting that you preferred Faisal.

'I wanted to crush your resistance, to force you to admit that you loved me, but always you eluded me, until at last I thought that you had guessed my feelings for you and were playing on them to make me accede to your betrothal to Faisal. Then I knew bitterness indeed. I admit now that I let my prejudice blind me, seeing only what I wanted to see—what experience had taught me to see. When you walked openly in the street I admit you played straight into my hands, but *I* didn't write to Faisal. I could not bring myself to denounce you to him, much as I longed to part you. When you accused me of knowing that your romance with him was at an end I had no idea what you meant. You see, I hadn't read his letter. While we were in the desert I meant to read it, but there never seemed to be time.' He shrugged. 'To tell the truth, I did not want to read it. I thought he would be begging me to allow him to return to further your romance, and I planned to keep you apart, hoping that you would turn from him to me.

'When I discovered that you were missing…. Never as long as I live do I want to go through that torment again. My relief at finding you, coupled with your own stubborn refusal to admit your response to me, drove me over the edge of sanity. This morning I telephoned Faisal and told him that I had received his letter—which I *have* now read.

It seems that Yasmin wrote to him after seeing us together in Kuwait, and her letter provided him with the loophole he had wanted. Unlike me, he had the wit to see your essential innocence, and he had decided that you would never enter the kind of impermanent relationship he most enjoys. When Nadia came to me and told me that you were leaving I knew I had to stop you. My pride was as the sand beneath my feet.... Marry me, Felicia,' he begged. 'I want you now and tomorrow and for all our tomorrows. I want to be the man who will unfasten the one hundred and one buttons of your bridal gown; the one who penetrates the final veil, the one whose child you bear, the one whose grave you share. I want you for my wife, Felicia—my only wife,' he promised. 'Many, many times my sister has pleaded for me to marry, but I could not. Perhaps it is a weakness in me, but I knew always that the woman I married must be the only woman, and when I saw you I knew you were she. Only let me, and I shall wipe away the bitterness of last night and teach you the true meaning of love.'

'But you told me that a marriage between East and West would never work,' Felicia reminded him, not daring to believe her ears.

'Between you and Faisal,' Raschid corrected. 'Because no sooner had I set eyes upon you than I knew that I could never allow you to waste yourself on Faisal, not when I could love you so much better. But you rejected me, and drove me insane with jealousy, tormented by images of you in Faisal's arms, when I longed to have you in mine.'

The ice that had invaded her heart melted, and Felicia looked up at him, giving herself trustingly into his care.

'Tell me you love me, Felicia,' he pleaded hoarsely.

'Tell me I am not deluding myself, misreading what I see in your eyes.'

She knew that this time she was not being deceived and her arms reached out to enclose him, her only protest a small murmur when his breath lost its cool, even tenor, and instead became the charged, uneven rasp of a lover.

Last night had all been a bad dream. Only this was real. There was reverence as well as desire in the sure touch of his hands and lips, as he whispered how desperate he had been when Achmed told him she was leaving.

A small smile touched Felicia's face. Achmed had told him. So Nadia had not really broken her promise after all. Clever Nadia!

He would never let her go, Raschid whispered fiercely. She would be his prisoner throughout their lives and beyond. They were two halves of an indivisible whole, and Felicia, lost in the wonder of his love, could only agree, her hands running lovingly over the satin smoothness of his back beneath the thin shirt.

'No, not now....' he muttered thickly, trapping her importuning hands. 'I cannot dishonour you.'

'But I want you,' Felicia pleaded.

Strong hands cupped her face, dark eyes understanding and stormy. 'Do you not think I want you?' Raschid whispered unevenly, groaning suddenly as he pulled her against him, letting her feel his need. Her fingers spread against his chest, as she pressed shy kisses against his skin. 'If I take you now, I shall be like a man consumed by thirst, who is given but one sip of water.' He smiled ruefully. 'I have denied myself this long, I can deny myself a little longer, but to taste water now and then have it withdrawn before

I have quenched my thirst will drive me to madness. Do you understand?'

If she had doubted the depth of his love, she did so no longer. Shyly she nodded, overwhelmed by the recognition of a need she had never suspected existed; a need only she had the power to arouse—and to assuage.

'It will not be long,' Raschid promised as he removed his shirt and gently fastened it over her. His eyes burned dark with desire as the damp fabric clung seductively to her swelling curves. 'Indeed it must not be long,' he added with a touch of self-mockery. 'My sister already knows of my hopes. Our betrothal shall be announced tonight. I will not give you an emerald,' he told her, betraying his knowledge of the stone Faisal had bought her. 'Do you remember the glass paperweight you gave me?' he asked suddenly. 'Well, I have it still, even though I knew you intended it for another. After you had gone I found it where you had thrown it. I keep it in my room so that I can always be reminded of you—little though I need to be. I have slept little since you invaded my life, Felicia Gordon, but soon I shall know the delights of your love.'

THREE WEEKS LATER, when the last of the wedding guests had drifted away, Felicia remembered his words, and trembled a little as wordlessly he lifted her into his arms and carried her through the now empty house.

She had begged to spend her honeymoon at the house by the oasis, and now they were alone, the faint light of the oil lamps throwing flickering shadows across the mosaic floor. Outside the Eastern night had veiled the skies in a shimmer of midnight gauze, studded with sparkling diamonds, like the tiny buttons fastening her robe.

Without a word Raschid knelt at her feet, and she held her breath as one by one he unfastened the tiny fastenings, pausing only when he reached the last one, to lift the heavy weight of her hair off her shoulders and remove the gold necklaces that had been placed there only hours earlier as a symbol of their eternal love. They had had a civil ceremony too, at the British Embassy, but these were their real marriage vows that they were to exchange now, Felicia thought dreamily.

At last she was free, stepping out of the rich fabric of her robe and walking into the hard warmth of the arms that opened to enclose her.

'Love me….' Raschid whispered passionately against her skin as he lifted her against him. 'Love me as I intend to love you, little dove. Trust me to make the night one of pleasure as well as initiation. Where there is pain, there is also pleasure, and there will be pleasure, Felicia. I love you, my little dove. So very, very much….'

She was gathered up against him and kissed tenderly and then passionately until every inch of her vibrated with a desire she made no attempt to hide from him as he carried her towards the divan and its silk cushions.

The Sheikh's Virgin Bride

PENNY JORDAN

CHAPTER ONE

'DID you check out the sexy windsurfer attendant like I told you?'

'Yeah! He was everything you said and more—much, much more. He's coming up to my room later. Mind you, he did say that he'd have to be careful. Apparently he's already on a warning from this Sheikh Rashid—the guy who co-owns the hotel—for fraternising with guests.'

'And you did more than just "fraternise", right?'

'Yeah, much, much more.'

From her seat under the protective sun umbrella of the rooftop bar of the Marina Restaurant where she had just finished lunch, the conversation of the two women standing next to her chair was plainly audible to Petra. Still discussing the sexual attributes of the Zuran resort complex's windsurfing instructor, they started to move away. Realising that one of them had dropped her wrap, Petra picked it up, interrupting their discussion to return it and earning herself a brief thank you from its owner.

As they walked away, still engrossed in their conversation, Petra grinned appreciatively to herself, murmuring wholeheartedly beneath her breath, 'Thank *you*!'

Although they didn't realise it, thanks to them she had just been given access to the very thing she had been looking for for the last two days!

As soon as they were out of sight she got up, collecting her own wrap, although unlike them she had chosen to eat her lunch wearing a silky pair of wide-legged casual trousers over her tankini top, instead of merely her swimwear.

5

Shading her eyes from the glare of the sun, she summoned the waiter who had served her her meal.

'Excuse me,' she asked him, 'can you tell me where the windsurfers are?'

Half an hour later Petra was lying on a sun lounger, carefully positioned by the attentive beach attendant who had asked her where she wanted to sit so that she had a direct and uninterrupted view of the stunning man-made bay which was home to the resort's pleasure craft, and an equally direct and uninterrupted view of the windsurfing instructor she had overheard discussed so enthusiastically over lunch!

She could certainly appreciate just why her fellow guests had waxed so lyrical about him!

Petra was used to seeing good-looking muscular men; she had attended an American university and, since the death of her parents in an accident when she was seventeen, she had travelled extensively both in Europe and Australia with her godfather, the senior British diplomat who had been her parents' closest friend. She'd become, therefore, quite familiar with the sexy beach bum super-stud macho type of man who thought he was heaven's gift to the female sex.

And this man certainly filled all the physical specifications for the type! And then some!

He could easily earn a living modelling designer underwear, Petra acknowledged as her own rush of sensual heat caught her discomfortingly off guard.

But as she watched him Petra was unwillingly forced to admit he had something else; something extra.

He was gathering up some discarded boards, and even the regulation smart hotel shorts had the effect of heightening his sexuality rather than discreetly concealing it.

Across the distance that separated them Petra could somehow sense his maleness, and almost feel the testosterone-
laden aura that surrounded him. The movement of his body
as he worked reminded Petra of the coiled suppleness of a
hunting panther—every movement, every breath a perfect
harmony of honed strength and focus, not one single jot of
energy wasted or superfluous.

She could see the way the sunlight highlighted the muscle structure of his arm as he held the windsurfer, the breeze
tousling the thick darkness of his hair. From beneath their
designer sunglasses she suspected that every woman on the
beach must be watching him, and perhaps holding their
breath as they did so, as she herself was doing. He had a
mesmerising presence about him that was wholly and
shockingly sexual, a rawness that Petra acknowledged was
compelling, challenging, and very, very dangerously exciting! Oh, yes! He was exactly what she needed! The more
she watched him, the more she was sure of it!

Compulsively she watched him from the safety of the
distance that separated them.

Over an hour later, on her way back to her luxurious hotel
suite, Petra was busily making plans. As she crossed the
busy *souq* area of the complex, Petra paused to watch in
admiration as a craftsman skilfully hammered a piece of
metal into shape.

It was no wonder that this particular complex had received such worldwide acclaim. From the seductive appeal
of its Moorish design, with its fragrant enclosed gardens,
to its palatial extravaganza of expensive boutiques and the
traditional flavour of its recreated *souq*, the complex
breathed magic and romance and most of all wealth.

Petra still could not get her head round the fact that in
all there were over twenty different restaurants situated

around the complex, serving food from virtually every part of the world, but right now food was the last thing on her mind.

From her hotel bedroom Petra could just about see the beach. The sexy macho windsurfer had disappeared midway through the afternoon, climbing aboard one of the gleaming and very obviously fast boats moored at the adjoining marina, and Petra's last sight of him had been of the sunshine gleaming on the thick darkness of his hair and the golden bronze of his tanned skin.

He was back now, though, even though the beach itself was deserted as the sun started to dip towards the horizon. Methodically he was collecting the abandoned windsurfers, and the other small pleasure craft the complex made available to its guests.

This was the perfect opportunity for her to do what she had been wanting to do ever since she had overheard the two women discussing him!

Before her courage could desert her she picked up her jacket and headed for her suite door.

Down on the beach it was almost dusk, the cool chill in the air reminding Petra that, despite the fact that the daytime temperature was in the high twenties, in this part of the world it was still winter.

For a second she thought she was too late, that the beach bum had gone, and her heart plummeted sharply with disappointment—her gaze searching the darkening beach.

As she stood looking out across the pretty marina Petra was so lost in her own thoughts that the sudden darkness of a shadow thrown across the fading light shocked her.

Spinning round, she sucked in her stomach on a shocked breath as she realised that the object of her thoughts was standing in front of her, and so close to her that a single step forward would bring them body to body.

Instinctively Petra wanted to step back, but the stubborn pride that her father had once insisted she had inherited directly from her grandfather refused to let her move.

Lifting her head, she took a deep breath, then exhaled it unsteadily as she realised that she had not lifted her head enough, and that right now instead of making contact with his eyes her gaze was resting helplessly on the curve of his mouth.

What was it they said about men with a full bottom lip? That they were very sensual, very tactile...men who knew all the secret nuances of pleasures the touch of those male lips could have on a woman?

Petra felt faintly dizzy. She hadn't realised he was so tall. What nationality was he? Italian? Greek? His hair was very dark and very thick, and his skin—as she had had every opportunity to observe earlier in the day—was a deep, warm golden brown. He was fully dressed now, in a white tee shirt, jeans and trainers, and somehow—despite his casual clothes—he was disconcertingly much more formidable and authoritative-looking than she had expected.

It was almost fully dark; tiny decorative lights were springing up all around them, illuminating the marina and its environs. Petra could see the searing flash of his eyes as his glance encompassed her. First almost dismissively, and then appraisingly, his body stiffening as though suddenly alerted to something about her that had caught his interest, awakened his hunting instinct, changing the uninterest she could have sworn she had initially seen in his eyes to a narrowed intense concentration that pinned her into wary immobility.

If she turned and ran now he would enjoy it—enjoy pursuing her, tormenting her, she decided nervily. He was that kind of man!

Despite the fact that she was wearing a perfectly respectable pair of jeans and a shirt, she suddenly felt as though he could see right through them to the flesh beneath her clothes, that already he knew every curve of her, every hidden secret and vulnerability. She was not used to experiencing such feelings and they threw her a little off guard.

'If you've come looking for one-to-one lessons, I'm afraid you've left it too late.'

The open cynicism in his voice was something she had not been prepared for, and both it and the look he was giving her burned her skin. Petra suspected she could hear a hundred generations of male contempt for a certain type of female wantonness.

'Actually, I don't need lessons,' she told him, immediately rallying her pride. She had learned to windsurf as a young teenager, and although he wasn't to know it she'd reached competition standard.

'No? Then what do you need?' his soft insultingly knowing response shocked through her.

Petra could understand how those women had been so excited by him! He possessed a sexual aura, a sexual magnetism that dizzied her senses. His air of control and self-assurance hinted tauntingly at the fact that he considered he had the power to overwhelm and dominate her if he chose to do so, that he knew precisely the effect he had on her sex! This was a man whose very existence spelled a very distinct kind of predatory male dangerousness in any language. Which was exactly why he was so perfect for what she wanted, she reminded herself as she tussled with an unfamiliar and ignominious urge to turn and run whilst she still had the option to do so.

Irritated by her own weakness, she refused to give in to it. In her time she had faced down a wide array of men for a wide variety of reasons, and there was no way she was going to be out-faced by this one! Even if it was the first time she had ever been made so overwhelmingly aware of a man's sexuality that she could barely breathe the air that surrounded them because it was so charged with raw rogue testosterone.

Ignoring what she was feeling, Petra took a deep breath and told him firmly, 'I have a proposition to put to you.'

In the silence that followed her statement he must have moved slightly, she recognised, because suddenly she could see his full face—and what she could see made the breath seize in her lungs. She had known this afternoon that he had the kind of powerful male allure that could neither be imitated nor acquired, but now she realised that he also had the kind of facial features that would have made a Greek god weep with envy.

The only thing she couldn't see was the colour of his eyes. But surely with such colouring they had to be brown. Brown! Inwardly Petra allowed herself to relax a little. Brown-eyed men had never appealed to her. Secretly she had always hankered for a man with the cool magnetism of pure silver-grey-coloured eyes, having fallen in love with the hero of a book she had read as a young teenager whose eyes had been that colour.

'A proposition?' The cynical uninterest in his voice made her face burn a little. 'I'm a man,' he told her bluntly. 'And I don't go to bed with women who proposition me. I like to hunt my own prey, not be hunted by it. Of course if you're really desperate I could give you directions to a place where you might have more luck.'

As she felt her fingers curling into small, angry fists, Petra had to resist the instinctive temptation to react to his insult in the most basic female way possible. Satisfactory though it might initially be, slapping his face was hardly going to be conducive to concluding her plan successfully, she reminded herself wryly. At least his attitude confirmed her assumption that he was a sexual predator—not the kind of man a potential husband would want consorting with the woman he wanted to make his wife. In short this man was ideal for her purpose.

'It isn't that kind of proposition,' she denied firmly.

'No…? So what kind is it, then?' he challenged her.

'The kind that pays well and isn't illegal,' Petra replied promptly, crossing her fingers and hoping inwardly that her comment would have piqued his interest.

He had moved again, and now Petra realised that it was her turn to have her features revealed to him in the increasing illumination of the decorative lights.

She wasn't a vain person, but she knew that she was generally considered to be attractive. But if this man found her so, he certainly wasn't showing it, she acknowledged as she was subjected to a cool visual inspection that made her itch to step back into the protective shadows, her arms wrapped protectively around her body.

'Sounds fascinating,' he mocked her laconically. 'What do I have to do?'

Petra allowed herself to begin to relax. 'Pursue me and seduce me—very publicly,' she told him.

Just for a second she had the satisfaction of seeing that she had surprised him. His eyes widened fractionally before he controlled the movement.

'Seduce you?' he repeated. And now it was Petra's turn to be surprised, and unpleasantly so, as she marked the sharp curtness in a male voice that had abruptly become disconcertingly chilly.

'Not for real,' she told him quickly, before he could say

anything more. 'What I want is for you to pretend to seduce me.'

'Pretend? Why?' he demanded baldly. 'Do you already have a lover you wish to make jealous? Is that it?' he guessed insultingly.

Petra glared at him.

'No, I do not. I want to pay you to ensure that I lose my...my reputation.'

For one unguarded moment Petra saw his face and wondered exactly what the sudden frown creasing his forehead and the complete stillness of his body meant.

'Am I allowed to ask why you want to lose it?' he asked her.

'You can ask,' Petra told him. 'But I don't intend to tell you.'

'No? Well, in that case, I don't intend to help you.'

He was already turning away from her and Petra started to panic.

'I'm prepared to pay you five thousand pounds,' she called out to him.

'Ten thousand and then we might...just might have a deal,' he told her softly as he stopped and turned to look at her.

Ten thousand pounds. Petra felt sick. Her parents had left her a very generous trust fund, but until she turned twenty-five, there was no way she could raise such a large sum without the approval of her trustees—one of whom was her godfather, who was after all part of the reason why she needed to do this in the first place.

Her body slumped in defeat.

He was still walking away from her, and had almost reached the end of the beach. In another few seconds he would be gone.

Swallowing against the bitter taste of her own failure, she turned away herself.

CHAPTER TWO

REFUSING to give in to the temptation of watching him disappear, Petra fixed her gaze on the sea.

Most people, on first seeing her, assumed that Petra carried either Spanish or Italian blood in her veins. Her skin had a soft creamy warmth and her dark brown hair was thick and lustrous, her bone structure elegant and delicately patrician. Only her brilliant green eyes and the narrow straightness of her small nose, combined with her passionate nature, gave away the fact that she possessed Celtic genes, inherited through her American father's Irish ancestry. Very few people guessed that her colouring came from an exotic blending of those genes with her mother's Bedouin blood.

She could feel the evening breeze lifting her hair, its coolness raising tiny goosebumps on her skin, but they were nothing to the rash of sensation that flooded atavistically through her body as she suddenly felt the pressure of a male hand on the nape of her neck.

'Five thousand, then—and the reason,' a now familiar silken voice whispered in her ear.

He had come back! Petra didn't know whether to be elated or horrified!

'No haggling!' the silken voice warned her. 'Five thousand and the reason, or no deal.'

Petra's throat had gone dry. She didn't want to tell him, but what option did she have? And besides, what harm could it really do?

'Very well.'

What was it that was making her voice sound so tremulous? Surely not the fact that his hand was still on her nape?

'You're trembling,' he told her, so accurately tracking and trapping her own thoughts that his intuitiveness shocked her. 'Why? Are you afraid? Excited?'

As he drawled the soft words with deliberate slowness, almost whispering into her ear, his thumb stroked against the side of her throat, trapping the pulse fluttering there.

Stalwartly Petra wrenched herself free and told him resolutely. 'Neither! I'm just cold.'

She could see the taunting cruelty in the mocking curve of his smile.

'Of course,' he agreed. 'So, you want me to publicly pursue and seduce you?'

He questioned her as though he had suddenly grown bored with tormenting her, like a domestic cat suddenly tiring of the prey it had caught as a plaything rather than for food. But this man was no domesticated fireside pet! No, everything he did had a raw, untamed danger about it, a warning of power mockingly leashed.

'Why? Tell me!'

Petra took a deep breath.

'It's a long and complicated story,' she warned him.

'Tell me!' he repeated.

Briefly Petra closed her eyes, trying to marshal her thoughts into logical order, and then opened them again, beginning quietly, 'My father was an American diplomat. He met my mother here in Zuran when he was posted here. They fell in love but her father did not approve. He had other plans for her. He believes that it is a daughter's duty to allow herself to be used as a pawn in her family's empire-building.' As she spoke Petra could hear the anger and the bitterness in her own voice, just as she could feel it surging inside her—a mixture of a long-standing old pain on behalf of her mother and a much newer, bitter anger for herself.

'My grandfather refused to have anything to do with my mother after she ran away with my father. And he forbade his family—my mother's brothers and their wives—from having anything to do with her either. But she told me all about him. How cruel he had been!' Petra's eyes flashed.

'My parents were wonderfully, blissfully happy, but they were killed in an accident when I was seventeen. I went to live in England with my godfather who, like my father, is a diplomat. That's how they met—when my godfather was with the British Embassy in Zuran. Everything was fine. I finished university and then I travelled with my godfather, I worked for an aid agency in the field, and I was…am planning to take my Master's. But then…

'A short time ago, my uncle came to London and made contact with my godfather. He told him that my grandfather wanted to see me. That he wanted me to come to Zuran. I didn't want to have anything to do with him. I knew how much he had hurt my mother. She never stopped hoping that he would forgive her, that he would answer her letters, accept an olive branch, but he never did. Not even when she and my father were killed. He never even acknowledged her death. No one from my family here came to the funeral. He would not allow them to do so!'

Tears of rage and pain momentarily filled Petra's eyes, but determinedly she blinked them away.

'My godfather begged me to reconsider. He said it was what my parents would have wanted—for the family to be reconciled. He told me that my grandfather was one of the major shareholders in this holiday complex and he had suggested that both I and my godfather come and stay here, get to know one another. I wanted to refuse, but…' She stopped and shook her head. 'I felt for my mother's sake that I had to come. But if I'd known then the real reason why I was being brought out here—!'

'The real reason?' There was a brusqueness in the male voice that rasped roughly against her sensitive emotions.

'Yes, the real reason,' she reiterated bitterly.

'The day we arrived my uncle came here to the hotel with his wife, and his son—my cousin Saud. He's only fifteen, and... They said that my grandfather wasn't well enough to come, that he had a serious heart condition, and that his doctor had said that he needed bed rest and no excitement. I believed them. But then, when we were on our own together, Saud accidentally let the cat out of the bag. He had no idea, you see, that I didn't know what was really going on!'

Petra shook her head as she heard her voice starting to tremble. 'Far from merely wanting to meet me, to put right the wrong he had done to my parents, what my grandfather actually wants is to marry me off to one of his business partners! And, unbelievably, my godfather actually thinks it's a good idea.

'Although at first he tried to pretend that I had got it wrong and misunderstood Saud, in fact my godfather thinks it's so much of a good idea that right now he's incommunicado in the far east—on official diplomatic business, of course—and he's taken my passport with him! "Just meet the chap, Petra, old thing."' She mimicked her godfather's cut-glass upper class British voice savagely. '"No harm in doing that, eh? Who knows? You might find you actually rather like him. Look at British nobility. All from arranged marriages, and with pretty good results generally speaking. All that love tosh. Doesn't always work y'know. Like to like, that's what I always say—and from what your uncle has to say—it seems like this Sheikh Rashid and you have lots in common. Similar cultural heritage. Bound to go down well with the Foreign Office. And the Prime Minister…awfully keen on that sort of thing, y'know. I've heard it on the grapevine that the White House is one hundred per cent behind the idea."'

'Your grandfather wants you to marry a man who is a fellow countryman of his, and a business colleague, as a PR exercise for diplomatic purposes? Is that what you're telling me?' He cut across Petra's angry outburst incisively.

Petra could hear the cynical disbelief in his voice and didn't really blame him for his reaction.

'Well, my godfather would like me to think that's the only motivation for my grandfather's behaviour, but of course he isn't anything like so high-minded or altruistic,' she told him scathingly.

'From what I've managed to find out from Saud, my grandfather wants me to marry this man because as well as being a fellow shareholder in this complex he is also very well connected—is in fact related to the Zuran Royal Family, no less! My mother was originally supposed to marry a second cousin of the Family before she met and fell in love with my father. Her father—my grandfather—considered it to be a very prestigious match, and one that would bring him a lot of benefits. I suppose in his eyes it is only fitting that since he couldn't marry my mother off to suit his own ends I should now take her place as a…a victim to his greed and ambition!'

'Does your mixed heritage disturb you?' His unexpected question threw Petra a little.

'Disturb me?' She tensed, anger and pride ignited inside her. 'No! Why should it?' she challenged him. 'I am proud to be the product of my parents' love for one another, and proud to be myself as well.'

'You misunderstand me. The disturbance I refer to is that

caused by the volatile mixing of the coldness of the north with the heat of the desert; Anglo Saxon blood mixed with Bedouin, the hunger for roots and the compulsion that drives the nomad and everything that those two polar opposites encompass. Do you never feel torn, pulled in two different ways by two different cultures? A part of both of them and at the same time alien to them?'

His words so accurately summed up the feelings that had bedevilled Petra for as long as she had been able to recognise them that they stunned her into silence. How could he possibly know that she felt like that? The tiny hairs on her skin lifted as though she were in the presence of a force she could not fully understand—a strength and insight so much more developed than her own that she felt in awe of it.

'I am what I am,' she told him firmly as she fought to ignore the way he was making her feel.

'And what is that?'

Anger darkened her eyes.

'I am a modern, independent woman who will not be manipulated or used to serve the ends of a machiavellian old man.'

She could see the shrug he gave.

'If you do not want to marry the husband your grandfather has chosen for you then why do you simply not tell him so?'

'It isn't that easy,' Petra was forced to admit. 'Of course I told my godfather that there was totally and absolutely no way I was going to agree to even meet this man. Never mind marry him. That was when he announced that he had to leave for the far east and that he was taking my passport with him. To give me time to get to know my grandfather and to rediscover my cultural heritage, was how he put it, but of course I know what he's really hoping for. He's hoping that by leaving me here, at my grandfather's mercy, he will be able to pressure me into doing what he wants. My godfather retires next year, and no doubt he's hoping that the government will reward him for his work—including arranging a high-profile marriage to Sheikh Rashid— with a Peerage in the New Year's honours list. And what makes it even worse is that, from what my cousin Saud has told me, it seems the whole family believe I should be thrilled to think that this…this…man is prepared to consider marrying me,' Petra concluded bitterly.

'Like normally marries like in such circumstances,' the cool, almost bored voice pointed out. 'I understand what you are saying about your grandfather's motivations, but what about those of your proposed husband? Why should this…?'

'Sheikh Rashid,' Petra supplied for him grimly. 'The same Sheikh Rashid who, from what I hear, does not approve of your…behaviour with his female guests!'

The quick, hard look he gave her caused Petra to say immediately, 'I heard two women discussing you earlier on—' She stopped. 'As to why the Sheikh should want to marry me…' Petra took a deep breath. 'You might well ask. But apparently he and I have something in common— we are both of mixed parentage, only in his case I believe that it was his father who provided his Zuran heritage and not his mother. More importantly, The Zuran Royal Family consider the marriage to be a good idea. My godfather says that it will cause great offence if he refuses a marriage they have given their seal of approval, and great offence to mine if he refuses me. However, whilst I know enough about Zuran culture to know that for either of us to refuse the other once negotiations have commenced is considered to be an unforgivable insult, I know too that if he were to have reason to believe that morally I am not fit to be his wife he could honourably refuse to accept me.'

'There's an awful lot of supposition going on here,' came the wry comment.

But when Petra shot him a fulminatingly angry look, and demanded, 'Are you trying to say that it's all in my imagination? Then there's no point in us wasting any more of one another's time!'

He gave her a small semi-placatory look and offered conciliatingly, 'So! I understand the motivation, but why choose me?'

Petra gave a small cynical shrug.

'Like I said, I heard a couple of female guests discussing you earlier, and from what they were saying it was obvious that...'

When she stopped speaking, he prompted her softly, 'That what?'

'That you have a reputation for enjoying the favours of the women who stay here. So much so, in fact,' she added, tilting her chin defiantly, 'that you have already been reprimanded for your behaviour by...by Sheikh Rashid, and are in danger of losing your job!' Petra gave a small shudder. 'I don't know how those women can cheapen themselves! I might not want an arranged marriage, but there is no way I would ever prejudice my own personal moral beliefs by indulging in a meaningless sexual fling a...a cheap sexual thrill!' Through the darkness Petra was suddenly acutely conscious of his gaze fixing intently on her.

'I see... So you don't want an arranged marriage and you don't want cheap sexual thrills. So what do you want?'

'Nothing!' As he turned his head Petra saw the mocking way he raised his eyebrows and defended herself immediately. 'What I mean is I don't want anything until I meet a man who...'

'Who matches up to your very high standards?' he suggested tauntingly.

Crossly Petra shook her head.

'Please don't put words into my mouth. What I was going to say was until I meet a man I can love and respect and…and want to…to commit myself to emotionally, mentally, cerebrally, sexually—every which way there is. That is the kind of relationship my parents shared,' she told him passionately. 'And that is the kind of relationship I want for myself and one day want to encourage my own children to aspire to.'

'A tall order, especially in this day and age,' came the blunt response.

'Perhaps, but one I think it worth waiting to fulfil,' Petra told him firmly.

'Aren't you afraid that if you finally meet this paragon he might be deterred by the fact that your reputation—?'

'No.' Petra interrupted him swiftly. 'Because if he loves me he will accept me and know and understand my values. And besides…' She stopped, her face burning as she realised just how close she had come to telling him that the fact that she had so far not met such a man and was still a virgin would tell its own story to the man who eventually claimed her love. 'Why are you asking me all these questions?' she demanded sharply instead.

'No reason,' he replied laconically.

Through the darkness Petra could sense him evaluating her.

'So,' he announced at last. 'You are offering to pay me five thousand pounds to pursue and seduce you and publicly ruin your reputation.'

'To pretend to,' Petra corrected him immediately.

'What's wrong?' he taunted her. 'Having second thoughts?'

'Certainly not!' Petra denied indignantly, and then gasped in shock as he closed the distance between them and took her in his arms, demanding shakily, 'What are you doing?'

He smelled of clean night air and warm male skin, of the dangerous heat of the desert and the cool mystery of the night, and her whole body quivered in helpless reaction to his maleness. The slow descent of his head blocked out the light and the glitter of his eyes mesmerised her into unmoving stillness.

'We have made a pact! A bargain!' she felt him murmuring against her lips.

'And now we must seal it. In the desert in times gone by such things were sealed in blood. Shall I prick your skin and release the life blood from your veins, to mingle it with my own, or will this suffice?'

Before Petra could protest his mouth was on her own, crushing the breath from her lungs. Oh yes, she had been right, she recognised weakly. He was as swift and as deadly as the panther she had mentally likened him to earlier...

A tiny frantic moan bubbled in her throat as she felt her body's helpless response to the mastery of his kiss. She had been right to fear the passionate expertise indicated by that full bottom lip. There was a slight roughness about his face that chafed slightly against her own soft skin, and she had to fight to control the instinctive movement of her hand towards his face to touch that distinctive maleness. As he released her lips it seemed for some inexplicable shaming reason that they were determined to cling to his. Panic flooded over her, and before she could stop herself she bit fiercely into his lip in defiant pride.

The shock of the taste of his blood on her tongue held her immobile.

As she tensed herself for his retaliation she felt his hand wrapping round the slenderness of her throat.

'So…you prefer to seal our bargain in blood after all? There is more of the desert in you than I had realised.'

And then before she could move his mouth was on hers again, crushing it with the pressure of a kind of kiss that was totally outside anything she had ever experienced. She could taste his blood, feel the rough velvet of his tongue, hear the frenzy of a desert storm in her own heartbeat and the relentless, unforgiving burn of its sun in the touch of his hand against her throat.

And then abruptly he had released her, and as he raised his head for a brief moment Petra saw his face fully illuminated for the first time.

His eyes were open and shock reeled through her as she discovered that they were not, after all, as she had imagined dark brown, but a pure, clear, cool, steely silver-grey.

'We have the whole morning at our disposal, Petra. I thought you might like to go shopping. There is an exclusive shopping centre nearby, which has some wonderful designer shops, and…'

With a tremendous effort Petra tried to concentrate on what her aunt was saying to her.

She had telephoned Petra the previous evening to suggest that she show her something of the city and its shops. Whatever she thought about her grandfather's behaviour, Petra could not help but like her aunt by marriage—even if she had been the one to speak to Petra self-consciously the very day her godfather had left.

'Your grandfather knows how disappointed you must be that his doctor's orders mean that he is unable to see you just yet, Petra, and so he has arranged for a…a family friend who…who has a major financial interest in it, to give

you a guided tour of the hotel complex and to show something of our country. You will like Rashid. He is a very
charming and very well-educated man.'

Petra had had to bite on her tongue to prevent herself
from bursting out angrily that she knew exactly who and
what Rashid was—thanks to Saud's innocent revelations!

She had been awake for what felt like virtually the whole
of the night, reliving over and over again those moments
on the beach and wondering how she could ever have been
stupid enough to allow them to happen, and had then fallen
into a deep sleep which had left her feeling heavy-eyed.

The combination of that and the nervous edginess that
was making her start at every tiny sound had exhausted
her, and shopping was the last thing she felt like doing.
Besides, what if *he* should try to get in touch with her?
Would he do that, or would he expect her to seek him out
on the beach and perhaps throw herself at him in the same
shameless way she had heard that the other women had
done? The thought made her stomach tense nauseously. No,
their arrangement was that he was the one who had to pursue her, she reminded herself. Pursue and seduce her, a tiny
inner voice whispered dangerously to her...

Seduce her. A fierce shudder ran through her, causing
her aunt to ask in concern if she was cold.

'Cold? In nearly thirty degrees of heat?' Petra laughed.
Her aunt might protest that in Zuran it was winter, but to
Petra it felt blissfully warm.

'Your grandfather hopes to be well enough to see you
very soon,' her aunt continued. 'He is very much looking
forward to that, Petra. He keeps asking if you look anything
like your mother...'

Petra tried not to be affected by her aunt's gentle words.

'If he really wanted to know he could have found out a

long time ago—when my mother was still alive,' she pointed out, remaining unforgiving.

It was so tempting to tell her aunt that she knew the real reason she was here in Zuran, but she had no wish to get her young cousin into trouble.

'What do you think of the hotel complex?' her aunt was asking her, tactfully changing the subject.

Petra toyed with the idea of fibbing but her conscience refused to allow her to do so.

'It's...it's breathtaking,' she admitted. 'I haven't explored all of it yet, of course. After all it's almost like a small town. But what I have seen...'

She particularly liked the traditional design of the interconnecting hotel and villa complexes, with their private courtyards filled with sweetly scented plants and fruit trees, and the musical sound of fountains which had reminded Petra immediately of both the Moorish style of Southern Spain's architecture and images her mother had shown her as a child of Arabian palaces.

'When Rashid shows you round you must tell him that. Although unfortunately it may be several days before he is able to do so. He sent word to your grandfather this morning that he has been called away on business on behalf of The Royal Family... Another project he is working on in the desert.'

'He works?' Petra made no attempt to conceal her disbelief. From what Saud had told her, her prospective suitor sounded far too wealthy and well-connected to do something so mundane.

'Oh, yes,' her aunt assured her. 'As well as having a large financial interest in this complex he also designed it. He is a very highly qualified architect and greatly in demand. He trained in England. It was his mother's wish that he should go to school there, and after her death his father honoured that wish.'

An architect! Petra frowned, but she had no intention of showing any interest in a man she had already decided to despise.

'It sounds as though he is a very busy man,' she told her aunt. 'There really is no need for him to give up his time to show me round the complex. I am perfectly capable of exploring it on my own.'

'No. You must not do that,' her aunt protested once they were on their own again.

'No? Then perhaps Saud could accompany me?' Petra could not resist teasing her.

'No...no! It is best that Rashid should show you. After all, he is the one who designed the complex and he will be able to answer any questions you might have.'

'And his wife?' Petra questioned innocently. 'Will she not mind him spending his precious free time with me?'

'Oh, he is not married,' her aunt assured her immediately. 'You will like him, Petra,' she assured her enthusiastically. 'You have much in common with one another, and—' She broke off as her mobile phone started to ring.

Her aunt reached beneath her robes to retrieve her phone. But as Petra listened to her speaking quickly in Arabic, she saw her aunt's face crease in anxiety. 'What is it?' she demanded as soon as the call was over. 'Is it my grandfather? Is he—'

Furious with herself for her unguarded reaction, and for her concern, Petra stopped speaking and bit her lip.

'That was your uncle,' her aunt told her. 'Your grandfather has suffered a relapse. He knows that he has been ordered to rest but he will not do so! I must go home, Petra. I am sorry.'

Just for a moment Petra was tempted to plead to be allowed to go with her—to be allowed to see her grandfather, the closest person to her in blood she had—but quickly she stifled her weakening and unwanted emotions. Her grandfather meant nothing to her. How could he when she so obviously meant nothing to him? She must not forget the past and his plans for her. No, she was certainly not going to be the one to beg to see him. Her mother had begged and pleaded and had suffered the pain of being ignored and rejected. There was no way that she, Petra, was going to allow her grandfather to do the same to her!

After a taxi had dropped her off outside the hotel, Petra made her way into the lobby. With the rest of the day to herself there were any number of things Petra knew she could do.

The complex had its own *souq,* filled with craftspeople making and selling all manner of deliciously irresistible and traditional things, or she could leave the hotel and enjoy a gondola ride through the man-made canals that bisected the complex, or walk in the tranquillity of its gardens. And of course she could simply chill out if she so wished, either by one of the several stunningly designed pools, including a state-of-the-art 'horizon pool', or even on one of the private beaches that belonged to the complex.

The pools and beaches were reached via a man-made 'cave' below the lobby floor of the hotel, where it was possible to either walk or be taken in one of the resort's beach buggies.

Once there, as Petra had already discovered, a helpful employee would carry her towel to the lounger of her choice, and position both it and her beach umbrella for her before summoning a waiter in case she wanted to order a drink.

Nothing that a guest might need, no matter how small—

or how large—had been left to chance in the planning of the complex or the training of its staff. Petra had travelled all over the world, both with her parents, her godfather, and on her own, and she had already decided that she had never visited anywhere where a holidaymaker's needs were catered for so comprehensively and enthusiastically as they were here.

But of course she was not here on holiday—even if her closest girlfriends at home had insisted on dragging her round some of London's top stores before she had left, to equip her with a suitably elegant wardrobe for her trip.

Baring in mind her own innate modesty, and the country she was travelling to, Petra had eschewed the more *outré* samples of resort wear her enthusiastic friends had pointed out to her—although from what she had seen of her fellow holidaymakers' choice she could have chosen the briefest and most minimal bikini and still have felt comparatively over-dressed compared with some of them.

Instead she had opted for cool, elegant linens and discreet tankini beach sets, plus several evening outfits including an impossible to resist designer trouser suit in a wonderfully heavy cream matt silk satin fabric, which the salesgirl and her friends had tried in vain to convince her she should wear with simply the one-button jacket fastened over her otherwise naked top half.

'You've got the figure for it,' the salesgirl had urged her, and her friends had wickedly agreed. But Petra had refused to give in, and so a simple cream silk vest with just a hint of a pretty gold thread running through it had been added to her purchases.

A rueful smile quirked her mouth as she remembered the more outrageous of her two friends attempts to persuade her to buy a trendy outfit they had seen in a London department store: a fringed and tasselled torso-baring top, with a pair of matching lower than hip level silky pants which had revealed her belly button, claiming mock innocently that it would be perfect for her to wear in a country that celebrated the art of belly dancing.

Petra had known when she was being wound up. Her smile deepened as she instinctively touched her smooth flat stomach with her fingertips. Hidden beneath her clothes was the discreet little diamond navel stud she had bought herself just before she'd left home to replace the one she had been wearing whilst her recently pierced flesh had healed up.

No one, not even her friends, knew of the uncharacteristic flash of reckless defiance which had led to her having her navel pierced the very day after her godfather had finally ground down her opposition and persuaded her to come to Zuran.

Secretly Petra had to acknowledge that there was something dangerously decadent and wanton about the way the tiny diamond she had bought for herself flashed whenever it caught the light, but of course no one was ever likely to see it, or to know of her rebellious emotional reaction at having to give in to her grandfather's desire for her to visit his country.

Thinking of her grandfather made Petra frown. Just how serious was his heart condition? She had assumed from her uncle's original calm, almost casual reference to it that it was not a particular cause for concern.

Was he as ill as her aunt seemed to believe? Or was it simply a ploy, a means of manipulating her and putting pressure on her? Petra was fiercely determined that she would not give one inch to the despot who had caused her mother so much pain, and she was convinced that he was playing the kind of cat and mouse game that her mother had often told her he was an expert at, using his supposed poor health as a means of keeping her in dark about his real plans for her. Naturally such behaviour on his part had put her on her mettle and alerted her most defensive and hostile reactions. But what if she had been wrong? What if her grandfather was genuinely very ill?

Although it would have been impossible for her not to be emotionally touched by the warmth of her aunt and uncle's reception of her, and their concern that she might be disappointed at being deprived of what they seemed to assume was a much longed for meeting with her grandfather, Petra's antipathy towards her grandfather had been intensified by his emotional manipulation and had caused her to harden her heart even more against him.

She had every right to both mistrust and dislike him, she reassured herself. So why was she feeling somehow abandoned and rejected—excluded from the anxious family circle which had gathered protectively around him? Why did she feel this sense of anxiety and urgency to know what was going on? Why did she feel this sense of pain and loss?

Her uncle or her aunt would ring her at the hotel if they thought it was necessary; she knew that. But that wasn't like being there, being part of what was happening, being totally accepted.

A family walked past her in the foyer, on their way to the piano lounge, its three generations talking happily together. A deep sense of anguish welled up dangerously inside Petra. Grimly she tried to suppress what she was feeling. She had always been too vulnerable to her emotions. Her Celtic inheritance was responsible for that! Against her will she discovered that she was remembering how she had felt as a child, knowing that she was different, sensing her mother's pain and helpless to do anything to alleviate it, envious of other children she knew who talked easily and confidently about their adoring grandparents.

She was letting her feelings undermine her common sense, she warned herself. Her grandfather had only brought her here for one reason and it had nothing to do with adoring her! To him she was merely a suddenly valuable pawn in the intricate game he so enjoyed playing with other people's lives, using them to advance his own lust for power.

But if he was ill…seriously ill…if…something should happen before she had the chance to meet him….

Swallowing against the sharp lump in her throat, Petra headed for the lift. She would go upstairs to her room and decide how she was going to spend the rest of the day.

The suite her family had booked her in to was elegantly luxurious and large enough to house a whole family. Not only did it have a huge bathroom, complete with the largest shower Petra had even seen, as well as a sunken whirlpool bath, it also had a separate wardrobe-filled dressing room, and a bedroom with the most enormous bed she had even slept in, as well as a private terrace overlooking one of the complex's enclosed gardens.

Letting herself into the suite, Petra walked over to the dressing table and put down her bag. As she did so she glanced into the mirror and then froze as in it she saw the reflection of the bed—and more importantly the man lounging on it: her would-be seducer and partner in crime! His hands were clasped behind his head as he watched her, his body covered in nothing more than the towel he had wrapped around his hips. Tiny drops of moisture still glinting on his skin testified to the fact that he must have only recently stepped out of the shower—her shower, Petra reminded herself, unable to stop her eyes widening in betraying shock as she turned round and stared at him in disbelief.

Her suite, like the others on the same floor, and like the palatial owners suite above them, could only be reached by a private lift for which one needed a separate security card!

But for a man like this one anything and everything was possible, Petra suspected.

Like someone in a trance, she watched as he swung his feet to the floor and stood up.

If that towel he had wrapped so precariously around his body should slip...

Nervously she wetted her suddenly dry lips with the tip of her tongue. His own mouth, she suddenly realised on a flush of dangerous raw heat, bore a small fresh scar. Mesmerised, she tried to drag her gaze away from it...from him...

Had someone turned off the air-conditioning? she wondered dizzily. The room suddenly seemed far too warm...

He was walking towards her now, and in another few seconds... Automatically she backed away.

CHAPTER THREE

As THOUGH it was someone else who was actually speaking, Petra heard her own voice, thick and openly panicky, demanding, 'What are you doing in here?'

She could have sworn that her nervousness was amusing him. There was quite definitely a distinct glint in his eyes as he replied easily, 'Waiting for you, of course.'

'In here and...and like that?' Petra couldn't stop the indignation from wobbling her voice. 'What if someone else had been with me...my aunt...?'

Carelessly he gave a small shrug.

'Then you would have achieved your purpose, wouldn't you? Besides, we needed to talk, and I needed to shower, so it made sense for me to deal with both those needs together.'

He looked so totally at home in her suite that she felt as though she was the interloper, Petra acknowledged, and she wasn't even going to begin to ask just how he had managed to gain access to it.

'You could have showered in your own accommodation,' she told him primly. 'And as for us talking—I had planned to come down to the beach later.'

'Later would have been too late,' he told her. 'This is my afternoon off. And as for my own accommodation— ' he gave her a wry look '—do you honestly suppose that the hotel staff are housed as luxuriously as its guests?'

Petra's throat had gone dry—not, she quickly assured herself, because of that sudden and unwanted mental image she had just had of him standing beneath the warm spray of the shower...his naked body gleaming taut and bronze-gold as he soaped the sculptured perfection of the six-pack stomach that was so clearly revealed by the brevity of the towel that did little more than offer the merest sop to modesty—hers and quite obviously not his, Petra reflected indignantly as he strolled round the room, patently unconcerned that the towel might slip!

'How...how did you manage to find me? I didn't tell you my name and you didn't give me yours.'

'It wasn't hard. Your grandfather is very well known.'

Petra's eyes widened. 'You know him?'

The dark eyebrows rose mockingly.

'Would a mere itinerant worker be allowed to "know" a millionaire?'

'And your name is?' Petra pressed him.

Was she imagining it, or had he frowned and hesitated rather longer than was necessary?

'It's Blaize,' he told her briefly.

'Blaize?' Petra looked at him.

'Something wrong?' he challenged her.

Petra shook her head.

'No, it—it's just that I had assumed that you must be Southern European—Italian, or...or Spanish or Greek. But your name...'

'My mother was Cornish,' he told her almost brusquely.

'Cornish?' Petra repeated, bemused.

'Yes,' he confirmed, boredom beginning to enter his voice as he informed her, 'According to my mother, her ancestors belonged to a band of wreckers!'

Wreckers. Well, that no doubt accounted for his colouring, and for that sharp air of danger and recklessness about him, Petra reasoned, remembering that Cornish wreckers were supposed to have pillaged galleons from the defeated Spanish Armada, taking from them not just gold but the high-born Spanish women who were sailing on them with their husbands as well.

Blaize. It suited him somehow. Blaize.

'So now that we've got the civilities out of the way, perhaps we can turn our attention to some practicalities. This plan of yours—'

'I don't want to discuss it now,' Petra interrupted him. 'Please get dressed and leave...'

She was beginning to feel increasingly uncomfortable, increasingly agitated and aware of the effect his virtual nudity was having on her!

'What's wrong?' he questioned her sharply. 'Have you changed your mind? Has your family perhaps managed to persuade you to consider this man they have chosen for you after all? After all, there are worse things to be endured than marriage to a very wealthy man...'

'Not so far as I am concerned,' Petra told him sharply. 'I can't imagine anything worse than...than a loveless marriage,' she told him passionately.

'Have you ever been in love?' he questioned her, answering his own question as he said softly, 'No, of course you haven't. Otherwise...'

There was a glint in his eyes that was making Petra's heart beat far too fast. She was still in shock from discovering him in her room and, even worse, her senses were still reacting to the totally relaxed and arrogant male way in which he was now lounging against the wall, arms folded across his chest, tightening the muscles in them in a way that for some reason refused to allow her to withdraw her fascinated female gaze from them.

'Whether or not I have ever been in love has nothing whatsoever to do with our...our business arrangement,' Petra reproved him sternly.

'When are you supposed to be being introduced to Rashid?'

Petra frowned. 'I...I don't know! You see at the moment I'm not even supposed to know what my grandfather has planned. My aunt has dropped several discreet hints about Rashid, pretending that he is just a kind family friend who has offered to...to show me round the complex, but...'

When Blaize's eyebrows rose, Petra explained defensively, 'It seems that he doesn't merely have a large financial interest in it, but that he helped design it as well. According to my aunt, he's a trained architect.'

Petra wondered uncomfortably if Blaize could hear the slight breathlessness in her voice. If so she hoped he would assume it was because she was impressed by her would-be suitor's academic qualifications rather than by the sight of Blaize's own muscles!

'When is he to show you around?'

Petra shrugged her shoulders.

'I don't know. According to my aunt, Rashid the Sheikh has been called away on business.'

'And you are no doubt hoping that by the time he returns enough damage will have been done to your reputation to have him questioning your suitability to be his wife? Well, if that is to be achieved we should not waste any time,' Blaize told her, without waiting for her response. 'Tonight everyone who is anyone on the Zuran social scene will be out and about, looking to see and be seen, and the current in place for that is a restaurant here on this complex called The Venue. It has a Michelin-starred chef and boasts a separate music room where diners can dance. I think that you and I should make our first public appearance there tonight. Dress is formal, and there is a strict admissions policy, but as a guest of the hotel and a woman that won't be a problem for you!'

'It sounds expensive,' Petra told him doubtfully.

'It is,' he agreed. 'But surely that isn't a problem? You did tell me that you are staying here at your family's request, and as their guest, and since the cost of dining in the restaurant can be debited to your room—'

'No! I couldn't possibly do that,' Petra denied immediately, unable to conceal either her distaste or her shock. But far from being contrite, Blaize merely looked amused.

'Why ever not? You have to eat, don't you?'

'I have to eat, yes,' Petra acknowledged. 'But I can't possibly expect my family to pay for...'

As she paused, struggling to find the right words to express her feelings, Blaize shrugged and told her bluntly, 'Either you were serious about this plan of yours or it was just a childish impulse that you're now regretting. In which case, you're wasting my time as well as your own—'

'I *am* serious,' Petra interrupted him quickly.

'Very well, then. We eat late here, so I shall meet you downstairs in the foyer at nine-thirty—unless of course you want me to come up to your room to collect you a little earlier, which would give us time to...'

'No,' Petra said firmly, her face burning as she saw the amused look he was giving her.

'How very much the epitome of a nervous virgin you look and sound right now! Are you one?'

Her face burning even hotter, Petra told him fiercely, 'You have no right to ask me that kind of question.'

Laughing softly, Blaize shook his head. 'Who would have thought it? Now you *have* surprised me! A nervous virgin who wants to be considered openly sexually available. You really don't want this marriage, do you?'

'I've just told you I am not prepared to discuss my...my personal private life with you...'

'Even though you expect me to publicly convince others

that I am very much a part of that personal private life...very, very much a part of it?' he said softly.

There was a look in his eyes that was making Petra's insides quiver with tension and indignation. How dared he make fun of her? It occurred to her that somehow or other he had managed to turn their relationship around so that he was the one who was in control of what was happening rather than her. A presentiment shiver brushed over her skin, warning her that she might be in danger of getting herself involved in a situation that she ultimately could not control. But before she could analyse her fears properly the doorbell to her suite suddenly rang, the shrilling sound activating her inner alarm system and throwing her body into immediate anxiety.

'It's okay,' Blaize informed her easily. 'That will be Room Service. I ordered something to eat.'

'*You* ordered...' Petra stared at him, and then looked frantically towards the suite door as the bell rang again. 'You can't—' she began, and then stopped, pink-cheeked, as she realised Blaize was laughing softly at her.

'You know,' he said, 'I think that this is going to be fun. Have you any idea how tempting it is to really shock you, little Miss Prim?'

Still laughing, he leaned forward and cupped her face with his hand, brushing her unsuspecting mouth with his own before releasing her and disappearing into the bathroom just before the suite door opened and the meal he had ordered was brought in.

'Panic over?'

Automatically Petra looked towards Blaize as he emerged from the bathroom, still wearing merely the towel, with an electric razor in one hand whilst he smoothed the skin of his newly shaved jaw with the other. Then she quickly looked away as her heart did a triple-flip before losing its balance and slamming heavily into her chest wall.

What on earth was the matter with her? So he was having a shave. So what?

So what? The voice of moral female indignation inside her retorted angrily; what he was doing was an act of deliberate male intimacy…shaving in her suite…in her bathroom…

'Mmm. I could get used to this,' he told her appreciatively as he studied the well-laden trolley. 'Pour me a cup of coffee, would you?' he called out to her as he turned back towards the bathroom. 'Black and strong, no sugar.'

Pour him a coffee! Who on earth did he think he was?

'Oh, by the way,' he told her, pausing as he reached the bathroom door. 'I've already booked us a table at The Venue for tonight, and told them to bill it to your room. We were lucky. They were virtually fully booked. Are you sure you don't feel like short-circuiting things? I could move in here and…'

'No!'

Petra's denial was an explosive sound of outrage and panic, but far from shaming him it just seemed to add to her tormentor's amusement.

Relaxing against the open doorway, he told her wickedly, 'You know, I think I could really enjoy making this seduction the real thing, if you want me to.'

'No.' This time her denial was even more vehement, her eyes huge and storm-lashed as she added in a strangled voice, 'Never.'

'Ah, yes! I forgot that you're saving yourself for the man of your dreams! Well, take care he doesn't turn into a nightmare… Is that my coffee?' he added easily, coming to rescue the cup that she was in danger of overfilling.

Furious with herself for her automatic response to his original request, Petra snatched the cup back from him.

'No, it isn't' she denied. 'It's mine. You can pour your own.'

Unperturbed, he shrugged and reached for the coffee pot, leaving Petra to digest her hollow victory along with the bitterly strong coffee she had claimed.

Broodingly she watched as Blaize tucked into the meal he had ordered with obvious relish. This wasn't what she had envisaged when she had initially approached him. What she had had in mind was an open and obvious flirtation on the beach, perhaps a couple of very public outings and maybe a meal together thrown in.

'Come and sit down and have something to eat. I ordered enough for both of us,' Blaize told her.

'So I see,' Petra agreed waspishly.

There was no way she could let her family pay for whatever Blaize had added to her bill. Thankfully she had come away with plenty of traveller's cheques and her credit cards, and her godfather—no doubt motivated by guilt—had pressed a very generous sum of money on her before he had left for the far east.

'I'm a working man,' Blaize told her cheerfully.

'I'm glad you reminded me,' Petra replied. 'And, talking of your work, shouldn't you...?'

'Don't worry,' he assured her. 'I had some leave owing to me, so I've arranged to take some time off. That way I can be free to do whatever you want me to do. If our Rashid is prepared to take you sight unseen, so to speak, then I dare say he's going to be pretty hard to shift. So you and I are going to have to make sure that we're convincing. Are you sure you don't want me to move in here?' he pressed, looking wistfully at her large bed.

'Perfectly sure,' Petra told him through gritted teeth.

'And just as soon as you've finished I would be grateful if you would get dressed and leave.'

'Leave? So soon? I thought we could spend some time getting to know one another a little better.'

To Petra's chagrin she knew that her expression had betrayed her even before he started to laugh.

'You're going to have to do much better than this if you expect to convince anyone that you've ever done anything more than exchange chaste kisses with a man—never mind that you and I are lovers,' he warned her when he had stopped laughing.

'The whole purpose of my paying you is that your reputation is dire enough to do the convincing for both of us!' Petra reminded him flintily.

'You look very hot and uncomfortable,' Blaize responded, ignoring both her comment and her ire. 'I can recommend the shower. In fact, if you like—'

'No! Don't you dare…' Petra stopped him, hot-cheeked.

'Dare what?' he asked her mock innocently. 'I was only going to say that I could alter the height of the shower head for you if you wanted me to.'

Petra gave him a fulminating look.

'Thank you, but I'm perfectly capable of doing that for myself,' she told him.

She bitterly regretted having let slip to him the fact that she was still a virgin. He obviously thought it hugely entertaining and would no doubt continue to goad and tease her about it. Unless she found a way of stopping him!

Petra tensed as the telephone in her suite started to ring. Before answering it she glanced at her reflection in the mirror. She had almost finished getting ready and she was wearing her new cream trouser suit. Warily she picked up the receiver, only to discover that her caller was her aunt.

'I meant to ring you earlier,' she apologised. 'Are you all right? I feel so guilty about leaving you on your own.'

As she assured her that she was fine, Petra waited for her aunt to make a firm arrangement for her to visit her family and finally meet her grandfather. But instead of issuing any invitation there was a small awkward silence from her aunt, and then an unconvincing and rushed explanation that certain family obligations meant it would not be possible for them to spend any time with her on the following day.

'At least your grandfather is feeling a little better. Although the doctor says that he must still rest. He is longing to see you, Petra, and—'

If anything her aunt's voice sounded even more unconvincing, Petra reflected bitterly.

Well she certainly wasn't going to turn herself into a liar by saying that she was longing to see *him*. She had no idea what he was hoping to achieve by what he was doing, unless it was to make her feel so isolated and alone that she practically fell into her proposed suitor's arms out of gratitude to him for rescuing her from her solitude.

'It is such a pity that my own family, my sisters and their children, are out of the country right now,' her aunt was continuing. 'But as soon as Rashid gets back—'

'You mustn't worry about me, Aunt,' Petra interrupted her. 'I am perfectly capable of entertaining myself. As a matter of fact...' Petra paused, wondering how much she ought to say.

But her aunt obviously wasn't listening properly because she cut across what Petra was saying, telling her, 'There are several escorted trips from the resort that you might enjoy taking, Petra, whilst you wait for Rashid to return. The gold *souq,* for one. Oh, I must go. I can hear your grandfather calling for me.'

There was barely time for Petra to wish her goodbye before her aunt had rung off.

As she turned towards the mirror to apply her lipstick Petra discovered that her hand was shaking slightly.

Because she was angry, she told herself—*not* because she was nervous at all at the thought of spending the evening with Blaize. She was angry because she knew instinctively that her aunt was not being entirely honest with her.

Mentally she tried to picture her grandfather, using the vivid verbal images her mother had drawn for her, and those she had gained herself from studying the robed men she had seen moving with imperious arrogance through the hotel. He would be bearded, of course, his profile hawk-like and his expression harsh, perhaps even vengeful as he confronted her, the child of the marriage he had fought against so bitterly and so unsuccessfully.

It was impossible for Petra to get her head round the mindset of a father who had turned from being protective and loving to one who refused so much as to hear his once beloved daughter's name spoken, simply because she had chosen to marry the man she loved.

In the mirror her own reflection confronted her. At home in England she was often conscious of looking out of place, her colouring and the delicacy of her fine-boned body giving her an almost exotic beauty, but here in her mother's country, conversely, she felt very Celtic.

Her mother! What would *she* think of the course of action Petra was taking? What would she think of Blaize?

Snatching up her purse, Petra refused to allow herself to pursue such potentially unsettling thoughts.

The lobby of the hotel was the busiest Petra had seen it since her arrival. A large group of designer-clad women and their male escorts were standing by the entrance to the piano lounge and Petra's eyes widened as she saw the jewellery the women were wearing.

Her own outfit was provoking a few assessing and appreciative female glances, as well as some much more openly male admiring ones, but Petra was unaware of them as she looked round anxiously for Blaize.

'There you are. I was just about to come up and collect you.'

Whirling round, Petra rounded her eyes as she stared at Blaize. He was dressed formally in clothes she immediately recognised as being the very best in Italian tailoring, and which she knew must have cost a small fortune. No wonder more than one of the diamond-decked women were studying him with such open sexual interest!

On the wages he must earn there was no way he could possibly afford such clothes, Petra decided, which must mean...

She didn't like the unpleasant cold feeling invading her stomach, or the lowering realisation that she was probably far from being the first woman to pay Blaize for his 'services'—although of course the services she was paying him for were no doubt very different from those normally expected by his benefactresses.

'What's wrong? You look as though you've just swallowed something extremely unpleasant.'

His intuitiveness triggered a sharp spiral of warning.

'I was just wondering what's going to be on the menu tonight,' she replied smoothly.

He might have caught her off guard this afternoon, but tonight was going to be different. This time she was going to make it plain to him that *she* was the one in charge of events and not him!

'These days Zuran is renowned for the variety and standard of its restaurants, as you are about to discover.'

As he spoke he was guiding her across the foyer, one hand protectively beneath her elbow. Petra would have liked to pull away, to put some distance between them, but the crush of people in the lobby made it impossible, and besides, she firmly reminded herself, the whole point of being with him was that she was *seen* to be with him!

However, instead of heading for the exit, as she had expected him to do, Petra discovered that he was guiding her in the direction of the large glass doors that opened out into one of the formal garden courtyards, beyond which lay the largest of the network of canals which criss-crossed the complex.

'I thought we were going out to dinner,' she said, hanging back a little as two uniformed men held open the doors for them.

'We are,' Blaize told her, giving her a quizzical look as he ushered her outside. 'What's wrong?' he teased her. 'Did you think I was taking you out into the courtyard so that I could indulge in a little private tuition before we faced our public?'

He laughed softly, the hand which had been beneath her elbow suddenly grasping her upper arm and holding her so close to his own body that she could feel the laughter vibrating as they walked out into the heavy satin warmth of the indigo-dark night.

'In a garden? Where anyone might see us. Oh, no... If *that* was my intention I would have taken you somewhere far, far more private...'

'Like your official accommodation, you mean?' Petra challenged him bitingly, determined not to let him think that she was in the least bit affected by what he was saying.

'You remind me of a little cat, all sharp claws and defensive temper. Take care that you don't tempt me to teach you how to purr with pleasure and use those claws only in the heat of passion...'

'We aren't in public, yet,' was all Petra could think of to say in retaliation and she mentally blessed the darkness for concealing her hectically flushed face. 'So you can save the practised seduction scenario until we are!'

They had almost crossed the garden now, and the canal lay in front of them. As they reached it Blaize raised his hand to summon one of the gondoliers waiting several yards away.

'This isn't the quickest way to reach the restaurant, but I think it is certainly the most...relaxing,' he informed her in a soft murmur as the gondola was brought to a halt in front of them.

As Blaize helped her into the gondola Petra wondered helplessly if anything could possibly be more romantic— or more hackneyed!

Clever lighting had transformed the daytime appearance of the resort into a place of magic and mystery, designed to appeal to the senses. Strawberry-scented vapour floated over their heads in a pale pink cloud, and in the distance Petra could see and hear fireworks. As they passed the *souq,* a fire-eater performed for a watching group of teenagers whilst a 'merchant' loaded his wares onto a waiting camel train, causing Petra's heart to give a small unsteady thump.

The one thing she wanted to do whilst she was in Zuran was take a trip into the desert. Her aunt might speak enthusiastically about shopping malls and the fabulous gold and diamond *souq,* but it was the desert that called most strongly to Petra in a siren song that whispered to her that to know it was her heritage.

Deep in her own private thoughts, she jumped when Blaize touched her arm. The gondola swung into an ornately decorated private landing from which a red carpet led towards a building so unmistakably Parisian in concept that Petra could only stare at it in bemusement.

Several other people were already standing in front of the entrance to the restaurant, and as she felt Blaize's hands on her body when he helped her from the gondola Petra immediately tensed in rejection of the sexual intimacy, instinctively uncomfortable about other people witnessing it.

'Don't do that!' she protested when Blaize bent his head and allowed his breath to graze intimately against her skin as he brushed her hair from her face. 'The women who paid for your clothes might have enjoyed being pawed in public, but I don't.'

The minute she had finished speaking Petra knew that she had gone too far. It was there in the sudden stiffening of his body and the glacial glitter in his eyes.

It was useless to try to explain that her own panic at her body's helpless reaction to him had motivated her rash words—and besides, her pride would not allow her to do so. So Petra tensed and bent her head beneath the savage lash of his softly spoken retaliation.

'For your information no woman has ever...ever...paid for my clothes. And as for your comment about "pawing"—be thankful that your innocence protects you from the consequences of such a comment—for now!'

In silence, but with her head held high, Petra turned towards the red carpet. Not for anything was she going to admit—even to herself—how much she longed for the protective warmth of Blaize's hand beneath her elbow as she watched the other diners entering the restaurant, the men in their robes and their women couturier-clad and holding themselves with a proud elegance Petra secretly envied.

'More wine?' Blaize asked as their waiter hovered solicitously, holding the wine bottle. Immediately Petra shook her head and covered her still half-full glass with her hand. The meal they had just been served had been outstandingly good—with every mouthful Petra had been reminded of her first grown-up meal in Paris, a birthday treat from her parents. Everything from the decor and the whole ambience of the place, right down to the subtle perfume of the candles on the tables, replicated the chicest of Parisian restaurants, and Petra knew she would not have been surprised to hear French itself being spoken.

'Coffee, then?' Blaize was asking as he signalled her refusal to the hovering waiter.

Nodding her head, Petra warned herself that if she was not careful she might be in danger of falling for her own fiction, so well was Blaize playing the part of attentive and adoring lover. But then, of course, no doubt he had had plenty of practice, she reminded herself grimly.

Petra dreaded to think about the impact the cost of the meal was going to make on her credit card, but there was no way she could feel comfortable allowing it to be debited to her suite.

As she waited for the waiter to bring her coffee she was suddenly aware of being studied by the occupants of a nearby table—a group of three couples.

The arrival of the waiter with her coffee momentarily distracted her, but as she glanced away from them Petra could have sworn that Blaize gave the tiniest warning shake of his head when one of the men started to get up, as though he was about to come over to their table.

As soon as the waiter had gone, Petra demanded, 'Who is that…?'

'Who do you mean?' Blaize questioned her, frowning slightly.

'The man you just looked at,' Petra said. 'He was about to come over, but you—'

'I didn't look at anyone,' Blaize denied.

'Yes, you did,' Petra insisted. 'I saw you...'

'You're imagining things,' Blaize told her. 'Which man do you mean? Point him out to me.'

Irately Petra did so, but when Blaize looked deliberately in his direction the man Petra had pointed out looked pointedly through them before averting his gaze.

Giving her an ironic look, Blaize shrugged his shoulders meaningfully whilst Petra's face burned. She had obviously been wrong after all, but she wasn't going to give Blaize the satisfaction of admitting it!

'When you have finished your coffee perhaps you would like to dance,' Blaize suggested. 'After all, we are supposed to be lovers, despite that virginal look of yours...'

Petra's mouth compressed and she put down her coffee cup with a small clatter.

'That's it!' she told him forcefully. 'From now on every time you so much as mention my...my...the word "virgin" I shall fine you five pounds, and deduct the money from your fee! I am paying you to help me escape from a marriage I don't want. Not to...to keep on bringing up something which has nothing whatsoever to do with our business arrangement!'

'No? I beg to differ,' Blaize informed her softly. 'I am supposed to create the impression that I am seducing you,' he reminded her. 'Who is going to believe that if you insist on looking like a—'

'Five pounds,' Petra warned him.

'Like a woman who does not know what it is to experience a man's passion,' Blaize finished silkily.

She had finished her coffee and Blaize had summoned the waiter to ask for the bill.

Immediately Petra reached for her bag to remove her credit card.

'What are you doing?' Blaize demanded curtly, when he saw what she was doing.

'I can't let my family pay for this. It would be... immoral...' Petra told him.

'Immoral... To allow them to pay for a meal? But not apparently immoral to allow them to believe that you are sleeping with me...a man you picked up on the beach...'

'My body is mine to do with as I wish,' Petra hissed furiously to him as the waiter arrived with the bill. She already had her credit card in her hand, but to her disbelief before she could place it on the saucer Blaize had picked up the bill.

'I shall deal with this,' he told her coolly, 'You may reimburse me later.'

Turning to the discreetly waiting waiter, he murmured something to him that Petra couldn't catch, handing the man the bill which he immediately walked away with.

Several minutes later, as they made their way to the separate music room, Petra felt as though everyone else in the restaurant was watching them. She was being over-sensitive, of course. She knew that. No doubt it was only the female diners who were watching Blaize, she told herself wryly.

The music room and its dance floor were very dimly lit, and as she heard the provocative strains of the sensual music that was being played, watched the way the dancers already on the floor were moving, she automatically pulled back. This wasn't dancing. It was...it was sex on the dance floor—and there was no way *she* was going to allow Blaize to hold *her* like that. No way she dared allow him to hold her like that.

Why not? It wasn't, after all, as though he was her type,

she reminded herself robustly, and she knew that no matter how outwardly sensual and romantic he might appear he felt nothing whatsoever for her. They were here for a purpose, and the sooner it was achieved the sooner she would be free to return home.

Squaring her shoulders, she allowed Blaize to guide her towards the dance floor.

Seconds later, held in his arms, her face pressed into his shoulder whilst his hand smoothed its way down her back, coming to rest well below her waist, Petra acknowledged that she had perhaps been over-confident about her ability to control her body's physical reaction to him.

He was a practised seducer, she told herself in her own defence. A man who had perfected his seduction technique on an unending stream of women...

'Relax... We're supposed to be lovers, remember...'

'I am relaxed,' Petra told him through gritted teeth.

'No, you aren't!' he corrected her. 'You're petrified that I'm going to do something like this to you...'

As he finished speaking he slid his hand into the hair at the nape of her neck, gently tugging her head so that his lips could graze along her throat and then nibble tormentingly against her ear. Just the feel of his breath made her whole body quiver in shocked delight as his thumb tracked the betraying pulse beating increasingly fast at the base of her throat.

'Have you any idea how very, very much I want you...?'

The throaty words he whispered against her mouth caused Petra's eyes to widen—until she remembered that he was simply acting...playing the part she was paying him to play.

'Shall I take you back to your room and show you how much? Remove the clothes from your delectable sexy body and stroke and kiss every inch of it before—'

Petra gasped as he reached for her hand and told her rawly, 'Feel what you're doing to me…'

She tried to pull free but it was too late. He was already placing her hand against his body, and she could feel the heavy thud of his heart against her palm.

'Come closer to me,' he said, drawing her deeper into his embrace, and then whispering, 'Closer than that! So close that I can pretend I have you naked in my arms, your silky skin next to mine…'

Petra knew that the heat filling her could not be blamed on the lack of air in the room, but stubbornly she refused to acknowledge what was really causing both it and the shivery, achy, tight pangs of longing that were running riot inside her body, inciting a rebellion she was terrified she might not be able to control.

Somehow she managed to put enough distance between them, to raise her head and tell him huskily, 'I want to leave.'

'So soon? It's only just gone midnight?'

Petra could feel her panic increasing. If he kept her here on the dance floor, holding her the way he was, for very much longer— It was all very well for her brain to know that he was simply acting, but her body seemed to be finding it almost impossible to differentiate between fact and fiction. It was responding to him as though…as though… she…actually wanted him!

'It's been a long day, and my aunt will probably be telephoning me early in the morning to update me on my grandfather's condition!'

'I thought you weren't interested in his health.'

'I'm not,' Petra denied immediately. 'It's just…'

Blaize had released her now, and was standing in front of her searching her face with far too sharp a gaze. Instinctively Petra wanted to hide herself—and her feelings—from him—to protect herself from something, someone she was rapidly coming to realise might potentially offer a far more serious threat to her future happiness than she felt comfortable acknowledging.

Why was he affecting her like this? After all, he wasn't the first male she had danced intimately closely with, or been kissed by; he was not even the first male who had caused her to want him! She might not as yet have had a lover, but she knew what it was to feel desire, to feel emotionally drawn to someone. She had gone through all the normal early teenage crushes on a variety of male icons, from popstars to football heroes, and she had even fancied herself in love a couple of times. But this was the first time she had been so powerfully and intimately aroused that she felt in fear of not being able to control those feelings!

'It's just what?' Blaize prompted her, breaking into her anxious thoughts.

'I don't want to talk about it,' Petra replied, stubbornly shaking her head.

'Very well, then. If you're sure you want to leave, and you're not just making an excuse to escape from my arms because you're afraid that you might enjoy being there too much...'

Petra glared at him, outwardly angry but inwardly horrified by his insouciant comment. He was probably just testing her...teasing her, she reassured herself. After all, he couldn't possible know what she was feeling...could he?

'Oh, I could never do that,' she told him firmly, giving him a carefully manufactured smile as she added sweetly, 'After all, I've never liked crowds!'

She had expected her put-down to silence him, but instead he simply demanded softly, 'Meaning?'

'Meaning that the space within your arms is crowded

with the women who have already been there,' Petra answered him forthrightly.

However, instead of being abashed, Blaize simply shrugged and told her carelessly, 'I am thirty-four years old. Naturally there have been...relationships...'

It was on the tip of Petra's tongue to tell him that it wasn't his 'relationships' she was referring to, but the other women whom she suspected had paraded in and out of his life—and his arms—in an unending and highly impermanent line. But instead she simply shook her head and started to walk away from him.

He caught up with her by the door, just as the doorman and his uniformed attendants sprang into action—almost as though they were royalty, Petra thought as she stepped onto the red carpet which led from the restaurant door to the pathway and the car park and canal.

'I think I'd rather be driven back,' Petra announced hurriedly. There was no way, in her present vulnerable mood, that she wanted to share the intimacy of a moonlit gondola ride back to her hotel with Blaize!

She had half expected him to talk her out of her decision, but instead he simply raised his hand to summon one of the waiting buggies.

Their silent return to the hotel was somehow more unnerving for Petra than even those moments on the dance floor. She couldn't understand how it was that a man in Blaize's position, who behaved as he did and who was after all being paid by her, could somehow manage to be so convincingly autocratic and superior!

Once inside the hotel, as he pressed the bell for the lift for her, Blaize told her firmly, 'The more obviously we are seen in public together, the better. So tomorrow I suggest that we make arrangements to that end. There are several organised trips we could take together.'

'Organised trips?' Petra interrupted him, frowning. 'But surely it won't be enough for you to simply be seen with me by my fellow visitors? We need to be seen together by people who are known to Rashid.'

'Zuran is a small place. I am sure that our... friendship...will soon come to his ears,' Blaize replied as the lift arrived.

He stepped into it with her and pressed the button for her floor.

'You don't need to come up with me,' Petra protested immediately, but the doors had already closed and the lift was in motion.

'What is it you are so afraid of?' Blaize mocked her when the lift had stopped. 'That I might kiss you, or that I might not?'

'Neither!' Petra denied forcefully.

'Liar!' Blaize taunted her softly. 'You are a woman, after all, and of course you want—'

'What I want,' Petra interrupted him angrily outside her suite door, 'is for you to remember that I am paying you to act as my lover in public, and that is all!'

As she spoke she was fumbling in her bag for her key card, thankfully finding it and swiping it.

Blaize's hand was on the door handle and Petra held her breath as he pushed the door open. What would she do if he insisted on coming into her room? If he insisted on doing even more than that? Her heart suddenly seemed to have developed an over-fast and erratic heartbeat, and instinctively Petra put her hand on her chest, as if she was trying to steady it.

As he held open the door for her Blaize switched on the suite lights. Petra's mouth felt dry, her body boneless and soft, the blood running hotly through her veins. She closed

her eyes and then opened them again as she heard the small
but distinctive click of the suite door closing.

Whirling round, she opened her mouth to tell Blaize that
she wanted him to leave, and then closed it again as she
stared at the empty space between her own body and the
closed door where she had expected him to be.

Blaize had gone. He had not come into her suite! He had
simply closed the door and left. Which was exactly what
she had wanted...wasn't it?

CHAPTER FOUR

PETRA had finished her breakfast and the waiter had cleared away the room service trolley, leaving her with a fresh pot of coffee and the newspaper she had ordered.

She had eaten her breakfast outside on her private patio, in the pleasurable warmth of the early morning sunshine, and by rights she ought to be feeling contently relaxed.

But she wasn't!

Her mobile phone started to ring and she picked it up.

'Petra?'

The unexpected sound of her godfather's voice banished her mood of introspection.

He was ringing from a satellite connection, he told her, and would not be able to stay on the line very long.

'How are you getting on with your grandfather?' he asked.

'I'm not,' Petra responded wryly. 'I haven't even seen him yet. He hasn't been well enough, apparently.'

'Petra—I can't hear you!' She heard her godfather interrupting her, his own voice so faint that she could barely hear it. 'The line's breaking up. I'm going to have to go. I'll be out of contact for the next couple of weeks. Government business…'

A series of sharp crackles distorted his voice so much that Petra couldn't make out what he was saying, although she thought he was telling her that he loved her. Before she could make any response the line had gone dead.

Miserably she stared at the now blank screen. There would be no point in her trying to ring back; she had no idea exactly where her godfather was and she didn't have a number.

It was a pity that she hadn't been able to beg him to send her her passport before the line had broken up! Now her only means of escape from her unwanted marriage was quite definitely via Blaize.

As a tiny shower of tingling excitement skittered dangerously down her spine Petra warned herself that she was being foolish—and gullible! Why had she allowed Blaize to manoeuvre her into agreeing to last night's expensive meal, when surely her purpose could have been just as easily if not even better achieved via a short interlude on the beach with him?

She glanced at her mobile. Perhaps out of good manners she ought to at least telephone to enquire after her grandfather's health. A little nervously Petra dialled the number of the family villa.

An unfamiliar male voice answered, throwing Petra into confusion. Hesitantly she asked for her aunt, and was asked for her own name. Several seconds later Petra breathed out in relief as she heard her aunt's voice.

A little uncomfortably, asked after her grandfather.

'He has had a good night,' her aunt told her. 'But he is still very weak. He insisted on going to morning prayers, although he was not supposed to do so. Unfortunately he had instructed his manservant to drive him there before I realised what was going on. I am so glad that you have rung, Petra. It will mean such a lot to him to know of your concern.'

The genuine warmth and approval in her voice was making Petra feel even more uncomfortable, and rather guilty as well, even though she tried to reassure herself that she had nothing to feel guilty about.

'You are being wonderfully patient,' her aunt continued.

'I promise you it won't be long now before you will be able to see him. I had intended to telephone you myself, to ask if you would like to go round the spice *souq* tomorrow morning, and then perhaps we could have lunch together?'

'I...that sounds very nice,' Petra accepted lamely. Feeling even more uncomfortable and guilty, she quickly ended the call.

She needed to see Blaize, she decided firmly, to make sure that he realised she was the one in charge of things and not him. He had said that he would make contact with her, but she was being driven by a sense of anxious urgency.

She wanted...needed to see Blaize now!

Half an hour later she stood on the beach, trying to cope with the frustration of explaining to the anxious to please lifeguard and the young man who was now in charge of the windsurfers what she wanted. But they didn't seem to recognise Blaize from her description, Petra slowly forced herself to count to ten.

It wasn't their fault that they didn't know Blaize! The fault lay with her, not with them, for not making sure that she was able to get in touch with him. Thanking the two young men for their attempts to help her, she made her way back to her hotel.

It was lunchtime but she wasn't really hungry; the emptiness inside her could not be satisfied with food! She had been infuriated by the way Blaize had tormented her about her virginity, and disturbed by her own physical reaction to him. Of course there was no way she had really wanted him to kiss her last night, but just supposing that he had.

Quickly Petra pressed the lift button, hoping that no one had noticed her flushed face or the fierce shudder that had gripped her body.

What on earth was the matter with her? Petra derided

herself scornfully as the lift carried her smoothly and effortlessly upwards. She might be a virgin but that did not mean she was sexually repressed or unaware—so naïve and vulnerable that all it took to arouse her was one look from a predatory experienced male!

But if Blaize *had* kissed her... If he had then she would have had the common sense to reject him and send him packing, she assured herself firmly. Theirs was a business relationship and that was the way she intended it to stay!

The lift had stopped. She got out and made her way to her suite, holding her breath as she opened the door. But this time there was no virtually naked man reclining on her bed. Much to her relief! Or so she told herself,

Half an hour later she was still trying to decide what she was going to do with the rest of her day. A little restlessly she paced her terrace. She wasn't really in the mood for the beach. The guidebook she had found suggested several walks through the city which took in various points of interest. Quickly she went to find it, picking it up and flicking through it.

There was one walk which took in the older parts of the town, including a tour of the home of a former ruler. It had now been turned into a museum documenting the social, cultural, educational and religious history of the area.

Firmly Petra told herself that it would do her good to have something other than her grandfather and the problems he was causing her to occupy her mind. After changing into a pair of white linen trousers and pulling on a loose long-sleeved cotton top, Petra left her suite.

Outside the afternoon sunshine was strong enough to have her reaching for her sunglasses whilst she waited for the concierge staff to summon her a taxi. Out of the corner of her eye she saw an immaculate shiny black stretch limousine pulling up a few yards away from her.

Curiously she watched as a flurry of anxious attendants hurried to open doors and several very important-looking robed men got out of the vehicle. Watching them discreetly, Petra suddenly stiffened, and then relaxed, shaking her head ruefully. Just for a second she had actually thought that in profile one of the robed men looked like Blaize! How ridiculous! Of course it couldn't possibly be him! It wasn't only her preoccupation with her grandfather she needed to clear out of her thoughts, she told herself grimly as she headed for her waiting taxi.

She had spent so much time inside the museum that outside it was going dark, Petra realised as she drew a deep breath of evening air into her lungs, her head full of everything she had just seen.

It wasn't just Zuran's history and past she had just experienced, it was also part of her own—which of course was why the contents of the museum had so absorbed her. Inside the museum, for the first time she had actually felt a sense of awareness and recognition of her Bedouin roots, and with that the first tentative, uncurling delicate tendrils of belonging. For the first time in her life she was actually recognising and acknowledging that she needed to know more about this country—not just for her mother's sake but for her own.

There was a faint scent on the wind that caused her to lift her head and look towards the desert. There on the wind was the scent of her past, her destiny, and instinctively her senses recognised it. She was part of a proud race of people who had roamed this land when Cleopatra had been Queen, when Marco Polo had made his epic journey along the silk road.

Without thinking about what she was doing Petra

reached down and scooped up a small handful of sand, letting it trickle slowly through her fingers. Her country...

Her eyes blurred with tears. Fiercely she blinked them away.

A group of people hurried past her, accidentally jostling her, and the mood was broken. It was almost dark and she was hungry. She hailed a cruising taxi and gave him the address of her hotel.

Hesitantly, Petra scanned the hotel foyer. She had booked herself a table for dinner at the complex's Italian restaurant, but now, standing in the foyer and realising that she was the only woman there on her own, she was beginning to have second thoughts. But Zuran was an extremely cosmopolitan and safe country, she reminded herself stoutly, and the complex was geared to the needs of the visitor—even a solitary female such as herself.

Tonight she had dressed a little less dramatically, in a simple black linen dress that buttoned down the front. Its neat square neckline showed off the delicate bones at the base of her throat and the proud arch of her neck, just as the plain gold bangle she was wearing on her wrist revealed the fragility of its bone structure. The bangle had originally belonged to her mother, and Petra touched it now, seeking its comforting reassurance.

She wasn't used to dining in public alone but she refused to eat a solitary meal in her suite!

The clerk at the hotel's guest relations desk assured her that she didn't have very far to walk to the Italian restaurant—which, he explained, was situated in its own private courtyard and could be reached on foot or by gondola.

Taking a gondola was too dangerous, Petra decided. It might remind her of last night and Blaize! She started to frown. All day she had been on edge, expecting Blaize to get in touch with her, but he had not done so. Because he had found someone more profitable to spend his time with, both financially and sexually? She had already seen that there was no shortage of admiring women eager for his company.

Pausing in mid-step, Petra firmly reassured herself that the funny little ache she was experiencing had nothing at all to do with any jealousy. Her? Jealous of Blaize's other women? How ridiculous!

The clerk had been right when he had told her that the restaurant wasn't very far away. Petra turned a corner and found herself in the courtyard he had mentioned to her.

The middle of the courtyard was filled with fountains and pools, the jets of water from them making intricate patterns suddenly broken by an unexpected powerful surge that sent one of the jets soaring into the air, much to the delight of a group of watching children who screamed and clapped their hands in excitement.

Smiling indulgently, Petra made her own way towards the restaurant.

Given her previous evening's experience, with the 'Parisian' Michelin-starred restaurant, she supposed she should have expected that the Italian trattoria would be equally authentic, and it certainly was—right down to the strolling musician and the appreciative genuinely Italian waiters, who ushered her to a table and handed her a menu.

Half an hour later, when Petra had just started to relax and feel comfortable as she sipped her wine and enjoyed the seafood starter she had ordered, the restaurant door opened and a group of brashly noisy young men burst in.

Petra could tell from the reactions of the restaurant staff that they were not entirely at ease with the loud-voiced demands of the new arrivals. To Petra, familiar with the behaviour of a certain type of European male, it was obvious that the men had been drinking. Their attitude towards the staff was bordering on the aggressive, and although none of them looked particularly intimidating they were in a pack, and like all pack animals they possessed a certain aura of volatility and danger.

They were speaking in English, demanding that they were given a table large enough to accommodate them all and refusing to listen when the *maître d'* tried to tell them that the restaurant was fully booked.

'Don't give us that, mate,' one of them objected. 'We can see for ourselves that you've got plenty of empty tables.'

Discreetly Petra affected not to notice what was going on when the waiter removed her empty plate and returned with her main course. But as she thanked him for her meal, she suddenly heard one of the men saying, 'Hey, look at that over there—the brunette sitting on her own. We'll have that table there, mate,' he continued, pointing to the empty one next to where Petra was seated.

She tensed warily. She could tell that the *maître d* was trying to persuade them to leave, but it was obvious that they had no intention of doing so. She tried not to betray her discomfort as they surged round her, sitting at three of the tables close to her own so that she was almost surrounded by them.

They were ordering more drinks whilst making crudely off-colour comments about their sexual proclivities and deliberately staring at her, trying to force her to return their eye contact.

Petra wasn't exactly frightened. She lived in London, after all, and considered herself to be relatively streetwise. But in London she would never have been eating on her own, or been in a situation which would have made her so vulnerable.

She was uncomfortably aware of the diners at the two other tables, young couples with children, getting up and leaving, whilst the raucous behaviour of the men around her became even more unpleasant.

Although she hadn't finished her meal, Petra recognised that it was impossible for her to stay. The newcomers were making no attempt to order a meal and instead were becoming even more disorderly. A bread roll flew past her head, quickly followed by another as two men on tables either side of her began to hurl them at one another.

'First to get one down her dress gets a free round!' one of the men sang out.

Petra had had enough.

As calmly as she could she stood up, but to her horror, instead of allowing her to walk past them, the men immediately surrounded her, making openly sexually suggestive comments both to her and about her to one another that made Petra's throat and face burn with disgust and anger.

She could see that the restaurant manager was on the telephone, and the *maître d'* was doing his best to assist her, begging the men to step back otherwise he would have to ask them to leave.

'Going to pick one of us, are you, sweetheart?' the most obnoxious of the gang smirked at Petra. 'Or shall we choose for you? Which one is going to be first, lads?' he demanded, turning to his friends.

The *maître d'* intervened, protesting, 'Please, gentlemen, I must ask you to leave—'

'We aren't going anywhere, mate,' Petra's tormentor told him drunkenly.

'Oh, but I think you are…'

The coolly incisive sound of Blaize's voice cut through

the loud-mouthed vulgarities like tempered steel slicing into flaccid flesh, his appearance shocking Petra even more than it obviously did the gang.

Instinctively she turned towards him, her expression betraying both her disbelief and her fear.

'In fact, I think I can safely say that not only are you going to leave the restaurant, you are going to leave the country as well.'

One of the gang started to laugh.

'Come off it, mate. You can't make us do anything! There's only one of you and a dozen or us, and besides...we're here for the races, see.'

'The restaurant manager has already summoned the police,' Blaize informed them coolly. 'There is a law in this country against men harassing women, and in Zuran laws are reinforced.'

Petra could hear sounds of new arrivals outside the restaurant, and it was obvious so could the gang.

Suddenly they began to look a lot less sure of themselves. Blaize was holding out his hand to her. Shakily Petra pushed her way past the men and went to his side, just as the restaurant door opened and several stern-looking uniformed police officers came in.

'Come on,' Blaize instructed Petra, taking hold of her arm. 'Let's get out of here...'

Petra was only too glad to do so. And only too glad of the protection of his firm grasp on her arm as he ushered her back to her hotel.

She could see the grim look on his face, and the way that his mouth had compressed, somehow making him look very austere and stern.

Once they were inside the hotel, Petra thought she saw him give a small curt nod in the direction of the guest relations desk and the clerk seated there, but as he bustled her towards the lift she decided that she must have imagined it.

As the lift moved upward, Petra expelled a small shaky sigh of relief.

'You don't know how pleased I was to see you—' she began, but Blaize stopped her, his expression forbiddingly grim.

'What the hell where you doing?' he demanded furiously. 'Why didn't you leave? Surely you must have realised…'

The unexpected harshness of his attack coupled with its unfairness shocked her into silence.

The lift stopped and they both got out. Her legs, Petra discovered, were trembling and she felt slightly sick.

Outside her suite, she tried to open her bag to find her key card, but her fingers were shaking so much she dropped it. As she bent down to retrieve it Blaize beat her to it, picking up her bag and opening it. Absently Petra noticed how tiny it looked in his hands. He had well-groomed nails, immaculately clean, and his fingers were long and lean. The fleshy pad just below his thumb mesmerised her, and she couldn't stop staring at it.

Distantly a part of her recognised that she was probably in shock, but that knowledge was too far away and vague for her to really comprehend it. Instead she simply accepted it gratefully as a rational explanation for the tremors that were now beginning to visibly shake her body, and the tight, aching pain that was locking her throat and preventing her from defending herself.

'Do you realise what could have happened if the manager hadn't…?'

'I tried to leave,' Petra told him, suddenly managing to speak. 'But they wouldn't let me.'

They were in the suite and the door was closed. Her

shock suddenly accelerated out of the distance and rico-
cheted towards her. Tears flooded her eyes and her body
shook violently.

'Petra!'

Now the anger she could hear in Blaize's voice sounded
different.

'Petra!'

As he repeated her name he made a sound, somewhere
between a groan and a growl and then suddenly he was
holding her in his arms.

Valiantly Petra forced back her tears. She could feel
Blaize's hand stroking her hair. Tilting back her head, she
looked up at him, and kept on looking, drowning in the
molten mercury glow of his eyes as her lips parted and her
head fell aback against his supporting arm.

'Petra...'

As he lowered his head she could feel the warmth of his
breath tantalising the quivering readiness of her lips. She
had wanted this...him...from the moment she had walked
into her room the previous day and seen him lying on her
bed, she acknowledged dizzily, as she breathed in and felt
the hard pressure of his mouth against her own.

Passion! It was just a word! How could it possibly convey all that she was feeling, all she was experiencing—
every nuance of sensation and emotion that burned and
ached through her as his mouth moved over her own, taking
her deeper and deeper into a world of dark velvet forbidden
pleasure?

There was nothing to warn her when the protective inner
barriers she had erected against him came tumbling down—
no flash of insight, no mental alarm call, no frantic conscience voice. Nothing to impede the delirious intoxication
of her senses running wild, her body clamouring for the
freedom to express its longings!

She could feel his lips moving against her mouth and then her ear as he spoke to her warningly. 'You're in shock, Petra, and this isn't—'

Frantically Petra blotted out what he was trying to say, closing her ears to it and then closing his mouth as she placed her hand against his jaw, moved her mouth back to his, her lips eagerly showing him what she wanted.

She felt him stiffen, heard his indrawn breath and held her own, suddenly sharply aware of his hesitation. But as she leaned against him, her body still trembling, but no longer out of any fear other than that he might leave her, she looked into his eyes and saw the fierce, predatory look of male hunger glittering there, and felt a sweetly powerful sense of female triumph.

She kissed him slowly, and then waited, whilst her glance slid longingly from his eyes to his mouth. Like someone in a dream she reached up and traced its shape with the tip of her finger, and caught her own bottom lip between her teeth as she felt—and saw—the shudder that rocked him.

'This isn't a good idea.' She heard him groan as he lifted her hand from his mouth and pressed a fiercely sensual kiss in its palm. Now his glance was on her face—and not just her face, she recognised as her heart gave a series of heavy, excited thuds when it dropped to her body.

'Why not?' she whispered dangerously back to him.

'Because,' he told her thickly, 'if I touch you now…here…like this…'

Petra quivered violently as his hand barely brushed against her breast and then returned to cup it gently, whilst even more tantalisingly his thumb rubbed slowly across her taut nipple.

'Then,' Blaize was continuing huskily, 'I shall need to touch you again and again, and then I will have to…'

Her flesh was melting like ice cream covered in the sensuality and irresistibility of pure hot chocolate, Petra decided, and what Blaize was doing to her was making her long to have his hands...his body against her own body. Her naked body...

The small sound of longing she made was smothered by the heat of his kiss. The sound of their mutually charged breathing filled the room, and then, disconcertingly, Petra heard the mood-destroying clatter of the fax machine. Automatically she tensed, just as Blaize released her and then stepped back from her.

'That should not have happened,' she heard him saying tersely as he turned his back to her. 'It isn't part of our deal.'

Not part of their deal! Chagrin, discomfort, shame and angry humiliation—Petra felt them all in an icy shock wave that brought her back to reality.

Stiffly she headed for the fax machine, more to give herself something to do than because she was anxious to read its message. When she eventually managed to get her gaze to bring it into focus properly, through the turbulence of her thoughts, it turned out to be merely a flyer from a local tour company, highlighting one of their special offers.

As she focused on the wavering print, willing herself not to turn round and look at Blaize, she heard the door to her suite quietly open and then close again.

Even though she continued to focus on her fax message Petra knew just from the feel of the air around her that Blaize had left.

Some time...one day, maybe...she would be glad that this had happened, she told herself fiercely. She would be glad that they had been interrupted and that he had left her! One day. But not now!

CHAPTER FIVE

MISERABLY Petra pushed her uneaten breakfast away and focused determinedly on the brilliantly sunlit scene beyond the windows of the hotel's breakfast room.

She had decided to eat here this morning rather than on her own in her room, primarily because she had hoped that the busyness of having other people around her would take her mind off the events of the previous evening—and Blaize.

Blaize! Every time she thought about him—which was far, far too often for her own peace of mind, she was swamped by opposing feelings of longing and angry self-contempt, plus a sense of bewilderment and disbelief that she could have ever got herself in such a situation. How could she possibly want him?

Petra frowned as she glanced from the informal breakfast dining area into the hotel foyer, which this morning seemed to be filled with far more uniformed and slightly on edge-looking members of staff than she could remember seeing there before.

The waiter had come to clear away her virtually untouched breakfast, and to spend time before going to meet her aunt Petra walked over to study the board outside a small private office, advertising the trips organised by the hotel. One in particular caught her eye, and she read the details of it a second and then a third time.

An escorted drive into the desert, plus an overnight stay at an exclusive oasis resort where it was possible to experience the wonder and majesty of the desert at first hand!

The desert... Quickly, before she could change her mind, Petra went into the office, emerging ten minutes later having made herself a booking. A full night away from Blaize should surely give her time to assess the damage her physical reaction to him was having on her moral beliefs and get herself back in balance again—give her some 'time out'.

As she walked towards the foyer a subtle voice whispered inside her head that there was an even more reckless and dangerous way of stopping a conflagration in its tracks: namely fighting fire with fire. But by using what? Her own sexual need to destroy itself? As in not just giving in to it but actively encouraging it, fanning it into an inferno that would turn and destroy itself?

There was just enough time for her to go to her suite and tidy up before meeting her aunt. Petra smiled at the nervous-looking group of uniformed staff hovering close to the private lift that went to the penthouse suite.

'Everyone looks very busy today,' she commented.

One of the uniformed men rolled his eyes and explained in a semi-hushed whisper. 'There is a meeting upstairs of the hotel owners.'

The hotel owners. Petra's heart did a nervous little shimmy. Did that mean that Rashid had returned? And if he had how long would it be before he sought her out?

'Mmm...it smells heavenly,' Petra acknowledged with a smile as she sniffed the golden nugget of frankincense her aunt was holding out to her. They were in the spice market, where her aunt had haggled determinedly and very professionally for some spices before picking up the frankincense and offering it to Petra to smell. A little wonderingly now, Petra studied the nugget in her hand.

There was something really awesome about standing

here in the new millennium handling something which had been familiar to people from civilisations so ancient it was barely possible to comprehend the time that separated them. There was something about this land that did that to a person, Petra recognised as she handed the nugget back to the robed vendor, nodding her head in agreement as her aunt suggested a cooling glass of pressed fruit juice.

'I have some good news for you.'

Petra saw that her aunt was beaming, as she handed Petra her drink.

'Your grandfather is feeling much better and he has asked me to invite you to visit him this afternoon.'

Petra almost spilled her drink. Was it merely a coincidence that her grandfather should invite her to visit him at the same time as Sheikh Rashid had returned to Zuran? Her body stiffened defensively.

'I'm sorry, but I'm afraid that won't be possible. I…I have other plans.' Petra was proud of the way she managed to keep her voice so calm and cool, even though she was unable to either meet her aunt's eyes or prevent herself from turning her glass round and round in her hands.

She could sense from the quality of silence that her response was not the one her aunt had been expecting, and immediately she felt guilty and uncomfortable. The last thing she wanted to do was upset or offend her aunt, who had been unstintingly kind to her—but she knew just what her grandfather's real plans for her were, Petra firmly reminded herself.

Her aunt was smiling, but Petra could see that her smile was a little strained.

'Your grandfather will be disappointed, Petra,' her aunt told her quietly. 'He has been looking forward to meeting you, but of course if you are busy…'

'I…I have arranged to take a trip into the desert tomorrow,' Petra heard herself explaining, almost defensively, 'and there are things I need to do beforehand...'

A little gravely her aunt inclined her head in acknowledgement of Petra's explanation.

Her aunt insisted on accompanying Petra back to her hotel, but once there refused Petra's suggestion of a cup of coffee.

Her aunt was on the verge of stepping into the taxi the concierge had summoned for her when, on some instinct she couldn't begin to understand, Petra suddenly hurried after her, telling her huskily, 'I've changed my mind. I...I will come and see my grandfather...'

Petra sank her teeth into her bottom lip, mortified by her own weakness as her aunt beamed her approval and gave her a warm hug.

'I know this cannot be easy for you, Petra, but I promise you your grandfather is not an ogre. He has your best interests at heart.'

A tiny little trickle of warning ran down Petra's spine as she absorbed her aunt's unwittingly ominous words. But it was too late for her to recall her change of mind now.

'Your grandfather rests after lunch, but I shall arrange for a car to collect you and bring you to the villa to see him. The driver will pick you up here at four thirty, if that is convenient?'

There was nothing Petra could do other than nod her head.

She had been half expecting that Blaize would try to make contact with her—after all she had as yet still not paid him anything for his services—but there were no messages waiting for her, and no Blaize either!

Petra tried to tell herself that the lurching sensation inside her chest was simply because she was anxious to discuss the day's developments with him—on a purely business basis, of course—and to determine what course of action should follow. It was only natural, surely, that she should feel both anxiety and a sense of urgency now that Sheikh Rashid had returned. And as for last night—well, what was a kiss, after all? If she had blown both it and her reaction to it a little out of proportion, only she knew it! She wasn't so naïve as to deceive herself that kissing her had meant anything special to Blaize.

So why hadn't he been in touch with her? And why hadn't she insisted on him furnishing her with a means of getting in touch with him?

It was gone two o'clock, but despite the fact that she had not been able to eat her breakfast she did not feel hungry. Her stomach was churning in apprehensive anticipation of her coming meeting with her grandfather, and her tension was turned up an unpleasant few notches by the added anxiety of Rashid's return and the lack of contact from Blaize.

It was time for her to get changed, ready for her meeting with her grandfather. Petra hesitated as she surveyed the contents of her wardrobe. The linen dress and jacket would be a good choice, modest but smart, or perhaps the cool chambray...or... Her hand trembled slightly as she removed a plain dark trouser suit from the cupboard. Simply cut in, a matt black fabric it was an outfit that would always be very special to her. It was the suit her mother had bought her just weeks before her death—a good luck present to Petra for her pre-university interviews.

Instead of wearing it for her interviews, Petra had actually worn it for her parents' funeral. But whenever she touched the soft fabric it wasn't that bleak, shocking day she remembered, but the teasing love in her mother's eyes as she had marched her into the boutique and told her that she was going to buy her a present—the happiness and pride in her smile as she'd insisted that Petra parade in front of her in virtually every suit in the shop before she had finally decreed that this particular one was the right one.

This suit held her very last physical memory of her mother's touch and her mother's love, and sometimes Petra would almost swear she could even smell her mother's scent on it—not the rich Eastern perfume that had always been so much a part of her, but *her* scent, her essence.

Sharp tears pricked Petra's eyes. Her mother might not be here with her now, but in wearing this suit Petra somehow felt that she was taking a part of her at least with her— that they were both together, confronting the man who had caused her so much pain.

The suit still fitted, and in fact if anything was perhaps slightly loose on her, Petra acknowledged as she studied her reflection in the mirror.

It was almost half past four. Time to go down to the foyer.

Her business-like appearance attracted several discreet looks as she made her way to the exit. Once again a red carpet was very much in evidence, leading to where several huge shiny black limousines were waiting, flags flying.

Petra studied them with discreet curiosity as she waited for her own transport to arrive, but her interest in the limousines and their potential occupants was forgotten as a sleek saloon car pulled up in front of her and her cousin Saud got out of the front passenger seat, grinning from ear to ear as he hurried towards her.

As she hugged him, Petra was vaguely aware of a sudden stir amongst the limousine chauffeurs, and the emergence of a group of immaculately robed men from the private entrance. But it was Saud who stopped to gaze at the group, grabbing hold of her arm as he told her in an excited voice, 'There's Rashid—with his great-uncle.'

'What? Where?' Her heartbeat had gone into overdrive, but as Petra craned her neck to look in the direction Saud was pointing the last of the robed men was already getting into the waiting limousine.

'Have you met him yet?' Saud demanded as the cars pulled away 'He's cool, isn't he…?'

Petra suppressed her grim look. It was becoming plain to her that her young cousin hero-worshipped her proposed suitor.

'No, I haven't,' she answered him, getting into the waiting car. But as they drove away from the hotel a sudden thought struck her. 'So, was Rashid wearing robes?'

'Yes that's right,' Saud confirmed.

'Despite his Western upbringing?'

Saud looked baffled. 'Yes,' he agreed, then smiled. 'Oh, I see! Rashid's father and his uncle—who is a member of our Royal Family—were very, very close. Rashid's great-uncle has acted as a…a sponsor to Rashid since his parents' death—they were killed when their plane crashed in the desert. I do not remember, since I was not even born then and Rashid himself was only young, but I have heard my father and my grandfather talk of it. Rashid was away in England at the time, at school, but his great-uncle welcomed him into his own family as though Rashid were his son. It is a great honour to our family that his great-uncle favours Rashid's marriage to you. It is just as well that you are a modest woman though, cousin, because Rashid does not approve of the behaviour of some of the tourists who come here to Zuran,' Saud told her.

'Oh, doesn't he?' She demanded with dangerous softness. 'And what about his own behaviour? Is that—'

'Rashid is a very moral man—everyone who knows him knows that. He has very strong values. Zara, my friend and second cousin, says that she feels embarrassed for her own sex when she sees the way that women pursue him. He is very rich, you know, and when they come to the hotel complex and see him they try to attract his attention. But he is not interested in them. Zara says that this is because...' He paused with a self-conscious look in Petra's direction, but she was too infuriated by his naïve revelations to pay much attention.

'Rashid is a very proud man and he would never permit himself or anyone connected with him to do anything to damage the name of his family,' Saud continued solemnly.

At any other time Saud's youthful fervour and seriousness would have brought an amused and tender smile to Petra's lips, but right now his innocent declaration had really got her back up and reinforced her fast-growing animosity to this as yet unmet man, who had patronisingly deigned to consider her as a potential wife.

Well, he was going to discover in no uncertain terms, and hopefully very soon, that she was exactly the type of woman he most despised!

In fact, Petra reflected grimly, the more she heard about Sheikh Rashid the more she knew that there was no way she could ever want to marry him!

They had reached the family villa now, and Petra held her breath a little as they drove through the almost fortress-like entrance into the courtyard that lay beyond it.

Her grandfather insisted on remaining in what had been the family's original home when Zuran had been a trading port and the family rich merchants—although, as her aunt had explained to her, in recent years Petra's uncle had persuaded him to add a large modern extension to the villa. In this older part, though, traditional wind towers still decorated the roofline.

The family no longer adopted the traditional custom of separate living quarters for women, as Petra's mother had told her had been the case when she was a girl, but her aunt quickly explained to Petra, once she had been ushered inside to a cool, elegantly furnished salon, that her grandfather still preferred to keep his own private quarters.

'Kahrun, his manservant, will take you to him,' her aunt informed her. 'He has been very ill, Petra,' she continued hesitantly, 'and I would ask that you…make allowances for…for his ways, even though they are not your own. He loved your mother very much, and her death…' She paused and shook her head whilst Petra forced herself to bite back on her instinctive fierce need to question what her aunt was saying.

A maid arrived with a welcome drink of strong fragrant coffee. Her mother had never lost her love of the drink, and just to smell it reminded Petra so much of her.

Several minutes later, when Petra had refused a second cup, a soft-footed servant arrived and bowed to her, before indicating that she was to follow him.

Her heart thudding but her head held high, Petra did so. They seemed to traverse a maze of corridors before he finally paused outside a heavily carved pair of wooden doors.

The room beyond them was cool and shadowy, its narrow windows overlooking an enclosed garden from which Petra could hear the sound of water so beloved by desert people. The air inside the room smelled of spices—the frankincense she had breathed in this morning, and sandalwood, bringing back to her vivid memories of the small box in which her mother had kept her most precious memories of her lost home and family.

As her emotions momentarily blurred her vision it was impossible for Petra to fully make out the features of the man reclining on the divan several feet away from her.

She could hear him, though, as he commanded, 'Come closer to me so that I may see you. My doctor has forbidden me to overtire myself and so I must lie on this wretched divan on pain of incurring his displeasure.'

Petra heard the small snort of derisive laughter that accompanied the complaint as she blinked away her emotional reaction.

Her mother had described her father in terms that had conjured up for Petra a mental vision of a man who was cruelly strong and stubborn—a man who had overwhelmed and overpowered her mother emotionally—and now that her vision was clearing she had expected to see all those things reflected in him now. But the man in front of her looked unexpectedly frail. One long-fingered hand lay on top of the richly embroidered coverlet, and Petra could see in his profile the pride her mother had described to her so often. But in the dark eyes whose scrutiny seemed to search her face with avid hunger she could see nothing of the rejection and anger that had hurt her mother so badly.

'I don't look very much like my mother,' Petra told him coolly.

'You do not need to look like her. You are of her, and that is enough. Child of my child! Blood of my blood! I have waited a very long time for you to come here to me, Petra. Sometimes I have feared that you would not come in time, and that I would never know you with my outer senses. Although I have always known you with my heart. You are wrong,' he added abruptly, his voice suddenly stronger. 'You are very like my Mija. She was the child of my heart—my youngest child. Her mother was my third wife.'

Angrily Petra looked away.

'You do not approve. No, do not deny it—I can see it in your eyes. How they flash and burn with your emotions! In that too you are like your mother.'

Petra couldn't trust herself to speak.

It had shocked her, though, to realise how frail he looked. She had known that he would be old—he had been in his forties when her mother had been born—but somehow she had convinced herself that he would still be the strong, fierce man her mother had remembered from her own childhood. Not this obviously elderly white-bearded person whose dark eyes seemed to hold a mixture of compassion and understanding that unsettled her.

Somehow the curt words she had intended to speak to him, the demands she had planned to make to know just why he had wanted to see her, the cynicism and contempt she had planned to let him see, refused to be summoned.

Instead…instead…

As she lifted her hand the gold bangle caught the light. Immediately her grandfather stiffened.

'You are wearing Mija's bracelet,' he whispered. 'It was my last gift to her… I have a photograph of her here, wearing it.'

To Petra's astonishment he reached out and picked up a heavy photograph album which Petra hadn't previously noticed, beckoning her to come closer so that she could see what he wanted to show her.

As his frail fingers lifted the pages Petra felt her heart turn over. Every photograph in the book was of her mother, and some of them…

She could feel her eyes starting to burn with tears as she recognised one of them. It was a photograph of herself as a very new baby with her mother. Her father had had exactly the same picture on his desk, in the room which had been his office when he'd worked at home!

Immediately she put out her hand to stop him from turning any more of the pages, unable to stop herself from demanding in a shaky voice, 'That photograph—how…?'

'Your father sent it to me,' he told her. 'He sent me many photographs of you, Petra, and many letters, too.'

'My father!' This was news to Petra, and it took her several minutes to absorb it properly. It was hard enough to accept that her father could have done such a thing, but what was even harder was knowing that he had kept his actions a secret from her. And from her mother? Petra felt cold. Surely not? What could have motivated him when he had known how badly her mother had been hurt by her father's actions?

As her glance met that of her grandfather Petra knew that he could see what she was thinking.

A little awkwardly he beckoned her to move closer to him. When she hesitated, he told her, 'There is a box, over there. I would like you to bring it to me.'

The box in question was sitting on an intricately carved table, its surface smooth and warm to Petra's touch. She could tell just by looking at it that it was very old.

'This belonged to my own grandfather,' her grandfather said as she took it to him.

'He was a merchant and this box went everywhere with him. He said that it had originally been made for one of the sultans of the great Ottoman Empire.' He gave a small smile. 'He was a great story-teller, and many times as a small child I would neglect my lessons to sit at his feet and listen to his tales. Whether they were true or not!'

As he was speaking he was reaching for a heavy bunch of keys, searching through them until he found the one he was looking for.

His fingers, obviously stiffened by old age, struggled to insert the key in the tiny lock and then turn it, but once he had done so and pushed back the lid Petra was aware of the mingled scents of sandalwood and age that rose from its interior.

She couldn't see what was inside the box, but waited patiently as her grandfather sighed and muttered to himself, obviously sifting through its contents until he had finally found what he wanted.

'Read this,' he commanded her brusquely, handing her a worn airmail envelope.

'It is your father's letter to me, telling me of your birth.'

Hesitantly Petra took the envelope from him. She wasn't sure she was ready to read what her father might have written. All her life she had looked up to him as a man of strong sturdy morals and infinite compassion, a man of the highest probity and honour. If she should read something that damaged that belief...

'Read,' her grandfather was urging her impatiently.

Taking a deep breath, Petra did so.

The letter was addressed to her grandfather with true diplomatic formality, using his titles.

'To he who is the father of my beloved wife Mija,

I have the felicitation of informing you that I am now the proud father of the most beautiful baby daughter. I had thought when Mija came into my life that there could be no place in it to love another human being, so great and all-encompassing is my love for her, but I was wrong. I write to you now as one father to another to tell you of the most wonderful, precious gift we have received in Petra's birth, and to tell you also that we now share common ground—we are both fathers—we have both been granted the unique privilege of being gifted with daughters.

And it is as a father that I write to you begging you to reconsider your decision regarding the exclusion of Mija from your family—for your own sake and not ours. I have made a solemn vow that I shall surround Mija

with all the love she will ever need. We have each other
and our beautiful daughter and our lives will be filled
with love and joy. But what of you? You have turned
away your own daughter and denied yourself her love
and that of the grandchild she has given you.

I beg you to think of this and to put aside your pride.
I know how much it would mean to Mija to have word
from you, especially at this time.

Whatever your decision, I have made a vow to my
daughter that I shall ensure that you, her grandfather, and
the rest of the family are kept informed of her life.

The letter bore her father's formal signature at its end,
but Petra could barely focus on it as the paper trembled in
her hand and her eyes stung with tears. It shamed her that
she could have doubted her father for so much as a single
heartbeat.

As he took the letter from her, returning it to its envelope
and replacing it carefully in the box before relocking it, her
grandfather said gruffly, 'Your father was a good man, even
though he was not the man I would have chosen for my
Mija.'

'My father was a wonderful, wonderful, very special
man,' Petra corrected him proudly.

Had her mother known what her father had done? If so
she had never spoken of it to her, but then neither had her
father! Suddenly, despite her private knowledge of her
grandfather's secret purpose in wanting her here in Zuran,
she was glad that she had come!

'He understood my feelings as a father,' her grandfather
acknowledged.

Petra had to close her eyes to conceal the intensity of
the emotions that rushed over her.

'You say that now! You claim to have loved my mother.

But you never made any attempt to contact her—to...'
Petra refused to say the word 'forgive', because so far as
she was concerned her mother was the one who had the
right to extend that largesse, not her grandfather! 'You must
have known how much it would have meant to her to hear
from you!'

Impossible for her to hold back her feelings—or her
pain—any longer. Petra knew that her grandfather must be
able to hear it in her voice just as she could herself.

'When she left you told her that you would never permit
her name to be spoken in your hearing ever again. You said
that she was dead to you and to her family, and you forbade
them to have anything to do with her. You let her die—'

Petra heard herself sobbing like a lost child. 'You let her
die believing that you had stopped loving her! How could
you do that?'

As Petra fought for self-control she could see the pain
shadowing her grandfather's eyes, and suddenly it seemed
as though he shrunk a little, and looked even older and
more fragile than he had done when she had first walked
into the room.

'There is nothing I can say that will ease your pain. No
words I can offer you will lighten either your burden—or
my own,' she heard him saying sombrely. 'It is still too
soon. Perhaps in time... But at my age time is no longer
either a friend or an ally. I am sorry that we have not been
able to make you properly welcome here in your mother's
home, Petra, but now that that old fool my doctor has
ceased his unnecessary fussing I shall give instructions that
a room is to be prepared for you. We have much to discuss
together, you and I.'

Like his desire to see her married to the man of his
choice? Petra wondered suspiciously, abruptly back on her
guard; he might look frail and sorrowful now, but she

couldn't forget the cunning and deceit which history had already proved him capable of.

And once she was living here beneath his roof she would virtually be a prisoner. With no passport she had no means of leaving the country! Which meant it was imperative that she persisted with her plan to have Rashid refuse to consider her as a wife.

Even if that meant seeing Blaize again and the risk that could entail?

Unable to give herself a truly rational answer, Petra diverted her own thoughts by telling her grandfather, in a cool voice she intended would make him fully aware of her determination to retain her independence, 'I have made arrangements for an overnight trip into the desert tomorrow, so—'

'The desert!' To her surprise, his eyes lit up with pleasure and approval. 'It is good that you wish to see the land that is so much a part of your heritage. I wish that it was possible for me to go with you! But you shall tell me all about it! I shall inform your hotel that Kahrun will be collecting you to bring you here once you return.'

He was beginning to look tired, but instinctively Petra sensed that his pride would not allow him to admit any weakness. Whatever else she had been lied to about, Petra could see now that so far as his health was concerned he had genuinely been ill. It was there in the greyish tinge to his skin, the vulnerability of his frail frame. An unexpected—and unwanted—emotion filled her: a sense of kinship and closeness, an awareness of the blood tie they shared that she simply had not been prepared for and which it seemed she had no weapons to fight against. He was her grandfather, the man who had given life to the mother she had loved so much, a potential bridge via which she could recapture and relive some of her most precious memories.

Swallowing against the lump in her throat, Petra got up, and as her grandfather reached out his hands to her, Petra placed hers in them.

'Beloved child of my beloved child,' he whispered brokenly to her, and then the door opened and Kahrun, his manservant, arrived to escort her back to the hotel.

It was only when she was finally being driven back to her hotel by Kahrun that Petra mentally questioned just why she had not challenged her grandfather with her knowledge of his plans for her. Had the emotions he had displayed been genuine and as overwhelming as they had seemed? Or had he simply been manipulating the situation and her for his own ends? Surely she wasn't foolish enough to be influenced by her own unwilling acknowledgement of his frailty, a long-ago letter from her father, and a few emotional words?

But there was more to the situation than that! A lot more! In his presence, in the home which had once been her mother's, Petra had abruptly been forced to recognise and acknowledge a deep subterranean pool of previously hidden emotions.

Her parents' deaths had forced her to grow up very quickly, to become mature whilst she was still very young, and in many ways had forced her to become her own parent. Her godfather, kind though he was, was a bachelor, a man dedicated to his career, who had had no real idea of the emotional needs of a seventeen-year-old girl. Had she been a different person, Petra knew, she might quite easily have gone off the rails. Her godfather's lifestyle meant that she had been allowed a considerable amount of unsupervised freedom, and she had been called upon to make decisions about her life and her future that should more properly have been made by someone far more adult. The result of this had been that she'd had to 'police' her own behaviour, and to take responsibility for herself, emotionally and morally.

Now, today, in her grandfather's room, she had suddenly realised just what a heavy burden those responsibilities had been, and how much she had yearned to have someone of her own to carry them for her—to counsel and guide her, to protect her, to love her! How much, in fact, she had needed the family which had been denied to her! And how much a small, weak part of her still did...

That was where her real danger lay, she recognised. It lay in her wanting the approval and acceptance of her 'family' so much that she could fall into the trap of allowing herself to exchange her freedom and independence for them!

The weight of her own thoughts was beginning to make her head ache.

CHAPTER SIX

GRIMLY Petra blinked the slight grittiness from her eyes as she studied her reflection in her bedroom mirror. She had barely slept, and when she had she had been tormented by confusing dark-edged dreams in which she was being pursued by a white-robed persecutor, his features hidden from her. In her nightmare she had called out to Blaize to rescue her, but although she could see him he had not been paying any heed to her pleas, had instead been engrossed with the scantily clad bevy of women surrounding him.

Only once had he actually turned to look at her, and then he had shaken his head and told her cruelly, 'Go away, little virgin. I do not want you.'

And now, even though the night was over, Petra felt as though its dark shadow still hung over her. There was hardly any time left for her to convince Rashid that she was not a suitable bride, and once again Blaize had made no attempt to get in touch with her.

Lethargically she moved away from the mirror. She had already packed an overnight bag, as instructed by the fax she had received from the tour operator, and she was dressed in what she hoped would be a suitable outfit of short-sleeved tee shirt and a pair of khaki combat-style pants with sturdy and hopefully sand-proof trainers. She had, as instructed, a long-sleeved top to cover her arms from the heat and the sand, a hat, a pair of sunglasses and a large bottle of water. But the sense of adventure and intrigue with which she had originally booked the trip had gone, leaving in its place a lacklustre feeling of emptiness.

Because she hadn't heard from Blaize? A man she had known less than a week? A man who quite patently cynically used his sexuality to fund a lifestyle that was in direct opposition to everything that Petra herself believed in! She couldn't possibly really be trying to tell herself that she was emotionally attracted to him? That in such a short space of time he had become so necessary to her that a mere twenty-four hours without him had left her feeling that her whole life was empty and worthless?

Now she was afraid, Petra admitted shakily, and with good reason! What she was thinking truly was cause for the horrified chills running down her spine! There was no way she could allow herself to be in love with Blaize.

Be in love? Since when had love entered the equation? she tried to mock herself.

Only two days ago she had been finding it hard to admit that she just might find him sexually attractive. Two days before that she had barely known that he existed. Yet here she was, trying to talk herself into believing she loved him! No, not trying to talk herself into it, trying to talk herself *out* of it, Petra corrected herself swiftly.

Her telephone rang. Quickly she picked up the receiver. It was the front desk informing her that her transport had arrived.

Picking up her overnight bag, Petra told herself sternly that a little breathing space would do her good. What a pity she was living in the modern century, though, and not a previous one where it might have been possible for a traveller attached to a camel train to pass through a country's borders without the necessity of producing a passport...

A group of newly arrived holidaymakers were filling the foyer, and the concierge staff had no time to do anything more than point Petra in the direction of the waiting vehicle she could see outside, a logo painted on its side.

Even with her sunglasses the sunlight was so strong that she was momentarily blinded as she headed for the four-wheel drive vehicle, and it was whilst she was still trying to accustom her eyes to the brilliance that she felt strong hands relieve her of her overnight bag, and then grasp her waist to help her into the front passenger seat of the vehicle.

She heard the slam of the passenger door, and then the closing rear door. As her driver climbed into the driving seat she turned her head to look at him, her eyes widening in shock as she realised just who her driver was!

'Blaize!' she exclaimed weakly. 'What are you doing here?'

Petra tried to drag her gaze away from him as she gulped in air. Her chest had gone so tight it hurt, and she could feel the heat surging through her body as it reacted with telltale swiftness to his presence.

'You booked a trip into the desert,' he told her laconically as he set the vehicle in motion and drove off.

'Yes... But...'

'But what?' he challenged her with an almost bored shrug. 'I thought it made more sense for me to take you. The desert can be a very seductive place, so I've been told, and your intended isn't going to like knowing that his bride-to-be has spent the night in the desert with another man. How did you get on with your grandfather? Is all forgiven?' he asked her flippantly.

'My mother is the one who is owed forgiveness,' Petra told him quietly. 'And she died believing that he had stopped loving her.'

There was a small silence before Blaize responded in a voice that sounded unfamiliarly serious.

'Then I imagine that your grandfather will find it extremely difficult to forgive himself.'

'His feelings are of no concern to me!' Petra told Blaize

angrily, and then stopped speaking as an inner voice told her that she was not being entirely truthful. 'I thought that he was pretending to be ill,' she heard herself telling Blaize.

'And was he?' he asked.

'No,' Petra acknowledged. 'But that still does not mean he has the right to do what he is trying to do to me—use me for his own selfish ends.'

'Perhaps he thinks this marriage will be beneficial for you,' Blaize suggested. 'His generation still believe that a woman needs a protector, a husband, and it would keep you here, close to your mother's family, and provide for you financially.'

'What?' Petra stared at him in disbelief. 'How can you say that after what I have told you? My feelings...my needs...are the last thing he is thinking about.'

'You mean *you* believe they are! If you were to leave Zuran now, what would you do...where would you go?'

Petra glared at him. Why was he suddenly trying to play the devil's advocate? For amusement?

'I would go home...to the UK. I'm twenty-three, and although I have a good degree I would like to get my Master's. There's so much social inequality in the world that needs addressing—working in the field for the aid agency showed me that. I would like to do something to help other people.'

'As a rich man's wife you could do far more than as a mere fieldworker.'

'I've already told you—I could never marry a man I did not love and respect. And from what Saud has told me it sounds as though I would be expected to treat Rashid as though he's a minor god! Saud hero-worships him, and can't wait for me to marry him so that he can officially claim Rashid as a relative. And of course he isn't the only one! From the sound of it, my whole family are delirious with joy at the prospect of this marriage. All I seem to hear is ''Rashid this'' and ''Rashid that''...'

'Your cousin seems to be a positive wealth of information about the man.'

There was a certain dryness in Blaize's voice that made Petra frown a little. 'Saud is young and impressionable. Like I said, he obviously hero-worships Rashid, and thinks he can do no wrong.'

'A young person sometimes benefits from a role model and mentor.'

'Oh, I agree. But if a man who quite plainly divides women into two separate groups—good and bad, moral and immoral—whilst no doubt maintaining for himself the right to live exactly as he chooses, is not, in my opinion, a good role model—'

'If you look to your left now, you might just catch a glimpse of the royal horses being exercised,' Blaize interrupted her calmly.

Stopped in mid-tirade, Petra was tempted to continue with her diatribe—but then she saw the horses and their jockeys, and the sheer thrill of seeing so much power and beauty kept her silent as she inwardly paid homage to the spectacle they created.

'You are still totally opposed to this marriage, then, I take it?' Blaize asked her several minutes later.

'Of course. How could I not be? I can't marry a man I don't love.'

'You might find you could come to love him after the marriage.'

Petra gave him a scornful look.

'Never,' she denied vehemently. 'And anyway even if I did, I somehow doubt that the Sheikh is likely to return my feelings. No, all our marriage would mean to him would be the successful conclusion to a diplomatic arrangement.

I've got to make him change his mind and refuse to even countenance the idea.'

'Have you thought that he may feel the same way about this situation as you do yourself? Have you thought of contacting him and perhaps discussing things with him?'

Petra gave him a withering look.

'Unlike me, he has had the chance to refuse to become involved! After all, without his tacit acceptance the whole situation could simply not exist. Anyway, why are you suddenly so keen to promote him? Don't you want to earn five thousand pounds any more?' she demanded.

Or was it perhaps that he wanted her out of his life because he had sensed how she felt about him? A man like him would quite definitely not want the complications of having a woman fall in love with him!

Fall in love? But she hadn't done that, had she? Petra closed her eyes in helpless self-anger. Hadn't she got enough unwanted emotional pain to carry through life as excess baggage already, without deliberately inviting more?

'Hang on tight. We'll be leaving the highway soon and going into true desert terrain,' Blaize warned her, without taking his eyes off the road.

Petra gasped and clung to her seat as they veered off the road and crested the first of a series of sand dunes, following what to her was a barely discernible track—although Blaize did not seem to be having any trouble in finding and following it.

Within minutes it seemed to Petra the road had vanished and the landscape had become a vast expanse of sand dunes, stretching from horizon to horizon. A little anxiously she swivelled round in her seat, craning her neck to look in the direction they had just come.

'How...how do you know the way?' she asked Blaize a little uncertainly.

'I can tell the direction we are travelling by the position of the sun,' he said with a small dismissive shrug, and then added derisively, 'And besides, these all-terrain vehicles are equipped with navigation systems and a compass. Essential in this type of country. A bad sandstorm can not only reduce visibility to nought, it can also wipe out existing trails. See that over there?' he commanded, pointing in the direction of where a bird was hovering motionless, a mere dot in the hot blue emptiness of the sky.

'What is it?' Petra asked him.

'A hunting falcon,' he told her, reaching into the compartment between them. As he did so his fingertips inadvertently brushed against her knee and immediately her body reacted, pouring a lava hot molten tide of sharp longing through her. Petra could feel her whole body tightening in wanton hunger for him. If she turned to him now, covered his hand with her own, his mouth with her own; if she reached out and touched him as she wanted him to touch her… But it was too late. He had already moved away and was producing a pair of binoculars, which he offered to her. Binoculars! When what she wanted him to offer her was…was himself!

'Take a closer look,' he instructed her. 'It will probably be a trained bird. A number of Zuran's richest inhabitants maintain their own falconries, where birds are reared and trained. It's an ancient craft which is still practised here.'

As Petra watched the bird suddenly turned and wheeled and was quickly out of sight, as though responding to some unseen summons.

'They often have displays of falconry at the desert village where we'll be spending the night,' Blaize informed her. 'Most people find the birds too fearsome to approach, but in actual fact the camels are probably more dangerous.'

'So my mother told me,' Petra replied.

She was finding it a little disconcerting that Blaize, the beach bum, should so suddenly and unexpectedly prove to be so knowledgeable about the local culture and history. Not wanting to be outdone, she was quick to remind him that she was, after all, a part of that culture, even if this was the first time she was experiencing it firsthand.

There was quite definitely a stirring awesomeness about the desert, but Petra was finding it difficult to give her exclusive attention to her surroundings because of the effect that Blaize himself was having on her.

But that did not mean that she had fallen in love with him, she reassured herself fiercely. Just because her heart was beating with an unfamiliar speed, and she dared not look properly at him because when she did she wanted to keep on looking...and do much, much more than just merely look, she admitted breathlessly. But that did not mean...anything. In fact it meant nothing—nothing at all other than that she was physically aware of him.

Aware of him and responsive to him... And surely, if she was truly honest with herself, not just physically...

'You look flushed,' she heard Blaize telling her brusquely. 'You must make sure that you drink plenty of water. The desert is the last place to get dehydrated.'

Perhaps she ought to be glad that he believed her heightened colour was caused by the sun's heat rather than guessing that it was caused by the unwanted sensuality of her own desire for him, Petra reflected inwardly.

She had believed that her mother's reminiscences of her own childhood trips into the desert had prepared her for what she might expect, but Petra still found that she was holding her breath and then expelling it in a sharp sound of excitement as they crested yet another sand dune. There before them, shimmering beneath the sun's heat like a mirage, lay the oasis and the encampment which had been recreated to give tourists like herself a taste of what desert living had been all about in the days when Nomad tribes had still roamed the desert, travelling from one oasis to another.

Several other four-wheel drive vehicles were already parked close to one another and Blaize pulled up next to them.

'Wait here,' Blaize told her. 'I'll go and find out which tent has been assigned to us.'

To *them*? Petra's stomach muscles were quivering with the effort of controlling her emotions when Blaize returned several minutes later and she walked into what was more properly a pavilion than a mere tent, at the farthest edge of the encampment. She discovered that it was divided inside into three completely separate sections, which comprised a living room area, complete with rich, patterned oriental carpets and silk-covered divans, as well as two separated bedrooms. The shower block, Blaize informed her, was more mundanely housed on its own, and provided up-to-the-minute facilities.

Petra was only half listening to him. She had unfastened the doorway leading to one of the bedrooms and was staring in disbelieving delight at its interior.

Unlike her very modern bedroom at the hotel, this really was straight out of an Arabian Nights fantasy.

The interior 'walls' of the pavilion were hung with a rich mixture of embroidered silks in shimmering oriental colours, embellished with gold thread which caught the light from the lamps placed on low, heavily carved chests dotted around the surprisingly spacious room.

The bed itself, whilst only slightly raised off the rug-covered floor, like the walls was covered in beautiful silk throws, and from the ceiling there hung sheer muslin voiles, currently tied back, which Petra suspected would cover the whole bed when untied. The effect was one of unsurpassable opulence and sensuality, and Petra was half afraid to even blink, just in case she discovered that the entire room was merely a mirage.

'Something wrong?' she heard Blaize asking from behind her.

Immediately Petra shook her head.

'No. It's…it's wonderful…'

'Arabian Nights meets MGM,' Blaize pronounced briefly and almost sardonically as he glanced past her into the room.

'It's beautiful.' Petra defended her new temporary home.

'Officially, it's the honeymoon suite,' Blaize informed her drily, adding, 'But don't worry—just in case they don't get any honeymooners—or if they do but they fall out— they keep the other room kitted out as a second bedroom.'

The honeymoon suite! Why had they been given that? Or had Blaize perhaps asked for it deliberately, to reinforce the idea that they were lovers?

'If you want to have a camel ride, now's the time,' Blaize was continuing, patently oblivious to the sensuality and allure of the silk-hung bedroom and the temptation that was affecting Petra so forcibly.

'More coffee?'

Smiling, Petra shook her head, covering her cup with her hand in the traditional gesture that meant that she had had enough.

It was nearly eleven o'clock in the evening, and the dishes had been cleared away following their evening meal, ready for the entertainment to begin.

Petra could feel the excited expectation emanating from the gathered onlookers as the musicians changed beat and out of one of the tents a stunningly beautiful woman shimmied, dressed in a traditional dancing costume, jewels sparkling on her fingers and of course in her navel as she swayed provocatively to the sound of the music. Her body undulated sensuously, her dark eyes flashing smoky temptation above her veil as she rolled her hips, her whole body, and most especially the bare, smooth, taut brown expanse of her belly in rhythmic time to the music.

To one side of her a group of tourists were passing a hubble-bubble pipe between one another, the girls giggling softly as they breathed in the sweet taste of the strawberry-flavoured smoke. Its effect was supposed to be mildly euphoric, and Petra hesitated a little when it was passed on to her.

'If you don't try it you have to pay a forfeit and get up and dance with our belly dancer,' the tour guide with the large party who had just passed her the pipe teased Petra.

Rather than appear standoffish, Petra took a quick breath, relaxing as she smelled the innocuous scent of the strawberries and then offering the pipe to Blaize, only to realise that he had got up and walked away. He was talking to the falconer, who was still holding one of his now hooded birds, the gold tooling on the leather gloves, gleaming in the firelight.

As she handed the pipe back to the waiting tour guide, Petra realised that she wasn't the only woman there looking at Blaize. The belly dancer was focusing her gaze and her openly inviting body movements on him, ignoring the rest of them and turning to face him, moving closer and closer to him.

And as for Blaize...! A sensation of sheer white-hot jealousy knifed through Petra as she saw the way he was watching the dancer and smiling at her.

Petra had believed that she knew pain, but now, shock-

ingly, she realised that all she had experienced was one of
its many dimensions. Right now, watching Blaize look at
another woman when she ached, yearned, needed to have
him look only at her, unlocked for her the door to an agonising new world of pain!

Thoughts, longings, needs hitherto denied and forbidden
broke loose from the control she had imposed on them, one
after the other, until she was exposed to an entire avalanche
of them. They buried for ever any possibility of her denying
what her feelings for Blaize really were!

Frantically she struggled to make sense of what was happening. In the eerie pristine silence that followed the inner
explosion, her thought processes were frozen.

How was it possible for her to love Blaize? Petra felt as
though she had suddenly become one of those small figures
in a child's snowstorm ball, who had just had her whole
world and all her perceptions of what was in it turned vigorously upside down. But say she had got it wrong. Say
she did not really love Blaize. Mentally she tried to imagine
how she would feel if she were never to see him again.

The intensity of her pain made her catch her breath. Was
this how her mother had felt about her father? It must have
been. But things had been different for her mother, Petra
had to remind herself. Her mother had known that her love
was returned...shared... That she was loved as much as
she herself loved.

The music was reaching a crescendo, and Petra shivered
as she felt and saw the raw sensuality of the dancer's movements, her passionate determination to make Blaize notice
her, choose her. Blaize himself had turned round and was
watching her. The girl danced faster and faster, and then
as the music exploded in climactic triumph she flung herself
bodily as Blaize's feet.

Petra could tell from the reaction of the guides and the

robed men watching that this was not the normal finale to the dance. Instinctively she knew that the girl did not normally offer herself with such sexual blatancy to one of the male onlookers the way she just had done to Blaize, and immediately her own jealousy burned to a white heat.

She wanted to run to the girl and push her away—to tell her that Blaize belonged to her. But of course he did not!

The audience were good-humouredly throwing money onto the floor for the dancer, as they had been encouraged to do, but the dancer remained prostrate in front of Blaize, not acknowledging their generosity. It was left to one of the male fire-eaters who had been entertaining them earlier to pick it up.

As Petra watched Blaize watching the girl she wondered what he was thinking. He said something to one of the men he had been speaking with, who inclined his head as though in deference to Blaize before going over to the girl and bending towards her.

What was the man saying to her? Petra wondered jealously. What message had Blaize given the man to give her? Had he told her that he would see her later? The girl was getting up. She looked at Blaize, a proud, challenging flash of dark eyes, before walking slowly away, her hips swaying provocatively as she did so, her spine straight.

How could any man resist such an invitation? Petra wondered bleakly. Why would a man like Blaize even try to do so? And why, oh, why did a woman like her have to fall in love with him?

The evening was drawing to a close. People were finishing off their drinks and retiring to their pavilions.

Petra looked towards Blaize, who was still talking to the falconer and some other men. The dancer had disappeared, and Blaize was showing no signs of coming over to her or even looking at her.

Tiredly Petra got up and made her own way to their pavilion, collecting her things and then heading for the shower block. Too much was happening to her too quickly. Since arriving in this country she had been forced to confront aspects of herself and her feelings that it was very hard for her to accept.

Suddenly, standing beneath the warm spray of the shower, she longed achingly to be able to turn back the clock and return to a time when she had known nothing of the complexities that meeting her grandfather would bring. A time when she would have laughed out loud in disbelief if anyone had suggested that she would fall in love with a man like Blaize.

The camp was settling down to sleep when she made her way back to her pavilion. The soft glow of the lamps added to the air of mystery and enticement of its interior.

Someone had placed a dish of dates on one of the low carved tables in the sitting area, and silk cushions were placed invitingly on the floor in front of it, but Petra had no stomach for the sweetness of the dates—no stomach for anything, really, she admitted, now that her heart was soured by the anguish of her unreturnable love for Blaize. After all, even if he were by some impossible means to return her feelings, how could there be any future for them?

It wasn't a matter of money. That didn't come into it. Blaize could have had nothing and she would have loved him proudly and joyously. But how could she feel anything other than disquiet and distress at loving a man who used himself in the way that Blaize did? It was that which hurt her more than anything else! Even more than thinking about him with another woman? The belly dancer for instance?

Petra curled her hands into small fists. Where was he now? He was not in his room. The fabric covering the entrance to it was tied back so that she could see that the space beyond was empty.

Unlike hers, the 'walls' of his room were hung with darker, heavier fabric, which if anything was even more richly embroidered in gold than her own. Opulent fur-mimicking throws were heaped on the bed. There was a beautiful rug on the floor and a dish of sweet almond cakes on the table in front of the divan, along with a pot of richly fragrant coffee.

It was a setting fit for an Arabian prince, Petra reflected admiringly. And a retreat to which that same prince could bring the dancing girl of his choice, a dangerous inner voice taunted her.

Quickly Petra suppressed it. Blaize was no prince, Arabian or otherwise, and as for the dancing girl...

But where was he? Virtually the whole camp seemed to have settled down to sleep, and yet there was no sign of him.

Restlessly Petra paced the small pavillioned sitting area, tensing as the opening flap was abruptly pushed back and Blaize came in. He was stripped to the waist, a towel round his shoulders, his hair damp, and as he came in he brought with him the scent of the night and the desert—and of himself.

Petra felt her insides turn softly, compliantly liquid, longing pulsing through her as she gazed helplessly at his body.

She hadn't truly appreciated its magnificence the first time she had seen it, hadn't been able to sense its male capacity for sensuality and female pleasure, but now she could.

Abruptly her eyes narrowed, her gaze focusing on the angry claw-marks on his arm, which were still oozing blood slightly. Immediately the earth rocked beneath her feet and she was savaged by her own jealousy.

He had been with the dancer, and she had clawed her mark of possession on him!

Her mark of passion!

Before she could even recognise what she was doing, never mind stop herself, Petra had clenched her hands into small fists and advanced on him, demanding furiously, 'Where have you been? As if I didn't know! Was she good? Better than the rich tourists who pay you for your favours?'

'What…?'

Like lightning the changing expressions chased one another across his face, frowning disbelief followed by a warning, taut concentration. In its place followed an even more dangerous flash of sheeting anger and his mouth compressed and a tiny nerve pulsed in his jaw.

But Petra was in no mood to heed warning signs, and her eyes glittered with a fury every bit feral as his as she stated sarcastically, 'Silly me! I thought the whole purpose of us being here together was to convince the outside world that *we* are lovers! But obviously I was wrong and it's not! No—what's obviously far more important to you than honouring the arrangement we made is enjoying the…the sexual favours of an…an oversexed belly dancer. But then of course the two of you have something in common, don't you? You both sell your sexual favours for money and—'

Petra gave a small squeak as she was suddenly lifted off her feet. Her arms were in a vice-like grip as Blaize held her so that their eyes were on the same level.

'You should check your facts before you start throwing insults like that around,' he told her, biting the words into small barbed insults, his mouth barely moving as he hurled them lividly at her. 'If you were a man— But you aren't, are you?' he demanded, his voice suddenly changing to a soft sneer as he added, 'You aren't even much of a woman…just an over-excited, over-heated virgin, aching with curiosity to know what it's all about. No, don't deny it. It's written all over you—all over every single one of those big-eyed looks you keep on giving me when you think I don't notice. You're just desperate to find out what sex is, aren't you? Well, I'm sorry to disappoint you, but you just don't have what it takes to encourage me to let you find out!'

Every single word he had uttered had found its mark, and Petra felt as though she was slowly dying from the pain of the wounds he had inflicted. But there was no way she was going to let him see that—no way she was going to stop fighting...

'You mean that I haven't offered you enough money?' she taunted him recklessly.

'Enough money?' To Petra's disbelief, he threw back his head and laughed harshly.

'Despite what you so obviously think, it isn't money that turns me on, Petra, that makes me want a woman, ache for her so I can't rest until I possess her in every way there is. Until I wake up with her beside me in the morning, knowing that her body still wears my touch, inside and out, that she is so much a part of me that she still smells of me. But you don't know anything about that, do you? You know nothing about a man's desire...the compulsion that drives him to want a woman. Shall I show you? Is that what you want?'

Petra knew that she ought to deny what he was saying...refuse what he was offering her. But all she could do was let her gaze cling helplessly to his, her body motionless in his arms as he lowered his head towards hers!

As his lips touched hers she made a tiny almost mute sound at the back of her throat. Now she knew what it was like to be driven by a need, a thirst so all-consuming that it burned the soul as well as the body—to crave something, someone, to the point where the pain of that craving was an eternal torment. No Nomad lost in the desert could crave water with anything like the same intensity as she craved Blaize right now!

She moaned as he kissed her, wrapping her arms as tightly around him as she could, savouring the hot, deep thrust of his tongue and pressing close to him.

She could feel the anger pulsing through his body, but she was beyond caring which emotion drove him just so long as he never, ever lifted his mouth from her own.

And then, before she could stop him, he was wresting his mouth from hers, telling her savagely, 'Why the hell am I doing this? I must be going crazy! The last thing I need—or want—right now is—' He had stopped speaking to shake his head, but Petra could guess what he was thinking! What he had been about to say!

The last thing he needed—or wanted—was her!

Driven by the pain of his abrupt rejection of her, held deep in the grip of a primitive urge, an emotional, immediate reaction to his cruel taunting words she couldn't control, Petra lashed out at him, her hand raised.

And when, more by accident than anything, her hand hit the side of his jaw his own shock was mirrored by the expression in her eyes as they rounded and darkened. She shuddered convulsively, as though he had been the one to hit her.

She felt him release her and her feet hit the ground. She knew she must have moved, because suddenly she was in her own bedroom, lying curled up in the centre of the lavish bed whilst her whole body trembled with shock and pain, but she had no awareness of having got there—no awareness of anything since that awful moment when she had felt as well as heard the crack of her open palm against his skin.

How could she have done such a thing? She was totally opposed to all forms of violence. It disgusted her to the point where she felt physically sick that she had acted in such a way, but her dry aching eyes refused to provide her with the comfort of cleansing tears to wash away her guilt.

CHAPTER SEVEN

PAINFULLY Petra stared into the emptiness surrounding her. It was barely twenty minutes or so since Blaize had left her, but to Petra each one of those minutes had felt like an hour as she fought to come to terms with the shock of her own uncharacteristic behaviour. She was being tormented—not just by her unwanted love for Blaize, but by her guilt at the way she had behaved as well.

No matter how righteous her cause or how much provocation she believed she had been made to suffer, she still could not excuse or forgive herself for what she had done. To have been so driven by her own demons that she had resorted to physical violence! A shudder of self-loathing and moral outrage gripped her body.

According to the code by which she had been brought up by her parents, she owed Blaize an apology. Never mind that his own behaviour was open to question—his behaviour was something she was not responsible for. Her own was a different matter.

Apologise to him? After what he had said? After what he had done? After the way he had inflamed her senses, her body, until she had ached so feverishly for him that her longing overwhelmed everything else and then rejected her! Never, never. Never, not even on pain of torture, Petra swore dramatically to herself.

But five minutes later, with her conscience digging into her painfully, refusing to be ignored no matter how tightly she cocooned herself in her righteous indignation and tried to smother its nagging little voice, Petra finally gave in. If she waited too much longer she would be disturbing Blaize in the middle of his night's sleep!

Nervously, she reached for her robe and took a deep breath.

In the outer room the oil lamps had burned low, casting soft long shadows against the darkness.

Surely her apology could wait until morning? a craven little voice urged her. Blaize might well already be asleep. But Petra refused to allow herself to listen to it. She had done something wrong and now she must make amends!

Taking a deep breath, Petra lifted back the entrance fabric to Blaize's bedroom. In the few seconds it took her eyes to adjust to the darkness she could hear the noisy, anxious slam of her own heart against her ribs, and instinctively she placed one hand against it, as though trying to silence it.

The full moon outside lifted the darkness just enough for her to be able to make out Blaize's sleeping form beneath the bedcovers. He was lying on his side, with his face towards her, but turned into the pillow so that she could not tell whether he was awake or not. Tentatively she whispered his name, but there was no response. Was he asleep?

If she left now he would never even know she had been here. Longingly she looked back towards the exit, but the stubborn pride her father had always teased her about, that she had inherited from her grandfather, refused to allow her to make a craven escape without first checking that he was actually sleeping.

Head held high, she walked over to the bed. Like her own it was easily wide enough for two people. Uncertainly she looked at Blaize. Was he asleep? He certainly wasn't moving. Quietly she crept a little closer, automatically balancing one knee on the bed as she did so in order to get a closer look at him.

Tentatively she whispered his name. If he didn't respond

and was asleep then she could return to her own bed with a clear conscience and save her apology until the morning, knowing that she had at least tried to deliver it!

He hadn't uttered a sound. Exhaling softly in relief, Petra started to back away—and then froze as with shocking speed he reached out and gripped her wrist, demanding tauntingly, 'Sleepwalking Petra?'

His fingers burned against her skin, and as though he had guessed his thumb probed the uncoordinated thud of her pulse as though he was monitoring her reaction to him.

'Your blood is racing through your body like a gazelle fleeing from the hunter.'

'You...you startled me. I thought you were asleep!'

She winced a little as he released her, gritting a soft expletive under his breath. Moving with the swift stealth of a panther, throwing back the bedclothes, he reached out to relight the oil lamp on the table beside the bed, taunting her softly, 'If you thought I was asleep then what exactly are you doing here?'

Far from being asleep, he sounded dangerously alert, Petra recognised.

As she gave a small nervous shudder his expression changed abruptly. Frowningly he questioned her, 'What is it? What's wrong? Don't you feel well? The desert air can sometimes...'

'I'm fine,' Petra assured him quickly. 'It isn't...' Catching her bottom lip between her teeth, she struggled to drag her distracted...besotted gaze away from his naked torso. Like her, he obviously did not favour pyjamas. But unlike her, she suspected, from the brief glimpse she had just had of one lean muscular hip and the telltale dark shadowing of hair running down over his taut flat stomach, Blaize did not even adopt the modesty of wearing briefs to sleep in!

'Fine?' he repeated. 'Then what…?'

He looked fully awake now. And fully alert too, Petra recognised with a sinking, almost queasy sensation gripping her stomach. Thinking about delivering a short but noble speech of apology in the privacy of her own bed was one thing: actually doing it whilst she was poised semi-crouched on the edge of Blaize's bed, with her mind more on the fact that he was undoubtedly naked beneath the silky throw than on what she was supposed to be doing, was very much another! And if she wasn't careful…if she wasn't very, very careful indeed…she might just be in grave danger of totally ignoring what she had come here to do…

The scratches on Blaize's upper arm caught her attention. They had stopped bleeding but they still looked raw, and even slightly inflamed.

As she dragged her gaze away it met Blaize's, and was held there trapped…hypnotised…

'For your information, they were *not* caused by Shara…the dancer,' he told her quietly. 'The falconer had a new young bird he was training and it became over-excited. I offered to help him.' He gave a small shrug. 'As I told him, once she matures she will make an enviably loyal bird. She resented being handled by someone who was not her master and she let me know it.'

'A falcon scratched you?' Petra breathed, her face flooding with guilty colour. Now she owed him not one but two apologies.

Helplessly she looked back to his arm, and then, unable to stop herself, she leaned forward and gently caressed the broken skin with her lips, tenderly kissing the line of each scratch.

As she kissed the last one she felt Blaize's body quiver. Sombrely she turned her head and looked into his eyes.

'I came to apologise,' she told him quietly. 'I should not have…have done what I did.'

There was a small tense pause through which she could feel her own emotions pulsing, as though they possessed a life force of their own, whilst she waited for him to speak, and once again she found that she was having to wet her dry lips.

His thickly groaned, 'Don't do that, Petra!' followed by an even thicker, 'Why…why did you have to come in here?' drove the colour from her face, redefining the delicacy of her bone structure and highlighting her fragility. She started to move away, her eyes widening as Blaize followed her, grasping hold of her wrists and holding them against his bare chest as he looked deep into her eyes, before his gaze dropped, heavy-lidded with sensuality, to her mouth.

In the thick, taut silence that enveloped them while Blaize lit the lamp next to the bed Petra made the interesting scientific discovery that it was possible to find that one could not breathe even with open airways, parted lips, and an ample supply of oxygen!

'You know that you shouldn't really be here, don't you, my little virgin?'

His little virgin? Petra's heart jumped like a hooked fish throwing itself against her ribcage.

'I…'

I can go, Petra had been about to say. But speech had suddenly become impossible because Blaize was kissing her…kissing her with a mind-drugging, slow, sweet simplicity that was nothing more than the merest touch of his lips against hers, over and over again, and then again, until all she wanted to do was live off their touch, to feel it for ever.

Somehow she was now kneeling upright on the bed, and

so too was Blaize, so that they were body to body. His naked body next to her very scantily clad one!

Petra could feel the heavy, fierce thud of his heart beneath her hands as he held them against his chest.

He was kissing the tip of her nose, her closed eyelids, with tiny butterfly kisses that brushed the taut planes of her cheekbones whilst the hands pinning her own set them free, lifted to cup her face, to push the hair back from it so that his lips and then his tongue could investigate the delicate and oh, so sensually sensitive whorls of her ears.

Petra heard herself whimpering, an unfamiliar distant sound that was a needy plea for even more of the pleasure he was inflicting on her. Blindly she turned her head, seeking the warmth of his mouth.

His hands shaped her throat, holding it, his thumb measuring the frantic leaping pulse at its base. Her small curled fists still lay against his chest, the rasp of his body hair against her skin disturbingly sexual.

His hands were on her shoulders, beneath her wrap, stroking her skin, sliding the fabric away.

In the soft light of the lamp he had lit Petra could see their reflection in a mirror. Her skin looked milky pale against the warm tan of his, her breasts surely swollen, its taut peak surely a deeper, hotter colour as it pressed against him, flushed and pulsing with the desire that ached right through her.

If he were to touch her there now, cup her breast, roll his fingertip around her nipple… Her whole body stiffened in response to her own thoughts and it was as though somehow he had read her mind and felt her desires. His hand cupped her breast and his mouth returned to hers, his lips brushing over it with tantalising and then tormenting delicacy, making her lips part with hungry longing and her body press into his.

Wantonly she ran her tongue-tip over his lips, until he captured it and drew it between his teeth, caressing it with his own before his tongue slid deeper and deeper into the moist sweetness of her mouth.

As she moaned her pleasure deep in her throat, Petra felt him jerk away from her.

'Petra, no!' he told her thickly. 'This isn't—'

Not wanting to hear what he was obviously going to say, Petra put her fingertips to his lips, silencing him, kissing his face wildly, with fierce, impassioned little kisses as she breathed in his ear, 'Yes... Yes, it is!'

Removing her fingers, she pressed her mouth to his, her body to his, rubbing herself sensuously against him. Virgin she might be, but that did not mean she didn't understand what passion was...what wanting him was!

As she slid her hands over his body, helpless to stop herself, she felt him tense and then shudder. His skin felt like hot oiled satin, and Petra knew she could never, ever get enough of the feel of it beneath her hands. She kissed his throat, lingering over the place where his Adam's apple pressed hard against his skin, stroking it with her tongue, nibbling at his skin, taunting him with her desire and daring him to refuse to share it.

When he didn't move she curled her fingers in the soft thick hair on his body, tugging wantonly on it and flicking her tongue against the tiny peak of his flat male nipple.

'Petra, you are a virgin,' she heard him protesting rawly. 'I can't...'

As she abandoned her torment of his throat, and her lips moved down along the line of hair toward his stomach, she could almost hear him grinding his teeth. Her tongue rimmed his flat belly button, her love for him filling her with a sensual bravado that normally would have shocked her. She had never dreamed that the first time she made love she would be the one taking the initiative, making moves so bold and provocative that they shocked her almost as much as they excited her.

'I don't want—' she heard Blaize groan thickly.

But her fingertips were already exploring the taut strength of his arousal, lending her the confidence to whisper daringly, 'Oh, yes, you do,' before returning to her task of laving the maleness of his flat belly with her inquisitive tongue.

There was a muscle pulsing there that fascinated and compelled her. Wickedly she traced it with lingering appreciation, so raptly lost in the pleasure of what she was doing that it caught her completely off guard when Blaize suddenly took hold of her, depositing her on the bed and holding her there whilst he looked down at her, his gaze skimming her face and then her body, her breasts, her narrow waist. She saw him frown and looked down at her own flesh, realising that he was staring at the tiny diamond glinting in her belly.

'Who gave you that?' she heard him demanding fiercely.

For a few seconds Petra was bemused, and her fingertip touched the diamond in confusion.

'Who was he, Petra?' she heard Blaize reiterating savagely—so savagely, in fact, that she was unable to prevent the entirely female thrill of excited pleasure rippling through her. He was jealous! She could tell. For a heartbeat she fantasised about pretending that he had a rival, that another man had looked at her body and laid claim to it, put his badge of possession on it. But her natural honesty reasserted itself.

'I bought it myself—for myself!' she told him truthfully. 'I heard a couple of girls discussing me at a party, saying that I was the type of person who was too pure and naïve to wear anything like this, and so...' She gave a small dismissive shrug.

'This is a gift that only a man would give a woman,' Blaize was insisting, his eyes smokily charcoal, hot with male possession and desire.

'Not these days,' Petra contradicted him wryly.

'Then where else have you adorned yourself?' Blaize was demanding softly, and his hand moved lower down her body, his head bent over her.

Now it was his turn to torment her, to kiss her with surely far more expertise and deliberate enticement and sensuality than she had done him as he traced a line of kisses from her breastbone right down to her quivering belly.

As she had done to him he rimmed her navel with tiny kisses, and then the tip of his tongue, but then, before Petra could stop him, he tugged delicately on the diamond whilst his hand covered her sex, his thumb slowly probing an entrance between its tightly furled outer covering in a way that made her heart turn over inside her chest whilst the whole of her body turned molten and fluid with arousal.

'Nowhere else,' she heard herself whisper, but even as she said them she knew that the words were not needed, that Blaize had discovered for himself that her body possessed no other form of adornment!

Withdrawing slightly, he looked down at her whilst she quivered from head to foot—but not with apprehension or regret.

'I want you,' she told him huskily. 'I want you now, Blaize.'

But as she reached for him he shook his head.

'Wait!' he told her, reaching out to open a small cupboard beside the bed.

'I just hope that whoever planned this as a lovers' retreat did some proper forward planning,' Petra heard him mutter.

Bewildered, she waited, trying to peer past his shoulder, and then when she did see what he had been searching for her face coloured self-consciously.

Until now all 'safe sex' had meant to her was an expression that applied to other people!

But of course Blaize was more experienced, far more worldly than she was herself, and shakily she admitted that she was thankful that he was being so conscientious!

She even felt a tiny little thrill of excitement, knowing what he was doing, what it was leading up to! And when he was ready and he turned back to her, wrapping her in his arms and kissing her slowly and thoroughly before caressing her body, she shivered in passionate urgency.

She had thought that she knew what wanting him, aching for him felt like! But she had been wrong!

Enshrined in the street lore of her girlhood, the received wisdom of a hundred magazine articles and books, she had carried a certain protective wisdom that 'first times were not good times'—but she had been wrong about that too!

She hadn't known just how proactive her own role would be, how proactive she would want it to be as she reached and touched, stretched and invited, as she shuddered in the exquisite indescribable sensation of having him slowly enter her, slowly fill her...

But she knew now.

She hadn't known either how easily she would find the words she could hear echoing the pace of his deepening thrusts, which told him all that she was feeling and wanting.

But she knew that now too.

Every breath he took as he filled and completed her—against her skin, in her ear, in the thud of his heartbeat against her own, deep inside her body, where it radiated out in golden waves—was the breath of life itself.

And then, just as she thought she had accustomed herself

totally to the feel of him, he changed the pace, increasing its intensity, deepening it, letting her feel the strength of its power, letting her see that her body was ready for such intimacy.

And it was!

Mindlessly Petra clung to him, lifting herself against him so that he could go deeper, fuller, stronger, so that the intimacy they were sharing was so intense, so sweetly, savagely unbearable that it had to shatter, hurling them both through paroxysm after paroxysm of pleasure and into the beautiful golden peace that lay beyond it.

'Mmm.' Sleepily, Petra drew a small heart on the smooth skin of Blaize's bare shoulder with her fingertip. He was asleep and she could see the dark fans his eyelashes made against the warmth of his tanned skin in the soft light of the lamp. She had been asleep herself until a couple of minutes ago, but it seemed that her body didn't want to waste a moment of the time it could have with Blaize in sleep when she could be awake, watching him, touching him…loving him.

There—she had acknowledged her love! Admitted it! Accepted it?

She closed her eyes, testing the words inside her head. I love him. I love Blaize.

Yes, it was true. She could tell that from the way her whole being responded to the inner vibration of the words. She loved him! She loved Blaize.

She moved closer to him, bending her head to replace her fingertip with her lips, slowly retracing her heart with tiny whisper-light kisses.

His skin felt so warm, his body so excitingly different from her own and yet now so wonderfully, preciously familiar.

From now until the very end of her life she would re-member tonight. Until the day she died she would be able to close her eyes and recreate his image inside her head. Her hands would never forget what it had felt like to touch him; her lips would never forget the taste of his, the heat of his mouth, the way he had kissed her.

Her eyes soft and dark with her own emotions, Petra traced the shape of his arm and then the length of his back, the curve of his buttock.

'Two can play at this game.'

Petra gasped as Blaize's hand suddenly slid over her, down to her waist and then up again to cup her breast, whilst his voice echoed in her ear.

'You wouldn't be trying to take advantage of a sleeping man, would you?' he teased her.

'I just wanted to see if you felt as good as I remembered,' Petra told him honestly.

She felt him move, tensing a little, as though her words had somehow touched a raw nerve, or were something he didn't really want to hear. But she decided that she must be wrong when he demanded, 'And do I?'

As he spoke his thumb was deliberately teasing the un-expectedly taut and excited peak of her breast.

The shock of discovering how easily and quickly he could make her feel so hungry for him distracted her. Her hands were already curling, weaving rhythmically against his skin as her body started to pulse and ache.

Eagerly she kissed his throat and then his mouth, making a soft, taut sound of need deep in her throat as she pulled his head down towards her breast.

The sensation of his lips covering her nipple, caressing it, drawing it deeper into his mouth, made her dig her fin-gers into the hard muscles of his back. Already she was imagining the feel of him inside her, aching for it and for him, so much that she reached out and ran her fingertips down his body, touching him with a knowing intimacy that would have shocked her twenty-four hours ago.

Against her breast he made a sound she couldn't decipher, smothered by the urgency of her compelling need as she arched against him and gloried in the swelling hardness of the male flesh beneath her touch.

Blaize had released her breast and rolled onto his back. She felt his hands on her waist. To lift her away? Swiftly she bent her head towards his body, her lips touching the hard shaft of flesh that compelled her, that she knew would complete her!

'Petra...Petra...'

Her name was a raw, tormented sound of broken male control that filled her with sweetly savage pleasure.

His hands were still on her waist, but this time as he lifted her it was not away from him but towards him.

As he positioned her Petra shuddered, her eyes huge and dark with the realisation of how quickly and wantonly her body had adjusted to its newly dominant role.

Slickly they moved together, deeper, stronger, faster, whilst she stared into the mask of agonised pleasure that was Blaize's face, his need openly revealed to her as he cried out and his body jerked in fierce spasms just as the pleasure exploded inside her.

She was trembling so much that she couldn't move, couldn't do anything other than lie against him whilst he wrapped his arms around her and rocked her.

'That shouldn't have happened,' she heard him telling her in a voice that was raw with emotions she didn't have the energy to analyse as a fog of exhaustion enveloped her.

'That should *not* have happened,' he repeated.

'Yuck, camel's milk! How totally disgusting!'

Petra forced herself to try and smile as the girl next to

her, sharing the communal breakfast they had been served at the tourist village, turned towards her, waiting for her to respond to her friendly comment.

Ordinarily Petra knew that she would have enjoyed joining in the good-natured atmosphere of the alfresco breakfast they had been served. But when she had woken up this morning she had woken up alone and in her own bed!

Blaize must have carried her there whilst she was asleep. Why hadn't he wanted her to stay with him? Why hadn't he wanted to keep her with him?

Now last night's euphoria had disappeared, leaving her feeling frighteningly hollow and cold inside.

What she needed right now more than anything else was Blaize's presence, Blaize's reassurance—and most of all Blaize's love!

CHAPTER EIGHT

'THANKS for the lift...'

Petra watched as the young tour guide reiterated his grateful thanks to Blaize, before jumping down out of the Land Rover.

They had all been on the point of departing from the oasis when the tour guide's Jeep had refused to start.

Places had been found for his passengers in other vehicles, but unfortunately there had not been enough room for him, so Blaize had offered to give him a lift back to the complex.

Of course his presence had made it impossible for Petra and Blaize to discuss anything personal, but Petra suspected that she minded this far more than Blaize did.

The truth was that he was probably relieved she couldn't say anything about last night, Petra acknowledged unhappily.

After all, if he had felt anything for her—even a more small percentage of the love she knew she had for him— then he would have told her so last night, instead of returning her to her own bed and then treating her this morning as though...as though she meant nothing to him!

She might mean nothing to him, but he meant everything to her!

Still, at least one good thing had come out of last night, she tried to tell herself with a brave attempt at cynical courage.

Rashid certainly wasn't going to want to marry her now. Not once he knew she had spent the night with another man! Given herself to another man! A man, moreover, who didn't love or want her!

Determinedly Petra tried not to give in to her own despair.

That wasn't true, she argued mentally with herself. Blaize had wanted her!

Her or just a woman…any woman?

Her pain was so intense that she didn't dare to even look at Blaize, just in case he might read her feelings in her eyes and feel even more contempt for her than he no doubt already did. All she meant to him was a meal ticket and a few hours of casual and no doubt quickly forgettable sex! She had known what he was all along, she reminded herself, so why had she been so stupid? So reckless with herself and her love? What had she been thinking? That with her he would be different? That her love would make it different? Why, why, why had she closed her eyes so deliberately to reality? Why had she ignored everything she knew about him and the way he lived his life?

Because her love for him had given her no choice, Petra recognised bleakly. Because, against her love, common sense and logic had no real weapons at all!

Acidly painful tears burned the back of Petra's throat. They were outside her hotel now, and without giving Blaize the opportunity to say anything she opened the door of the Land Rover and got out.

As she walked away she thought she heard Blaize calling her name, but she refused to stop.

It might be too late to stop herself from loving Blaize, but it was not too late for her to salvage her pride and her self-respect!

If she had meant anything to him…anything at all…he would have told her so last night.

*   *   *

An hour later, having exhausted every rational and several very irrational combinations of reasons and excuses for Blaize's behaviour, and still had to return to the unwanted, unbearable truth that he had simply been using her and, having done so now, no longer wanted her, Petra heard someone knocking on the door to her suite.

Immediately, despite everything she had just told herself, her heart leapt, whilst relief and joy poured through her. It was Blaize! It had to be! She had got it all wrong! There was a rational explanation for the distance he had put between them, and he had now come to explain everything to her—to apologise for hurting her and to tell her how much he wanted her, how much he loved her.

Her whole face illuminated with happiness and love, Petra ran to open the door.

Only it wasn't Blaize who was standing outside; it was her cousin Saud. In the shock of her disappointment Petra could only stand and stare at him uncomprehendingly.

'Are you packed yet?' she heard him asking her.

'Packed?'

'I told my mother she should have rung ahead to check that you were ready!'

Ready! Guiltily Petra realised that today was the day she was due to move in to the family villa. She had been so wrapped up in her love for Blaize and what had happened between them that she had totally overlooked the plans that had been made.

'I...I'm running a bit late, Saud,' she told him. After all, it was technically the truth. 'I'm sorry...'

'That's okay,' Saud assured her easily. 'I'm not in any rush. Did you enjoy your trip into the dessert with Rashid? I saw him driving you there,' he added casually.

Petra stared at him, her body completely immobile, like

that of someone caught up in the dark power of a sorcerer's spell.

'Rashid?' she questioned. Her lips were having trouble framing his name, and her heart had started to beat with heavy-doom laden thuds that rocked her whole body. 'You saw me with Rashid?'

'Yes, in one of the safari company's Land Rovers,' Saud confirmed.

'But I wasn't with—' Petra began to protest, and then stopped as Saud continued with a wide grin.

'My mother's already planning the wedding. She thinks...'

'Rashid,' Petra mouthed, forcing her lips to accommodate themselves to his name, whilst her body shook with the enormity of what Saud had said. 'But...'

But what? she asked herself numbly. But she had not been with Rashid. She had been with Blaize! Blaize who was not Rashid...who could not be Rashid...

'I suppose Rashid is working upstairs in the Presidential Suite now, is he?' Saud was chattering on happily. 'Has he taken you to see his new villa yet? The one he has just had built out by the private oasis he bought?' Saud was asking her excitedly. 'Did he show you his horses? And his falcons? I'd love a falcon of my own, but Dad says it's out of the question—especially if I'm to go to university in America.'

'Saud, I'm not...I'm not packed yet. Could you come back a little later, say in an hour?' she asked him jerkily, interrupting his enthusiastic and excited conversation.

'Sure!'

Petra stared blankly at the door Saud had closed behind him.

Saud had said that he had seen her with Rashid. But the

man she had been with was Blaize. Which meant either that Saud had been mistaken or...

There was a vile sickening sensation clawing coldly at the pit of her stomach, a suspicion inside her head that wouldn't go away.

The Presidential Suite. That was on the top floor. White-faced, but determined, Petra opened the door of her suite and headed for the lift.

What she was thinking couldn't be true, it just couldn't! Saud had to be mistaken, but she had to find out, she had to know...to be sure!

Only one lift went all the way to the Presidential Suite, and when she got out of it Petra was trembling violently—although whether from shock, fear or fury, she didn't really know.

Blaize could not be Rashid. It was totally implausible that he might be, totally impossible! But somehow the re-assurances she was trying to give herself had a disconcert-ingly hollow and empty sound to them.

In the private hallway to the suite, a thick, lushly rich carpet muffled her footsteps—but not her racing heartbeat. Nervously Petra stared at the closed door in front of her.

What was she doing here? Blaize was a beach bum, a chancer, an adventurer who lived on his wits and other people's money, a man with no moral beliefs, who made his own rules—and then broke them. Rashid, in contrast, from what she had heard about him, was a seriously suc-cessful businessman, a man ruthlessly focused on his own goals, a man prepared to marry a woman he did not know for his own advancement and benefit.

They could not be one and the same person. It was un-thinkable that they might be. Unthinkable, unsustainable, unendurable! Of course it was! Saud had simply made a mistake.

Feeling slightly calmer, Petra pressed the doorbell and waited.

The door swung inwards, and a male voice demanded curtly, 'Yes?'

The voice was the same, but the businesslike crispness certainly wasn't!

Her throat muscles virtually paralysed with shock and disbelief, Petra stared up into Blaize's face. Only he wasn't Blaize. He was... He was...

Ignoring the bare arm that Blaize had placed across the half-open doorway, Petra pushed her way past him and into the suite.

She had obviously disturbed Blaize, or rather Rashid, as she now knew him to be in mid-shower, to judge from the rivulets of moisture still running over his skin down to the towel he had draped round his hips.

'How could you?' she demanded chokily. 'How dare you? Why did you do it? Why...? Let go of me,' she spat as he suddenly took hold of her arm, her face white with shock and fury. 'Let go of me,' she repeated, as Blaize— Rashid, she corrected herself bitterly—virtually dragged her into the elegant sitting room.

If she had either shocked or shamed him, he certainly wasn't showing it.

'Not until you've calmed down and you're ready to listen to reason,' Rashid told her calmly. 'Come and sit down and I'll get you a cool drink. You look as though you need one.'

A cool drink! Petra tried to pull free of him and found that she could not.

'What I need,' she told him through gritted teeth, 'is an explanation of...of what is going on...of why you pretended to be someone you quite obviously are not...'

'I was going to tell you,' Rashid interrupted her curtly. 'But—'

'Liar!' Petra cut across him. 'You're lying to me. Just like you've lied to me all along! Let go of me,' she demanded fiercely. 'I can't bear having you touch me. I—'

'That wasn't what you said last night,' Rashid reminded her grimly.

Petra shuddered, unable to stop herself from reacting—not just to his words, but also to her own feelings, her memories...

'In fact, last night, as I recall, you seemed to find my touch a good deal more than merely bearable! Remember?'

When Petra refused to answer Rashid goaded her.

'Shall I help you to do so?'

As Petra gave a sharp gasp of shock he drew her closer to him. Petra tensed as she felt the dampness of his skin through her thin top. Her mind knew how gravely, how devastatingly, how unforgivably he had behaved towards her, but her body seemed only to know that he was its lover, its love.

'If I were to kiss you now,' he began softly, the words whispering tormentingly against her tightly closed lips, 'then...'

He stopped speaking and lifted his head as the suite door suddenly opened and a tall grey-bearded man strode in, his bearing immediately marking him out as a person of eminence and rank.

'Rashid, our new American project—how long do you think—' he began, and then stopped as he took in the scene in front of him, its apparent intimacy.

Eyes as sharp and dark as a falcon's made Petra feel as though she was as pinioned beneath their gaze as she was by Rashid's grip.

'Highness, please allow me to present to you Miss Petra Cabbot.'

Highness!

Petra gulped, sensing the cool air of regal disapproval emanating from the newcomer as he looked from Rashid to Petra and then back to Rashid again before saying quietly, 'I see!'

He left a brief but telling pause before asking Petra politely, 'Your godfather is well, I trust, Miss Cabbot? He and I were at Eton together.'

'He's—he's in the Far East,' Petra managed to croak, wondering if she dared add that he was there with her passport—which right now she needed very much.

'Indeed.' The princely head was inclined towards her. 'He is a very shrewd statesman, as was your father. Statesmen of world-class stature with far-seeing eyes are very much needed in these turbulent times.'

Her face burning, Petra moved out of earshot of the two men whilst the Prince spoke with Rashid.

Despite the Prince's politeness, Petra was uncomfortably aware of his evident, if unexpressed disapproval of her presence unchaperoned in Rashid's suite.

The moment the Prince had left, Petra made to leave herself. But immediately Rashid shook his head, closing the door firmly and standing in front of it as he said grimly, 'You do realise what this means, don't you? What will have to happen now that the Prince has seen you here alone with me?'

'You were the one who introduced me to him,' Petra reminded him defensively, ignoring his question.

'Because I had no other option,' Rashid told her savagely. 'If I had chosen not to introduce you it would have been a tacit admission that it was because honourably I could not do so…because you were my whore! There is nothing else for it now. You will have to marry me! Nothing less can save your reputation or that of your family!'

Petra stared at him in shocked disbelief.

'What?' she croaked. 'We can't!'

'We can and we are,' Rashid assured her grimly. 'In fact, we don't have any other option—thanks to you!'

'Thanks to me?' Petra glared at him. 'Thanks to me? What does that mean? I wasn't the one...'

'It means that since His Highness found you here in my apartment unchaperoned, I now have no other option than to marry you. It was obvious what he thought.'

'What...? That's...that's ridiculous,' Petra protested. 'Why didn't you just tell him the truth?'

'Which truth?' Rashid demanded scornfully. 'The truth that says last night you gave yourself to me? Last night...'

'Stop it...stop it.' Petra demanded in anguish, before accusing him recklessly, 'You've done all this deliberately, haven't you? Just so that you can get your own way and force me to marry you—for the financial benefit you'll get out of it! Just as a matter of interest, what is marriage to me worth to you, Rashid?' Her temper was burning white-hot. 'A good deal more than the traditional camels, I am sure! One hotel...two...an office block and perhaps a dozen or more villas thrown in? And why stop there? I know that the Royal Family's hotel interests extend all over the world, and—'

'You're overreacting.' Rashid cut across her increasingly emotional words curtly. 'If you would just allow me to explain—'

'Explain what?' Petra demanded bitterly. 'Explain that you deliberately lied to me and...and plotted and planned to...to use me for...for your own ends?'

'Me—use *you*. I wasn't the one who came into your

room,' Rashid reminded her icily. 'Into your bed! If anything, if anyone is to blame for the situation we now find ourselves in, Petra, it is you and your wretched virginal curiosity! And, contrary to what your juvenile imagination has decided, it is for that reason that I have no option other than to do the honourable thing and marry you.'

'Because I was a virgin! That's crazy!'

'No. You are crazy if you honestly believe there can be any other outcome to what happened. We have to marry now. Apart from any other consideration there is the fact that you could have a child.'

Petra stared at him.

'But…but that isn't possible,' she started to stammer. 'You…you…took precautions…'

She tensed as she heard him draw an exaggeratedly deep breath.

'Indeed I did—the first time!' he told her derisively. 'The second time I did not, and the second time I…'

'You planned all this, didn't you?' Petra repeated furiously, panicked by both the situation and Rashid's grim anger. 'You deliberately lied to me and—'

'Do you really think I like or want this any more than you do? And as for planning it! You obviously haven't listened properly to me, Petra. As I've just told you, I wasn't the one who crawled into your bed! Nor was I the one who begged—'

With a small chagrined moan Petra forced back the shocked emotional tears that were already stinging her eyes.

'How many more times do I have to tell you that for me not to marry you now would not just relegate you to the status of a…a plaything, it would humiliate your grandfather and his whole family?' Rashid said bitingly. 'Quite apart from the fact that you were alone in here with me in an intimate situation—do you really think the fact that we spent the night together last night went unnoticed? Has it really not occurred to you yet that this morning you so obviously looked...'

'No! I won't listen to any more,' she protested.

Every word he said was like a knife in her heart. She could hardly take in what was happening. What he had said. She had enough to do trying to come to terms with the fact that the man she had thought of as Blaize was in actual fact someone quite different, without having to cope with this additional shock!

'None of this need have happened if you had just been honest with me that evening down on the beach,' she threw at him wildly. 'If you had told me then.'

'When you first approached me I had no idea who you were. I had just returned from a business trip to discover that the idiotic young man who looked after the wind-surfers, who I had already had to warn on more than one occasion about his familiarity with the female guests, had been discovered by one of our guests in bed with his wife. Naturally I had had to sack him, and I had gone down to the beach simply to walk and think.'

'You were putting away the windsurfers,' Petra accused him bitterly.

Rashid gave a small shrug.

'An automatic habit. I worked on a Californian beach as a student, and just seeing them lying untidily there...'

'You could have told me who you were! Stopped me...' Petra persisted. 'You may think that you have been very clever, tricking me like this, but I won't marry you, Rashid.'

'You don't have any other choice,' he told her starkly. 'Neither of us do! Not now! I cannot—'

'You cannot what?' Petra demanded, refusing to allow him to finish speaking. 'You cannot afford to offend the

Royal Family? Well…well, tough! No way am I going to marry you just to…to save your precious reputation—'

She stopped in mid-sentence as Rashid cut across her, his voice sharply cynical. '*My* reputation? Haven't you listened to anything I have just said? It is your own you should be thinking about! Your own and that of your family. Because what I cannot do, Petra, unless I marry you, is protect you from the gossip that is now bound to occur. And not just about you! I have far too much respect for your grandfather to want to publicly humiliate him by having it known that I have not offered you marriage.'

'Fine! Your conscience is clear, Rashid! You have offered me marriage. And I am refusing to accept!'

'Despite the fact that you could be carrying my child?'

For a moment they looked at one another. Petra could feel herself weakening, remembering… But then she made herself face reality. He had lied to her, totally and without compunction, tricked and deceived her, and she could never overlook that, not if she wanted to retain her own self-respect, what little there was left of it!

Determinedly she told him, 'It could also be that I am not carrying your child! I won't marry you, Rashid,' she reinforced.

'Unfortunately, I am tied up with business meetings which cannot be cancelled or delayed until the day after tomorrow. But rest assured, Petra, on that day I shall be calling on your grandfather to formally request your hand in marriage.'

So intense was her sense of fury and frustration that Petra simply couldn't speak. Giving Rashid a savagely bitter look, she headed for the door.

To her relief he allowed her to pass through it without making any attempt to stop her or to say anything else.

Calling on her grandfather to request her hand in marriage. She had never heard of anything so archaic! Well, she would soon make it plain to him that his proposal was neither wanted nor acceptable!

CHAPTER NINE

'AUNT SORAYA,' Petra exclaimed warmly as she saw her aunt approaching her. 'I thought you were going out to spend the day with your friend.'

Her aunt had already told Petra with some excitement that she had been invited to visit an old schoolfriend whose daughter had just become betrothed to an extremely wealthy and highly placed prince.

To Petra's concern her aunt immediately looked not merely flustered but also acutely distressed, with large tears filling her soft brown eyes.

Taking hold of her hands in her own, Petra begged her, 'Aunt, what is it? What's wrong? Please tell me—has something happened to your friend or her daughter?'

Emotionally her aunt shook her head.

'Please,' Petra urged her. 'Tell me what's wrong?'

She had, she realised, become closer to her aunt than she had imagined she would, and the older woman's air of vulnerability made her feel very protective of her.

'Petra. I did not wish to tell you this,' her aunt was saying unhappily. 'The last thing I want to do is to hurt or anger you.'

Hurt or anger her?

Petra began to frown as a cold finger of icy intuition pressed warningly against her spine.

'I was to have seen my friend and her daughter today,' her aunt admitted, 'But she has telephoned to say that the visit must be cancelled. It is nothing personal against you, Petra. At least not intentionally! My friend understands that

136

you did not mean to… Well, she knows you have had a European upbringing. It is just that she has her daughter to protect, and the family of her husband-to-be are…are very traditional in their outlook.'

She was beginning to stumble slightly over her explanation in very obvious embarrassment, but Petra had already guessed what was coming.

Even so it was still a shock to have her aunt confirm her fears.

'There has been gossip about you, Petra! I know, of course, that there will be a perfectly acceptable reason for…for…everything…but my friend has heard that you are known to have been alone with Rashid, and that you and he—'

She broke off, blinking away her tears and pressing her hand to her mouth as though she could hardly bring herself to say any more.

'I cannot believe that Rashid would knowingly behave in such a way, that he would expose you to…that he should not behave honourably and…'

'Offer to marry me?' Petra suggested grimly. 'Well, as a matter of fact, Aunt, that is exactly what he has done. Although I…'

'He has!' Suddenly her aunt's face was wreathed in a relieved smile. Reaching out, she hugged Petra warmly, patently oblivious to the cynicism Petra had been intending to convey in her voice. 'Oh, Petra I am so happy… So overjoyed for you…for you both. He will make you a wonderful husband. Your grandfather will be so very very pleased.'

'No, Aunt, you don't understand,' Petra tried to protest, suddenly beginning to panic as she realised the interpretation her aunt had put on her admission. It was one thing for her to tell her aunt for the sake of her own pride and her aunt's comfort that Rashid had offered to marry her, but she had never intended that her aunt should assume she was pleased or, more importantly, that she actually intended to accept.

However, having made her own interpretation of Petra's words her aunt proved stubbornly hard to change!

Rashid had proposed! Of course it was impossible that Petra might have refused, and every attempt Petra made to tell her that she had done just that was greeted with amused laugher and comments about Petra's 'teasing' until Petra herself fell silent in despairing exasperation.

'I should have trusted Rashid, of course,' her aunt was saying. 'Although it was very thoughtless of you both to put your reputation at so much risk, Petra. Your mother would have hated knowing that people were beginning to talk about you the way they were,' she reproved her gently.

Her mother! Petra's heart suddenly ached. Her mother would have hated knowing that her daughter's name was being bandied about in a scurrilous way, that was true, but she would not have condemned her for what had happened. Petra knew that as well.

'So, you and Rashid are betrothed,' her aunt was saying happily. 'We are going to be so busy, Petra. Oh, my, dear,' she said, giving Petra another hug. 'I had not meant to tell you this, but now that you have put my mind at ease with the news of your betrothal I feel that I can. Had Rashid not offered you marriage, it would have done our family a very great deal of harm, and lowered our standing in the community to such an extent that my own husband's business would have been badly affected—as would your cousin's chances of making a good marriage. And as for your grandfather... I do not exaggerate, Petra, when I tell you that I think the shame might have killed him.'

Killed him!

Petra stood frozen within her aunt's warm embrace, feeling as though she had suddenly walked into a trap which had sprung so tightly around her that she would never be able to escape. And it made no difference at all that she had unwittingly and foolishly been the one to spring that trap herself!

There was no way out for her now. For the sake of her family she had no alternative other than to marry Rashid!

'Oh, Petra! You look so beautiful,' her aunt whispered emotionally. 'A perfect bride.'

They were standing together in Petra's bedroom at the family villa, waiting for Petra's grandfather to escort her to the civil marriage ceremony that would make her Rashid's wife.

After the civil ceremony there was to be a lavish banquet held in their honour in the specially decorated banqueting suite of the hotel.

Petra's aunt had spent virtually the whole of the last three days there overseeing everything, along with some of Rashid's female relatives, but despite her exhortations Petra had not been able to bring herself to go and view the scene of her own legal entrapment.

There was no point, she knew, in trying to tell her aunt that she did not want to marry Rashid. The older woman had a ridiculously high opinion of him and would, Petra knew, simply not be able to accept that Petra herself hated and despised him.

Rashid knew it, though—she had made sure of that the day he had come to formally ask her grandfather for her hand in marriage.

Unable to refuse him outright as she had wished, for the sake of her aunt and her family, she had had to content herself with a bitterly contemptuous and hostile glare at him when her grandfather had summoned her to receive his proposal.

'I am pleased to see that you have had the good sense to realise there is no alternative to this—for either of us,' he had managed to tell her grimly, gritting the words to her so quietly that no one else could hear them.

And, as though that hadn't been bad enough, she had then had to endure the miserable, humiliating parody of being forced to pretend that she wanted to accept his proposal!

However, she had managed to avert her face when he had leaned towards her to kiss her, so that his mouth had merely grazed her cheek instead of touching her lips.

Beneath his breath he had taunted her, 'How very modest! A traditional shrinking bride! However, I already know just how passionate you can be beneath that assumed cold exterior!'

And now there was no escape for her.

Her attendants—a swarm of pretty chattering girls from her aunt's extended family and Rashid's—had already left for the hotel in their stunning butterfly-hued outfits, and soon Petra herself would be leaving with her grandfather. She tensed as her bedroom door opened and her grandfather came in.

Giving her veil a final twitch, her aunt left them on their own.

As he came towards her Petra could see that her grandfather's eyes were shining with emotion. 'You are so like your mother,' he whispered. 'Every day I see more and more of her in you. I have something I would like you to wear today,' he told her abruptly, producing a leather jewellery box and removing from it a diamond necklace of such delicate workmanship that Petra couldn't help giving a small murmur of appreciation.

'This is for you,' she heard her grandfather telling her. 'It would mean a great deal to me if you would wear it today, Petra.'

Now Petra could understand her aunt's insistence on choosing a fabric for her wedding gown which was sewn with tiny crystals. Originally, when the silk merchant had come to the house with a selection of fabrics, Petra had wondered bitterly just what kind of fabric would best suit a sacrificial offering. It had been her aunt who had fallen on the heavy matt cream fabric with its scattering of tiny beads with an exclamation of triumph.

Petra could feel her grandfather's hands shaking as he fastened the necklace for her. It fitted her so perfectly that it might have been made for her.

'It was your mother's,' he said. 'It was my last gift to her. She left it behind. She would have been so proud of you today, Petra. Both your parents would, and with good reason.'

Proud of her? For allowing herself to be tricked into a soulless, loveless marriage?

Panic suddenly filled her. She couldn't marry Rashid. She wouldn't! She turned to her grandfather, but before she could speak her aunt came back into the room.

'It is time for you to leave,' she told them both.

As her grandfather walked towards the stairs Petra made to follow him, but her aunt suddenly stopped her. 'You are not wearing Rashid's gift,' she chided her.

Petra stared at her.

'The perfume he sent you, which he had specially blended for you,' her aunt reminded her, clicking her tongue as she hurried over to the table and picked up the heavy crystal bottle.

'No...I don't want to wear it...' Petra started to say, but her aunt wasn't listening to her.

Petra froze as the warm, sensual scent surrounded her in a fragrant cloud.

'It is perfect for you,' her aunt was saying. 'It has the youthfulness of innocence and the maturity of womanliness. Rashid has chosen well. And your mother's necklace is perfect on you, Petra. Your grandfather has never stopped missing her or loving her, you know.'

As her throat threatened to close up with tears, Petra demanded huskily, 'If he loved her so much then why didn't he at least come to the funeral? Even if he could not have been there he could have sent a message... something...anything...'

All the pain she had felt on that dreadful day, when she had stood at her parents' graveside surrounded by their friends and her father's family and yet feeling dreadfully alone, was in her voice.

She heard her aunt sigh.

'Petra, he would have been there. But there was his heart attack—and then when your godfather wrote that he did not think it a good idea that you should come here to us, that you had your own life and friends, he was too proud to...to risk a second rejection.'

Petra stared at her. She had known that her grandfather had made a very belated and seemingly—to her—very reluctant offer to give her a home, following her parents' death, but she had had no idea that he had been prevented from attending their funeral by a heart attack.

'A heart attack?' she faltered. 'I...'

'It was his second,' her aunt informed her, and then suddenly looked acutely uncomfortable, as though she had said something she should not have said.

'His second?' Petra had known nothing of this. 'Then...when...when did he have his first?' she demanded with a small frown.

Her aunt was becoming increasingly agitated.

'Petra, I should not have spoken of this. Your grandfather never wanted... He swore us all to secrecy when it happened because he didn't want your mother to feel...'

'My mother?'

She gave her aunt a determined look.

'I am not leaving this room until you tell me everything,' she informed her sturdily.

'Petra, you will be late. The car is waiting, and your grandfather...'

'Not one single step,' Petra warned her.

'Oh, dear. I should never... Very well, then. I suppose it can do no harm for you to know now...after all, it was your mother your grandfather wanted to protect. He loved her so much, you see, Petra... He loved his sons, of course, but he had that love for her that a father will often have for his girl-child. According to my husband he spoiled her outrageously, but then I suppose that is an older brother speaking. When she left like that, your grandfather was beside himself...with anger...and with despair. He had planned so much for her...

'Your uncle—my husband—found him slumped across his desk, holding your mother's photograph. The doctor did not think he would survive. He was ill for a very, very long time. Oh...I should not have told you—not today,' her aunt said remorsefully as she saw how pale Petra had gone.

'All those wasted years,' Petra whispered. 'When they could have been together—when we could all have been together as a family!'

'He missed her dreadfully.'

'But my father wrote, sent photographs...'

Her aunt sighed.

'You have to understand, Petra. Your grandfather is a very proud man. He couldn't bear to accept an olive branch extended by your father. He wanted...needed to know that your mother still wanted him in her life, that she still loved him.'

'She believed that he would never forgive her,' Petra told her chokily, shaking her head.

'When the news came that your parents were dead, your grandfather...' Her aunt paused and shook her head. 'It was a terrible, terrible time for him, Petra. He couldn't believe it. Wouldn't accept that she was gone, that he had lost her. When he had his second heart attack we honestly believed that it was in part because he simply no longer wanted to live. But mercifully he recovered. It was his greatest wish then that you might come to us, but your godfather— wisely, perhaps, in the circumstances, thought it best for you that you remained in an environment that was familiar to you. But your grandfather never gave up hoping, and when he knew that your uncle was to meet your godfather he begged him to try to persuade you to come here. I can't tell you how happy you are making him today, Petra. I wish you every happiness, my dearest girl, for you most certainly deserve it.'

As her aunt leaned forward to embrace her Petra felt her eyes burn with emotional tears.

In a daze she made her way out to the waiting car and her grandfather. Suddenly she was seeing him with new eyes. Loving, compassionate eyes. As she sat beside him she reached out and touched his hand. Immediately he clasped hers.

'You may kiss the bride!'

Petra felt her whole body clench against the pain of what was happening. Unable to move, she felt the coldness thrown by Rashid's shadow as he bent towards her.

She waited until the last possible second to turn her head

away, so that his dutiful kiss would only brush her cheek and not her lips. But to her shock, as though he had known what she would do, as she moved so did he, lifting his hand so that to their audience it looked at though he were cupping the side of her face in the most tender gesture of a lover, unable to stop himself from imbuing even this, a formal public rite, with the possessive adoration of a man deeply in love.

Only she knew that what he was actually doing was preventing her from turning away from him, that he was reinforcing to her his right, his legally given right as her husband, to demand her physical acceptance of him.

His mouth touched hers, and she trembled visibly with the force of her anger. She had believed in him, trusted him, loved him, but all the time he had been deceiving her, lying to her. How could she ever trust her own judgement again?

She would have to be constantly on her guard against it! And against him?

He moved, the smallest gesture that brought his nose against hers in the merest little touch, as though he wanted to offer her comfort and reassurance. Another lie…another deceit…and yet for an instant, caught up in the intensity of the moment, she had almost swayed yearningly towards him, wanting it to be real!

Suddenly Petra felt desperately afraid. She had thought in her ignorance that it would be enough simply for her to know what Rashid was to stop herself from continuing to love him, but now, shockingly, she wasn't so sure!

She hated him for what he had done; she knew that! So why did he still have the power to move her physically, to make her want him?

What was she thinking? Was she going crazy? She did

not want him. Not one tiny little bit! Fiercely she pushed against him. To her relief he released her immediately.

The ceremony was over. They were man and wife!

'I never knew that Rashid's middle name was Blaize.' That was her cousin Saud, flushed and excited, openly proud of his new relationship with his hero.

'Petra, my dear, your father would have been so proud had he been here today.'

Numbly Petra smiled automatically at the American Ambassador.

'Petra, you look so breathtakingly beautiful,' his wife, an elegant Texan with a slow drawl said with a warm smile. 'Doesn't she Rashid?' she demanded, causing Petra to stiffen, the tiny hairs on the back of her neck lifting as Rashid turned to look at her.

'She is my heart's desire,' Rashid responded quietly, without taking his gaze off her.

'Petra, take him away and hide him before I turn green, you lucky girl,' the Ambassador's wife teased.

'I am the one who is lucky,' Rashid corrected her.

'He certainly is,' Petra chimed in brittly. 'Today he isn't just gaining a wife, are you, Rashid? He's gaining the opportunity to design a new multi-million-pound-complex, and—'

'I'm certainly going to need some good commissions if I'm to keep you in the style your grandfather is accustoming you to.' Rashid cut across her outburst in a light drawl that masked the icy, glittering look of warning only she could see. 'At least if that necklace you're wearing is anything to go by.'

'Yes, it's gorgeous,' another of the guests enthused.

Petra tensed as she felt Rashid's hand beneath her elbow.

'I don't know why you're so determined to play the adoring husband,' she told him bitterly.

'No, I don't suppose you do,' he agreed.

'Why didn't you tell me that your second name was
Blaize?'

He gave a small dismissive shrug.

'Does is it matter? Rashid or Blaize—I am still the same
man, Petra. The man who—'

'The man who lied to me and trapped me,' Petra snapped
at him. 'Yes, you are.'

Out of the corner of her eye she could see his mouth
compress.

'We're married now, Petra, and—'

'For better, for worse… Don't remind me. We both know
which it will be, don't we?'

'Look, it doesn't have to be like this, Petra. After all, we
both already know that we have something in common,
some shared ground…'

'And what ground would that be? The ground you're
hoping to design another billion-pound complex on?
Money! Is that all you can think about?'

Petra tensed as she felt his grip move from her elbow to
her upper arm and tighten almost painfully on it as he bent
his head and whispered with menacing silkiness in her ear,
'I would have thought that I had already proved to you that
it is not. But if you wish me to show you again…'

Petra jerked away from him as though she had been
scalded.

'If you ever, ever try to force me to…to accept you as
my husband physically, then—'

'Force you?'

For a minute he looked as though she had somehow
shocked him, but then his expression changed, hardening.

'Now you are being ridiculous,' he told her curtly. 'There

has never been any question of my doing any such thing. Even though…'

'Even though what?' Petra challenged him bitterly. 'Even though legally it is your right?'

She was almost beside herself with misery and anguish mixed to a toxic consistency by an over-active imagination and the fear that she was not as indifferent to him as she wanted to be.

Now that the ceremony was over she was face to face with the knowledge that tonight she would be his wife—his bride. He was a sensually passionate man; she already knew that! If he chose to consummate their marriage would she have the strength to reject and deny him?

'Rashid, your uncle has been looking for you…'

Petra released her breath in a sigh of relief as he moved away from her.

Several hours later, blank-eyed with exhaustion and misery, Petra stared bitterly in front of her, wishing she was anywhere but where she was and anyone but who she was—or rather who she was now.

Her godfather had not been able to join them. No doubt he would save his celebrations until after the New Year and the announcement of his peerage, Petra reflected savagely.

Her marriage to Rashid had been trumpeted in the press as the romance of the year, but of course she knew better! She hated Rashid more than she had ever thought it possible for her to hate anyone, she decided wearily, and she knew she would never, ever forgive him for what he had done to her.

Finally the celebrations were drawing to a close. Finally her attendants were coming to carry her away to the suite that had been set aside for her to change out of her wedding dress and into her 'going-away' clothes.

'Where is Rashid taking you on honeymoon? Do you know?' one of the girls, a married niece of her aunt, asked Petra before shushing the knowing giggles of some of the younger bridesmaids.

Petra was tempted to reply that she neither knew nor cared, but good manners prevented her from doing so.

'I don't really know,' she replied instead.

'It's a secret. Oh, how romantic,' another of the girls exclaimed enviously.

Yet another chimed in, more practically, 'But how did you know what clothes to pack if you don't know where you are going?'

'She's going on honeymoon, silly,' another one submitted. 'So clothes won't—'

'Stop it, all of you,' the oldest and most sensible of her attendants instructed. 'You are supposed to be helping Petra, not gossiping like schoolgirls. You must not worry. A man as experienced as Rashid will know exactly what to do!' she soothed Petra. 'I can remember how nervous I was on my wedding night. I had no idea what to expect, and I was terrified that my husband would not know what I needed, but I should have had more trust in him…or rather in my mother.' She grinned. 'She had ensured that I had all the right clothes—although I suspect if it had been left to Sayeed I might not.'

Clothes! She was talking about clothes! Petra didn't know whether to laugh or cry!

At last it was over and she was ready, dressed in the simple cream trouser suit she had bought in the exclusive shopping centre nearby. The plain diamond ear studs which had been her mother's, and which she had worn since her death, had been removed from her ears and replaced by the much larger pair which had been part of Rashid's wedding present to her. She felt like ripping them out and destroying them, but of course that wasn't possible, with her attendants exclaiming excitedly over the clarity and perfection of the stones, obviously chosen to complement the diamonds in her platinum engagement and wedding rings.

She had been misted with a fresh cloud of Rashid's perfume, and handed the minute scraps of silk and lace that her aunt was pleased to call underwear—Petra still couldn't believe that such minute scraps of fabric could cost so very, very much. Her manicure and pedicure had been checked by her eagle-eyed chief attendant, who seemed to believe that it would be a lifelong reflection on her if Petra was not handed over into the hands of her new husband looking anything less than immaculate. Now she was apparently ready to be handed into the care of her husband like a sweetmeat to be unwrapped and enjoyed—or discarded as he saw fit!

'Come—it is time. Rashid is waiting,' her chief attendant announced importantly.

As Petra looked towards the closed door to the suite the busy giggles fluttering around her died away.

'Be happy,' the chief attendant told her as she kissed her.

'May your life be full of the laughter of your children and the love of your husband,' the second whispered, as all the girls queued up to offer her their good wishes for her future and exchange shy embraces with her.

'May the nights of your marriage be filled with pleasure,' the boldest-eyed and most daring told her.

The noise from outside her suite was becoming deafening.

'If we do not open the door soon Rashid might break it down,' someone giggled, and there was an instant flurry of excited and delighted female panic as the door was pulled open and Petra was prodded and pushed through it.

The assembled wedding guests standing outside cheered

exuberantly when they saw her, but Petra barely noticed their enthusiasm. Across the small space that separated them her bitter gaze clashed with Rashid's.

Like her, he was dressed in Western-style clothes. Designers the world over would have paid a fortune to have Rashid wearing their logo, Petra decided with clinical detachment, refusing to allow her heartbeat to react to the casual togetherness of his appearance. Place him in any city in the world and he would immediately be recognised as a man of style and class, a man of wealth and knowledge. Wealthy, educated people like Rashid shared a common bond, no matter what their place of birth, Petra acknowledged distantly.

Silently he extended his hand towards her.

The crowd started to cheer. Briefly Petra hesitated, her glance going betrayingly to the windows, as though seeking freedom, but someone gave her a firm little push and her fingertips touched Rashid's hand and were swiftly enclosed by it.

With almost biblical immediacy, the crowd parted to allow them to pass through. The huge double doors to the private garden of the banqueting suite were flung open, and as they stepped out into the softness of the night perfectly timed fireworks exploded, sending sprays of brilliantly coloured stars showering earthwards.

At the same time they were deluged with handfuls of scented rose petals, and the air was filled with a pink-tinged cloud of strawberry scented *shisha* smoke. Doves swooped and flew, and a cloud of shimmering butterflies appeared as if by magic—music played, people laughed and called out good wishes to them, and Rashid drew her relentlessly towards the exit to the garden.

As he touched her arm and held her for one last second to face their audience, he whispered wryly in her ear, 'Your aunt wanted me to whisk you away on an Arab steed, complete with traditional Arabic trappings, but I managed to dissuade her.'

Caught off guard by the note of humour underlining his words, Petra turned automatically to look at him. 'You mean like a prince from an Arabian fairytale? Complete with medieval accoutrements including your falcon?'

'I suspect she would have wanted to pass on the falcon—for the sake of the doves—and I certainly would not have wanted to expose my prize birds to this fairground.'

As she looked at him Petra felt her heart suddenly miss not one beat but two.

As though a veil had abruptly lifted, giving her a clear view of something she had previously only perceived in a shadowy distorted fashion, she recognised an unwanted, unpalatable, unbearably painful truth!

In believing that logic, reality, anger and moral right were enough to destroy her unwanted love for Rashid she had deceived herself even more thoroughly and cruelly than Rashid himself could ever have done.

Had she married Rashid because secretly deep down inside she still wanted him? Still loved him? Petra was filled with self-contempt and loathing, her fiery pride hating the very idea!

She had believed that her most dangerous enemy lay outside the armed citadel of her heart, in the shape of Rashid himself, but she had been wrong. Her worst enemy lay within herself, within her own heart, in the form of her love for him.

But Rashid must never ever know that. She must forever be on her guard to protect herself and her emotions. She and they must become a fortress which Rashid must never be allowed to penetrate!

*   *   *

'Welcome to your new home!'

For the first time since they had left the hotel Rashid broke the silence between them. They had driven into the courtyard of the villa several seconds earlier, its creamy toned wall, warmed to gold by the discreet nightscape lighting. Her whole body rigid with the effort of maintaining the guard she was clinging to so desperately, Petra had discovered that her throat had locked so tensely that she couldn't even speak!

Once inside the villa she felt no more relaxed—quite the opposite.

'It's late, and it has been a very long day,' she heard Rashid saying calmly. 'I suggest that we both get a good night's sleep before you begin another round of hostilities. I have arranged for you to have your own suite of rooms. Not exactly the traditional way to conduct a wedding night, perhaps, but then it is not as though it would be our first time together.' Her gave a small dismissive shrug whilst Petra struggled to assimilate a feeling which was not entirely composed of relief! 'This has been a stressful time for you, and you need a little breathing space, I suspect, to accustom yourself to what is to be. Despite your comments earlier, I can assure you that there is no way I intend to…to force the issue between us, Petra!'

Petra stared at him. He sounded so controlled, so calm, so…so laid-back and casual almost. And as for his comment about arranging for her to have her own rooms—that was not at all what she had been expecting!

From the moment he had proposed formally to her this night had been at the back of Petra's mind. This moment when they would be alone as husband and wife. Fiercely she had told herself that no matter what kind of pressure he put on her to break down her resolve she would not allow him to touch her!

And yet now he was the one telling her that he did not want her!

A distinctly unpleasant mix of emotions filled her. Shock, disbelief, chagrin…and…

Disappointment? Most certainly not! Relief—that was what she felt. Yes, she was perhaps just a touch disappointed that he had stolen her thunder by not allowing her the satisfaction of being the one to tell him that she didn't want him. But at the end of the day what really mattered was that she was going to be free to sleep on her own…without him. Sleeping in her own bed and not his…just as though they were not married at all. And that was just what she wanted. Exactly what she wanted!

At last she was on her own. Which was just what she wanted. So why couldn't she go to sleep? Why was she lying here feeling so…lost and abandoned? So unwanted…and unloved and so hurt?

What was it that she longed for so much? Rashid? Blaize?

No! What she ached for, so much that it hurt, Petra acknowledged tormentedly as she burrowed into the emptiness of her huge bed, was to be able to trust the man she loved. Because without such trust, without being able to be open and honest with one another, how could two people possibly claim to share love?

CHAPTER TEN

A LITTLE apprehensively, Petra surveyed the other women crowding into the exclusive enclosure.

It was the start of the horse racing season and Petra suspected that by now, after over a month of marriage, she ought to be familiar with the high-octane and very glamorous nature of the social events to which her position as Rashid's wife gave her an entrée.

In the short time they had been married they had already had the tennis championships, and a celebrity golf tournament, in addition to a whole host of business events sponsored by the Royal Family in which Rashid, as one of their most favoured architects and a business partner, had played a high-profile role.

And now, within a few days, it would be the most prestigious event of the Zuran social calendar—the Zuran Cup, the world's most glamorous horse race.

Horses, trainers, jockeys, owners and their elegant wives had been pouring into Zuran all month—the whole city was in a state of excited expectancy over the race and its eventual winner.

Rashid was entering his own horse, an American-bred and Irish-trained three-year-old stabled at his training yard close to the racecourse. Along with a mere handful of other specially favoured owners, Rashid was permitted to use the actual racecourse itself for training purposes.

Petra and Rashid were due to entertain a group of businessmen and diplomats and their partners from America and Europe, and for the duration of Race Week they would be staying at the hotel complex with their guests.

Unlike some of the other wives, Petra had not found it necessary to fly to Paris or Milan to order a series of one-off couture outfits for the event—although she had taken her aunt's advice and been to see a visiting top milliner to ensure that her hat for the occasion was 'special' enough for her position as the wife of an owner of one of the competing horses.

At the breathtakingly stunning villa he had designed and had built, in its equally breathtaking setting of his private oasis, they had entertained a variety of prominent politicians, sportsmen and women and businessmen from all over the world, including the UK, and never once on any of those occasions had Rashid faltered in enacting his own chosen role of devoted husband.

But in private things were very different. Rashid kept to his own suite of rooms in the villa, as she did hers, and when they were not entertaining or being entertained Petra hardly saw him.

He was either working, visiting various projects he was involved in virtually all over the world or, when he was at home, he would be down in the stables where he kept the racehorses he had in training, discussing their progress with his racing manager.

Of course Petra had commitments of her own. She had been invited to join the Zuran Ladies Club, headed by Her Highness—the club's remit being to provide a common ground for the exchange of ideas between women belonging to different nationalities and cultures. She had gone to women's lunches and fund-raising events, and an embryo friendship was developing between her and her most senior wedding attendant—a relative of her aunt by marriage. But these were the outer layers of her married life.

The inner ones were very different and very painful.

Common sense told her that the discovery she had not conceived Rashid's child should have been greeted with relief. Instead she had spent the night silently weeping with anguished disappointment. His child would at least have been something of him she would have been allowed to publicly love.

And that was the private pain which was slowly destroying her.

Outwardly, in the eyes of other people, she must seem as though she had everything anyone could possibly want, Petra reflected as she checked her appearance in her bedroom mirror.

Rashid, who was currently away on business and was not due to return for another two days, had kept his promise not to touch her. Indeed, he quite obviously found it a very easy promise to keep; his relaxed calm politeness whenever they were together made her grit her teeth together against the fury of physical and emotional confusion she herself was enduring.

How was it possible for her to want him so much when he quite obviously did not want her? She lay in bed at night aching for him. Longing for him, thinking about him—fantasising about him, if she was honest—and then in the morning was filled with such a sense of self-revulsion and despair at her own lack of self-control that she despised herself even more than she did him.

He treated her as distantly as though she were merely a visiting house guest—an outsider to his world and life to whom he was obliged to be polite. She had absolutely no idea what he might be thinking or feeling about their marriage, or about her, and that further intensified her sense of loneliness and frustration. It was not natural to live in the way they were doing, and her body, her mind, her heart, her spirit rebelled against it.

She wanted to share her life and herself fully with the man she loved, but how could she do that when that man was Rashid, a man who did not love her in return? A man she could not trust!

She paused in the process of packing her clothes for their Race Week stay in the hotel complex, a tiny, fine tremble of sensation electrifying her at the thought of seeing Rashid. Angrily she dismissed it. She reminded herself firmly instead that she was due to visit the racecourse stables to discuss with Rashid's trainer what arrangements needed to be made with regard to guests visiting the stables to view the horses.

Already, although they were still in March, the temperature had climbed well into the high thirties, and Petra dressed accordingly, in cotton jeans and a long sleeved tee shirt, plus a hat to protect her head from the sun.

The young man Rashid had appointed as her driver smiled happily at her as he opened the car door for her.

Petra had timed her visit to coincide with the end of the morning exercise session, and when she walked into the yard it was bustling with activity as the newly exercised horses were returned to their stables.

Rashid's manager and trainer were standing together on the far side of the stable yard talking to one another as Petra walked in. Several other groups of people were in the stable yard, including two small dark-haired children.

Smiling at them, Petra started to make her way towards Rashid's manager and trainer, but as she did so she saw one of the children suddenly dart across the yard, right into the path of the highly strung, nervously sweating young horse being led across the yard by his handler.

As the horse reared up Petra reacted instinctively, making a grab for the child and snatching him from beneath the horse's hooves.

She could hear the uproar going on all around her; the shrill squeal of fear from the horse and the even shriller scream of panic from the child, the groom's anxious voice, the voices of the onlookers, and then the breath was driven out of her lungs as the world exploded in an agonising red mist of searing pain followed by a terrifying sensation of whirling darkness as she hit the ground.

Blearily Petra opened her eyes.

'Ah, good, you've finally come round properly.'

A uniformed nurse smiled at her. Weakly Petra began to move, and then winced as she felt the pain in her shoulder.

'Don't worry, it isn't serious. Just a very nasty bruise, that's all,' the nurse comforted her cheerfully. 'You were lucky, though, and the little boy you rescued was even luckier.'

The child! Petra sat up anxiously and then gasped as pain ripped through her shoulder.

'Are you sure he's okay?' she pressed the nurse.

'He's fine—in fact I think his father is in a worse state of shock than he was. They are related to the Royal Family, you know. Cousins, I think. The father couldn't sing your praises highly enough. He is convinced that if you hadn't acted so promptly the horse might have killed his son.'

'It wasn't the horse's fault!' Petra protested. 'The yard was busy, and he was obviously nervous... Ouch!' She winced as the nurse readjusted the strapping holding the protective pad in place against her skin.

'Don't worry, I'm just checking to see if you've stopped bleeding.'

'Bleeding?' Petra frowned.

'The horse's shoe caught your shoulderblade, and as well

as inflicting a wonderful-looking bruise it's also broken the skin. It looks fine now, though.'

'Good—in that case, I can get dressed and go home,' Petra said.

'Not until the doctor has given you the all-clear,' the nurse warned her.

Half an hour later Petra was sitting fully dressed on the side of her bed, frowning mutinously at the young doctor confronting her.

'Look, I can't stay in overnight,' she told him firmly. 'We're less than a week away from Race Week, and I've got a hundred things I have to do. You've said yourself that you're ninety-nine per cent sure that I don't have concussion, and—'

'I would still prefer you to stay in overnight, just to be on the safe side,' the doctor was telling her insistently.

Petra shook her head.

'There really isn't any need. I promise you I feel fine.'

'We should at least alert your husband to what has happened,' the doctor persisted.

Rashid. Petra tensed. Right now he was in London, overseeing some problem with the alterations to the hotel which the Royal Family had just acquired to add to their portfolio of hotel properties. He wasn't due back for another two days, and she could just imagine how he was going to feel if he was dragged back on account of a wife who emotionally meant nothing whatsoever to him at all!

Determinedly she set about convincing the young doctor that there was no reason why Rashid should be unnecessarily alarmed about a mere minor accident, when he would be home within a couple of days anyway, and to Petra's relief he seemed to accept her argument.

When it came to allowing her to go home, though, he

was harder to persuade, but in the end he gave in and said that provided she was not going to be left on her own, and that there was someone there to keep an eye on her, he would agree to discharge her.

Assuring him that there was, Petra held her breath whilst he checked her bruised shoulder, and then wrote her a prescription for some painkillers, before finally agreeing to her discharge.

An hour later she was on her way home, gritting her teeth against the unexpectedly intense pain in her shoulder as she was driven slowly and carefully back to the villa by her very protective and anxious young driver.

Once there, she was fussed over by Rashid's staff to an extent that made her grit her teeth a little and insist that they stop treating her as though she was a fragile piece of china.

Within an hour of her return she had received so many concerned telephone calls that she was refusing to take any more, and the largest reception room of the villa was filled with floral tributes—including an enormous display from the Royal Family, thanking her for rescuing one of their family.

Ignoring the dull, nagging ache which even the strong painkillers she had been given at the hospital had not totally suppressed, Petra went into the room she used as her office and started to go through the sample menus submitted to her by the hotel's senior chef.

Their guests would be dining in one of the hotel's private dining rooms, and Petra worked into the evening, meticulously checking the profiles she had been given of their guests against the chef's suggested menus, stopping only to eat the light meal which Rashid's housekeeper brought her and to reassure her that she was feeling completely fine apart from having an aching shoulder. At midnight Petra decided that she had had enough and tidied away her papers before making her way to her suite.

The live-in staff had their own quarters, separate from the main villa. Quite what the housekeeper thought of a newly married couple who slept apart Petra had no idea, but the housekeeper had confided to her that Rashid had had her suite of rooms completely redecorated prior to their marriage, even though the villa was brand-new and the rooms had previously been unoccupied.

The villa embraced the best of both Eastern and Western cultures, and had a clean, almost minimalistic look that reminded her of certain exclusive West Coast American homes belonging to friends of her parents, where modern simplicity was broken up and softened by the intriguing addition of single antique pieces. In the case of Rashid's villa, there was an underlying sense of traditional Moorish décor which really appealed to Petra's senses. Even the colours he had chosen were sympathetic to the eye and the landscape: pale sands, soft terracottas, a delicate watery blue-green here and there to break up the neutral natural colours.

Stunning sculptures and pieces of artwork made subtle statements about Rashid's wealth and taste, fabrics made to delight the touch as well as the eye softened any starkness—and yet the villa felt alien and unwelcoming to Petra.

Despite its elegance and comfort, something essential was missing from it. It was a house empty of love, with no sense of being a home, of having a heart! To Petra, acutely sensitive about such things, it lacked that aura of being a place where people who loved one another lived.

She winced a little as she removed the bandage from her back and shoulder, but when she peered over her shoulder to study her reflection in the mirror in her bathroom she was relieved to see that, despite the livid bruising swelling her skin, the raw scrape on her flesh looked clean and had stopped bleeding. As she stood beneath the warm spray of a shower that was large enough for two people to share with comfort she winced a little with pain. She would have some discomfort for some days to come, the doctor had warned her.

It was the horse she felt most sorry for, Petra decided ruefully a little later as she discarded her wrap and slid naked into her bed. The poor animal had been nervous enough before the incident.

Her bed felt deliciously cool. It had been made up with clean, immaculate linen sheets that day. Forlornly Petra turned onto her side. The bed was huge, making her feel acutely conscious of the fact that, despite her marriage, she was still living the life of a partnerless woman. A woman whose husband did not want her, did not desire her, did not love her. Whilst she...

Whilst she had not gone one single night since her marriage without longing for Rashid to be here with her, without giving in to the hopeless, helpless temptation to recreate those hours she had spent in his arms at the oasis. Tiredly Petra closed her eyes against the slow fall of threatening tears.

Abruptly Petra opened her eyes, wincing as she tried to move her painfully stiff shoulder.

'Petra, are you all right?'

She gave a small gasp of shock as she stared into the darkness to where Rashid was sitting beside the bed.

'Rashid!'

Immediately she struggled to sit up, ignoring the dull nagging ache from her shoulder as she clutched the bed-clothes to her body, her heart thudding furiously.

'You weren't supposed to be coming back yet! What are you doing here?'

'What do you think I'm doing here?' he answered her grimly. 'I received a message to say that you had been involved in an accident and that there were grave concerns that you could be suffering from concussion. Naturally I caught the first flight back that I could.'

'You didn't need to do that.' Petra protested. 'I'm perfectly all right…apart from a stiff shoulder,' she added ruefully.

Whilst she had been speaking Rashid had switched on the lamp at the side of her bed.

Petra sucked in her breath as she saw him properly for the first time. She had never seen him looking so formidably severe, harsh lines etched from his nose to his mouth, his expression wintry and bleak.

'I'm sorry that you had to come back—' she began.

'What on earth were you thinking about?' Rashid overrode her apology. 'Is marriage to me really so unbearable that you prefer to throw yourself under the hooves of a horse and be trampled to death?'

Petra stared at him, stunned by the bleak bitterness in his voice.

'It wasn't like that,' she protested. 'There was a child…I simply acted instinctively, as anyone would have done.'

His frown deepened.

'I hadn't heard about a child, only that there had nearly been a terrible tragedy and that you had insisted on leaving the hospital even though there was concern that you might not be well enough to do so.'

'I have a bruised shoulder, that is all.' Petra told, him making light of her injury. The truth was that she was far more interested in discovering why the thought of her being injured had brought him all the way home from London than in discussing her very minor bruises with him.

'When I spoke to the hospital the doctor said that he was concerned there was a risk that you might experience concussion.'

'You came back because of that?' Petra was openly incredulous.

'He warned you that you should not be on your own,' Rashid told her grimly.

'He admitted that the risk was minimal and that he was virtually one hundred per cent sure that I would be okay. And anyway I'm not on my own—the staff—' Petra began.

'Are not here to keep a proper watch over you,' Rashid interrupted her. 'But I am.'

As he spoke he moved, and Petra saw how tired he looked.

'Rashid, I'm fine,' she told him. 'Look, why don't you go to bed and—'

'I'm staying right here,' he told her flatly.

Petra sighed. 'I promise you, there is no need. If I hadn't felt completely well I would not have come back to the villa.'

'That's fine. But, like I just said, until I'm convinced that you're okay I'm staying here,' Rashid reiterated.

Petra sighed again, hunching her uninjured shoulder defensively as she told him tiredly, 'Have it your own way, Rashid, but honestly there's no need for you to stay.'

As he reached out to switch off the light Rashid instructed her flatly, 'Go back to sleep.'

Quietly Petra moved her head. She could hear Rashid breathing, but she couldn't see him sitting in the chair beside her bed. And then, as she looked across the bed, she saw him.

He was lying on his back on the bed beside her fast asleep.

The moon was up and full, casting a soft silvery light through the gauzy curtains of her room. Propping herself up on one elbow, she studied Rashid's sleeping form. Watching him sleep and seeing him so vulnerable sent a huge wave of tenderness aching through her.

At some stage he had unfastened the shirt he had been wearing and the white fabric was a pale blur against the darkness of his skin. There was evidence of his long day in the dark shadow bearding his jaw, and her muscles tensed a little in female response to such evidence of his maleness. Before she could stop herself she was reaching out to touch his jaw experimentally with her fingertips, and she felt her tenderness give way to sharply spiked desire.

As her fingers started to tremble she snatched them away, curling them into a fist and imprisoning them with her other hand. But, although she had managed to stop herself from touching him, she couldn't stop herself from looking at him, her love-hungry gaze fastening greedily on his mouth, his throat, the exposed flesh of his torso.

Now it wasn't just her fingers that were trembling, it was her whole body! She could feel the hot urgency of her own desire seeping into every nerve-ending—seeping, flowing, flooding through her until it swamped her completely.

Rashid! Tormentedly she mouthed his name, and then jumped back as he stirred in his sleep, his eyes starting to open.

By the time he had fully opened them she had retreated to her own side of the bed and was lying defensively still as she tried to feign sleep.

'Petra?' She heard the anxiety in his sleep-thickened voice as he leaned towards her. His hand touched her throat, checking her pulse, monitoring its frantic race.

'Petra, wake up,' he was commanding her.

'Rashid, it's all right—I do not have concussion,' she told him briefly, guessing what he was thinking, turning her head to look at him and trying to shrug off his hand as she did so.

But suddenly he had gone completely still, his hand lying against her throat with heavy immobility. His gaze was fixed on her breasts, naked and exposed by her inadvertent negligence in failing to pull the covers up over her body.

She knew immediately and instinctively that he wanted her, and she knew just as instinctively that he would keep to the promise he had made her on the day of their wedding not to force himself on her.

All she needed to do was to reach for her covers and turn away from him. If that was what she wanted...

And if it wasn't? Hardly daring to acknowledge what was going through her mind, Petra held his gaze. She could feel the longing and need curling through her, gaining force and power, filling her until her whole body felt like a highly tuned instrument of desire, openly aching for his touch. She could feel her breasts swell and lift, her nipples tighten and ache, her belly sink in slightly against the desire flooding her sex.

Lifting her hand, she curled her fingers around his forearm, slowly caressing it, her eyes wide open as she gazed up into his.

She could feel the open tremor of his body at her touch, see the way he was fighting to draw extra air into his lungs. What was he thinking? Feeling? A fierce surge of excitement and power filled her as she read the answer in the hot gleam of his eyes and the immediate response of his body!

'Hold me, Rashid,' she commanded him boldly, shuddering violently as he did so, tightening his arms around her so that they were body to body, so that she could feel the heavy, exciting thud of his heart.

'Love me!' she whispered passionately against his hot skin, knowing that he could not hear the betraying words, only feel the warmth of her breath.

She heard—and felt—the low growl of sound he made deep in his throat! Frustration? Longing?

Her body responded to it immediately, her lips parting eagerly for the savage sweet pleasure of his kiss.

Instantly she was plunged into a spiral of aching need, a swift descent into the thick velvet heat of her own most primitive longings. Her hand pressed to the back of Rashid's head, she urged him to increase the pressure of his mouth against her own, until all rational thought was suspended beneath its bruisingly passionate heat.

Petra knew that she should have been horrified by and contemptuous of her own behaviour, that she should have totally resisted her own desire. But instead she could feel her heart turning over inside her chest and then slamming heavily into her ribs as shockingly elemental and savage emotions exploded into life inside her. She had wanted this so much, she recognised dizzily. She had wanted, needed him so much!

'Petra,' Rashid groaned against her mouth. 'This isn't...'

He moved, his hand accidentally brushing against her breast, and Petra froze. In the darkness she could feel his gaze searching the distance between them, penetrating the moon-silvered darkness and then fixing unerringly on the betraying peak of her nipple, where it pouted with deliberate invitation so dangerously close to his stilled hand.

'Petra?' This time when he said her name it held a different note, a male huskiness and timbre that her sensitive female ears interpreted as an open acknowledgement of his desire for her.

She could feel the power that his desire for her gave her. She was all Eve, a wanton temptress, holding her breath whilst she willed him to reach out to her, for her, already knowing the pleasure he would give her.

Very slowly his hand moved back towards her breast. Petra exhaled shakily, and then closed her eyes as he stroked her skin with the lightest of touches—so light that it was little more than a breath, and yet so sensual that her whole breast seemed to swell and yearn towards him.

'Petra.'

This time her name was muffled beneath the slow, lingering kisses he was threading around the base of her throat like a necklace. A necklace that reached down between her breasts and was then strung from the upper curve of one breast to the other.

At some stage Petra had started to tremble. Tiny little inner secret tremors at first, but by the time Rashid was cupping one breast in his hand, laving the delighted pink-flushed crest of the other with his tongue, they had turned into galvanic shudders of uncontrollable mute delight. And then not so mute, when Petra was forced to bite down hard on her bottom lip to prevent herself from crying out aloud.

When Rashid saw what she was doing he lifted his mouth from her nipple to watch her, and then slid his finger into her mouth, freeing her bottom lip whilst he told her thickly, 'Taste me instead, Petra!'

Her whole body reacted to his words, swept with a molten need that burned openly in her eyes.

'Yes! *Yes!*' he told her savagely, even though she had said nothing, spoken no question. But Petra knew that he had heard the silent hungry longing of her body, seen her need for him in her eyes.

'Yes,' he repeated more softly. 'Whatever... However...

Every which way you want, Petra. Every way, until you beg me to end our mutual torment.'

As he was speaking he was kissing her. Tiny slow kisses that were a torment in themselves as his hands shaped her body, effortlessly drawing from it everything that it ached so wantonly to give him and everything that she herself did not.

Her need, herself, her life. Her love...

She cried out in shocked denial under the touch of his tongue against her sex, and then cried out again in a low, guttural woman's cry of acknowledgement of the pleasure he was showing her. But when he moaned in response, and placed her hand on his body, her reaction caused him to lift his head and demand rawly, 'Did you think you are the only one to have pleasure in what I'm doing, in the feel of you, the heat of you, the taste of you? I've hungered for you like this Petra, for this intimacy with you...this possession of you.'

As he stopped speaking he turned his head and kissed the inside of her thigh. Petra trembled and then moaned as he kissed her again, more intimately. Her longing for his physical possession of her overwhelmed every other emotion she felt surging through her in an unstoppable, undammable torrent.

Petra didn't know if she had actually reached for Rashid or if he had simply known how she felt, how she ached...how she loved and needed. But suddenly he was there, where she most wanted him to be. Where she most needed him to be. Filling her with surge after powerful surge of exquisite sensation and unparallelled ecstasy.

She wanted it to never end. And yet she knew she would die if she did not reach the summit, the frantic crescendo of her completion. She thought she already knew the sensation, the pleasure, the fulfilment, but when the spasms began and she felt the hot sweet thickness of Rashid's own release within her she knew that all she had known had been a pale remembered shadow of real pleasure.

CHAPTER ELEVEN

'PETRA, are you sure you are all right?'

'Grandfather, I am fine,' Petra fibbed as she turned away from him to prevent him from seeing her tears.

He had arrived unexpectedly that morning, just after Rashid had left to visit the stables, anxious to find out how Petra was for himself.

'No, you aren't,' he insisted, coming up to her and turning her towards him. 'You are crying. What's wrong?' he asked sternly.

Petra bit her lip. She still felt seared, scorched, shamed by her memories of the previous night! And there was no point in her trying to mentally blame Rashid! She had been the one to instigate things...even if he had carried them...and her...to a point...place...she had never imagined existed!

She was furious with herself for her weakness, unable to accept her own behaviour. How could she have been so weak-willed as to give in to temptation? Why couldn't she make herself stop loving him? Especially when she knew there was no future for them; when she knew she couldn't trust him.

He didn't love her. He might have returned early from his business trip. He might have made love with her last night...he might even have stayed with her until she had fallen asleep. But he had never made any attempt to talk to her, to tell her...

To tell her what? That he loved her? But she already

172

knew that he did not, didn't she? She already knew that he had been forced to marry her!

They were trapped in a marriage which could only cause them both misery. And now, thanks to her behaviour last night, there could be additional complications. What if this time she *had* conceived his baby?

'You are not happy,' her grandfather was persisting. 'You are too thin...too pale. This was not what I expected when you and Rashid married. You are so obviously suited to one another in so many ways.' He started to frown.

Petra stared at him. Suited to one another! How could he think that?

'In your eyes, perhaps,' she told him unhappily. 'But no...! We should never have married. Rashid feels nothing for me. He doesn't love me and...I—'

'Petra, what nonsense is this?' her grandfather demanded immediately. 'Of course Rashid loves you! That has never been in any doubt! It is quite obvious how he feels about you from the way he talks about you, from the way he has behaved towards you.'

'No!' Petra stopped him in disbelief 'You're wrong! How can you say that he loves me? The only reason Rashid married me is because he...he had to!'

'Had to?' To Petra's consternation her grandfather actually laughed. 'What on earth gave you that idea? It was most certainly not the case at all!'

He gave her a wry look. 'It is, of course, true that the pair of you would logically be expected to marry, having spent so much time together unchaperoned, but I can assure you that there was no obligation for Rashid to marry you other than his own desire to do so! And I can also tell you that that desire sprang entirely from his love for you!'

Her grandfather shook his head. 'And, besides, Rashid would never have allowed himself to be involved in such a potentially compromising situation if he had not been passionately in love with you!'

Her grandfather spoke with such conviction that Petra was dumbfounded.

'There is only one reason Rashid married you, Petra,' he repeated. 'And that is quite simply that he loves you.'

'If that is true then why has he never told me so himself?' Petra asked emotionally, reluctant to allow herself to trust what she was hearing.

'Have you told him of your love for him?' her grandfather challenged her gently.

Biting her lip, Petra had to confess that she had not.

'But you do love him?' her grandfather persisted.

Petra could not bring herself to reply. She could see that her grandfather was frowning.

'If I have misjudged your feelings, Petra, then you must say so,' she heard him telling her with gentle firmness. 'Much as I like and respect Rashid, you are my granddaughter. If you have discovered that you do not love him, if you are in any way unhappy, then you can come home with me now and I shall speak to Rashid if you wish.'

Petra's eyes darkened with emotion.

'I feel so confused. There is so much I...I believed...I thought...' She stopped and took a deep breath. 'I thought that Rashid married me because of the financial benefits our marriage would bring him,' she confessed, blurting out her despair.

'The financial benefits?' Her grandfather looked bemused. 'Petra—' he began, but Petra stopped him, rushing on fiercely.

'Saud told me everything, Grandfather. You mustn't be cross with him. He didn't realise that I didn't know there was a...a plan to have me marry Rashid—whether I wanted to or not! Saud hero-worships him so much that he thought

I would be pleased…thrilled. I know all about…everything. Even my godfather seemed to think it was a good idea. So much so that he abandoned me here without my passport so that I couldn't leave…'

'Petra, Petra. My dear child. Please! You are distressing yourself so unnecessarily!'

Petra fell silent as she heard the pain in her grandfather's voice. 'Come and sit down here beside me,' he commanded her gently.

A little reluctantly she did so.

'You are right in thinking there was a suggestion that you and Rashid should meet one another, and that it was felt that…that you had a great deal in common—but you must understand that a suggestion was all it was, made more in jest than anything else. Saud obviously eaves-dropped on that conversation and leapt to incorrect as-sumptions…' He frowned. 'You may be sure that I shall have some strong words to say to him about his behaviour and his actions in passing on his totally unfounded as-sumptions to you. As you say, he greatly admires Rashid… But I can assure you that Rashid immediately insisted that what was being suggested was totally out of the question. Rashid has far too much pride, too much of the same spirit I can see so clearly in you, to ever allow anyone else to make that kind of decision for him,' he told her ruefully.

'As for your godfather.' He gave a small rueful shrug. 'He is a statesman and a diplomat—who knows what such men think? Intrigue is their bread and meat. If it does not exist then they create it!'

Petra had to acknowledge that there was some truth in his assessment of her godfather, even if his description of him leaned towards the slightly over-cynical.

Shaking his head, he continued, 'After losing Mija there was no way I would ever want to repeat the mistake I made with her. There was only one reason I wanted you to come to Zuran, Petra, and that is because you are my grandchild and because I longed so much to see you!'

'Grandfather, I know that you and Rashid are in business together,' Petra persisted. 'And that he is dependent on the patronage of the Royal Family! I know that there were diplomatic reasons…'

Petra stared at her grandfather as he started to laugh.

'Why are you laughing?' she demanded, offended.

'Petra, Rashid is a millionaire many times over in his own right, from the inheritance left to him by his father. We do have business interests in common, yes—and indeed the Royal Family are great admirers of his work—but Rashid is dependent on no one's patronage!'

Shaking his head, he added huskily, 'Petra, I did your mother a terrible wrong, but the price I paid is one I shall pay to the end of my days. There is never a sunrise when I do not think of your mother, nor a sunset when I do not mourn her loss.'

Petra blinked, her eyes wet with fresh tears. Instinctively she knew that her grandfather was telling the truth.

'Are you still feeling unhappy? Do you want to come home with me now?' he asked her. 'I shall speak with Rashid for you, if you wish. The decision is yours, but it seems to me that it would be a pity if two such well-matched people should lose one another through a simple matter of pride, and lack of communication and trust.'

Her grandfather made it all sound so easy!

'No… No, I do not wish you to speak to Rashid,' she answered him.

'I…I…can do that myself…'

The smile he was giving her made her colour self-consciously.

'It isn't for me to interfere, but you are my granddaughter,' he told her gently. 'It seems to me that you and Rashid are very well suited. You are both strong-minded, you are both proud, you share a spirit of independence; these are all good things, but sometimes such virtues can lead to a little too much self-sufficiency—claimed not because that is what a person necessarily wants but because they believe it is what they have to have in order to protect themselves. I think that both you and Rashid are perhaps afraid to admit your great love for one another because you fear the other will think you weak and in need.'

His intuitive reading of her most private and hidden feelings astonished Petra.

Part of the reason she had fought so hard to resist her love for Rashid *had* been because she feared its intensity. Could it be true, as her grandfather had implied, that Rashid felt exactly the same?

She was, she recognised, still trying to come to terms with the fact that she had made such an error of judgement in assuming why he had married her. But he had made no attempt to defend himself to her, had he? Out of pride? Or because he didn't really care what she thought? And he had deceived her about who he really was!

'Sometimes in life we are tested where we are most vulnerable. There are many ways of being strong, many reasons for being proud,' her grandfather was continuing gently. 'Only you can decide whether or not your love for Rashid is worth fighting for, Petra—whether it means enough to you for you to take the risk of reaching out to him, openly and honestly. Rashid has already taken that risk by marrying you. It is his way of saying how much he wants to be with you. Remember he has married you in free will and of his own choice. Perhaps it is now time for you to take your risk!'

Silently Petra absorbed his words. He had given her an

insight into the workings of Rashid's mind and heart that she had not previously contemplated, and the possibilities springing to life from that insight were giving her an entrancing, an intoxicating, an impossible to resist picture of what they could share together.

'I have additionally been instructed to give this to you,' her grandfather continued, changing the subject. He handed her a beautifully decorated piece of rolled parchment and a flat oblong package.

Petra frowned. 'What is it?'

'Open it and see,' he said with a smile.

Hesitantly Petra did so, her glance skimming the letter written on the parchment and then studying it more slowly a second time, before she turned to the package and quickly unfastened it.

'It's a letter from the father of the little boy—the one at the stables,' she told her grandfather. 'He has written to thank me and he has...' Her voice tailed away and she gave a small gasp as she studied the contents of the package.

'It's ownership papers for a...a horse...a yearling...'

'Bred out of the Royal stables,' her grandfather supplied for her. 'They are very grateful to you for what you did, Petra. You saved the life of a very precious child...and at no small risk to your own.'

'But a horse!' Petra was overwhelmed.

'Not just a horse,' her grandfather corrected her with a smile. 'But a yearling whose breeding means that he may one day earn you, his owner, the Zuran Cup!'

From the balcony of the Presidential Suite Petra could see down to the beach. Race Week and all its excitement and busyness was over. She and Rashid had said goodbye to their last guests and in the morning they were due to leave the hotel for the villa.

Rashid's horse had come in a very respectable fourth, and Petra's grandfather had teased him that he might soon find himself in the position of having his wife's horse competing with his own

There had been no opportunity for them to be on their own together since the night Rashid had made love to her at the villa, or for Petra to raise the subject she was desperately anxious to talk to him about.

According to her grandfather, Rashid loved her!

On a sudden impulse Petra left the suite and hurried towards the lift.

It was already almost dusk, the sun loungers around the pool empty, the beach deserted apart from one lone figure collecting the discarded windsurfers.

For a second his unexpected appearance checked Petra, and then she took a deep breath. She had initially intended to come down here merely to think, but perhaps fate had decided to take a hand in events.

The sand muffled her footsteps, but even so something must have alerted Rashid to her presence because he turned round to watch her in silence.

His formal clothes had been discarded and he was wearing a tee shirt and a pair of jeans.

Trying to control her nervousness, Petra walked up to him. His silence unnerved her, and she moistened her lips with the tip of her tongue, her face flushing as his gaze trapped the small betraying movement.

'I...I...have a proposition I want to put to you,' she told him, superstitiously crossing her fingers behind her back as she spoke.

How was he going to react? Was he going to walk away? Was he going to ignore her? Was he going to listen to her? Petra knew which she wanted him to do!

'A proposition?'

Well, at least he was responding to her, even if she could hear a grim note of cynicism in his voice.

'What kind of proposition?'

'I have a problem and I think you could be the very person to help me,' she said.

It was a relief that it was now fully dusk and he couldn't see her face—although she suspected that he must be able to hear the anxiety and uncertainty in her voice. If she had felt nervous the first time she had propositioned him then she felt a hundred—no, a thousand times more so now. Then all that had been at stake had been her freedom; now it was her whole life...her love...everything!

'I need you to help me find out if the man I love loves me. Until today I believed that he didn't, but now it seems I might have been wrong.'

'The man you love?' he questioned, and there was a new note in his voice that sent Petra's pulses racing.

'Yes. I love him so much that I'm almost afraid to admit just how much—even to myself, never mind to him—and I thought...'

'Yes?'

He had moved so swiftly and silently, and she had been so engrossed in her own anxiety, that his sudden proximity to her caught her off-guard.

'I thought you might be able to show me a way to show him just how I feel...' she said huskily.

'Oh, you did, did you? What inducement exactly were you planning to offer me in return for my co-operation?'

There was a distinct huskiness in his voice now, and Petra allowed herself to relax just a little.

'Oh...' She pretended to consider. 'I was rather thinking in terms of...er...payment in kind...'

'Uh-huh...'

Uh-huh. Was that going to be his only response? Nothing

more? Nothing more positive? More encouraging? Fresh uncertainty gripped her.

'If you aren't interested—' she began.

'Did I say that?' He was standing even closer to her now.

'No,' she admitted. 'But…'

'If you really wanted to prove to him that you do love him, I think a good place to start would be right here,' she heard him murmur. 'Right here, in his arms, like this…'

His arms were closing round her, holding her tight. Relief melted the tension from her bones.

'Like this?'

Was that thrilled little squeak really her voice?

'Uh-huh. And then you might show him that you liked being here by putting your arms around his neck, looking up in his eyes and…'

'Like this, you mean?' Petra whispered.

'Sort of… You're on the right track—but it would be even better if you did this!' Rashid told her, showing her what he meant as he brushed her lips with his own.

'Mmm… But what if I want to kiss him properly?' Petra asked him.

'Well, then I think you should go right ahead,' Rashid replied. 'But I ought to warn you that if you do that, he could very well want to…'

Sometimes actions could speak far more informatively than words, Petra decided dizzily as she daringly silenced Rashid's soft-voiced instructions with the loving pressure of her mouth against his.

It was a long, long time before either of them wanted to speak again, but when they had finally managed to stop kissing one another Rashid told her masterfully, 'I think our negotiations might be better conducted somewhere more…private.'

'Oh?' Petra gave him a mischievous look. 'Have you anywhere specific in mind? Only I am staying at the hotel.'

'What I have in mind,' Rashid responded softly, with an erotic undertone to his voice that made her heart dance in excited anticipation, 'is a very large bed, in a room that is preferably soundproofed so that no one can hear your cries of pleasure other than me...'

Since he was threading each word on a necklace of kisses round her throat, in between teasing her lips with the briefest of sensual contacts with his mouth, Petra was not really able to focus on too many specifics—although the words 'bed' and 'pleasure' did manage to penetrate her dizzying mist of euphoria.

As he kissed his way up the side of her neck and nibbled on her earlobe she demanded huskily, 'So it is true, then—you do love me?'

So abruptly that it shocked her, Rashid released her. For a moment Petra went icy cold with fear, but then she saw the expression in his eyes.

'I fell in love with you here on this beach, the evening you propositioned me,' Rashid told her quietly. 'Up until then you had just been a name I had heard mentioned in connection with your grandfather—someone who shared a similar parental background to my own, yes, but there are many, many offspring of mixed marriages living here.' He gave a small dismissive shrug. 'And then you accosted me here, and told me your wild tale of believing you were about to be forced into marriage to a man I admit even I was beginning to despise after I had listened to your description of him! And I thought that Saud liked me!' he commented drolly.

Petra had the grace to give him an abashed look.

'My grandfather told me that I'd got it all wrong, and that Saud had misunderstood what he had overheard!'

'A passing comment, between business partners, that was never intended to be taken seriously. Knowing how concerned your family was about your grandfather's health, and the effect your visit might have on it, I volunteered to show you something of the complex. But never for one moment did I intend to do so with a view to seeing if you might be a suitable wife!'

'Did you really fall in love with me that night?' Petra couldn't resist asking him.

'When I asked you what kind of man you wanted, and you told me...' He paused and looked away from her, before looking back again. 'I am a very wealthy man, Petra, and naturally I have been pursued by the kind of woman who sees a man only in terms of the financial benefits she can gain from him. When you spoke so passionately of your feelings and your beliefs, your hopes and desires for the way you wanted your life and your love to be, they so closely mirrored my own that I knew I could not let you walk away from me. And then I kissed you.'

'And you knew then?'

Petra knew that her voice was trembling, and that Rashid would be able to hear quite clearly the joy and incredulity in it, but now she felt no need to hide her feelings or to feel ashamed of them.

'Yes,' Rashid acknowledged simply.

'I knew then, and I was determined to court you...and woo you...but unfortunately I hadn't reckoned on your stubborn determination not to fall in love with the man you believed me to be. I was beginning to panic. I was afraid that I might lose you. And then you found out who I was and I thought I *had* lost you. I wasn't going to allow that to happen. Not when I knew just how good things could be for us.'

Petra gave him a wry look. 'So you had made up your mind that I loved you, had you?'

'Quite simply I could not bear to think of how my life would be if you didn't!'

His admission dissolved any potential suspicion of arrogance or lack of respect for her feelings so immediately that Petra could only look softly at him.

'And,' Rashid continued huskily, 'I hoped—especially after the way you had given yourself to me with such wonderful passion and completeness—that you loved me. But I knew that time was running out for me, that as Rashid I could not continue to be "away on business" for much longer. And then came the desert.'

'When you couldn't take your eyes off the belly dancer!' Petra reminded him challengingly.

'I know her—after all, she is an employee of the hotel complex and she knew who I was! I was afraid that she might inadvertently give me away! But then you came to me...to my bed...and I knew I had to take a chance and find some way of keeping you permanently in my life. When you came to the hotel suite, to confront me, I seized on the opportunity it gave me to insist that we marry out of desperation.'

'But you said nothing, Rashid... You were so cold—so indifferent...'

'I felt guilty,' he admitted. 'I had railroaded you into marriage to get what I wanted...and I knew that I shouldn't have done that.'

'There are lots of things you shouldn't have done,' Petra mock reproved him. 'Including giving me a separate suite of rooms and tormenting me by letting me think that you didn't care.'

'But now you know that I do care,' Rashid whispered softly. 'You are the oasis of my life, Petra, the cool enriching gift of water to my parched desert. You and you alone have the power to make my heart bloom and flower.'

Misty-eyed, Petra listened to him.

'I want to go home, Rashid,' she told him shakily.

'Home!' He didn't try to hide either the starkness in his voice or the tormented, anguished pain in his eyes. 'You want to leave me! Perhaps I deserve it, after what I have done, but I cannot bear to let you go, Petra. Please, just give me a chance to show you, prove to you, how much I want to make you happy, to give you love. If you are not happy here in Zuran then we can live somewhere else—anywhere else that you choose—so long as you let me live there with you!'

Immediately Petra realised that he had misunderstood her, but his reaction was all the proof she could have asked for of just how much he did love her.

'I meant I want to go home with you, to our home,' she corrected his misunderstanding. 'To our home, our room, our bed...home to you, Rashid. You are my home, and wherever you are that is where my home is,' she told him with quiet sincerity.

As he wrapped her in his arms and proceeded to kiss her with fierce passion Petra could feel the fine tremble of his body.

'You know that I shall never, ever let you go now, don't you?' Rashid whispered to her. 'You are mine, Petra. My wife, my love, my life, my heart!'

One Night With the Sheikh

PENNY JORDAN

PROLOGUE

'You won't forget your mummy whilst I'm away working, will you, my precious baby girl?'

Mariella watched sympathetically as her younger half-sister Tanya's eyes filled with tears as she handed her precious four-month-old daughter over to her.

'I know that Fleur couldn't have anyone better to look after her than you, Ella,' Tanya acknowledged emotionally. 'After all, you became my mother as well as my sister when Mum and Dad died. I just wish I could have got a job that didn't mean I have to be away, but this six-week contract on this cruise liner pays so well that I just can't afford to give it up! Yes, I know you would support us both,' she continued before Mariella could say anything, 'but that isn't what I want. I want to be as independent as I can be. Anyway,' she told Mariella bitterly, 'supporting Fleur financially should be her father's job and not yours! What I ever saw in that weak, lying rat of a man, I'll never know! My wonderful sexy dream fantasy of a sheikh! Some dream he turned out to be—more of a nightmare.'

Mariella let her vent her feelings, without comment, knowing just how devastated and hurt her half-sister had been when her lover had abandoned her.

'You don't have to do this, Tanya,' she told her gently now. 'I'm earning enough to support us all, and this house is big enough for the three of us.'

'Oh, Mariella, I know that. I know you'd starve

5

yourself to give to me and Fleur, but that isn't what I want. You've done so much for me since Mum and Dad died. You were only eighteen, after all, three years younger than I am now, when we found out that there wasn't going to be any money! I suppose Dad wanted to give us all so much that he simply didn't think about what would happen if anything happened to him, and with him remortgaging the house because of the stock market crisis.'

Silently the sisters looked at one another.

Both of them had inherited their mother's delicate bone structure and heart-shaped face, along with her strawberry-blonde hair and peach perfect complexion, but where Tanya had inherited her father's height and hazel eyes, Mariella had inherited intensely turquoise eyes from her father, the man who had decided less than a year after her birth that the responsibilities of fatherhood and marriage simply weren't for him and walked out on his wife and baby daughter.

'It's not fair,' Tanya had mock complained to her when she had announced that she was not going to go to university as Mariella had hoped she would, but wanted to pursue a career singing and dancing. 'If I had your eyes, I'd have a ready-made advantage over everyone else whenever I went for a part.'

Although she knew how headstrong and impulsive her half-sister could be, Mariella admired her for what she was doing, even whilst she worried about how she was going to cope with being away from her daughter for six long weeks.

Whatever small differences there might ever have been between them, in their passionate and protective love for baby Fleur they were totally united.

'I'll ring every day,' Tanya promised chokily.

'And I want to know everything she does, Ella… Every tiny little thing. Oh, Ella…I feel so guilty about all of this…I know how you suffered as a little girl because your father wasn't there; because he'd abandoned you and Mum…and I know too how lucky I was to have both Mum and Dad and you there for me, and yet here is my poor little Fleur…'

Holding Fleur in one arm, Mariella hugged her sister tightly with the other.

'The taxi's here,' she warned, before releasing Tanya and tenderly brushing the tears off her face.

'Ella! I've got the most fab commission for you.'

Recognising the voice of her agent, Mariella shifted Fleur's warm weight from one arm to the other, smiling lovingly at her as the baby guzzled happily on her bottle. 'It's racehorses, dozens of them. The client owns his own racing yard out in Zuran. He's a member of the Zuran royal family, and apparently he heard about you via that chap in Kentucky, whose Kentucky Derby winner you painted the other year. Anyway—he wants to fly you out there, all expenses paid, so that you can discuss the project with him, see the beasts *in situ* so to speak!'

Mariella laughed. Kate, with her immaculate designer clothes and equally immaculate all-white apartment, was not an animal lover. 'Ella, what is that noise?' she demanded plaintively.

Mariella laughed. 'It's Fleur. I'm just giving her her bottle. It does sound promising, but right now I'm pretty booked with commissions, and, to be honest, I don't really think that going to Zuran is on. For a start, I'm looking after Fleur for the next six weeks, and—'

'That's no problem—I am sure Prince Sayid

wouldn't mind you taking her with you and February
is the perfect time of year to go there; the weather will
be wonderful—warm and mild. Ella, you can't turn this
one down. Just what I'd earn in commission is making
my mouth water,' she admitted frankly.

Ella laughed. 'Ah, I see…'

She had begun painting animal 'portraits' almost by
accident. Her painting had been merely a small hobby
and her 'pet portraits' done for friends, but her reputation had spread by word of mouth, and eventually
she had decided to make it her full-time career.

Now she earned what to her was a very comfortable
living from her work, and she knew she would normally have leapt at the chance she was being offered.

'I'd love to go, Kate,' she replied. 'But Fleur is my
priority right now…'

'Well, don't turn it down out of hand,' Kate warned
her. 'Like I said, there's no reason why Fleur shouldn't
go with you. You won't be working on this trip, it's
only a mutual look-see. You'd be gone just over a
week, and forget any idiotic ideas you might have
about potential health hazards to any young baby out
there—Zuran is second to none when it comes to being
a world-class cosmopolitan city!'

One of the reasons Mariella had originally bought
her small three-storey house had been because of the
excellent north-facing window on the top floor, which
she had turned into her studio. With Fleur contently
fed she looked out at the grey early February day. The
rain that had been sheeting down all week had turned
to a mere drizzle. A walk in the park and some fresh
air would do them both good, Mariella decided, putting
Fleur down whilst she went to prepare her pram.

It had been her decision to buy the baby a huge old-fashioned 'nanny' style pram.

'You can use the running stroller if you want,' she had informed Tanya firmly 'But when I walk her it will be in a traditional vehicle and at a traditional pace!'

'Ella, you talk as though you were sixty-eight, not twenty-eight,' Tanya had protested. Perhaps she was a little bit old-fashioned, Mariella conceded as she started to remove the blankets from the running stroller to put in the pram. Her father's desertion and her mother's consequent vulnerability and helplessness had left her with a very strong determination to stand on her own two feet, and an extremely strong disinclination to allow herself to be emotionally vulnerable through loving a man too much as her mother had done.

After all, as Tanya had proved, it was possible to inherit a tendency!

She frowned as her fingers brushed against a balled-up piece of paper as she removed the bedding. It could easily have scratched Fleur's delicate skin. She was on the point of throwing it away, when a line of her sister's handwriting suddenly caught her eye.

The piece of paper was a letter, Mariella recognised, and she could see the name and address on it quite plainly.

'Sheikh Xavier Al Agir, No. 24, Quaffire Beach Road, Zuran City.'

Her heart thudded guiltily as she smoothed out the note and read the first line.

'You have destroyed my life and Fleur's and I shall hate you for ever for that,' she read.

The letter was obviously one Tanya had written but not sent to Fleur's father.

Fleur had always refused to discuss her relationship with him other than to say that he was a very wealthy Middle Eastern man whom she had met whilst working in a nightclub as a singer and dancer.

Privately Mariella had always thought that he had escaped far too lightly from his responsibility to her sister and to his baby...

And now she had discovered he lived in Zuran! Frowning slightly, she carefully folded the note. She had no right to interfere, she knew that, but... Would she be interfering or merely acknowledging the validity of fate? How many, many times over the years had she longed for the opportunity to confront her own father and tell him just what she thought of him, how he had broken her mother's heart and almost destroyed her life?

Her father, like her mother, was now dead, and could never make reparation for what he had done; but Tanya's lover was very much alive, and it would give her a great deal of satisfaction to tell him just what she thought of him!

Blowing Fleur a kiss, she hurried over to the telephone and quickly dialled her agent's number.

'Kate,' she began. 'I've been thinking...about that trip to Zuran...'

'You've changed your mind! Wonderful... You won't regret it Ella, I promise you. I mean, this guy is mega, mega rich, and what he's prepared to pay to have his four-legged friends immortalised in oils...'

Listening to her, Mariella reflected ruefully that on occasion Kate could show a depressing tendency to favour the material over the emotional, but she was an excellent agent!

CHAPTER ONE

ZURAN had to have the cleanest airport in the world, Mariella decided as she retrieved her luggage and headed for the exit area, and Kate had been right about Prince Sayid's willingness to spare no expense to get her to Zuran. In the first-class cabin of their aircraft Fleur had been treated like a little princess!

Arrangements had been made for her to be chauffeur-driven to the Beach Club Resort where she would be staying along with Fleur in their own private bungalow, and, thanks to the prince's influence with the right diplomatic departments, all the necessary arrangements to get Fleur a passport, with Tanya's permission, had also been accomplished at top speed!

Craning her neck, Mariella looked round the busy arrivals area searching for someone carrying a placard bearing her name.

Behind her she was vaguely aware of something going on, not so much because of an increase in the noise level but rather because of the way it suddenly fell away. Alerted by some sixth sense, Mariella turned round, her eyes widening as she watched the way the crowds parted to make way for the small phalanx of white-robed men. Like traditional outriders, they carved a wide path through the crowd to allow the man striding behind them to cross the marble floor unhindered. Taller than the others, he looked neither to the right nor the left so that Mariella's artist's eye was able

11

to observe the patrician arrogance of a profile that could only belong to a man used to being in command.

Instinctively, without being able to substantiate her reaction, Mariella didn't like him. He was too arrogant, too aware of his own importance. So physically and powerfully male, perfect in a way that sent a hundred unwanted sexual messages skittering over her suddenly very sensitive nerve endings. He had drawn level with her, and, whether because she sensed her antagonism or because Mariella had gripped her just a little bit more tightly, Fleur suddenly broke the silence with a small cry.

Instantly the dark head turned in their direction whilst the equally dark eyes burned into Mariella's. Mariella registered his gaze as her body gave a small, tight shudder.

The dark eyes stripped her, not of her clothes, but of her skin, her defences, Mariella recognised shakily, leaving them shredded down to her bones; her soul! But his gaze lingered longest of all on her face. Her eyes, she realised as she returned his remote and disdainful look of contempt with one of smouldering fury.

Fleur made another small sound and immediately his gaze switched from her to the baby and stayed there for a while, before it switched back to her own as though checking something.

Whatever it had been it brought a sneering look of contempt to his mouth that curved it into an even more dangerous line, Mariella noticed as her body responded to his reaction with a slow burn of colour along her cheekbones.

How dared he look at her with such contempt? She didn't care who or what he was! Once she imagined her father must have looked so at her mother before walking out on her, before leaving her to sink into the needy despair and dependence that Mariella remembered so starkly from her childhood, until her stepfather with his love and kindness had come to lift them both out of the dark, mean place her father had left them in.

As swiftly and as silently as they had arrived the small group of men swept through the hall and left. As a production it had been ridiculously overdone and theatrical, Mariella decided as she found the chauffeur patiently waiting for her and allowed herself to be carefully driven along with Fleur in the air-conditioned luxury of the limousine.

The Beach Club Resort was everything a five-star resort should be and more, Mariella acknowledged a couple of hours later when she had finished her exploration of her new surroundings.

The bungalow she had been allocated had two large bedrooms, each with its own bathroom, a small kitchen area, a living room, a private patio complete with whirlpool, but it was the obvious forethought that had gone into equipping the place for a very young baby that most impressed Mariella. A good-sized cot had been provided and placed next to the bed, the bathroom was equipped with what was obviously a brand-new baby bath, baby toiletries had been added to the luxurious range provided for her own use, and in the fridge was a very full selection of top-of-the-range baby foods. However, it was the letter that had been left for her stating that the Beach Club's chef would prepare fresh organic baby food for Fleur on request that really made Mariella feel she could relax.

Having settled Fleur, who fell asleep as easily and comfortably as though she was in her own home,

Mariella checked her watch and then put a call through to her sister. Tanya's cruise liner was on an extended tour of the Caribbean and the Gulf of Mexico.

'Ella, how's Fleur?' Tanya demanded immediately.

'Fast asleep,' Mariella told her. 'She was fine on the flight and got thoroughly spoiled. How are you?'

'Oh…fine… Very busy…we're doing two shows each evening, with no time off, but as I said the money is excellent. Ella, I must go… Give Fleur a big kiss for me.'

A little guiltily, Mariella looked at the now-silent mobile. She hadn't said anything to Tanya about her determination to confront her sister's faithless ex-lover and tell him just what she thought about him! Tanya might have gone willingly to his bed, but Mariella knew she hadn't been lying to her when she had told her that she had believed that he loved her, and that they had a future together.

Mariella struggled to wake up from a confused and disjointed dream in which she was being dragged by her guards to lie trembling at the feet of the man who was now her master. How she hated him. Hated him for the way he stood there towering over her, looking down at her, looking over her so thoroughly that she felt as though his gaze burned her flesh.

He was looking deep into her eyes. His were the colour of the storm-tossed skies and seas of her homeland, a cold, pure grey that chilled her through and through.

'You dare to challenge me?' he was demanding softly as he moved closer to her. Behind her Mariella was conscious of the threatening presence of the guards.

She hated him with every sinew of her body, every pulse of blood from her heart. He left the divan where he had been sitting and came towards her, bending down, extending his hand to her face, but as his fingers gripped her chin Mariella turned her head and bit sharply into the soft pad of flesh below his thumb.

She felt the movement of the air as the guards leapt into action, heard them draw their swords, and her body waited for the welcome kiss of death, but instead the guards were dismissed whilst her tormentor stepped back from her. One bright spot of blood glistened on the intricately inlaid tiled floor.

'You are like a wildcat and as such need to be tamed,' she heard him telling her softly.

She could feel the cleanliness of her hair on her bare skin and froze as he slowly circled her, standing behind her and sliding his hand through her hair and then wrapping it tightly around his fingers, arching her back against his body so that her semi-naked breasts were thrown into taut profile. His free hand reached for the clasp securing her top and her whole body shook with outrage. And then abruptly he released her, turning to face her so that she could see the contempt in his eyes.

Swimming up through the layers of her dream Mariella recognised that his face was one she knew; that his cynical contempt was something she had experienced before...

In the half heartbeat of time between sleeping and waking she realised why. The man in her dream had been the arrogant, hawk-eyed man she had seen earlier at the airport!

Getting out of bed, she went into the bathroom, shaking her head to clear her thoughts, and then, when that tactic did nothing to subdue their dangerous, clinging tentacles of remembered sensuality, she turned on the shower, deliberately setting it at a punishing 'cool,' before stepping into it.

The minute the cool spray hit her overheated skin she shuddered, gritting her teeth as she washed the slick film from her body, and then stepping out of the shower, to wrap herself in a luxuriously thick, soft white towel. In the mirror in front of her she could see the pale, pearlescent gleam of her own skin, and dangerously she knew that if she were merely to close her eyes, behind her closed eyelids she would immediately see her tormentor, tall, cynically watchful, as he mocked her before reaching out to take the towel from her body and claim her.

Infuriated with herself, Mariella rubbed her damp skin roughly with the towel, and then re-set the air-conditioning. In her cot Fleur slept peacefully. Going to the fridge, Mariella removed a bottle of water and opened it. Her hand was shaking so much some of it slopped from the bottle onto the worktop.

Mariella and Fleur had just finished eating a leisurely breakfast on their private patio when a message came chattering through the fax machine. Frowning, Mariella read it. The prince had been called away on some unexpected business and would not now be able to see her for several days. He apologised to Mariella for having to change their arrangements, but asked her to enjoy the facilities of the Beach Club at his expense until his return.

Carefully smoothing sun-protection lotion onto Fleur's happy, wriggling little body, Mariella bent her head to kiss her tummy, acknowledging that this would be an ideal time to seek out Fleur's father. She had his address, after all! So all she needed to do was summon a taxi to take her there!

Kate had been quite correct when she had described Zuran's February weather as perfect, Mariella admitted half an hour later as she carried Fleur out into the warm sunshine. Since she was here on business and not holiday she had packed accordingly, and was wearing a pair of soft white linen trousers and a protective long-sleeved top. When she showed the taxi driver the sheikh's address he smiled and nodded. 'It will take maybe three quarters of an hour,' he told her. 'You have business with the sheikh?' he asked her conversationally.

Having learned already just how friendly people were, Mariella didn't take offence, replying simply tongue in cheek, 'You could say that.'

'He is a famous man. Revered by his tribe. They admire him for the way he has supported their right to live their lives in the traditional way. Although he is an extremely successful businessman it is said that he still prefers to live simply in the desert the way his people always have. He is a very good man.'

Mariella reflected inwardly that the picture the driver had just drawn for her was considerably at odds with the one she had gained from her half-sister.

Tanya had met the man in a nightclub, after all. Mariella had never liked the fact that Tanya worked there—although she had been employed as a singer, it openly advertised the sexual charms of its dancers, and Tanya had freely admitted that the majority of the customers were male.

And, certainly, during the twelve months they had been together, Mariella had never heard Tanya mention any predilection on her sexy sheikh's part to spend quality time in the middle of the desert! In fact, if she was honest, she had gained the impression that he was something of a 'playboy,' to use a perhaps now outdated word.

It took just under forty minutes for them to reach the impressive white mansion, which the taxi driver assured her was the correct address.

A huge pair of locked wrought-iron gates prevented them from going any farther, but as if by magic an official stepped out of one of the pair of gatehouses that flanked the gates, and approached the car.

As firmly as she could Mariella explained that she wished to see the sheikh.

'I am sorry but he is not available,' the official informed her. 'He is away at the oasis at the moment and not expected back for some time.'

This was a complication Mariella had not been expecting. Fleur had woken up and was starting to grizzle a little.

'If you would care to leave a message?' the official was offering courteously.

Ruefully Mariella acknowledged inwardly that the nature of the message she wanted to give to the sheikh was better delivered in person!

Thanking him, she asked the taxi driver to take her back to the hotel.

'If you want, I can find someone to drive you to this oasis?' he suggested.

'You know where it is?' she questioned him.

He gave a small shrug. 'Sure! But you will need a four-wheel drive vehicle, as the track can be covered with sand.'

'Could I drive there myself?' Mariella asked him.

'It is possible, yes. It would take you two, maybe three hours. You wish me to give you the directions?'

It made more sense to drive to the oasis under her own steam than to go to the expense of paying a driver for the day as well as hiring a vehicle, Mariella decided.

'Please,' she agreed.

Methodically, Mariella checked through everything she had put on one side to pack into the four-wheel drive for her trip into the desert. The Beach Club's information desk staff had assured her that it would be perfectly safe for her to drive into the desert, and had attended to all the necessary formalities for her, including ensuring that a proper baby seat was provided for Fleur.

The trip should take her around three hours—four if she stopped off at the popular oasis resort for lunch as recommended by the Beach Club. But just in case she decided not to, they had provided her with a packed lunch in the form of a picnic hamper.

If it hadn't been for the serious purpose of her trip, she could quite easily have felt she were embarking on an exciting adventure, Mariella thought. Like everything else connected with the Beach Club, the four-wheel drive was immaculately clean and was even provided with its own mobile telephone!

The road into the desert was clearly marked, and turned out to be a well-built, smooth road that was so easy to navigate that Mariella quickly felt confident.

The secluded oasis where apparently the sheikh was staying was located in the Agir mountain range.

The light breeze, which had been just stirring the air when she had left the Beach Club, had increased enough to whip a fine dust of sand over her vehicle and the road itself within an hour of her setting out on her journey. The sand particles were so fine that somehow they actually managed to find their way into the four-wheel drive, despite the fact that Mariella had the doors and windows firmly closed. She had left the main road, now branched out onto a well-marked track across the desert itself.

It was a relief when she reached the Bedouin village marked on her map. It was market day and she had to drive patiently behind a camel train through the village, but fortunately it turned off towards the oasis itself, allowing her to accelerate.

In another half an hour she would stop for some lunch—if she hadn't reached the second oasis, marked on her map, she and Fleur would have their picnic instead.

The height of the sand dunes had left her feeling surprised and awed; they were almost a mountain range in themselves. Fleur was awake and Mariella turned off the radio to play her one of her favourite nursery rhyme tapes, singing along to it.

It was taking her longer than she'd estimated to reach the tourist base at the oasis where she had planned to have lunch—it was almost two o'clock now and she had expected to be there at one. A film of sand dust had turned the sky a brassy red-gold colour, and as she crested a huge sand dune and looked down into the emptiness on the other side of it Mariella began to panic slightly. Surely she should be able to at least see the tourist base oasis from here?

Ruefully she reached for the vehicle's mobile, realising that it might be sensible to ask for help, but to her dismay when she tried to make a call to the number programmed into the phone the only response was a fierce crackling sound. Stopping the vehicle she reached for her own mobile, but it was equally ineffective.

The sky was even more obscured by sand now, the wind hitting the vehicle with such force that it was physically rocking it. As though sensing her disquiet Fleur began to cry. She was hungry and needed changing, Mariella recognised, automatically attending to the baby's needs whilst she tried to decide what she should do.

It was impossible that she could be lost, of course. The vehicle was fitted with a compass and she had been given very detailed and careful instructions, which she had followed to the letter.

So why hadn't she reached the tourist oasis?

Fleur ate her own meal eagerly, but Mariella discovered that she herself had lost her appetite!

And then just as she was beginning to feel truly afraid she saw it! A line of camels swaying out of the dust towards her led by a robed camel driver.

Relieved, Mariella drove towards the camel train. Its leader was gravely polite. She had missed the turning to the oasis, he explained, something that was easily done with such a wind blowing sand across the track. To her alarm he further explained that, because of the sudden deterioration in the weather, all tourists had been urged to return to the city instead of remaining in the desert, but since Mariella had come so far her best course of action now was to press on to her ultimate destination, which he carefully showed her how to do using the vehicle's compass.

Thanking him, she did as he had instructed her, grimly checking and re-checking the compass as she drove up and down what felt like an interminable series of the sand dunes until eventually, in the distance through the sand blowing against her windscreen, she could just about see the looming mass of the mountain range.

It was already four o'clock and the light seemed to be fading, a fact that panicked Mariella into driving a little faster. She had never dreamed that her journey would prove so hazardous and she was very much regretting having set out on it, but now at last its end was in sight.

It took her almost another hour of zigzagging across the sand dunes to reach the rocky thrust of the beginnings of the mountain range. The oasis was situated in a deep ravine, its escarpment so high that Mariella shuddered a little as she drove into its shadows. This was the last kind of place she had expected to appeal to the man who had been her sister's faithless lover.

Would his villa here be as palatial as his home in Zuran? Mariella frowned and checked as the ravine opened out and she saw the oasis ahead of her. Remote and beautiful in its own way, it was very obviously a place of deep solitude, the oasis itself enclosed with a fringing of palms illuminated by the eerie glow of the final rays of the setting sun. Shielding her eyes, Mariella stopped the vehicle to look around. Where was the villa? All she could see was one solitary pavilion tent! A good-sized pavilion, to be sure, but most definitely not a villa! Had she somehow got lost—again?

Fleur had started to cry, a cross, tired, hungry noise that alerted Mariella to the fact that for Fleur's sake if nothing else she needed to stop.

Carefully she drove the vehicle forward over the

treacherously boulder-rutted track, which seemed more like a dry river bed than a roadway! Sand blowing in from the desert was covering the boulders and the thin sparse grass of the oasis.

There was a vehicle parked several yards from the pavilion and Mariella stopped next to it.

A man was emerging from the pavilion, alerted to her arrival by the sound of her vehicle.

As he strode towards her, his robe caught by the strong wind and flattened against his body revealing a torso muscle structure that caused her to suck in her own stomach in sharply dangerous womanly response to its maleness.

And then he turned his head and looked at her, and the earth halted on its axis before swinging perilously in a sickening movement as Mariella recognised him.

It was the man from the airport. The man from her dream!

CHAPTER TWO

HIS hand was on the door handle of the four-wheel drive. Wrenching it open, he demanded angrily, 'Who the devil are you?'

He was looking at her eyes again, with that same look of biting contempt glittering in his own as he raked her with a gritty gaze.

'I'm looking for Sheikh Xavier Al Agir,' Mariella responded, returning his look with one of her own—plus interest!

'What? What do you want with him?'

He was curt to the point of rudeness, but then, given what she had already seen—and dreamed—of him, she wouldn't have expected anything else.

'What I want with him is no business of yours!' she told him angrily.

In her seat Fleur's cries grew louder.

Peering into the vehicle, he demanded in disbelief, 'You've brought a baby out in this?'

The disgust and anger in his voice made her face sting even more than the pieces of sand blown against it by the wind.

'What the hell possessed you? Didn't you hear the weather warning earlier? This area was reported as being strictly out of bounds to tourists because of the threat of sandstorms.'

Hot-faced, Mariella remembered how she had switched off the radio to play Fleur's tapes.

'I'm sorry if I've arrived at an inconvenient time,'

she responded sarcastically to cover her own discomfort, 'but if you could just give me directions for the Oasis Istafan, then—'

'This is the Oasis Istafan,' came back the immediate and cold response.

It was? Then?

'I want to see Sheikh Xavier Al Agir,' Mariella told him again, gathering her composure together. 'I presume he is here?'

'What do you want to see him for?'

Mariella had had enough. 'That is no business of yours,' she said angrily. Inwardly she was worrying how on earth she was going to get back to the city and the comfort of her Beach Club bungalow and what on earth a man as wealthy as the sheikh was reputed to be was doing out here with this...this...this arrogant predator of a man!

'Oh, I think you'll find that anything concerning Xavier is very much my business,' came the gritted reply.

Something—Mariella wasn't sure what—must have alerted her to the truth. But she was too shocked by it to voice it, looking from his eyes to his mouth and then back again as she swallowed—hard—against the tight ball of shock tightening like ice around her heart. 'You...you...can't be the sheikh,' she told him defiantly, but her voice was trembling lightly, betraying her lack of confidence in her own denial.

Was this man her sister's lover...and Fleur's father? What was that sharp, bitter, dangerous feeling settling over her like a black cloud?

'You are the sheikh, aren't you?' she acknowledged bleakly.

A brief, sardonic inclination of his head was his only response but it was enough.

Turning away from him, she reached into the baby carrier and tenderly removed Fleur. Her whole face softened and illuminated with love as she hugged her and then kissed her before looking him straight in the eyes and saying fiercely to him, 'This is Fleur, the baby you have refused to both acknowledge and support.'

She had shocked him, Mariella realised, even though he had concealed his reaction very quickly.

As he stepped back from the vehicle for a second Mariella thought he was going to tell her to leave—and cravenly she wanted to do so! The man, the location, the situation were so not what she had been anticipating and prepared herself for. Each one of them in their different ways shattered not just her preconceptions but also her precious self-containment.

The man—try as she might she could just not envisage him in the club where Tanya had performed. The location made her ache for her painting equipment and brought her artistic senses to quick hunger. And her situation! Oh, no... Definitely no! This man had been her sister's lover, and was Fleur's father—

The shadowy fear that had stalked her adult years suddenly loomed terrifyingly sharply in front of her. She would not be like her mother; she would not ever allow herself to be vulnerable in any way to a man who could only damage her emotionally. The ability to fall in love with the wrong man might be learned, but it was not, to the best of Mariella's knowledge, inherited!

'Get out!'

Get out? With pleasure! Gripping the steering wheel, Mariella reached for the door, slamming it closed and then switching on the ignition at the same time, then she threw the vehicle into a furious spurt of reverse speed.

The tyres spun; sand filled the air. She could hear a thunderous banging on her driver's door as the car refused to budge. Looking out of the window, she saw Xavier looking at her in icy, furious disbelief.

Realising that she was bogged down in the swirling sand, Mariella switched off the engine. If he wanted her to leave he would have to move the vehicle for her, she recognised in angry humiliation.

As the engine died he was yanking the door open, demanding, 'What the hell do you think you are trying to do?'

'You told me to get out!' Mariella reminded him, equally angry.

'I meant get out of the car, not...' As he swore beneath his breath, to her shock he suddenly reached into the vehicle and snapped off her seat belt, grasping her so tightly around her waist that it actually hurt.

As he pulled her free of her seat and swung her to the ground she had a sudden shocking image of the two of them in her dream!

'Let go of me,' she demanded chokily, pushing him away. 'Don't touch me...'

'Don't touch you?'

Now that she was on the ground she realised just how far she had to look up to see the expression in his eyes.

'From what I've heard it isn't often those words leave your lips.'

Instinctively Mariella raised her hand, taking refuge in an act of female rebuttal and retaliation as ancient as the land around her, but immediately he seized her wrist in a punishing grip, his eyes glittering savagely as he curled his fingers tighter. 'Hell cat!' he taunted her mercilessly. 'One attempt to use your claws on me and, I promise you, you will regret it.'

'You can't go anywhere tonight,' he told her bluntly. 'There's a sandstorm forecast that would bury you alive before you could get even halfway back to the city. In your case it would be no loss, but for the sake of the child...'

The child...Fleur!

An agonised sound of distress choked in Mariella's throat. She could not stay here in this wilderness with this...this...savagely dangerous man, but her own common sense was telling her that she had no other option. Already the four-wheel drive was buried almost axle-deep in sand. She could taste it in her mouth, feel it on her skin. Inside the vehicle, Fleur had begun to cry again. Instinctively Mariella turned to go to her, but Xavier was there before her, lifting Fleur out.

The baby looked so tiny held in his arms. Mariella held her breath watching him... He was Fleur's father after all. Surely he must feel something? Some remorse, some guilt...something... True, he did pause to look at her, but the expression on his face was unreadable.

'She has your hair,' he told Mariella, before adding grimly, 'The wind is picking up. We need to get inside the tent. Where are you going?' he demanded as she turned back to the vehicle.

'I want to get Fleur's things,' she told him, tensing as he gave a sharp exclamation of irritation and overruled her.

'Leave them for now. I shall come back for them.'

Mariella couldn't believe how strong the wind had

become! The sand felt like a million tiny particles of glass shredding her skin.

By the time they reached the safety and protection of the pavilion, her leg muscles ached from the effort of fighting her way through the shifting sand.

Once inside the pavilion she realised that it was much larger than she had originally thought. A central area was furnished with rich carpets and low divans. Rugs were thrown over dark wood chests, and on the intricately carved tables stood oil lamps and candles. In their light Mariella could see two draped swags of cloth caught back in a dull gold rope as though they covered the entrance to two other inner rooms.

'Fleur needs something to eat, and a change of clothes,' she announced curtly, 'and I want to ring the Beach Club to tell them what has happened.'

'Use a telephone—in this intensity of sandstorm?' He laughed openly at her. 'You would be lucky to be able to use a landline, never mind a mobile. As for the child...'

'The child!' Mariella checked him bitterly. 'Even knowing the truth you still try to distance yourself from her, don't you? Well, let me tell you something—'

'No, let me tell you something... Any man could have fathered this child! I feel for her that she should have a mother of such low morals, a mother so willing to give herself to any and every man her eye alights on, but let me make it plain to you that I do not intend to be blackmailed into paying for a pleasure that was of so little value, never mind paying for a child who may or may not be the result of it!'

Mariella went white with shock and disbelief, but before she could defend her sister, Fleur started to cry in earnest.

Ignoring Xavier, Mariella soothed her, whispering tenderly. 'It's all right sweetheart, I know you're hungry…' Automatically as she talked to her Mariella stroked her and kissed the top of her head. She was so unbearably precious to her even though she was not her child. Being there at her birth had made Mariella feel as though they shared a very special bond, and awakened a maternal urge inside her she had not previously known she had.

'I don't know what she has to eat, but there is some fruit and milk in the fridge, and a blender,' he informed her.

Fridge? Blender? Mariella's eyes widened. 'You have electricity out here?'

Immediately he gave her a very male sardonic look.

'Not as such. There's a small generator, which provides enough for my needs.' He gave a brief shrug. 'After all, I come out here to work in peace…not to wear a hair shirt! The generator can provide enough warm water for you to bathe the child, although you, I am afraid, will have to share my bathing water.'

He was waiting for her to object, Mariella could see that. He was enjoying tormenting her.

'Since I shall only be here overnight, I dare say I can manage to forgo that particular pleasure,' she told him grittily.

'I shall go to your vehicle and bring the baby's things. You will find the kitchen area through that exit and to your right.'

Mariella had brought some dried baby food with her as well as some tinned food, which she knew would probably suit Fleur's baby digestion rather better than raw fruit, no matter how well blended! Even so, it would do no harm to explore their surroundings.

As she stepped through the opening she found that she was in a narrow corridor, on the right of which was an unexpectedly well equipped although very small kitchen, and, to the left, an immaculately clean chemical lavatory, along with a small shower unit.

The other opening off the main room must lead to a sleeping area, she decided as she walked back.

'What is all this stuff?' she heard Xavier demanding as he walked in with his arms full.

In other circumstances his obvious male lack of awareness of a small baby's needs might have been endearing, but right now...

Ignoring him and still holding Fleur, she opened the cool-bag in which she had placed her foods.

'Yummy, look at this, Fleur,' she murmured to her. 'Banana pudding...our favourite... Yum-yum.'

The look of serious consideration in Fleur's hazel eyes as she looked at her made her smile, and she forgot Xavier for a second as she concentrated on the baby.

'I suppose I shouldn't be surprised that she isn't receiving the nutrition of her mother's own milk,' she heard Xavier announcing critically.

Immediately Mariella swung round, her eyes dark with anger.

'Since her mother had to go back to work that wasn't possible!'

'How virtuous you make it sound, but isn't it the truth that the nature of that work—is anything but? But of course you will deny that, just as you will claim to know who the child's father is.'

'You are totally despicable,' Mariella stopped him. 'Fleur does not deserve to be treated like this. She is an innocent baby...'

'Indeed! At last we are in agreement about something. It is a pity, though, that you did not think of that before you came out here making accusations and claims.'

How could he be so cold? So unfeeling! According to the little Tanya had said about him, she had considered him to be a very emotional and passionate man.

No doubt in bed he was, Mariella found herself acknowledging. Her face suddenly burnt hotly as she recognised the unwanted significance of her private thoughts, and even worse the images they were mentally conjuring up for her; not with her sister as Xavier's partner—but herself!

What was happening to her? She was a cool-blooded woman who analysed, rationalised and resisted any kind of damaging behaviour to herself. And yet here she was...

'Just how long is this sandstorm going to last?' she asked abruptly.

The dark eyebrows rose. 'One day...two...three...'

'Three!' Mariella was aghast. Apart from the fact that Tanya would be beside herself if she could not get in touch with her, what was the prince going to think if he returned and she wasn't there?

'I have to feed and change Fleur.'

Luckily she had brought the baby bath with her as well as the changing mat, and Fleur's pram cum carry-cot, mainly because she had not been quite sure what facilities would be available at the oasis.

'Since it is obvious that you will have to stay the night, it is probably best that you and the child sleep in my... In the sleeping quarters,' Xavier corrected himself. Mariella's mouth went dry.

'And…where will you sleep?' she asked him apprehensively.

'In here, of course. When you have fed and bathed the child I suggest that we both have something to eat. And then—'

'Thank you, but I am perfectly capable of deciding for myself when I eat,' Mariella told him sharply.

She was far more independent, and a good deal more fiery, than he had anticipated, Xavier acknowledged broodingly when Mariella had disappeared with Fleur. And quite definitely not his younger cousin's normal type.

Thinking of Khalid made his mouth tighten a little. He had been both furious and disbelieving when Khalid had telephoned him to announce that he had fallen in love and was thinking of marrying a girl he had met in a dubious nightclub. Khalid had been in love before, but this was the first time he had considered marriage. At twenty-four Khalid was still very immature. When he married, in Xavier's opinion it needed to be someone strong enough to keep him grounded—and wealthy enough not to be marrying him for his money.

His frown deepened. It had been his cynical French grandmother who had warned him when he was very young that the great wealth he had inherited from his father would make him a target for greedy women. When he had been in his teens his grandmother had insisted that he spent time in France meeting the chic daughters of her own distant relatives, girls who in her opinion were deserving of inheriting the 'throne' his grandmother would have to abdicate when Xavier eventually married.

Well-born though they were, those girls had held

very little appeal for him, and, practical though he knew it would be, he found himself even less enamoured of the idea of contracting an arranged marriage.

Because of this he had already decided that it would be Khalid who would ultimately provide the heir to his enormous fortune and, more importantly, take his place as leader of their historically unique tribe. But he hadn't been in any hurry to nudge Khalid in the direction of a suitable bride—until he had learned of his plans *vis-à-vis* the impossible young woman who had forced her way into his private retreat!

He didn't know which of them had angered him the most! Khalid for his weakness in disappearing without leaving any indication of where he had gone, or the woman herself who had boldly followed up her pathetic attempt at blackmailing him via the letter she had sent Xavier, with a visit to his territory, along with the baby she was so determined to claim his cousin had fathered!

Physically he had not been able to see any hint in the child's features that she might be Khalid's; she was as prettily blonde as her mother, and as delicately feminine. The only difference was that, whilst her mother chose to affect those ridiculous, obviously false turquoise-coloured contact lenses, the baby's eyes were a warm hazel.

Like Khalid's?

There was no proof that the child was Khalid's, he reminded himself. And there was no way he was going to allow his cousin to marry her mother, without knowing for sure that Khalid was the father, especially now that he had actually met her. It was a wonder that Khalid had ever fallen so desperately in love with her in the first place!

'She has the grace of a gazelle,' he had written to him. 'The voice of an angel! She is the sweetest and most gentle of women...'

Well, Xavier begged to differ! At least on the two eulogising counts! Had he known when he had seen her at the airport just who she was he would have tried to find some way of having her deported there and then!

Remembering that occasion made him stride over to the opening to the pavilion, pulling back the cover to look outside. As had been forecast the wind was now a howling dervish of destruction, whipping up the sand so that already it was impossible to see even as far as the oasis itself. Which was a pity, because right now he could do with the refreshing swim he took each evening in the cool water of the oasis, rather than using the small shower next to the lavatory.

It both astounded and infuriated him that he could possibly want such a woman—she represented everything he most detested in the female sex: avarice, sexual laxity, selfishness—so far as he was concerned these were faults that could never be outweighed by a beautiful face or a sensual body. And he had to admit that, in that regard, his cousin had shown better taste than he had ever done previously!

Xavier allowed the flap of the tent to drop back in place and secured it. It irked him that Mariella should have the gall to approach him here of all places, where he came to retreat from the sometimes heavy burden of his responsibilities. A thin smile turned down the corners of his mouth. From what Khalid had described of the luxury-loving lifestyle they had shared, he doubted that she would enjoy being here. However little he cared about her discomfort, though there was the child to be considered.

The child! His mouth thinned a little more. Little Fleur was most definitely a complication he had not anticipated!

With Fleur fed, clean and dry, Mariella suddenly discovered just how tired she felt herself.

She had not expected Xavier to be pleased to be confronted with her accusations regarding his treatment of Tanya and Fleur, but the sheer savagery and cruelty with which he had verbally savaged her sister's morals had truly shocked her. This was after all a man who had very eagerly shared Tanya's bed, and who, even worse, had sworn that he loved her and that he wanted her to share a future with him!

In her opinion Tanya and Fleur were better off without him, just as she had been better off without the father who had deserted her!

Now that she had confronted him, though—and witnessed that he was incapable of feeling even the smallest shred of remorse—she longed to be able to get away from him, instead of being forced to remain here with him in the dangerous intimacy of this desert camp where the two of them...

Those ridiculous turquoise eyes looked even more theatrical and unreal in the pale triangle of her small exhausted face, Xavier decided angrily as he watched Mariella walking patiently up and down the living area of the pavilion whilst she rocked Fleur to sleep in her arms.

No doubt Khalid must have seen her a hundred or more times with her delicate skin free of make-up and those haunting, smudged shadows beneath her eyes as he lay over her in the soft shadows of the early morning, waking her with his caresses.

The fierce burst of anger that exploded inside him infuriated him. What was the matter with him? When he broke it down what was she after all? A petite, small-boned woman with a tousled head of strawberry-blonde hair that was probably dyed, coloured contact lenses to obscure the real colour of her eyes, skin the colour of milk and a body that had no doubt known more lovers than it was sensible for any sane-thinking adult to want to own to, especially one as fastidious in such matters as he was.

It would serve her right if he proved to Khalid just exactly what she was by bedding her himself! That would certainly ensure that his feckless cousin, who had abandoned his desk in their company headquarters without telling anyone where he was going or for how long, would, when he decided to return, realise just what a fate he had protected him from!

The child, though was a different matter. If she should indeed prove to be his cousin's, then her place was here in Zuran where she could be brought up to respect herself as a woman should, and to despise the greedy, immoral woman who had given birth to her!

CHAPTER THREE

MARIELLA woke up before Fleur had given her first distressed, hungry cry. She wriggled out from under the cool pure linen bedding to pad barefoot and naked to where she had placed the carry-cot.

Her khaki-coloured soft shape trousers could be re-worn without laundering, but the white cotton tee shirt she had worn beneath her jacket, and her underwear—no way.

Fastidiously wrinkling her nose at the very thought, Mariella had rinsed them out, deciding that even if they had not dried by morning wearing them slightly damp was preferable to putting them back on unwashed!

Picking Fleur up, she carried her back to the bed…Xavier's bed, a huge, low-lying monster of a bed, large enough to accommodate both a man and half his harem without any problem at all!

Sliding back beneath the linen sheets, Mariella stroked Fleur's soft cheek and watched her in the glow of the single lamp she had left on. She could tell from the way the baby sucked eagerly on her finger that she was hungry!

She had seen water in the fridge, and she had Fleur's formula. All she had to do was to brave the leopard's den in order to reach the kitchen!

And in order to do that she needed to find something to wear.

Whilst she was deciding between one of the pile of

soft towels Xavier had presented her with or the sheet itself, Fleur started to cry.

'Hush,' she soothed her gently. 'I know you're hungry, sweetheart...'

Xavier sighed as he heard Fleur crying. It was just gone two in the morning. The divan wasn't exactly the most comfortable thing to sleep on. Outside the wind shrieked like a hyena, testing the strength of the pavilion, but its traditional design had withstood many centuries of desert winds and Xavier had no fears of it being plucked away.

Throwing back the cover from his makeshift bed, he pulled on the soft loose robe and strode towards the kitchen, briskly removing one of the empty bottles Mariella had left in the sterilizer and mixing the formula.

His grandmother—an eccentric woman so far as many people were concerned—had sent him to work in a refugee camp for six months after his final year at school and before he went on to university.

'You know what it is to be proud,' she had told him when he had expressed his disdain for her decision. 'Now you need to learn what it is to be humble.

'Without humility it is impossible to be a great leader of men, Xavier,' she had informed him. 'You owe it to your grandfather's people to have greatness, for without it they will be swamped by this modern world and scattered like seeds in the wind.'

One of his tasks there had been to work in the crèche. For the rest of his life Xavier knew he would remember the emotions he had experienced at the sight of the children's emaciated little bodies.

Snapping the teat on the filled bottle, he headed for the bedroom.

The baby's cries were noticeably louder. Her feck-less mother was no doubt sleeping selfishly through them, Xavier decided grimly, ignoring the fact that he himself had already noticed just how devoted Fleur's mother was to her.

Fleur was crying too much and too long to be merely hungry, Mariella thought anxiously as she caught the increasing note of misery in the baby's piercing cry.

To her relief, Fleur seemed to find some comfort as Mariella sat up in the bed and cuddled her against her own body.

'What's wrong, sweetheart?' she whispered to her. 'Are you missing your…?'

She froze as the protective curtain closing off the room swung open, snatching at the sheet to cover her-self, her face hot with embarrassment as she glared at Xavier.

'What do you want?' she demanded aggressively.

'So you are awake. I thought—'

Fleur's eyes widened as she saw that he was carrying Fleur's bottle.

'What have you put in there?' Mariella demanded suspiciously, holding Fleur even tighter as he held the bottle out to her.

'Formula,' he told her curtly. 'What did you think was in it…hemlock? You've been reading too many idiotic trashy books!'

As she took the bottle from him and squirted a few drops onto the back of her hand, tasting it, he watched her.

'Satisfied?'

Looking fully at him, Mariella compressed her lips.

'My word,' she heard him breathe in disbelief. You even go to bed in those ridiculous coloured contact lenses! Hasn't anyone ever told you that no one actually has eyes that colour? So if it's your lovers you are hoping to impress and deceive...'

As Fleur seized eagerly on her bottle Mariella froze in outraged fury.

Coloured contact lenses. How dared he?

'Oh, is that a fact?' she breathed. 'Well, for your information, whether you consider it to be ridiculous or not this just happens to be the real colour of my eyes. I am not wearing contact lenses, and as for wanting to impress or deceive a lover—'

Fleur gave a wail of protest as in her agitation Mariella unwittingly removed the teat from her mouth. Apologising to the baby, and comforting her, Mariella breathed in sharply with resentment.

Real? The only thing about her that was real was her outrageous lying! Xavier decided lowering his lashes over his eyes as he discreetly studied the smooth swell of her breasts as her agitated movements dislodged the sheet.

No wonder she had not wanted to feed her child herself. With breasts so perfectly and beautifully formed she would be reluctant to spoil their shape. He could almost see the faint pink shadowing of the areolae of her nipples.

Uncomfortably he shifted his weight from one foot to the other, all too conscious of the effect she was having on him. She was doing it deliberately, he knew that... She was that kind of woman!

When he came here it was to withdraw from the fast-paced city life and concentrate on more cerebral matters, Xavier reminded himself sharply.

The sheet slipped a little farther.

Her flesh was creamy pale, untouched by the sun.

He frowned. Khalid had said specifically that he had taken her to the South of France. Surely there she must have exposed herself, as so many did, to the hot glare of its sun and the ever hotter lustful looks of the men who went there specifically to enjoy the sight of so much young, naked flesh?

Knowing his cousin as he did, he couldn't imagine that Khalid would be attracted to a woman too modest to remove her bikini top!

He, on the other hand, found something profoundly and intensely sensual about the thought of a woman only revealing her bare breasts to her lover, her only lover...

Worriedly Mariella studied Fleur's suddenly flushed face, reaching out to touch her cheek. It burned beneath the coolness of her own fingertips. Her heart jumped with anxiety.

Xavier's stomach muscles clenched as she removed her arm, revealing the full exposed curve of her breast. As he had known it would be, her nipple was rose-pink and so softly delicate that he ached to reach out and touch it, explore its soft tenderness, feel it hardening in eager demand beneath his caress.

In her anxiety for Fleur, Mariella had all but forgotten that he was there, only alerted to his sudden departure by the brief swirl of air eddying the doorhanging as he left.

The minute he had gone Fleur started to cry again and nothing Mariella could do would soothe her.

In the end, terrified that he would reappear at any minute and demand that she silence the baby or else, Mariella got out of the bed and, wrapping the sheet around herself, started to pace the floor, gently rocking Fleur as she did so.

To her relief after about ten minutes Fleur began to fall asleep. Gently carrying her back to her cot she started to lie her down, but the minute she did so the baby began to cry again.

Resolutely Mariella tried again...and again...and again...

Three hours later she finally admitted just how afraid she was. Fleur was crying pitifully now, her cheeks bright red and her whole body hot and sweaty. Mariella's own eyes ached and her arms were cramped with holding her as she walked up and down the bedroom.

Outside the wind still howled demoniacally.

'Oh, poor, poor baby,' Mariella whispered anxiously. Tanya had entrusted her precious child to her. How would she feel if she knew what Mariella had done? How she had brought her to the middle of the desert where there was no doctor and no way of getting to one? What if Fleur had something really seriously wrong with her? What if she had picked up some life-threatening infectious disease? What if...? Sick with anxiety and guilt, Mariella prayed that Fleur would be all right.

In the outer part of the pavilion Xavier could hear the fretful cry of the baby but he dared not go in to find out what was wrong. He could not trust himself to go in and find out what was wrong he admitted grimly.

An hour later, still trying to soothe and comfort Fleur, Mariella felt desperately afraid. It was obvious that Fleur wasn't well. The fear tormenting her could not be ignored any longer. Her hands trembling, Mariella relit all the oil lamps and then carefully undressed Fleur, slowly checking her for any sign of the rash that would confirm her worst fears and indicate that the baby could somehow have contracted meningitis.

Not content with having checked her skin once without finding any sign of a rash, Mariella did so again. When once again she could not find any sign of a rash, she didn't know whether to feel relieved or simply more anxious!

Tenderly wiping the tears from Fleur's hot face, she kissed her. Fleur grabbed hold of her finger and was trying to suck on it. No, not suck, Mariella realised— she was trying to bite on it. Fleur was cutting her first tooth!

All at once relief and recognition filled her. Fleur was teething—that was why she had been so uncomfortable. Mariella could well remember Tanya at the same age, her mother walking up and down with her as she tried to soothe her, explaining to Mariella just how much those sharp, pretty little teeth cutting through tender flesh hurt and upset the baby.

Naturally Mariella had tucked a good supply of paediatric paracetamol suspension into her baby bag before leaving home and, still holding Fleur, she went to get it.

'This will make you feel better, sweetheart,' she crooned, adding lovingly, 'And what a clever girl you are, aren't you, with your lovely new tooth? A very clever girl.'

Within minutes or so of the baby having her medicine, or so it seemed to a now totally exhausted Mariella, she was fast asleep. Patting her flushed face, Mariella smothered a yawn. Tucking Fleur into her cot, she made for her own bed.

Xavier frowned. It was well past daylight. He had showered and eaten his breakfast and switched on the laptop he had brought with him to do some work, but his mind wasn't really on it. Every time he thought about his cousin's mistress he was filled with unwanted and dangerous emotions There hadn't been a sound from the bedroom in hours. No doubt working in a nightclub she was used to sleeping during the day... And very probably not on her own!

The very thought of the woman sleeping next door in his bed drove him to such an unfamiliar and furious level of hormone-fuelled rage that he could barely contain himself. And he was a man who was secretly proud of the fact that he was known for his fabled self-control!

Khalid should think himself very fortunate indeed that he had prevented him from marrying that turquoise-eyed seductress.

But Khalid did not think himself fortunate! Khalid thought himself very far from fortunate and had, in fact, left his cousin's presence swearing that he would not give up the woman he loved, no, not even if Xavier did try to carry out his threat and disinherit him!

His cousin was quite plainly besotted with the woman, and now that Xavier had met her for himself he was beginning to understand just how dangerous she was.

But not even Khalid's love would be strong enough to withstand the knowledge that she had been his cousin's lover. That she had given herself willingly to him! That the thought of ensnaring an even richer man than Khalid, in Xavier himself, had been enough to have her crawling into his bed.

That knowledge would hurt Khalid, but better that he was hurt quickly and cleanly now than that he spent a lifetime suffering a thousand humiliations at her hands! As he undoubtedly would do!

Surely the silence from the bedroom was unnatural. The woman should be awake by now, if only for the sake of her child!

Irritably Xavier strode towards the bedroom area, and pulled back the hanging.

Mariella was lying on the bed deeply asleep, one arm flung out, her pale skin gleaming in the soft light.

The thick strawberry-blonde hair was softly tousled, a few wisps sticking to her pink-cheeked face, lashes, which surely must be dyed to achieve that density of colour, surrounding the turquoise she insisted on claiming was natural.

In her sleep she sighed and frowned and made a little moue of distress before settling back into sleep.

Unable to drag his gaze from her, Xavier continued to watch her. There was nothing about what he knew of the type of person she was that could appeal to his aesthetic and cultured taste. But physically...

Physically, hormonally, she exerted such a pull over his senses that right now...

He had taken a step towards the bed without even realising it, the ache in his groin immediately a fierce, primal surge of white-hot need. If he took her in his arms and woke her now, would it be Khalid's name he heard on her lips?

That thought alone should have been enough to freeze his arousal to nothing, but instead he was filled with a savage explosion of angry emotion at the thought of any man's name on her lips that wasn't his own!

As he battled with the realisation of just what that

meant, his attention was suddenly distracted by the happy gurgling coming from the cot.

Striding over to it, he stared down at Fleur. Her child. The child another man had given her! A surge of primitive aching pain filled him.

Fleur had kicked off her blankets and was playing with her bare toes, smiling coquettishly up at him.

Xavier sucked in his breath. She was so small, so delicate…so very much like her mother.

Instinctively he bent to pick her up.

Mariella didn't know what woke her from her deep sleep, some ancient female instinct perhaps, she decided shakily as she stared across the room and saw Xavier bending over Fleur.

Gripping the bedclothes, she burst out frantically, 'Don't you dare hurt her.'

'Hurt her?' Tight-lipped, Xavier swung round. 'You dare to say that when she has already been hurt immeasurably simply by being brought into being as the child of a woman who…'

Unable to fully express his feelings, he compressed his mouth.

'I suppose she is used to being left to amuse herself whilst her mother sleeps off the effects of her night's work!'

Mariella could scarcely contain her fury.

'How dare you say such things, after the way you have behaved? You are the most loathsome, the most vile man I have ever met. You are totally lacking in any kind of compassion, or…or responsibility!'

Her eyes really were that colour, Xavier recognised in disbelief as he watched them darken from turquoise to inky blue-green.

Did they turn that colour when she was lost in passion? Was she as passionate in her sexual desire as she was in her anger? Of course she was…he knew that instinctively, just as he knew equally instinctively that if she were his…

'It is nearly eleven o' clock, the child must be hungry,' he told her tersely, infuriated by his own weakness in allowing such thoughts to creep into his head.

Eleven o'clock—how could it be? Mariella wondered guiltily, but a quick glance at her watch showed her that it was.

She couldn't wait to get back to the city and the sooner she and Fleur were on their way back there, the better, she decided as Xavier strode out of the room.

CHAPTER FOUR

MARIELLA frowned as she walked into the empty living area of the pavilion. Where was Xavier?

A laptop hummed quietly on a folding campaign table to one side of the pavilion. Xavier had obviously been working on it.

As she looked round the pavilion with its precious carpets and elegant few pieces of furniture, which she recognised as being expensively antique as well as functional, Mariella tried to imagine her dizzy half-sister in such a setting. Tanya was totally open about the fact that she was a girl who loved the bustle of cities, holidays in expensive, fashionable locations, modern apartments as opposed to traditional houses. Although she adored Fleur, self-indulgence was her by-word, and Mariella was finding it increasingly hard to visualise her sister ever being compatible with a man like Xavier, who she could not imagine truly sharing Tanya's tastes. He was too austere, surely. Too…

Tanya loved him, she reminded herself stubbornly, although she was finding that equally hard to imagine! He was just so totally not Tanya's type! Tanya liked happy-go-lucky, boyish, fun-loving men!

Fleur was sound asleep, and Mariella decided she would go outside to check on what was happening. She could no longer hear the sound of the wind battering against the walls of the pavilion, which hopefully meant that she would be able to make her way back to the city.

49

As she stepped outside she saw to her relief that the wind had indeed dropped. The air was now totally still and the sky had a dull ochre tinge to it. She could see her four-wheel drive, its sides covered in sand.

On the far side of the oasis, the rock face of the gorge rose steeply, its almost vertical face scarred here and there by the odd ledge.

There was a raw, elemental beauty about this hidden place, Mariella acknowledged, seeing it now with an artist's eye rather than the panicky apprehension of a lost traveller.

A scattering of palm trees fringed the water of the oasis, and beyond them lay a rough area of sparse, spiky grass. The rutted track she had driven down probably was a dried-out river bed, she could see now.

The quality of the stillness and the corresponding silence were almost hypnotic.

A movement on the other side of the oasis caught her eye, her body tensing as she recognised Xavier. He was dressed not in traditional robes, but in jeans and a tee shirt. He seemed to be checking the palm trees, she realised as he paused to inspect one before walking to another. He had obviously not seen her, but instinctively she drew farther back into the shadow cast by the pavilion.

He had turned away from the trees now and was staring across the oasis, shading his eyes as he looked up into the sky.

The storm hadn't weakened the roots of any of the palm trees, Xavier acknowledged. There was no reason why he shouldn't go back to the pavilion and continue with his work. And in fact pretty soon he would have to do so. Right now they were in the eye of the storm, but as soon as it moved on the wind would return with even greater force.

But he couldn't go back inside. Not whilst he was still visualising *her* lying on the bed...his bed...

Angrily he stripped off his tee shirt, quickly followed by the rest of his clothes. And began to wade out into the water.

Mariella couldn't move. Like someone deeply beneath the spell of an outside force she stood, muscles clenched, hardly daring to breathe as she fought to repel the sensation coiling through her, and shivering to each and every single sensitive nerve ending as her gaze absorbed the raw male beauty of Xavier's nudity.

As an artist she was fully aware of the complexities and the beauty of the human form, she had visited Florence and wandered lost in rapt awe as she studied the work of the great masters, but now she recognised she was seeing the work of the greatest Master of all.

Xavier was wading out into the water, the dull glaring sunlight glinting on flesh so warmly and evenly hued that it was immediately obvious that such nudity was normal for him.

As he moved through the water she could see the powerful sinews in his thighs contracting against its pressure. Trying to distract herself she visualised what lay inside that heavy satin male flesh, the bones, the muscles, the tissues, but instead of calming her down, it made her awareness of him increase, her wanton thoughts fiercely pushing aside the pallid academic images she was trying to conjure, in favour of some of their own: like a close-up of that sun-warmed flesh, roped with muscle, hard, sleek, rough with the same fine dark hair she could see so clearly arrowing down the centre of his body.

Only his buttocks were a slightly paler shade than the rest of his skin, taut and man-shaped, packed with the muscles that would drive...

Mariella shuddered violently, feeling as though she herself were sinking into a pool of sensation so deep and dangerous that she had no means of freeing herself from it.

Helplessly she watched as Xavier moved farther into the oasis until all she could see above the water were his head and shoulders. He ducked his whole body beneath the water and she held her breath, expelling it when she saw him break the surface several yards away, cleaving through it with long, powerful over-arm strokes that propelled him at a fierce and silent speed away from her.

She felt sick, shocked, furiously angry, terrifyingly vulnerable, aching from head to toe and most of all, deep down inside the most female part of her body, tormented by a need, a knowledge that ripped apart all her previous beliefs about herself.

She could not possibly want Xavier! But that...that merciless message her body had just given her could not be denied.

It sickened her to think of wanting a man who had hurt her sister so much; a man Tanya still loved so much. Such a feeling was a betrayal of everything within herself she most prided herself on. It was inconceivable that such a thing could be happening, just as it was inconceivable too that she, a woman who took such pride in her ability to mentally control the sexual and emotional side of her nature, could allow herself to feel so...so...

Dragging her gaze away from the oasis, Mariella closed her eyes.

Go on, admit it, she taunted herself mentally. You are so hungry for him that if he came to you now, you would let him do whatever he wanted with you right here and right now. Let him? You would urge him, encourage him, entice him...

Frantically Mariella shook her head, trying to shake away her own tormenting thoughts, the tormenting inner voice that was mocking her so openly.

Blindly she headed back for the pavilion, not seeing the hot breaths of wind tugging warningly at the topmost fronds of the palm trees, and not noticing, either, the bronze ring of light dulling the sun so menacingly.

Once inside the pavilion she hurried to check on Fleur who was still sleeping. She had only been outside for around half an hour, but it felt somehow as though she had passed through a whole time zone and entered another world. A world in which she no longer knew exactly who or what she was.

Quickly she started to get together their things. She didn't want to be here when Xavier came back. She couldn't bear to be here when he came back; she couldn't bear to face him, to be in the same room with him, the same space with him; in fact she wasn't sure right now if she could even bear to be in the same life with him.

She had never imagined that there could be anyone who could make her feel so threatened, so appalled by her own feelings, and so afraid of them. Flushed and sticky, she surveyed her uncharacteristically chaotic packing.

She would put their things in the four-wheel drive first, and then pop Fleur in and then she would drive back to the hotel and not stop until she got there.

Mariella took a deep breath. Once she was there she

would no doubt come to her senses and think of Xavier only as the man who had betrayed her sister, the man who was Fleur's father!

The wind was beginning to bend the palms as Mariella hurried out to the vehicle with their things, but she was oblivious to it as she wrestled with the heavy door and started to load the car.

Xavier saw her as he turned to swim another length. Treading water, he watched in furious disbelief as she struggled with the vehicle's door and then started to push the bulky container she had brought with her inside it.

There! Now all she had to do was go back for Fleur and then they could leave, hopefully whilst Xavier was too busy swimming to notice! And anyway, if he had wanted a swim that badly why couldn't he have worn…well, something? Why had he had to—to flaunt his undeniably supremely male and very, very sexy body in the way he had?

Engrossed in her thoughts, she failed to see Xavier wade out of the water and pull on his tee shirt and jeans without wasting time on anything else, before starting to run towards the pavilion into which she had already disappeared.

'Come on, my beautiful baby,' Mariella crooned lovingly to Fleur as she wrapped her up. 'You and I are going—'

'Nowhere!'

Turning round, white-faced and clutching Fleur protectively to her, Mariella glared at him. The fine cotton tee shirt was plastered to his very obviously still damp body and her skittering gaze slid helplessly downward to rest indiscreetly on the groin of his jeans at the same time as her heart came to rest against her chest wall in a massive breathtaking thud.

He was standing in the exit blocking her way, but infuriatingly, instead of registering this vitally important fact first, her senses seemed to be far too preoccupied with taking a personal inventory of the way he looked clothed and the way he had looked...before!

Reminding herself that she was an adult, mature businesswoman, well used to running her own life and making her own decisions, and not the sad female with her hormones running riot that she was currently doing a good impression of, she drew herself up to her full height and told him determinedly, 'I am taking Fleur back to the city and there is no way you are going to stop me. And anyway, I can't imagine why you would want us to stay after the way you have behaved! The things you have said!'

'Want you to stay? No, I don't!' Xavier confirmed harshly. 'But unfortunately you are going to have to, unless, of course, you want to condemn yourself and the baby to almost certain death.'

Mariella stared at him. What did he mean? Was he trying to threaten her? 'We're leaving,' she repeated, making for the exit, and trying to ignore both the furious thud of her heart and the fact that he was standing in the way.

'Are you mad? You'd be lucky to get above half a dozen miles before being buried in a sand drift. If you thought the wind coming here was bad, well, let me tell you that was nothing compared with what's blowing up out there now!'

Mariella took a deep breath.

'I've just been outside. There is no wind,' she told

him patiently, slowly spacing each word with immense care. 'The storm is over.'

'And you would know, of course, being an expert on desert weather conditions, no doubt. For your information, the reason that there was no wind, as you put it, is because we are, or rather we were in the eye of the storm. And anyone who knows anything about the desert would know that. Couldn't you feel the stillness? Didn't you notice the sand haze in the sky?' The look he shot her could have lit tinder at fifty paces, Mariella recognised shakily.

'You're lying,' she told him stubbornly, determined not to let him get the better of her. 'You just want to keep us here because—'

When she stopped he looked derisively at her.

'Yes. I want to keep you here because what?'

Because you know how dangerously much I want you, a treacherous little voice whispered insidiously inside Mariella's head, and you feel the same way.

Shuddering, she pushed her thoughts back into the realms of reality—and safety.

'You're lying,' she repeated doggedly, eyeing the exit rebelliously.

'Am I?' Moving to one side, he swept back the tent flap so that she could see outside.

The palms were bending so much beneath the strength of the wind that their fronds were brushing the sand.

As she stared in disbelief Mariella could hear the strength of the wind increasing until it whistled eerily around the oasis, physically hurting her ears.

Out of nowhere it whipped up huge spirals of sand, making them dance in front of her. She could hardly see the sun or differentiate any longer between sand and sky.

Disbelievingly she took a step outside and cried out in shock as she was almost lifted off her feet when the wind punched into her. In her arms, Fleur screamed and was immediately removed to the protection of a much stronger and safer pair as Xavier snatched Fleur from her.

The thought of what would have happened to them if they had been caught in the open desert in such conditions drove the colour from Mariella's face.

'Now do you believe me?' Xavier demanded grimly when they were both back inside and he had secured the tent flap.

Reaching out to take Fleur from him, Mariella, whose fingers had inadvertently come into contact with the damp heat of his tee-shirt-clad chest, withdrew her hand so fast she almost lost her balance.

Immediately Xavier gripped her arm to steady her, supporting whilst he did so, so that it looked almost as though he were embracing them both, holding them both safe.

Against all rationality, given what she knew about him, Mariella discovered that her eyes were burning with emotional tears. She should be crying, she acknowledged grimly, for her own stupidity in allowing her emotions to be aroused so much for so little real reason! Pulling back from him, she demanded, 'Just how long is this storm going to last?'

'At least twenty-four hours, perhaps longer. Since the storm is making it impossible to receive any kind of communication signal, it is impossible to know.

Such storms are rare at this time of year, but when they do occur they are both unpredictable and fierce.'

As was Xavier himself, Mariella decided as she took Fleur from him.

CHAPTER FIVE

GETTING up from the bed where she had been lying reading one of the research books she had brought to Zuran with her, Mariella went to check on Fleur.

A brief glance at her watch showed her that it was nearly eight p.m. Fleur was awake but obviously quite content, and happy to oblige when Mariella checked her mouth to look at the small pearly white tooth just beginning to appear. Her face was still a little bit swollen and flushed, but the paracetamol seemed to have eased the pain she had suffered the previous night.

Mariella had retreated to 'her bedroom' late in the afternoon, desperate to escape from the highly charged atmosphere in the main living area.

It had become impossible for her to look at Xavier without imagining him as he had been earlier: naked...male.

He had retrieved the things she had carried out to the four-wheel drive and put them back in the bedroom, and when Mariella had come across a sketch-book and pencils she had forgotten she had brought, along with her book, she had fallen on the book with a surge of relief.

Apart from the fact that she genuinely found the subject interesting, it gave her a perfect excuse to distance herself from Xavier, who had been busily working on his laptop.

On the pretext of Fleur needing a nap she had come

into the sleeping quarters and had remained there ever since.

A thorough understanding of anatomy was essential for any painter in her type of field, and she had quickly become totally engrossed in trying to trace the development of the modern-day racehorse from the original Arabian bloodstock.

As Kate had said, the potential commission from the prince was indeed a prestigious one.

Picking up her sketch-book, Mariella started to work. Those incredible muscles that powered every movement... Her pencil flew over the paper, her absorption in what she was doing only broken when Fleur started to demand her attention.

Smiling, she discarded the sketch-book and then frowned sharply as she looked at what she had done, her face burning mortified and disbelieving scarlet.

How on earth had that happened? How on earth had she managed to sketch, not a horse, but a man... Xavier...Xavier, swimming, Xavier standing, Xavier: his body lean and naked, clean-muscled and powerful.

Guiltily, Mariella flipped over the page. Fleur was blowing kisses at her and becoming increasingly vociferous.

Tucking the sketch-pad safely out of sight, Mariella went to her and picked her up, fastening her into her car seat and then carrying her into the kitchen.

'Look at this yummy dinner you're going to have,' Mariella crooned to Fleur as she prepared her food.

It had been her intention to take Fleur back into the bedroom to feed her, but instead Mariella carried her into the living area.

Fleur was Xavier's daughter, after all, and perhaps

they both needed reminding just what that meant, albeit for very different reasons! Perhaps too he ought to be made to see just what he was missing out on by not acknowledging her.

He was working on the laptop when Mariella walked in and put Fleur down in her seat so that she could feed her.

She was a strong, healthy baby with a good appetite, who thankfully no longer seemed to be too bothered by the tooth she had been cutting.

Absorbed in her own enjoyable task, Mariella didn't realise that Xavier had stopped work to turn and study them until some sixth sense warned her that they were being watched.

His abrupt, 'She has your nose,' made Mariella's hand tremble slightly. She and Tanya shared the same shaped nose, which they had both inherited from their mother. Fleur had their nose, but, according to Tanya, her father's deliciously long thick eyelashes.

Mariella could feel her face starting to burn. What was it about a certain type of man that enabled him to behave so uncaringly towards the child he had fathered?

The way Xavier was behaving towards Fleur was so reminiscent of the way her father had behaved towards her! She knew all too well what it was like to grow up feeling rejected and unloved by one's father and she couldn't bear to see that happen to Fleur!

Xavier ought to be made to see that she was at least in part his responsibility instead of being allowed to just walk away from her. The way she felt had nothing whatsoever to do with money, Mariella recognised, and everything to do with emotion.

Fleur had finished her meal and was beginning to

drift off to sleep. Bending down to double check that she was comfortably fastened into her seat, Mariella tenderly kissed her downy cheek, then straightened up and headed for the kitchen to wash out her feeding things.

Left on his own with Fleur, Xavier studied her frowningly. She was far fairer skinned than his cousin and, whilst Xavier could see an unmistakable physical resemblance to Mariella in her, he could see none to Khalid. Fast asleep now, Fleur gave a small quiver.

Immediately Xavier went over to her. Desert nights could be unbelievably cold—she felt warm enough, but perhaps she needed an extra cover?

He could hear Mariella in the kitchen and so he went through into the bedroom area, to get an extra blanket from the carry-cot.

Mariella had tucked her sketch-pad in between the carry-cot and the box of baby equipment, and as Xavier reached for a blanket he saw the sketch-pad, and its very recognisable sketches.

Frowning, he picked it up and studied it.

Having washed Fleur's feeding cup, Mariella walked into the bedroom intending to put it away, coming to an abrupt halt as she saw Xavier bending towards the carry-cot.

'Where is Fleur?' she demanded immediately. 'What— ?'

'She's fast asleep where you left her,' Xavier answered her adding, 'From looking at her, it is plain to see her resemblance to you, but as to there being a similarity to her supposed father...'

Mariella had had enough.

'How can you deny your own flesh and blood?' she

demanded bitterly. 'I can't imagine how *any* woman could ever desire you, never mind—'

Before she could say 'Tanya' he had cut her off as he asked with cutting brutality, 'Indeed? Then, what may I ask, are these?'

Mariella felt the breath wheeze from her lungs like air squeezed from a pair of bellows as he held up in front of her her own sketches.

Chagrin, embarrassment, guilt and anger fused into one burning, searing jolt of emotional intensity had her lunging frantically towards him, intent on snatching her betraying sketches from him. But Xavier was withholding them from her, holding them out of her reach with one hand whilst he fended her attempt to repossess them with the other.

Furiously Mariella redoubled her efforts, flinging herself at him, and trying to shake off his hard grip of her wrist as she did so.

'Give those back to me. They are mine,' she insisted breathlessly.

As she tried to reach up for them she overbalanced slightly, her fingers curling into his arm, her fingernails accidentally raising livid weals on his olive skin.

'Why, you little...'

Shocked as much by her own inadvertent action as his reaction to it, Mariella went stiff with disbelief as he suddenly dropped the sketches and grabbed hold of her waist with both hands.

'Other men might have been willing to let you get away with such behaviour, but I most certainly do not intend to!' she could hear Xavier grating at her as he gave her a small, angry shake.

Mariella could feel the edge of the bed behind her as she turned and twisted, frantically trying to break free, but Xavier was refusing to let her go and suddenly she was lying on the bed, with Xavier arching over her, pinning her down.

He was angry with her, Mariella recognised as she stared into the lava-grey heat of his eyes, but her senses were telling her something else as well and a savage little quiver then ran unmistakably through her own body as she realised that something else had nothing whatsoever to do with fear.

Xavier wanted her! Mariella could sense, feel it, breathe it in the sudden tension that filled the air, engulfing, locking them both in a place out of time.

This was fate, Xavier decided recklessly, a golden opportunity given to him to prove to his cousin beyond any shadow of a doubt that this woman was not worthy of his love, but, strangely, as he lowered his mouth to Mariella's it wasn't his duty towards his cousin that was filling his thoughts, driving him with an intense ferocity that a part of him recognised was more dangerous than anything he had previously experienced.

This was wrong, desperately wrong, the very worst kind of betrayal, Mariella acknowledged as her whole body was savaged by a mixture of anguish and hunger.

Xavier's mouth burned hers, its possession every bit as harsh and demanding as she had expected, barely cloaking a hunger that scorched right through her body to her fingertips.

Helplessly her mouth responded to the savage demand of his, her body quivering as his tongue probed her closed lips demanding entry. Somehow, some time she had lifted her hands to his body so that she was gripping his shoulders. To push him away, or to draw him closer?

His teeth tugged ruthlessly at her bottom lip and her

resistance ebbed away, like the inner tears of shame and guilt she was silently crying inside for her inability to resist giving in to flames of her own desire as they licked and darted inside her, burning down her pathetically weak defences. Without knowing how she knew, she knew that this man, this moment was something a part of her had been waiting for, for a very long time. Even the merciless intent of his sensual need was something that a part of her was fiercely responsive to.

Her eyes, magnificent in their emotional intensity, shimmered from turquoise to dark blue-green. Xavier was mesmerised by them, caught in their brilliance. How could such cool colours glow so hotly? But not nearly so hotly as his own body.

Without knowing what she was doing, Mariella raked the taut flesh of his arm—deliberately this time— her body galvanised by deep, urgent shudders as his kiss possessed her mouth, his tongue thrusting into its warm softness.

Mariella tried to deny what she was feeling, pulling frantically away from Xavier, in a desperate attempt to escape and to save them both from the very worst kind of betrayal, but having shared her surrender Xavier refused to let her go, pinning her to the bed with the weight of his body hot and heavy on hers, making her melt, making her ache, making her writhe in helpless supplication and moan into his mouth, a tiny keening sound lost beneath the greater sounds of their bodies moving on the bed. The rustle and rasp of fabric against flesh, of two people both revealing their hunger in the accelerated sound of their breathing, and the frantic thud of their heartbeats.

Xavier's mouth grazed her skin, exploring the curve of her jaw, the soft vulnerability of her throat as she automatically arched her whole body. The hot, fevered feel of his mouth against her flesh made her arch even more, shuddering in agonised pleasure.

Just a few kisses, that was all it was... And yet she felt as possessed by him, as aching for him as though he had touched her far more intimately and for far, far longer. The desire she was feeling was so acute, so very nearly unbearable, that Mariella dared not allow herself to imagine how she was going to feel when he did touch her more intimately. And yet at the same time she knew that if he didn't—

When his hand covered her breast she cried out, unable to stop herself, and felt his responding groan shudder through his body. She could hear herself making small, whimpering sounds of distress as she tugged at his clothes, her own body consumed by a need to be completely bare to his touch, to be open to him...

And yet when he had finally removed them and she was naked, a sense of panic that was wholly primitive and instinctive ripped through her, causing her to go to cover her naked breasts protectively with her own hands. But Xavier was too quick for her, his fingers snapping round her wrists, pinioning her hands either side of her head as he knelt over her.

Mariella felt the heavy thread of her own hungry desire. She just had time to see the molten glitter of Xavier's answering hunger before he looked down at her exposed breasts. A sinful desire slid hotly through her veins, her face burning as she watched him absorbing the taut swell of her breasts as her nipples tightened and darkened, openly inciting the need she could hear and feel in his indrawn breath, even before he lowered his head to her body.

The feeling of him slowly circling first one and then

the other nipple with the moist heat of his tongue, whilst she lay powerless beneath him, should surely have inflamed her angry independence instead of sending such a sheet of white-hot sensuality pouring through her that her belly automatically concaved under its pressure whilst her sex ached and swelled.

Mariella closed her eyes. Behind her closed eyelids she could see him as she had done in the oasis, just as she wanted to see him again now, she recognised as her body began to shudder. Slow, deep, galvanic surges of desire that ripped rhythmically through her, her body moving to the suckle of his mouth against her breast.

She could feel his knee parting her thighs her body already aching for the aroused feel of him, hot, heavy, masculine as he urgently moved against her.

He was losing himself, drowning in the way she was making him feel, his self-control in danger of being burned away to nothing. Just the sight of her swollen breasts, their nipples tight and aroused from his laving of them, made him ache to possess her, to complete and fill her, to complete himself within her.

The moment Xavier released her wrists, Mariella tugged impatiently at his clothes, answering her demanding need for him. Immediately Xavier helped her, guiding her hands over buttons and zips and then flesh itself as she moaned her pleasure against the hot skin of his throat when her fingertips finally tangled with the soft, silky hair she had ached to touch earlier.

His body, packed hard with muscle, was excitingly alien and overpoweringly male. His impatience to be a part of her made her gasp and shudder as he kissed her throat, her shoulder and then her mouth, whilst he wrapped her tightly in his arms so that they were lying intimately, naked body to naked body.

The feel of him pressing against her. Hot and hard, aroused, his movement against her urgently explicit, was more than she could withstand.

Eagerly she coiled herself around him, opening herself to him, crying out as she felt him enter her, each movement powerful and sure, strong and urgent.

Already her own body was responding to his movement, her muscles clinging to him. Sensually stroking him and savouring each thrust, she could feel him strengthening inside her, filling her to completion, picking up the rhythm of her body and carrying...driving them both with it.

'Never mind the child he has given you, has my cousin given you this? Has he made you feel like this when he holds you? When he possesses you? When he loves you? Was *this* how it was between you when you made Fleur together?'

Mariella's whole body stiffened.

'Did you give yourself to him as easily as you did to me? And how many others have there been?'

With a fierce cry, she pulled away from him, her brain barely able to take in what he was saying, her body and emotions in such deep shock that removing herself from him made her feel as though she were physically dying.

The shock of her rejection tore at Xavier's guts. He wanted to drag her back into his arms, where surely she belonged, to roll her into the bed beneath him and to fill her with himself, to make her admit that no other man had ever or could ever give her or share with her what he could. But most of all he wanted to fill her with the life force that would ultimately be his child.

A part of him recognised that there was no more elemental drive than this, to fill a woman's body with one's child in order to drive out her commitment to another man and the child he had already given her. The barbaric intensity of his own emotions shocked him. He had done what he had done for Khalid's sake, to protect him, he reminded himself, and to reinforce that fact he told her, 'It's a little too late for that now! You have already proved to me just what you are, and once Khalid learns how willing you were to give yourself to me he will quickly realise how right I was to counsel him against you.'

He had taken her to bed for that? Because of that? So that he could denounce her to another man?

In the outer room Fleur suddenly started to cry. Dragging on her clothes, Mariella hurried in to her, picking her up and holding her tightly as though just holding her could somehow staunch the huge wound inside her that was haemorrhaging her life force. She was shaking from head to foot with reaction, both from what had happened and from what she had just learned.

Fleur was not Xavier's child! Xavier's cousin was Fleur's father! But Xavier believed that she was Fleur's mother. And because of that he had taken her to bed, out of a cold-hearted, despicable, damnable desire to prove to his cousin that she was a...a wanton who would give herself to any man!

Fate had been doubly kind to her, she told herself staunchly: firstly in ensuring that she had not betrayed her sister, and secondly in giving her incontrovertible proof of just what manner of man Xavier was!

CHAPTER SIX

As SHE stepped inside the welcome familiarity of her Beach Club bungalow, Mariella allowed herself to expel a shaky sigh of relief. Her first since she had left the oasis!

Now that she was safely here, perhaps she could allow herself to put the events of the last forty-eight hours firmly behind her. Lock them away in a very deep sealed drawer marked, 'Forget for ever.'

But how could she forget, how could any human being forget an act as deliberately and cold-bloodedly cruel and damaging as the one Xavier had perpetrated against her?

If she herself had been a different kind of woman she might have taken a grim sense of distorted pleasure in knowing that, for all he might try to deny it, Xavier had physically wanted her. In knowing it and in throwing that knowledge back at him! Instinctively she knew that he would be humiliated by it, and if any man deserved to be humiliated it was Xavier!

Just thinking about him was enough to have Mariella's hands curling into small, passionately angry fists. As her heart drove against her ribs in sledgehammer blows. How could he possibly not have recognised that she would never, ever, ever under any circumstances betray her love, and that if she had been another man's lover nothing he could have done would have tempted her to want him? Hadn't her body itself proclaimed to him the unlikeliness, the impossibility of her being Fleur's mother and any man's intimate lover?

But believing that he had been Tanya's lover hadn't stopped her, had it?

She would carry that shame and guilt with her to her deathbed, Mariella acknowledged.

The message light on the bungalow's communications system was flashing, indicating that she had re ceived several telephone calls, all from the prince's personal assistant, she discovered when she went to check them. Before answering them, the first thing she intended to do now that she was safely back at the hotel was ring her sister and double check that she had not misunderstood Xavier—he was not Tanya's lover or Fleur's father!

And once she had that confirmation safely in her possession, then Xavier would be history!

It took her several attempts to get through to Tanya, who eventually answered the phone sounding breathless and flustered.

'I'm sorry, Ella,' she apologised quickly. 'But things are really hectic here and... Look, I can't really talk right now. Is Fleur okay?'

'Fleur is fine. She's cut her first tooth, but, Tanya, there's something I've got to know,' Mariella told her, firmly overriding her attempts to end the call.

'I must know Fleur's father's name, Tanya. It's desperately important!'

'Why? What's happened? Ella, I can't tell you...'

Hearing the panic in her sister's voice, Mariella took a deep breath. 'All right! But if you won't tell me who he is, Tanya, then please at least tell me that his first name isn't Xavier...'

'Who?' Tanya's outraged shriek almost hurt her eardrums. 'Xavier? You mean that horrid cousin of Khalid's? Of course he isn't Fleur's father. I hate him... He's the one responsible for parting me and Khalid! He sent Khalid away! He doesn't think that I'm good enough for him! Anyway...how do you know about Xavier, Ella? He's an arrogant, overbearing, old-fashioned, moralistic beast, who lives in the Dark Ages! Look, Ella, I've got to go... Love to Fleur and lots of kisses.'

She ended the call before Mariella could stop her, leaving her gripping the receiver tensely.

But at least she had confirmed that Xavier was not Fleur's father.

Determinedly Mariella made herself turn her attention to her messages.

The prince had now returned to Zuran and wanted her to get in touch with his personal assistant.

'Don't worry,' the prince's personal assistant reassured Mariella when she rang him a few minutes later to explain why she had not returned his calls.

'It is just that the prince is hosting a charity breakfast tomorrow morning at the stables and he wanted to invite you as his guest. His Highness is very enthusiastic about his project of having the horses painted, but of course this is something you will be having formal discussions with him about at a later date. The breakfast is a prestigious dressy event, although we do ask all our guests not to wear strong perfumes, as this can affect the horses.'

'It sounds wonderful,' Mariella responded. 'However, there is one small problem. I have brought my four-month-old niece to Zuran with me, as the prince knows. I am looking after her for my sister, and—'

'That is no problem at all,' the PA came back promptly. 'Crèche facilities are being provided with fully trained nannies in attendance. A car will be sent to collect both you and the baby, of course.'

Mariella had previously attended several glitzy society events at the invitation of her clients, including one particularly elegant trip to France for their main race of the season at Longchamps—a gift from a client, which she had repaid with a 'surprise' sketch of his four-year-old daughter on her pony, and, recalling the sophistication and glamour of the outfits worn by the Middle Eastern contingent on that occasion, she suspected that she was going to have to go shopping.

Two hours later, sitting sipping coffee in the exclusive Zuran Designer Shopping Centre, Mariella smiled ruefully to herself as she contemplated her assorted collection of shiny shopping bags.

The largest one bore the name, not of some famous designer, but of an exclusive babywear store. Unable to choose between two equally delicious little outfits for Fleur, Mariella had ended up buying her niece both.

She had been rather less indulgent on her own account, opting only to buy a hat—an outrageously feminine and eye-catching model hat, mind you!—a pair of ridiculously spindly heeled but totally irresistible sandals, which just happened to be the exact shade of turquoise-blue of the silk dress she had decided to wear to the charity breakfast, and a handbag in the same colour, which quite incredibly had the design of a galloping horse picked out on it in sequins and beads.

And best of all she had managed not to think about

Xavier at all…well, almost not at all! And when she
had thought about him it had been to reiterate to herself
just what a total pig he was, and how lucky she was
that all she had done was give in to a now unthinkable
and totally out of character, momentary madness,
which would never, ever be repeated. After all, there
was no danger of her ever allowing herself to become
emotionally vulnerable to any man—not with her father's behaviour to remind her of the danger of falling
in love—never mind a man who had condemned himself in the way that Xavier had!

Having drunk her coffee, she gathered up her bags
and checked that Fleur was strapped securely in her
buggy before heading for the taxi rank.

It had been a long day. She had hardly slept the night
before, lying awake in Xavier's bed, her thoughts and
her emotions churning. And then there had been the
long drive back to Zuran this morning after her prayers
had been answered and the storm had died away.

True, she had had a brief nap earlier, but now, even
though it was barely eight in the evening, she was already yawning.

Xavier paced the floor of the pavilion. He should, he
knew, be rejoicing in his solitude and the fact that that
woman had gone! And of course he would have no
compunction whatsoever in telling Khalid just how easily and quickly she had betrayed the 'love' she had
claimed to have for him!

That ache he could feel in his body right now meant
nothing and would very quickly be banished!

But what if Khalid refused to listen to him? What
if, despite everything he, Xavier, had said to him, he
insisted on continuing his relationship with her?

If Fleur was Khalid's child then it was only right that he should provide for her. Xavier tried to imagine how he would feel if Khalid were to set his mistress and their child up in a home in Zurau. How he would feel knowing that Khalid was living with her, sharing that home...sharing her bed?

Angrily he strode outside. Even the damned air inside the tent was poisoned by her perfume—that and the scent of baby powder! He would instruct his staff to dispose of the bedding and replace it with new, just in case her scent might somehow manage to linger and remind him of an incident he now wanted to totally forget!

But even outside he was still haunted by his mental images of her. Her ridiculous turquoise eyes, her creamy pale skin, her delicate bone structure, her extraordinarily passionate response to him that had driven him wild, driven him over the edge of his control to a place he had never been before. The sweet, hot, tight feel of her inside, as though she had never had another lover, never mind a child! No wonder poor, easygoing Khalid had become so ensnared by her!

Fleur was certainly attracting a lot of attention, Mariella reflected tenderly as people turned to look at the baby she was carrying in her arms, oblivious to the fact that it was her own appearance that was attracting second looks from so many members of the fashionably dressed crowd already filling the stable yard.

Her slim silk dress had originally been bought for a friend's wedding, its soft, swirling pattern in colours that ranged from palest aqua right through to turquoise. Over it, to cover her bare arms, Mariella was wearing a toning, velvet-edged, silk-knit cardigan, several shades paler than her hat and shoes.

A member of the prince's staff had been on hand to greet her as she stepped out of the limousine that had been sent to collect her, and to pass her on to a charming young man, who was now taking her to introduce her to the prince.

The purpose-built stables were immaculate, the equine occupants of the stalls arching their long necks and doing a good deal of scene stealing, as though intent on making the point that they were the real stars of the event and not the humans who were invading their territory.

The breakfast was to be served in ornamental pavilioned areas, off which was the crèche, so Mariella had been informed.

Her stomach muscles tightened a little as she saw the group of people up ahead of her. People of consequence and standing, no matter how they were dressed, all possessed that same air of confidence, Mariella acknowledged as the crowd opened up and the man at the centre of it turned to look at her.

'Miss Sutton, this is his Royal Highness,' her young escort introduced her to the prince, her potential client.

'Miss Sutton!' His voice was warm, but Mariella was aware of the sharp, assessing look he gave her.

'Your Highness,' she responded, with a small inclination of her head.

'I have been very impressed with your work, Miss Sutton, although I have to say that, especially in the case of my friend and rival Sir John Feinnes, you have erred on the side of generosity in the stature and muscle you have given his "Oracle".'

A small smile dimpled Mariella's mouth.

'I simply reflect what I see as an artist, Highness,' she told him demurely.

'Indeed. Then wait until you have seen my animals. They are the result of a breeding programme that has taken many years' hard work, and I want them to be painted in a way that pays full tribute to their magnificence.'

And to his own, Mariella decided, but tactfully did not say so.

'My friend Sir John also tells me that you have some very innovative ideas... The finishing touches are currently being put to an exclusive enclosure at our racecourse, which will bear my family name, and it occurs to me that there could be an opportunity there for...' He paused.

Mariella suggested, tongue in cheek, 'Something innovative?'

'Indeed,' he agreed. 'But this is not a time to discuss business. I have invited you here as my guest, so that you can meet some of your subjects informally, so to speak...'

Fleur, who had been staring around in wide-eyed silence, suddenly turned her head and smiled at him.

'You have a beautiful child,' he complimented her.

'She is my niece,' Mariella informed him. 'I am looking after her for my sister. I think my agent did explain.'

'Yes. I am sure she did! I seem to remember that my personal assistant did mention the little one.'

Some new guests were waiting to be presented to him, and Mariella stepped discreetly to one side. In the distance on the racecourse she could see a string of horses being exercised, whilst here in the yard there were grooms and stable hands all wearing khaki shorts or trousers, and tee shirts in one of the prince's three racing colours denoting their status within the hierarchy of the stables.

'If you would care to take the baby to the crèche,' the prince's assistant was asking politely.

Firmly Mariella shook her head. Such was her sense of responsibility towards her niece that she preferred to keep her with her for as long as she could, and, besides, the yard was far too busy for her to be able to do even the briefest of preliminary sketches of the animals. The event was providing her with a wonderful opportunity to do some people watching, though.

Surveying the crowd filling the prince's racing yard, Xavier wondered what on earth he was doing here. This kind of social event was normally something he avoided like the plague! It was much more Khalid's style than his, and if Khalid had not taken leave of absence without warning he would have been the one to attend the event! However, since Xavier was involved in shared business interests with the prince, he had felt that perhaps he should attend the breakfast—especially as it was in aid of a charity that he fully supported.

Several people had already stopped him to talk with him, including various members of the royal family, but he now felt that he had done his duty and was on the point of leaving when he suddenly frowned as he caught sight of a silky flash of turquoise-blue as the crowd in front of him momentarily parted.

Grimly he started to stride towards it.

People were starting to move towards the pavilioned area where the breakfast was about to be served, but Mariella hesitated a little uncertainly, suspecting that it would be a diplomatic move now to take Fleur over to the crèche area rather than into the pavilions. A little uncertainly she glanced round, unsure as to what to do, and hoping that she might see the prince's helpful assistant.

Xavier saw Mariella before she saw him, his eyebrows snapping together in seething fury as he realised his suspicions had been confirmed. It was her! And he had no difficulty in guessing just what she was doing here! Some of the richest men in Zuran were here, and very few of them were unlikely to at least be tempted by the sight of her! From the top of the confection of straw and tulle she was wearing on top of her head to the tip of the dainty little pink-painted toenails revealed by shoes so fragile that he was surprised that she dared risk wearing them, especially when carrying her child, she looked a picture of innocent vulnerability. But of course she was no such thing! And dressing the baby in an outfit obviously chosen to match hers seemed to proclaim their mother and baby status to the world.

Unaware of the fact that Nemesis and all the Furies were about to bear down on her with grim zeal in the shape of a very angry and disapproving male, Mariella shifted Fleur's weight in her arm.

'Very fetching! Trust you to be here, and with the very latest European accessory—I have to tell you, though, that you've misjudged its effect in Zuran!'

'Xavier!' Mariella felt her legs wobble treacherously in her high heels as she stared at him in shock.

'I don't know how you managed to get past the security staff—although I suspect I can guess how!' he told her cynically. 'Kept women and those who sell their favours to the highest bidder are normally kept out of such events.'

Kept women! His condemnation stung not just her pride, but her sense of sisterly protection for Tanya. She knew that if this conversation were to continue, she would have to explain she was not Fleur's mother, but right now she was due in the pavilion for breakfast. She was here on business and she would not jeopardise the commission by having an argument with Xavier in front of the prince! 'I refuse to speak with you if you are going to be so rude,' she said tersely. 'Now, if you'll excuse me, I must go and join the others.' A flash of light to her left made her gasp as she realised a photographer had just caught the two of them on camera!

'Don't think I don't know what you're doing here,' Xavier told her challengingly. 'You know that Khalid is going to come to his senses and realise just what you are, and you're looking for someone to take his place, and finance you.'

'Finance her!' The feathers nestling in the swathes of chiffon on Mariella's hat trembled as she shook with outrage.

'For your information, I do not need anyone to finance me, as you put it. I am completely financially independent.' As she saw his expression Mariella turned on her heel.

Hurrying away from him, she tensed as she suddenly felt a touch on her arm, but when she looked round it was only the prince's assistant.

'The Prince would like you to join his table for breakfast, Miss Sutton.' he told her. 'If I may escort you first to the crèche,' he added tactfully.

Angrily Xavier watched as the crowd swallowed her up. How dared she lie to him and claim to be financially independent, especially when she knew he knew the truth about her?

She was the most scheming and deceitful woman he had ever met, a woman he was a total fool to spare the smallest thought for!

The conversation around the breakfast table was certainly very cosmopolitan, Mariella decided as she listened to two other women discussing the world's best spa resorts, whilst the men debated the various merits of differing bloodstock.

After the breakfast was over and people were beginning to drift away, the prince came over to Mariella.

'My assistant will telephone you to make formal arrangements for us to discuss my commission,' he told her.

'I was wondering if it would be possible for me to visit your new enclosure?' Mariella asked him. 'Or, failing that, perhaps see some plans?'

She had the beginnings of a vague idea which, if the prince approved, would be innovative, but first she needed to see the enclosure to see if it would work.

'Certainly. I shall see that it is arranged.'

As he escorted her outside Mariella saw Xavier standing several yards away, her face beginning to burn as he looked at the prince and then allowed his glance to drift with slow and deliberate insolence over her, assessing her as though...as though she were a piece of...of flesh he was contemplating buying, Mariella recognised.

'Highness!'

'Xavier.' As the two men exchanged greetings Mariella turned to leave, but somehow Xavier had moved and was blocking her way.

'I see that you do not have Fleur with you!'

'No,' Mariella agreed coldly. 'She is in the crèche. I am just on my way to collect her.'

'You know Miss Sutton, Xavier? I hadn't realised. I am about to avail myself of her exceptional services, and she has promised me something extremely innovative.'

Mariella winced as she recognised from his expression just what interpretation Xavier had put on the prince's remarks. Excusing herself, she managed to push her way past Xavier, but to her consternation he only allowed her to take a few steps into the shadows cast by one of the pavilions before catching up with her and taking hold of her arm.

'My word, but you are a witch! The prince is renowned for his devotion to his wife and yet he speaks openly of entering a relationship with you!'

Mariella did not dignify that with an answer. Instead she bared her teeth at him in a savage little smile as she told him sweetly, 'There, you see, you need not have gone to all that trouble to protect your cousin. There is no need for you to go running to him now to tell him all about your sordid and appalling behaviour towards me. After all, once he gets to hear about the fact that the prince is paying for my…expertise…'

'You dare to boast openly about it?' Xavier was gripping her with both hands now, his fingers digging into the vulnerable flesh of her upper arms.

To her own surprise Mariella discovered that winding Xavier up was great fun and she was actually enjoying herself.

'Why shouldn't I?' she taunted him. 'I am proud of the fact that my skills are so recognised and highly thought of, and that I am able to earn a very respectable living for myself by employing them!'

As his fingers bit even harder into her arms she viewed the ominous white line around his mouth with a dangerous sense of reckless euphoria.

'In fact, in some circles I have already made quite a name for myself.'

She had gone too far, Mariella realised as her euphoria was suddenly replaced with apprehension.

'You are proud of being known as a high-class whore? Personally I would have classed you merely as an expensive one!'

Mariella was just about to slap him when he said, 'If you strike me here you could well end up in prison, whereas if I do this...'

She gasped as he bent his head and subjected her to a savagely demanding kiss, arching her whole body back as she fought not to come into contact with his, and lost that fight. In the shadows of the pavilion he used his physical strength to show her what she already knew—that despite his rage and contempt he was physically aroused by her! Just as she was by him?

He released her so abruptly that she almost stumbled. As he turned away from her he reached into his robe and removed a wallet, opening it to throw down some money.

White-faced, Mariella stared at him. Deep down inside herself she knew that she had deliberately incited and goaded him, but not for this.

'Pick it up!' he told her savagely.

Mariella took a deep breath and gathered what was left of her dignity around her. 'Very well,' she agreed calmly. 'I am sure the charity will be grateful for it,

Xavier. I understand it helps to support abandoned children.'

She prayed that he would think the glitter in her eyes was caused by her contempt and not by her tears.

Silently Xavier watched her go. His own behaviour had shocked him but he was too stubbornly proud to admit it—and even more stubbornly determined not to acknowledge what had actually caused it.

How could he admit to jealousy over the favours of such a woman? How could he acknowledge that his own desire to possess her went far, far beyond the physical desire for just her body? He could not and he did not intend to do so!

CHAPTER SEVEN

'A FRIEZE?'

The prince frowned as he looked at Mariella.

It was three days since the charity breakfast, and two since she had visited the new enclosure.

After what had happened with Xavier, the temptation to simply pack her bags and return home had been very strong, but stubbornly she had refused to give in to it.

It wasn't her fault that he had totally misinterpreted things. Well, at least not entirely! And besides... Besides, the commission the prince was offering her had far too much appeal for her as an artist to want to turn it down, never mind what her agent was likely to say!

So instead of worrying about Xavier she had spent the last two days working furiously on the idea she had had for the prince's new enclosure.

'The semi-circular walkway that leads to the enclosure would be perfect for such a project,' she told him. 'I could paint your horses there in a variety of different ways, either in their boxes, or in a string. I have spoken to your trainers and grooms and they have told me that they all have their individual personalities and little quirks, so if I painted them in a string I could include some of these. Solomon in particular, they tell me, does not like anyone else to lead the string, and then Saladin will not leave his box until his groom has removed the cat who is his stable companion. Shazare can't tolerate other horses with white socks, and—'

The prince laughed. 'I can see how well you have done your research, and, yes, I like what you are suggesting. It will be an extremely large project, though.'

Mariella gave a small shrug.

'It will allow me to paint the animals lifesize, certainly.'

'It will need to be done in time for the official opening of the stables.'

'And when will that be?' Mariella asked him.

'In around five months' time,' he told her.

Mariella did a quick mental calculation, and then exhaled in relief. That would give her more than enough time to get the work completed.

'It would take me about a month or two to finish. It has to be your decision, Highness,' she informed him diplomatically.

'Give me a few days to think about it. It is not that I don't like the idea. I do, but in this part of the world, we still put a great deal of store on ''face'', and therefore, no matter now innovative the idea, if it is not completed on time, then I shall lose face in the eyes of both my allies and my competitors. I certainly have no qualms about your work or your commitment to it, though.'

He needed time to check up on her and her past record of sticking to her contracted time schedules, Mariella knew, but that didn't worry her. She was always extremely efficient about sticking to a completion date once it was agreed.

The nursemaid provided by the prince to look after Fleur whilst she had been working smiled at her as she went to collect the baby.

'She is a very good baby,' the young woman told Mariella approvingly.

Once she was back in the Beach Club bungalow, Mariella tried to ring Tanya to both update her on Fleur's progress and to tell her about her work, but she was only able to reach her sister's message service.

If the prince did give her this commission, then at least she would be earning enough to ensure that Tanya did not have to work away from home. She knew her sister wanted to be independent, but there were Fleur's needs to be considered as well, and besides...

She was going to miss Fleur dreadfully when the time came to hand her back to her mother, Mariella acknowledged. She was just beginning to realise what her determination never to become involved in a permanent relationship was going to mean to her in terms of missing out on motherhood.

A little nervously, Mariella smoothed down the fabric of her skirt. She had arrived at the palace half an hour ago to see the prince, who was going to give her his verdict on whether or not he wanted her to go ahead with the frieze.

A shy nursemaid had already arrived to take Fleur from her, and now Mariella peeped anxiously at her watch. Fleur hadn't slept very well the previous night and Mariella suspected that she was cutting another new tooth.

'Miss Sutton, His Highness will see you now.'

'Ah, Mariella...'

'Highness,' Mariella responded as she was waved onto one of the silk-covered divans set around the walls of the huge audience room.

Almost immediately a servant appeared to offer her

coffee and delicious-looking almond pastries glistening with honey and stuffed with raisins.

'I am pleased to inform you that I have decided to commission you to work on the frieze,' the prince announced. 'The sooner you can complete it, the better—we have lots of other work to do before the official opening.'

Quickly Mariella put down her coffee-cup and then covered it with her hand as she saw that the hovering servant was about to refill it.

Whilst he padded away silently the prince frowned.

'However, there is one matter that is of some concern to me.'

He was still worrying about her ability to get the work finished on time, Mariella guessed, but instead of confirming her suspicions the prince got up and picked up a newspaper from the low table in front of him.

'This is our popular local newspaper,' he told her. 'Its gossip column is a great favourite and widely read.'

As he spoke he was opening the paper.

'There is here a report of our charity breakfast, and, as you will see, a rather intimate photograph of you with Sheikh Xavier Al Agir.'

Mariella's heart bumped against the bottom of her chest, her fingers trembling slightly as she studied the photograph the prince was showing her.

It took her several seconds to recognise that it had been taken when she and Xavier had been quarrelling, because it looked for all the world as though they were indeed engaged in a very intimate conversation, their heads close together, her lips parted, Xavier's head bent towards her, his gaze fixed on her mouth, whilst Fleur, whom she was holding in her arms, beamed happily at him.

Even though she had not eaten any of the pastries, Mariella was beginning to feel sick.

The article accompanying the photograph read:

Who was the young woman who Sheikh Xavier was so intimately engaged in conversation with? The sheikh is known for his strong moral beliefs and his dedication to his role as leader of the Al Aglr tribe, and yet he was seen recently at the prince's charity breakfast, engaged in what appeared to be a very private conversation with one specific female guest on two separate occasions! Could it be that the sheikh has finally chosen someone to share his life? And what of the baby the unknown young woman is holding? What is her connection with the sheikh?

'In this country, unlike your own, a young woman alone with a child does cause a certain amount of speculation and disapproval. It is plain from the tone of this article that the reporter believes you and Xavier to be Fleur's parents…' the prince told Mariella, his voice very stern.

'But that is not true, Your Highness. We are not,' Mariella protested immediately. 'Fleur is my niece.'

'Of course. I fully accept what you are saying, but I think for your own sake that some kind of formal response does need to be made to this item. Which is why I have already instructed my staff to get in touch with the paper and to give them the true facts and to explain that Fleur is in fact your niece and that you are in Zuran to work for me. Hopefully that will be an end to the matter!'

*   *   *

Mariella frowned as for the third time in as many hours her sister's mobile was switched onto her message-taking service.

Why wasn't Tanya returning her calls?

Because of the length of time it was going to take her to complete the frieze, it had been decided that, instead of her returning to England as had originally been planned, she and Fleur should remain in Zuran so that she could commence work immediately.

The prince had announced that she would be provided with a small apartment and the use of a car, and Mariella was planning a shopping trip to equip both herself and Fleur for their unexpected extended stay.

Fleur's new tooth had now come through and the baby was back to her normal happy self.

Someone was knocking on the door of the bungalow and Mariella went to open it, expecting to see a member of the Beach Club's staff, but instead to her consternation it was Xavier who was standing outside.

Without waiting for her invitation he strode into the room, slamming the door closed behind him.

'Perhaps you can explain the meaning of *this* to me,' he challenged her sarcastically, throwing down the copy of the newspaper she had been reading earlier, open at the gossip column page.

'I don't have to explain anything to you, Xavier,' Mariella replied as calmly as she could.

'It says here that you are not Fleur's mother.'

'That's right,' she agreed. 'I'm not! I'm her aunt. My sister Tanya is her mother…and the woman who I have had to listen to you denouncing and abusing so slanderously and unfairly! And, for your information, Tanya is not, as you have tried to imply, some…some…

she is a professional singer and dancer, and, whilst you may not consider her good enough for your precious cousin, let me tell you that in my opinion he is the one who isn't good enough for her…not for her and certainly not for Fleur!' All the anger and anguish Mariella had been bottling up inside her was exploding in a surge of furious words.

'Your cousin told Tanya that he loved her and that he was committed to her and then he left her and Fleur! Have you any idea just what that did to Tanya? I was there when Fleur was born, I heard Tanya cry out for the man she loved. It's all so easy for a man, isn't it? If he doesn't want the responsibility of a woman's love or the child they create together, he can just walk away. You don't know what it means to be a child growing up knowing that your father didn't want or love you, and knowing too that your mother could never again be the person she was before her heart was broken. I would never, ever let any man hurt me the way Tanya has been hurt!'

'You wantonly and deliberately let me think that you and Khalid were lovers,' Xavier interrupted her savagely, ignoring her emotional outburst.

'Well, at first I thought you were Fleur's father, so I assumed you knew I wasn't Fleur's mother. But, face it, you wanted to think the worst you could about me, Xavier. You enjoyed thinking it! Revelled in it. I tried to warn you that you were getting it wrong, when you totally misinterpreted those comments by the prince! Remember?'

'Have you any idea just what problems this is causing?' he demanded harshly.

'What I have done?' Mariella gave him a disbelieving look. 'My sister is a modern young woman who lives a modern young woman's life. Her biggest mistake, in my opinion, was to fall in love with your wretched cousin, and yet you have talked about her as though—!' Mariella compressed her lips as she saw the flash of temper darkening his eyes.

'Are you trying to say to me that you too are a modern young woman who lives a modern young woman's life, because if you are I have to tell you—!'

Xavier broke off abruptly, remembering the character references the prince had insisted on him reading when he had stormed into the palace earlier in the afternoon, demanding an immediate audience with him.

Mariella was not only a very highly acclaimed artist, she was also, it seemed, a young woman of the highest moral integrity—in every facet of her life!

'That is none of your business,' Mariella told him angrily.

'To the contrary. It is very much my business!'

Mariella stared at him, her heart thumping.

'Fleur is my cousin's child, which makes her a member of my family. Since you are also of her blood, that also makes you a member of my family. As the head of that family I am, therefore, responsible for both of you. There is no way I can allow you to live here in Zuran alone, or work unchaperoned for the prince. Our family pride and honour would be at risk! It is my responsibility!'

'What?' Mariella looked at him in open angry contempt. 'How can you possibly lay claim to any right to pride or honour? You, a man who was quite prepared to take the mother of his cousin's child to bed, just so that you could enforce your wish to keep them apart? This has got to be some kind of joke! I mean, you…you abuse me verbally, and physically. You in-

sult and denigrate me and…and now you have the gall
to turn round and start preaching to me about pride or
honour! And as for your so-called sense of responsibility! You don't even begin to understand the meaning
of the word, as decent people understand it!'

Mariella could see the tension in his jaw, but she
suspected that it was caused by anger rather than any
sense of shame.

'The situation has now changed!'

'Changed? Because you have discovered that instead
of being, and I quote, your cousin's "whore" paid to
have sex with men, I am a career woman.'

'I have received a…a communication from Khalid
confirming that he is Fleur's father, and because of
that—' his mouth tightened '—I have to consider
Fleur's position, her future…her reputation!'

'Her reputation!' Mariella gave him a scathing look.
'Fleur is four months old! And anyway, His Highness
has already done everything that is necessary to stem
any potential gossip.'

'I have been to see His Highness myself to inform
him that, whilst you are here in Zuran, you will be
living beneath the protection of my roof! Naturally he
is in total agreement!'

Mariella couldn't believe her ears.

'Oh, no,' she denied, shaking her head vigorously
from side to side. 'No, no, no. No way!'

'Mariella. Please see it as a way for me to make
amends by offering you my hospitality. Besides, you
have no choice—the prince expects it.'

He meant it, Mariella recognised as she searched his
implacable features.

'I shall wait here until you have packed and then we
will return to my home. I have arranged for my wid-

owed great-aunt to act as your chaperone for the duration of your stay in Zuran.'

Her chaperone!

'I am twenty-eight years old,' she told him through
gritted teeth. 'I do not need a chaperone.'

'You are a single woman living beneath the roof of
a single man. There will already be those who will look
askance at you having read that article.'

'At me, but not, of course, at you!'

'I am a man, so it is different,' he told her with a
dismissively arrogant shrug that made her grind her
teeth in female outrage.

Mariella couldn't wait to speak to her sister to tell
her what had happened!

Right now, though, Mariella dared not take the risk
of defying him! He could, after all, if he so wished,
not merely put his threats into action, but also take
Fleur from her here and now if he chose to do so!

It took her less than half an hour to pack their things,
a task she performed in seething silence whilst Xavier
stood in front of the door, his arms folded across his
chest, watching her with smoulderingly dangerous
eyes.

When she had finished she went to pick Fleur up,
but Xavier got there first.

Over Fleur's downy head their gazes clashed and
locked, Xavier's a seething molten grey, Mariella's a
brilliantly glittering jade.

The limousine waiting for them was every bit as opulent looking as the one the prince had sent for her,
although Mariella was surprised to discover that Xavier
was driving it himself.

Somehow she had not associated him with a liking
for such a luxurious showy vehicle. She had got the
impression that his tastes were far, far more austere.

But, as she had discovered, beneath his outwardly
cold self-control a molten, hot passion burned, which
was all the more devastating for being so tightly
chained.

It didn't take them long to reach the villa, but this
time the gates were opened as they approached them
and they swept in, crunching over a gravel drive
flanked by double rows of palm trees.

The villa itself was elegantly proportioned, its design
restrained, and Moorish in inspiration, Mariella noticed
with unwilling approval as she studied its simple lines
with an artist's eye.

A pair of wrought-iron gates gave way to a gravelled
walled courtyard, ornamented with a large central stone
fountain.

Stopping the car, Xavier got out and came to open
her own door. A manservant appeared to deal with her
luggage, and a shy young girl whom Xavier introduced
to her as Hera, and who, he told her, would be Fleur's
nanny. Smiling reassuringly at the nanny he handed
Fleur to her before Mariella could stop him.

She certainly held Fleur as though she knew what
she was doing, Mariella recognised, but even so! A
pang of loss tightened her body as she looked at Fleur
being held in another woman's arms.

'Fleur doesn't need a nanny,' she told Xavier
quickly. 'I am perfectly capable of looking after her
myself.'

'Maybe so, but it is customary here for those who
can afford to do so to provide the less well off amongst
our people with work. Hera is the eldest child in her

family, and her mother has recently been widowed. Are you really willing to deprive her of the opportunity to help to support her siblings, simply because you are afraid of allowing anyone else to become emotionally close to Fleur?'

As he spoke he was ushering her into the semi-darkness of the interior of the villa. Mariella was so shocked and unprepared for his unexpectedly astute comment that she stumbled slightly as her eyes adjusted to the abrupt change from brilliant sunlight to shadowy darkness.

Instantly Xavier reached for her, his hand gripping her waist as he steadied her. Her dizziness must be something to do with that abrupt switch from lightness to dark, Mariella told herself, and so too must her accompanying weakness, turning her into a quivering mass of over-sensitive nerve endings, each one of them reacting to the fact that Xavier was touching her. Confused blurred images filled her head: Xavier, naked as he swam, Xavier leaning over her as he held her down on the bed, Xavier kissing her until she ached for him so badly her need was a physical pain.

Her need? She did not need Xavier. She would never, never need him. Never… She managed to pull herself free of him, her eyes adjusting to the light enough for her to see the cold disapproval with which he was regarding her.

'You must take more care. You are not used to our climate. By the end of this month the temperature will be reaching forty degrees Celsius, and you are very fair-skinned. You must be sure always to drink plenty of water, and that applies to Fleur as well.'

'Thank you. I do know not to allow myself to get dehydrated,' Mariella told him through gritted teeth. 'I am a woman, not a child, and as such I am perfectly capable of looking after myself. After all, I've been doing it for long enough.'

The look he gave her made her feel as though someone had taken hold of her heart and flipped it over inside her chest.

'Yes. It must have been hard for you to lose your mother and your stepfather having already lost your father at such a young age...'

'Lost my father?' Mariella gave him a bitter look. 'I didn't "lose" him. He abandoned my mother because he didn't want the responsibilities of fatherhood. He was never any true father to me, but he broke my mother's heart— '

'My own parents died when I was in my early teens—a tragic accident—but I was lucky enough to have my grandmother to help me through it. However, as we both know, the realisation that one is without parents does tend to breed a certain...independence of spirit, a certain protective defensiveness.' He was frowning, Mariella recognised, picking his words with care as though there was something he was trying to tell her. He broke off as Hera came into the reception hall carrying Fleur.

'If you will go with Hera, she will show you to your quarters. My aunt should arrive shortly.'

He had turned on his heel and was striding away from her, his back ramrod straight in the cool whiteness of his robe, leaving her no alternative other than to follow the timidly smiling young maid.

The villa obviously stretched back from its frontage to a depth she had not suspected, Mariella acknowledged ten minutes later, when she had followed the maid through several enormous reception rooms and up a flight of stairs, and then along a cloistered walk-way through which a deliciously cool breeze had flowed and from which she had been able to look down into a totally enclosed private courtyard, complete with a swimming pool.

'This is the courtyard of Sheikh Xavier,' Hera had whispered to her, shyly averting her gaze from it and looking nervous when Mariella had paused to study it.

'Normally it is forbidden for us to be here, as the women of the household have their own private en-trance to their quarters...'

'Let me take Fleur,' Mariella told her, firmly taking her niece back into her own arms and relishing the deliciously warm weight of her.

A door at the end of the corridor led to another clois-tered walkway, this time with views over an immacu-late rose garden.

'This was the special garden of the sheikh's grand-parents. His grandmother was French and the roses were from France. She supervised their planting her-self.'

For Mariella the rigid beds and the formality of the garden immediately summoned up a vivid impression of a woman who was very proud and correct, a true martinet. Her grandson obviously took after her!

The women's quarters, when they finally got to them, proved to be far more appealing than Mariella had expected. Here again a cloistered walkway opened onto a private garden, but here the garden was softer, filled with sweet-smelling flowers and decorated with a pretty turreted summer house as well as the custom-ary water features.

They comprised several lavishly furnished bed-rooms, each with its own equally luxurious bathroom

and dressing room, a dining room, and a salon—
Mariella could think of no other word to describe the
delicate and ornate antique French furniture and decor
of the two rooms, which she suspected must have been
designed and equipped for Xavier's French grandmother.

On the bookshelves flanking the fireplace she could
see leather-bound books bearing the names of some of
France's most famous writers.

'The sheikh has said that you will wish to have the
little one in a room next to your own,' Hera was telling
her softly. 'He has made arrangements for everything
that she will need to be delivered. I am not sure which
room you will wish to use...'

Ignoring the temptation to tell her that she wished to
use none of them, and that in fact what she wished to
do was to leave the villa with Fleur right now—after
all, none of this was Hera's fault and it would be unfair
of her to take out her own resentment on the maid—
Mariella gave in to her gentle hint and quickly inspected each of the four bedrooms.

One of them, furnished in the same Louis Fifteenth
antiques as the salon, had quite obviously been
Xavier's grandmother's and she rejected it immediately. Of the three others, she automatically picked the
plainest with its cool-toned walls and simple furniture.
It had its own private access to the gardens with a small
clear pool only a few feet away and a seat next to it
from which to watch the soothing movement of the
water.

'This room?'

When Mariella nodded, Hera smiled.

'The sheikh will be pleased. This was his mother's
room.'

Xavier's mother's room! It was too late for her to change her mind, Mariella recognised.

'What...what nationality was she?' she asked Hera, immediately wishing she had not done so.

'She was a member of the tribe... The sheikh's father met her when he was travelling with them and fell in love with her...'

Fleur was beginning to make hungry noises, reminding Mariella that it was her niece she should be thinking about and not Xavier's family background.

CHAPTER EIGHT

MARIELLA stared worriedly at her mobile phone. She had just tried for the fourth time since her arrival at the villa to make contact with Tanya, but her sister's mobile was still switched onto messaging mode. She had left a message saying that she was staying at Xavier's villa, and had asked Tanya to contact her at the villa or call her cell phone. Mariella realised to her consternation that it was days since she had actually spoken to Tanya. A little tingle of alarm began to feather down her spine. What if something had happened to her sister? What if she wasn't well or had hurt herself. Or…

Quickly Mariella made up her mind. It took her quite some time to get the telephone number for the entertainments director of her sister's cruise liner, but eventually she managed to get through.

'I'm sorry, who is this speaking, please?' The firm male voice on the other end of the line checked her when Mariella had asked for Tanya, explaining that she had been unable to make contact with her via her mobile.

'I am Tanya's sister,' Mariella explained.

'I see… Well, I have to inform you that Tanya has actually left the ship.'

'Left the ship!' Mariella repeated in disbelief. 'But…where? Why…?'

'I'm sorry. I can't give you any more details. All I can say is that Tanya left of her own accord and without giving us any prior warning.'

From the tone of his voice Mariella could tell that he wasn't very pleased with her sister!

Thanking him for his help, she ended the call, turning to look at Fleur, who was fast asleep in her brand-new bed.

As Hera had already warned her, Xavier had instructed a local baby equipment store to provide a full nursery's worth of brand new things, all of which Mariella had immediately realised were far, far more expensive and exclusive than anything she or Tanya could have afforded.

Tanya! Where was her sister? Why had she left the ship? And why, oh, why wasn't she returning her calls?

It was imperative that she knew what was happening, and, for all her faults, her impulsiveness and hedonism, Tanya genuinely loved Fleur. It was unthinkable to Mariella that she should not make contact with her to check up on her baby.

In Tanya's shoes there was no way she would not have been on the phone every hour of every day... No way she could ever have brought herself to be parted from her baby in the first place, Mariella recognised, but then poor Tanya had had no alternative! Tanya had been determined to pay her own way.

Emotionally, she stood over Fleur looking down at her whilst she slept. Increasingly she ached inside to have a child of her own. When she had made her original vow never to put herself in a position where she could be emotionally hurt by a man, she had not foreseen this kind of complication!

Xavier frowned as he paced the floor of his study. A flood of faxes cluttered his desk, all of them giving him the same information—namely that his cousin had not been seen in any of his usual favourite haunts! Where on earth was Khalid?

Xavier was becoming increasingly suspicious that his cousin had been deliberately vague about Fleur's true paternity. Out of a desire to protect Fleur and her mother, or out of a desire to escape his responsibilities?

Surely Khalid knew him well enough to know that, even if he couldn't approve of or accept Fleur's mother, he would certainly have insisted that proper financial arrangements were made for her and Fleur, and if necessary by Xavier himself? Of course he did, which was no doubt why he had now written to Xavier informing him that he was Fleur's father.

It irked him that he had been so dramatically wrong-footed in assuming that Mariella was Fleur's mother. The security information the prince had revealed to him had made it brutally clear just how wrong he had been about her.

Here was a young woman who had shouldered the responsibility, not just of supporting herself, but of supporting her younger half-sister as well. Not a single shred of information to indicate that Mariella had led anything other than the most morally laudable life could be found! There were no unsavoury corpses mouldering away in the dusty corners of Mariella's life; in fact, the truth was that there were not even any dusty corners! Everyone who had had dealings with her spoke of her in the most glowing and complimentary terms.

And yet somehow he, a man who prided himself on his astuteness and his ability to read a person's true personality, had not been able to see any of this! True, she had deliberately deceived him, but...

But he had behaved towards her in a way that, had

he heard about it coming from another man, he would have had no hesitation in immediately denouncing and condemning him!

There were no excuses he could accept from himself! Not even the increasingly insubstantial one of wanting to protect Khalid.

Wasn't it after all true that the last thing, the last person who had been in his thoughts when he had taken Mariella to bed had been his cousin? Wasn't it also true that he had been driven, possessed... consumed by his own personal physical desire?

He could find no logical excuse or explanation for what he had done. Other than to tell himself that he had been driven by desert madness, and he felt riddled with guilt, especially for the way he had coerced her into staying with him at his villa. He would of course have to apologise formally to Mariella!

A woman who already had proved how strong her sense of duty and responsibility was. A woman with whom a man could know that the children he gave her would be loved and treasured...

He had sworn not to marry, rather than risk the hazards of a marriage that might go wrong, he reminded himself austerely.

Surely, though, it was better to offer Mariella the protection of his name in marriage rather than risk any potential damage to her reputation through gossip?

He had already provided her with sufficient protection in the form of his great-aunt as a chaperone, he reminded himself grimly. If he continued to think as he was doing right now, he might begin to suspect that he actually wanted to marry her! That he actually wanted to take her back into his bed and complete what they had already begun.

Angrily he swung round as the sudden chatter of the fax machine broke into his far too sensually charged thoughts.

'So, here we are, then. Xavier has summoned me to be your chaperone, and I am to accompany you to the palace whilst you paint pictures for His Highness, *non?*'

'Well, not exactly,' Mariella responded wryly. It was impossible for her not to like the vivacious elderly Frenchwoman who was Xavier's great-aunt and who had arrived half an hour earlier, complete with an enormous pile of luggage and her own formidable looking maid.

'I am not actually working at the palace, but at the new enclosure at the racecourse, and, to be honest, I don't agree with Xavier—'

'Agree? But I am afraid that here in Zuran we have to comply with the laws of the land, *chérie,* both actual and moral.' Rolling her eyes dramatically, she continued, 'I know how difficult I found it when I first came to live here. My sister was already married to Xavier's grandfather for several years by then. She was older than me by well over a decade. Since the death of my husband, I live both in Paris and here in Zuran. The child I understand is Khalid's?' she commented, with a disconcerting change of subject. 'He is a charming young man, but unfortunately very weak! He is fortunate that Xavier is so indulgent towards him, but you probably know Xavier does not intend to marry and he intended for Khalid's son to ultimately take over his responsibilities! It is such foolishness...'

'Xavier does not intend to marry?' Mariella questioned her.

'So he claims. The death of his own parents affected him very seriously. He was at a most impressionable age when they perished and of course my sister, his grandmother, was very much a matriarch of the old school. She was determined that he would be brought up to know his responsibilities towards his people and to fulfil them. Now Xavier believes that their needs are more important than his own and that he cannot therefore risk marrying a woman who would not understand and accept his duty and the importance of his role. Such nonsense, but then that is men for you! They like to believe that we are the weaker sex, but we of course know that it is we who are the strong ones!'

'You have great strength, I can see that! You will miss the child when you eventually have to hand her back to her mother,' she added shrewdly.

The speed of her conversation, along with the speed of her perceptiveness, was leaving Mariella feeling slightly dizzy.

'I see that you have chosen not to occupy my late sister's room. Extremely wise of you if I may say so…I could never understand why she insisted on attempting to recreate our parents' Avenue Foche apartment here! But then that was Sophia for you! As an eldest child she was extremely strong-willed, whilst I…' she paused to dimple a rueful smile at Mariella '…am the youngest, and, according to her at least, was extremely spoiled!

'You would not have liked her,' she pronounced, shocking Mariella a little with her outspokenness. 'She would have taken one look at you and immediately started to make plans to make you Xavier's wife. You do not believe me? I assure you that it is true. She would have seen immediately how perfect you would be for him!'

Her, perfect for Xavier? Fiercely squashing the treacherous little sensation tingling through her, Mariella told her quickly, 'I have no intention of ever getting married.'

'You see? Already it is clear just how much you and Xavier have in common! However, I am not my sister. I do not interfere in other people's lives or try to arrange them for them! *Non!* But tell me why is it that you have made up your mind not to marry? In Xavier's case it is plain that it is because of the fear instilled in him by my sister that he will not find a woman to love who will share his dedication to his commitment to preserve the traditional way of life of the tribe. Such nonsense! But Sophia herself is very much to blame. When he was a young and impressionable young man she sent Xavier to France in the hope that he would find a bride amongst the daughters of our own circle. But these girls cannot breathe any air other than that of Paris. The very thought of them doing as Xavier has done every year of his life and travelling through the desert with those members of the tribe who had chosen to adhere to the old way of life would be intolerable to them!

'Xavier needs a wife who will embrace and love the ways of his people with the same passion with which he does himself. A woman who will embrace and love him with even more passion, for, as I am sure you will already know, Xavier is an extremely passionate man.'

Mariella gave her a wary look. What was his great-aunt trying to imply? However, when she looked at her face her expression was rosily innocent and open.

Madame Flavel's comments were, though, arousing both her interest and her curiosity.

Hesitantly she told her, 'You have mentioned the tribe and Xavier's commitment to it, but I do not really know just what...'

'*Non?* It is quite simple really. The tribe into which Xavier's ancestor originally married is unique in its way of life, and it was the life's work of Xavier's grandfather, and would have been of his father had he not died, to preserve the tribe's traditional nomadic existence, but at the same time encourage those members of it who wished to do so to integrate into modern society. To that end, every child born into the tribe has the right to receive a proper education and to follow the career path of their choice, but at the same time each and every member of the tribe must spend some small part of every year travelling the traditional nomadic routes in the traditional way. Some members of the tribe elect to live permanently in such a fashion, and they are highly revered by every other member of the tribe, even those who, as many have, have reached the very peak of their chosen career elsewhere in the world. Within the tribe recognition and admiration are won, not through material or professional attainment, but through preservation of the old ways and traditions.

'Xavier's role as head of the tribe means, though, that he has a dual role to fulfil. He must ensure that he has the business expertise to see that the money left by his grandfather generates sufficient future income to provide financially for the tribe, and yet at the same time he must be able to hold the respect of the tribe by leading it in its ancient traditional ways. Xavier has known all his life that he must fulfil both those roles and he does so willingly, I know, but nevertheless it will be a very lonely path he has chosen to follow unless he does find a woman who can understand and share his life with him.'

Mariella had fallen silent as she listened. There was a poignancy about what she was hearing that was touching very deep emotional chords within. The Xavier his great-aunt was describing to her was a man of deep and profound feelings and beliefs, a man who, in other circumstances, she herself could respect and admire.

'*Madame,* I assure you there is really no need for you to remain here with me,' Mariella told her chaperone firmly as she studied the long corridor that was to be her canvas.

Fleur was lying in her pram playing with her toes and Mariella had pinned up in front of her, on the easel she had brought with her, the photographs she had taken of the prince's horses.

'It is for this purpose that Xavier has summoned me to his home,' Madame Flavel reminded her.

'You will be bored sitting here watching me work,' Mariella protested.

'I am never bored. I have my tapestry and my newspaper, and in due course Ali will return to drive us back to the villa for a small repast and an afternoon nap.'

There was no way she intended to indulge in afternoon naps, Mariella decided silently as she picked up her charcoals and started to work.

In her mind she already had a picture of how she wanted the frieze to look, and within minutes she was totally engrossed in what she was doing.

The background for the horses, she had now decided,

would not be the racecourse itself, but something that she hoped would prove far more compelling to those who viewed it. The background of a rolling ocean of waves from which the horses were emerging would surely prove irresistible to a people to whom water was so very, very important. Mariella hoped so. His Highness had certainly liked the idea.

It wasn't until her fingers began to ache a little with cramp that she realised how long she had been working. Madame Flavel had fallen asleep in the comfortable chair with its special footstool that Ali had brought for her, her gentle snores keeping Fleur entranced.

Smiling at her niece, Mariella opened the bottle of water she had brought with her and took a drink. Where was Tanya? Why hadn't she got in touch with her?

The door to the corridor opened to admit Hera and Ali.

'Goodness, is it lunchtime already?' Madame Flavel demanded, immediately waking up.

Reluctantly Mariella started to pack up her things. She would much rather have continued with her work than return to the villa, but she was very conscious of Madame Flavel's age and the unfairness of expecting her to remain with her for hours on end.

CHAPTER NINE

BY THE end of the week Mariella was beginning to find her enforced breaks from her work increasingly frustrating.

'It disturbs me that you are so determined not to marry, *chérie*,' Madame Flavel was saying to her as she worked. 'It is perhaps because of an unhappy love affair?'

'You could say that,' Mariella agreed wryly.

'He broke your heart, but you are young, and broken hearts mend...'

'It wasn't my heart he broke, but my mother's,' Mariella corrected her, 'and it never really mended, not even when she met and married my stepfather. You see, she thought when my father told her that he loved her he meant it, but he didn't! She trusted him, depended on him, but he repaid that trust by abandoning us both.'

'Ah, I see. And because of the great hurt your father caused you, you are determined never to trust any man yourself?' Madame Flavel commented shrewdly. 'Not all men are like your father, *chérie*.'

'Maybe not, but it is not a risk I am prepared to take! I never want to be as...as vulnerable as my mother was...never.'

'You say that, but I think you fear that you already are.'

Mariella was glad of Ali's arrival to put an end to what was becoming a very uncomfortable conversation.

*　　*　　*

It was two o'clock in the afternoon and Madame Flavel was taking her afternoon nap.

Mariella walked restlessly round the garden. She was itching to get on with the frieze. She paused, frowning slightly. And then, making up her mind, hurried back inside, pausing only to pick up Fleur.

Ali made no comment when she summoned him to tell him that she intended to go back to the enclosure, politely opening the door of the car for her. Stepping outside was like standing in the blast of a hot hair-dryer at full heat.

The car was coolly air-conditioned, but outside the heat shimmered in the air, the light bouncing glaringly off the buildings that lined the road.

Like the car, the enclosure was air-conditioned, and as soon as Ali had escorted her inside and gone Mariella began to work.

A moveable scaffolding had been erected to allow her to work on the upper part of the wall, and she paused every now and again to look down from it to check on Fleur, who was fast asleep. Her throat felt dry and her hand ached, but she refused to allow herself to stop. In her mind's eye she could see the finished animal, nostrils flaring, his mane ruffled by the wind, the sea foaming behind him as he emerged from the curling breakers.

Somewhere on the edge of her awareness she was vaguely conscious of a door opening, and quiet but ominously determined footsteps. Fleur made a small sound, a gurgle of pleasure rather than complaint, which she also registered, her hand moving quickly as she fought to capture the image inside her head. This horse, the proudest and fiercest of them all, would not tolerate any competition from the sea. He would challenge its power, rearing up so that the powerful muscles of his quarters and belly were visible... Fleur was chattering happily to herself in baby talk, and Mariella was beginning to feel almost light-headed with concentration. And then just as she was finishing something a movement, an instinct made her turn her head.

To her shock she saw that Xavier was standing beside Fleur watching her.

'Xavier...'

She took a step forward and then stopped, suddenly realising that she was still on the scaffolding.

'What...what are you doing here?' she demanded belligerently to cover her own intimate and unwanted reaction to him.

'Have you any idea just how much you distressed Cecille by ignoring my instructions?' he demanded tersely.

Mariella looked away from him. She genuinely liked his great-aunt, and hated the thought that she might have upset her.

'I'm sorry if she was upset,' she told him woodenly, her own feelings breaking through her tight control as she gave a small despairing shake of her head.

'I promised His Highness that the frieze would be completed as soon as possible; your aunt is elderly. She likes to spend the afternoon resting, when I need to be here working! Whether you believe this or not, Xavier, I too have a...a reputation to protect.'

'In that case why didn't you simply come to me and explain all of this to me instead of behaving like a child and waiting until my aunt's back was turned?'

Mariella frowned. What he was saying sounded so...so reasonable and sensible she imagined that anyone listening to him would have asked her the same question!

'Your behaviour towards me has hardly encouraged me to...to anticipate your help or co-operation,' she reminded him as she went to climb down from the scaffolding, surreptitiously trying to stretch her aching muscles.

'Although she herself refuses to acknowledge it, my aunt is an elderly lady,' Xavier was continuing, breaking off suddenly to mutter something beneath his breath she couldn't quite catch as he strode forward.

'Be careful,' he warned her sharply. 'You might...'

To her own chagrin, as though his warning had provoked it, the scaffolding suddenly wobbled and she began to slip.

As she gave a small instinctive gasp of shock Xavier grabbed hold of her, supporting her so that she could slide safely to the floor.

Mariella knew that the small near-accident was her own fault and that she had worked for too long in one position, without stopping to exercise her cramped muscles, and her face began to burn as she anticipated Xavier's triumphant justification of his insistence that she was chaperoned, but instead of saying anything he simply continued to hold her, one hand grasping her waist, the other supporting the small of her back, where his fingers spread a dangerously intoxicating heat right through her clothes and into her skin.

Dizzily Mariella closed her eyes, trying to blot out the effect the proximity of him was having on her, but, to her consternation, instead of protecting her all it did was increase her vulnerability as sharply focused mental images of him taunted and tormented her, their effect on her so intense that she started to shake in reaction to them.

'Mariella? What is it? What's wrong?' she heard Xavier demanding urgently. 'If you feel unwell...'

Immediately Mariella opened her eyes.

'No. I'm fine,' she began and then stopped, unable to drag her gaze away from his mouth, where it had focused itself with hungry, yearning intensity.

She knew from his sudden fixed silence that Xavier was aware of what she was doing, but the shrill alarm bells within her own defences, which should have shaken her into action, were silenced into the merest whisper by the inner roar of her own aching longing. No power on earth, let alone that of her own will, could stem what was happening to her and what she was feeling, Mariella recognised distantly, as her senses registered the way Xavier's grip on her body subtly altered from one of non-sexually protective to one of powerfully sensual. She could feel the hot burn of his gaze as it dropped to her own mouth, and a sharp series of little shivers broke through her. Without even thinking about it she was touching her lips with the tip of her tongue, as though driven by some deep preprogrammed instinct to moisten them. She was trembling, her whole body galvanised by tiny sensual ripples of reaction and awareness that made her sway slightly towards him.

She saw a muscle twitch in his jaw and raised her hand to touch it with her fingertips, her eyes wide and helplessly enslaved.

'Mariella!'

She felt him shudder as he drew breath into his lungs, her body instinctively leaning into his as weakness washed over her.

His mouth touched hers, but not in the way she had remembered it doing before.

She had never known there could be so much sweet tenderness in a kiss, so much slow, explorative warmth, so much carefully suppressed passion just waiting to burn away all her resistance. She wanted to lose herself completely in it...in him.

She gave a small cry of protest as Xavier's ears, keener than hers, picked up the sound of someone entering the gallery, and he pushed her away.

Caught up in the shock of what she had experienced, Mariella watched motionless as Xavier went over to where Ali, his chauffeur, was hovering.

Lifting her hand, she touched her own lips, as though unable to believe what had happened...what she had wanted to happen. She had wanted Xavier to kiss her, still wanted him to kiss her, her body aching for him in a hundred intimate ways that held her in silent shock. She and Xavier were enemies, weren't they?

He was walking back to her and somehow she had to compose herself, to conceal from him what was happening to her.

She felt as though she were drowning in her own panic.

'We must get back to the villa, immediately,' he told her curtly.

Instantly her panic was replaced by anxiety.

'What is it?' she demanded. 'Has something happened to your aunt?'

She started to gather up her things, but he stopped her, instructing her tersely, 'Leave all that.'

He was already picking up Fleur, his body language so evident of a crisis that Mariella forbore to argue. Her stomach was churning sickly. What if something had happened to his great-aunt, perhaps brought on by her own stubborn determination to ignore his dictates? She would never forgive herself!

Falling into step beside him, Mariella almost had to run to keep up with him.

They drove back to the villa in silence, Mariella's anxiety increasing to such a pitch that by the time they finally turned into the courtyard of the villa she felt physically sick.

Giving some sharp order to Ali, in Arabic, Xavier got out of the car, turning to her and telling her equally shortly, 'Come with me.'

Even Fleur seemed to have picked up on his seriousness, and fell silent in his arms, her eyes huge and dark.

Please let Cecille be all right, Mariella prayed silently as the huge double doors to the villa were thrown open with unfamiliar formality and she followed Xavier into its sandalwood-scented coolness.

Without pausing to see if she was following him, Xavier headed for the anteroom that opened out into what Mariella now knew was the formal salon in which he conducted his business meetings.

Unusually two liveried servants were standing to either side of the entrance, their expressionless faces adding both to Mariella's anxiety and the look of stern formality she could see on Xavier's face, giving it and him an air of autocratic arrogance so reminiscent of the first time she had seen him that she automatically shivered a little.

Expecting him to stride into the room ahead of her, Mariella almost bumped into him when he suddenly turned towards her. A little uncertainly she looked at him, unable to conceal her confusion when he reached out his hand to her and beckoned her to his side.

Holding Fleur tightly, she hesitated for a second before going to join him. Wide as the entrance to the salon was, it still apparently necessitated Xavier standing so close to her that she could feel the heat of his body against her own as he gave the servants an abrupt nod.

The doors swung open, the magnificence of the room that lay beyond them dazzling Mariella for a moment, even though she had already peeped into it at Madame Flavel's insistence.

It was everything she had ever imagined such a room should be, its walls hung with richly woven silks, the cool marble floor ornamented with priceless antique rugs. The light from the huge chandeliers, which Madame Flavel had told Mariella had been made to Xavier's grandmother's personal design, dazzled the eyes as it reflected on the room's rich jewel colours and ornate gilding. Luxurious and rich, the decor of the salon had about it an unmistakable air of French elegance.

It was a room designed to awe and impress all those who entered it and to make them aware of the power of the man who owned it.

As her eyes adjusted to the brilliance Mariella realised that two people were standing in front of the room's huge marble fireplace, watching Xavier with obvious apprehension as they clung together.

Disbelievingly Mariella stared at them.

'Tanya,' she whispered, her voice raw with shock as she recognised her sister.

Her sister looked tanned and expensive, Mariella noticed, the skirt and top she was wearing showing off her body. She was wearing her hair in a new, fashionably tousled style, and it glinted with a mix of toning blonde highlights.

She was immaculately made up, her fingernails and toenails shining with polish, but it was the man standing at Tanya's side on whom Mariella focused most of her attention. He was shorter than Xavier and more heavily built, she guessed immediately that he must be Khalid, Xavier's cousin and Fleur's father.

'Khalid,' Xavier acknowledged curtly, with a brief nod in the other man's direction, confirming Mariella's guesswork. 'And this, I assume, must be...'

'My wife,' Khalid interrupted him, holding tightly to Tanya's hand as he continued, 'Tanya and I were married three days ago.'

'Honestly, Mariella, I just couldn't believe it when we docked at Kingston and Khalid came on board. At first I totally refused to have anything to do with him, but he kept on persisting and eventually...'

It was less than twenty-four hours since Mariella had learned that her sister and Khalid were now married, and Tanya was updating her on what had happened as they sat together in the garden of the villa's women's quarters, whilst Fleur gurgled happily in her carrier.

'Why didn't you tell me what was going on when I telephoned you?' Mariella asked her.

Tanya looked self-conscious.

'Well, at first I wasn't sure just what was going to happen—I mean...Khalid was there and he was being very sweet, admitting that he loved me and that he regretted what he had done, but...

'And then you left that message on my cell phone saying you were here with Xavier, and I was worried that you might say something to him and that he would find a way of parting me and Khalid again...'

'Have you any idea how worried about you I've been?' Mariella asked her.

Tanya flushed uncomfortably.

'Well, I had hoped that you'd just think I wasn't returning your calls because I was so busy... It didn't occur to me that you'd ring the entertainments director...'

'Tanya, you didn't ring me to check on Fleur for days. Of course I was worried...'

'Oh, well, I knew she'd be fine with you, and I did listen to your messages. But Khalid... Well, we needed some time to ourselves, and Khalid insisted... Please don't be cross with me, Ella. You've never been in love so you can't understand. When Khalid left me I thought my life was over. I'm not like you. I need to love and be loved. I don't think I'll ever forgive Xavier for what he did.'

'Xavier didn't physically compel Khalid to abandon you and Fleur, Tanya,' Mariella heard herself pointing out to her sister almost sharply.

The look Tanya gave her confirmed her own realisation of what she had done.

'How can you support him, Ella?' Tanya demanded. 'He threatened to stop Khalid's allowance; he would have left me and Fleur to starve,' she added dramatically.

'That's not true, Tanya, and not fair either,' Mariella felt bound to correct her, but she couldn't quite bring herself to tell her sister that it was her own opinion that Khalid was both weak and self-indulgent and that he had selfishly put his own needs before those of his lover and their child. She could see already the beginnings of a sulky pout turning down the corners of Tanya's mouth and her heart sank. She had no wish to quarrel with her sister, but at the same time she couldn't help feeling that Tanya wasn't treating her own behaviour with regard to her maternal responsibilities towards Fleur anywhere near as seriously as she should have been doing.

'Well, we're married now and there's nothing that Xavier can do about it! And he knows it!'

Mariella knew that this was not true and that Xavier could have carried out his threat to stop paying Khalid his allowance, and also remove him from his sinecure of a job. However, she also knew from what Madame Flavel had innocently told her that Xavier had not done so because of Fleur.

'Oh, and you'll never guess what,' Tanya told her excitedly. 'I haven't had the opportunity to tell you yet, but Khalid is insisting on taking me for an extended honeymoon trip. We're going to take Fleur with us, of course, and then once we get back I suppose we will have to make our home here in Zuran, but Khalid has promised me that we'll get away as often as we can. He says that we can have our own villa and that I can choose everything myself! Oh, and look at my engagement ring. Isn't it beautiful?'

'Very,' Mariella agreed cordially as she studied the huge solitaire flashing on her sister's hand.

'I can't tell you how happy I am, Ella,' Tanya breathed ecstatically. 'And you have looked after my darling baby so well for me. I have missed you so much, my sweet,' Tanya cooed, blowing kisses to her daughter. 'Your daddy and I can't wait to have you all to ourselves.'

As she listened to her sister a small shadow crossed

Mariella's face, but she was determined not to spoil Tanya's happiness by letting her see how much she was dreading losing Fleur.

'It all sounds very exciting,' she responded, forcing a smile as she looked up and saw the expectant look on her sister's face.

'When will you be leaving?'

'Tomorrow! Everything's already arranged. Khalid just wanted to come to Zuran to tell Xavier about our marriage, and to collect Fleur, of course...'

'Of course,' Mariella agreed hollowly.

'Ella, I can't thank you enough for looking after Fleur for me. We're both really grateful to you, aren't we, Khalid?'

'Yes, we are,' her new brother-in-law agreed.

Mariella was still holding Fleur, not wanting to physically part with her until she absolutely had to, whilst Tanya said her goodbyes to Madame Flavel and Xavier.

Tanya was still behaving very coolly towards Xavier, only speaking to him when she had to do so.

'Darling, can you take Fleur out to the car?' she instructed Khalid.

Mariella could feel herself stiffening as Khalid went to take the baby from her, and, whether because of that or because as yet Fleur was not used to her father, as he reached for her the little baby suddenly screwed up her face and started to cry.

Immediately Khalid pulled back from her looking flustered and irritable.

'Here, let me take her!'

Xavier quietly removed Fleur from Mariella's arms, before she could object. He smiled down at Fleur and soothed her, whilst she gazed back at him wide-eyed, her tears immediately ceasing.

Out of the corner of her eye Mariella saw that Tanya had started to glower at Xavier, obviously resenting the fact that Fleur was more comfortable with him than with her father, but before she could say anything Khalid was urging her to hurry.

They went out to the car together, Xavier still holding Fleur, Mariella wincing in the blast of hot air.

As soon as she got into the car, Tanya held out her arms to him for Fleur, but to Mariella's surprise, instead of handing Fleur to Tanya, Xavier gave her to Mariella.

Mariella could feel her eyes burning with emotional tears, her throat closing up as her feelings threatened to overwhelm her. It was almost as though Xavier could sense how she felt and wanted to give her one last precious chance to hold Fleur before she had to part with her.

Bending her head, she kissed her niece and then quickly handed her over to her sister.

When the car taking them to the airport finally pulled away, Mariella could only see it through a blur.

'Let's get out of this wind,' she heard Xavier telling her when the car had finally disappeared from sight.

If he was aware of her tears he was discreet enough not to show it, simply ushering her back to the villa without making any other comment.

However, once they were inside, Mariella took a deep breath and made her voice sound as businesslike as she could as she told him, 'I'll make arrangements to leave just as soon as I can arrange somewhere else to stay.'

'What on earth are you talking about?' Xavier demanded sharply. 'Nothing has changed. You are still a single young woman who is a member of my family, and as such your place is still here beneath my roof and my protection! This should be your home whilst you're in Zuran,' Xavier told her.

Mariella opened her mouth to argue with him and then closed it again. It was just because she was feeling so upset about losing Fleur that his statement was giving her this odd sense of heady relief, she told herself defensively. It had nothing to do with…any other reason. Nothing at all!

Mariella was dreaming. She was dreaming that she was all alone in an unfamiliar room, lying on a large bed and crying for Fleur, and then suddenly the door opened and Xavier came in. Walking over to the bed, he sat down beside her and reached out for her hand.

'You are crying for the child,' he told her softly. 'But you must not. I shall give you a child of your own to love. Our child!' As she looked at him he started to touch her, smoothing the covers from her naked body with hands that seemed to know just how to please her. Bending his head, he started to kiss her, a slow, magically tender kiss, which quickly began to burn with the heat of a fierce passion. She could feel her whole body trembling with need and longing! And not just for the child he had promised her, but for Xavier himself!

His hands cupped her breasts, his grey eyes liquid with arousal as he gazed at them, shockingly sensual words of praise falling from his lips as he whispered to her how much he wanted her. He kissed each rosy crest, savouring their shape and sensitivity with his lips and tongue until she was clinging to him, digging her nails into his back as she submitted to her own desire.

Possessively she measured the strong length of his arms with her fingertips, expelling her breath on a shuddering sigh as his tongue rimmed her belly and his hand covered her sex, waiting, aching, wanting. Beneath her hand she could feel him harden as she touched him, torn between wanting to explore him and wanting to feel him deep inside her as he ignited the spark of life that would be their child. But as she reached for him, suddenly he pulled away, abandoning her. Desperately she cried out to him not to leave her, her body chilled and shaking, tears clogging her throat and spilling from her eyes. Abruptly Mariella woke up.

Somehow in her sleep she had pushed away the bed-clothes, which was why she was now shivering in the coolness of the air-conditioning. The tears drying stick-ily on her face and tightening her skin were surely caused by the fact that she was missing Fleur and not because she had been dreaming about Xavier... about loving him and losing him! She would never allow her-self to be that much of a fool! But physically she was affected by him, she could not deny that! Fiercely she tried to tense her body against its own betraying ache of longing. Xavier was a man who, even she had to acknowledge, took his responsibilities and his commit-ments very seriously. A man whose passions...

Stop it, she warned herself frantically. What was she doing thinking like this? Feeling like this?

Wide awake now, she got out of bed, and was half-way toward Fleur's now empty cot before she realised what she was doing. It was only right that Fleur should be with her parents, but she ached so to be holding her small body. She ached so for a child of her own, she admitted.

Tiredly Mariella flexed the tense, aching muscles in her neck and shoulders as she sat beside the small pool in the women's courtyard. She had worked relentlessly on the frieze over the last two weeks, driven by a compulsion she hadn't been able to ignore, and now knew that she would be able to finish the project well ahead of time.

The prince had arrived to inspect her progress just before she had left and she had seen immediately from his expression just how impressed he was by what she was doing.

'It is magnificent…awe-inspiring,' he had told her enthusiastically. 'A truly heart-gripping vision.'

'I'm glad you like it,' Mariella had responded prosaically, but inwardly she had been elated.

Elated and too exhausted to eat her dinner, she reminded herself ruefully as she reached up to try and massage some relief into her aching neck, tensing as she saw Xavier walking towards her.

'I have just come from seeing His Highness,' he told her. 'He wanted to show me your work. He is most impressed, and rightly so. It is magnificent!'

His uncharacteristic praise stunned Mariella, who stared at him, her turquoise eyes shadowed and wary.

'Has your sister been in touch with you yet to reassure you that Fleur is well?' Xavier continued.

Not trusting herself to speak, Mariella shook her head and then winced as her tense, locked muscles resisted the movement.

Quick to notice her small betraying wince, Xavier

demanded immediately, 'You're in pain. What is it? What's wrong?'

'My muscles are stiff, that's all,' Mariella replied.

'Stiff. Where? Let me see?'

Before she could object he was sitting down next to her, his fingers moving searchingly over her shoulders, expertly finding her locked muscles.

'Keep still,' he said when she instinctively tried to pull away. 'I am not surprised you are in so much pain. You work too hard! Drive yourself too hard. Worry too much about others and allow them to abuse your sense of responsibility towards them!'

Swiftly Mariella turned her head to look at him.

'You are a fine one to accuse me of that!' she couldn't help pointing out.

For a moment they looked at one another in mutual silence. She was learning so much about this man, discovering so many things about him that changed her whole perception of what and who he was.

He couldn't have been more wrong about Mariella, or misjudged her more unfairly, Xavier acknowledged as he looked down into her eyes. Her sister, in contrast, was exactly what he had expected her to be, and typical of his cousin's taste in women. The more cynical side of his nature felt that, not only were they suited to one another, but that they also deserved one another in their mutual selfishness and lack of any true emotional depth.

Mariella, on the other hand... He had never met a woman who took her responsibilities more seriously, or who was more fiercely protective of those she loved. When she committed herself to a man she would commit herself to him heart and soul. When she loved a man, she would love him with depth and passion and her love would be for ever...

'Your sister should have been in touch with you. She must know how much you are missing Fleur,' he told Mariella abruptly.

Mariella tensed, immediately flying to Tanya's defence as she told him fiercely, 'She is Fleur's mother. She doesn't have to consult me about...anything. This holiday will give the three of them an opportunity to bond together as a family. Tanya and Khalid are Fleur's parents and...'

'I miss Fleur too,' Xavier stopped her gruffly, his admission astonishing her. 'And in my opinion she would be much better off here in a secure environment with those who know her best, rather than being dragged to some fashionable resort where she will probably be left in the care of hotel staff whilst her parents spend their time enjoying themselves!'

'You are being unfair,' Mariella protested, and then winced as Xavier started to knead the knots out of her muscles, making it impossible for her to move.

'No. I am being honest,' he corrected her. 'And when Khalid returns you may be sure that I shall be making it very plain to him that Fleur needs a secure family environment!'

Xavier would make a wonderful father, Mariella conceded, and then stiffened as she tried to reject the messages that knowledge was giving her! After all, like her, Xavier had no intentions of ever getting married!

'Your muscles are very badly knotted,' she heard him telling her brusquely as his thumbs started to probe their way over the tight lumps of pain.

It was heaven having the tension massaged from her body, Mariella acknowledged, and no doubt what he was doing would be even more effective if she wasn't trying to tense herself against those dangerous sensations that had nothing whatsoever to do with any kind of work-induced muscle ache, and everything to do with Xavier himself.

The longer he touched her, the harder she was finding it to control her sexual reaction to him.

His thumbs stroked along her spine, causing her to shudder openly in response. Immediately his hands stilled.

'Mariella.'

His voice sounded rough and raw, the sensation of his breath against her skin bringing her out in a rash of sensual goose-bumps. Was she only imagining that she could hear a note of hungry male desire in his voice?

She couldn't trust herself to speak to him, just as she didn't dare to turn round, but suddenly he was turning her, holding her, finding her mouth with his own and kissing her with a silent ferocity that made her tremble from head to toe as her body dissolved in a wash of liquid pleasure that ran through her veins, melting any resistance.

The hands that had so clinically massaged her shoulders were now caressing her flesh beneath her loose top in a way that was anything but clinical! A savage, relentless ache began to torment her body. The warm, perfumed night air of the garden was suddenly replaced by the aroused male scent of Xavier's body and Mariella reacted to it blindly, wrenching her mouth from beneath his and burying her face in the open throat of his robe so that she could breathe it—him— in more deeply, her lips questing for the satin warmth of his skin, her moan of pleasure locked in her throat as she gave her senses their head.

Beneath her lips his flesh felt firm and hot, the muscles of his throat taut, the curve where it met his shoulder tempting her to bite delicately into it. She heard him groan as his hand covered her breast, her nipple swelling eagerly against his palm. She felt the warmth of the night air against her skin as he pushed her simple cotton robe out of the way, her whole body shuddering in agonised pleasure as he cupped her breast and lowered his mouth to her waiting nipple.

The pleasure that surged through her tightened her body into a helpless yearning arc of longing, exposing her slender feminine flesh to his gaze and touch, offering her up to them, Mariella recognised distantly as she shook with hunger for him. Wanting him like this seemed so natural, and right, so inevitable, as though it were something that had been destined to happen.

Lifting her hand, she touched his face, their gazes meeting and locking, silently absorbing one another's need. The look in his eyes made her body leap in eager heat, the sensation of the slightly rough rasp of his jaw against her palm as he turned his face to kiss it filling her with a thousand erotic images of how it was going to feel, to have him caressing even more sensitive and intimate parts of her body. She was, she realised, trembling violently, as Xavier stroked his hands down her back and lifted her against his body so that she could feel its hard arousal. She ached so badly for the feel of him inside her, for the fulfilment of his possession of her, the completion. His mouth was on her breast, her nipple, caressing it in a way that made her cry out for the hot, deep suckle of a more savage pleasure.

In the moonlight Xavier could see the swollen softness of her mouth and her breast, his breath catching in his lungs as his gaze travelled lower, to where the delicate mound of her sex seemed to push temptingly against the fine cotton of her briefs.

The thought of sliding his hand beneath them and holding her, parting the delicately shaped lips and opening up her moist inner self to his touch, his kiss, sent a shudder of hot need clawing through him. In the privacy of this garden he could show her, share with her, give her the pleasure he could see and feel her body was aching for. But here in his garden, in his villa, where she was under his protection, a member of his family…a woman as off limits as any of the carefully guarded daughters of his friends.

His hand was already splaying across her sex, his thumb probing tantalizingly.

Hot shafts of molten quivers darted from the point where Xavier's hand rested so intimately on her to every sensitive nerve ending in her body. Within herself Mariella could feel her own femaleness expanding rhythmically in longing. More than anything else she wanted him there inside her. More than anything else she wanted him…

Her raw sound of shocked protest broke the silence as Xavier suddenly released her.

'I already owe you one apology for my…my inappropriate behaviour towards you,' she heard him telling her curtly. 'Now it seems that I am guilty of repeating that behaviour. It will not…must not happen again!'

As he stood up and turned away from her, Mariella wondered if he was trying to reassure her—or warn her! Her face and then her whole body burned hot with mortified misery.

Her throat was too choked with emotion for her to

be able to say anything, but in any case Xavier was already leaving, walking across the garden to the small, almost hidden doorway that led through into his own quarters, and to which only he had the key.

Was she too destined to be a secret garden to which only he held the key?

Fiercely she resisted the dangerous and unwanted thought. It was simply sex that had driven her…a physical need…a perfectly normal response to her own sexuality. There was nothing emotional about what she had felt. Nothing.

Pacing the floor of his own room, Xavier came to an abrupt decision. Since he couldn't trust himself to be in the same place as Mariella and not want her, then he needed to put a safe distance between them, and the best way for him to do that would be for him to return to his desert oasis.

CHAPTER TEN

'IT IS almost a week since he left and still Xavier remains at the oasis.'

Mariella forced herself to concentrate on her work instead of reacting to Madame Flavel's comments.

The prince had come to see how she was progressing earlier in the week and he had brought his wife and their young family with him. The sight of the four dark-haired and dark-eyed children clustering round their parents had filled her with such a physical ache of longing that she had felt as though her womb had actually physically contracted.

She was desperate to have her own child, Mariella recognised. And not just because she was missing Fleur. Fleur's birth might have detonated her biological clock, setting it ticking away with such frantic urgency, but the longing she felt now was beginning to consume her, eating into her dreams and her emotions.

Now she felt she understood why she had wanted Xavier so much. Her body had recognised him as a perfect potential baby provider! Knowing that had in a way eased a lot of the anxiety she had been feeling; the fear she couldn't bear to admit that she might actually have fallen in love with him. Now, though, she felt secure that her emotional defences had not been breached. Now it was easy for her to admit to herself just how much she had wanted him and how much she still wanted him. She wanted him because she wanted him to give her a child!

It made so much sense! Didn't she remember reading somewhere that a woman naturally and instinctively responded to the ancient way in which nature had programmed her and that was to seek the best genes she could for her child? Quite obviously her body had recognised that Xavier's genes were superlative and her brain fully endorsed her body's recognition.

And this of course was why she was being bombarded by her body and her brain with messages, longings, desires, images that all pointed in the same direction. Xavier's direction! Her maternal urges were quite definitely on red alert!

'Xavier has telephoned to say that he will be remaining at the oasis for another week,' Xavier's great-aunt informed Mariella with a small sigh as they sat down for dinner. 'It must be dull here for you, *chérie* with only your work to occupy you and me for company.'

'Not at all,' Mariella denied.

'*Non?* But you do miss *la petite bébé?*'

Now it was Mariella's turn to sigh.

'Yes, I do,' she admitted.

'Then perhaps you should consider having *enfants* of your own,' Madame Flavel told her. 'I certainly regret the fact that I was not blessed with children. I envied my sister very much in that respect. I have to confess I cannot understand why two people like Xavier and yourself, who anyone can see are born to be parents, should decide so determinedly against marriage.

'You are working very hard on your frieze. It would do you good to have a few days off.'

She *had* been working very hard—but if truth were

told, the frieze was practically finished. But Mariella
had been painstakingly refining it to make sure it was
absolutely perfect. Could she take a few days off? To
do what? Have even more time to miss Fleur and to
ache for a child of her own? Even more time to wish
passionately that Xavier had not brought an end to their
intimacy before they had... If only she had pressed him
a little harder, persuaded...seduced him to the point
where he had not been able to stop, she considered
daringly, then right now she could already be carrying
within her the beginnings of her own child!

Restlessly her thoughts started to circle inside her
head. Once they had finished eating Madame Flavel
retired to her own room, leaving Mariella to walk
through their private garden on her own. If only Xavier
were here in the villa now, she could go to him. And
what? Demand that he take her to bed and impregnate
her?

Oh, yes, she could just see him agreeing to that!

Why would she have to demand? She was a woman,
wasn't she? And Xavier was a man... He had already
shown her that he could be aroused to desire for her...

But he wasn't here, was he? He was at the oasis.

The oasis... Closing her eyes, Mariella allowed herself to picture him there. That night when he had
thought that she was Tanya, he had come so close to
possessing her. Her whole body was aching for him
now, aching with all the ferocity of a child-hungry
woman whose womb was empty!

Irritably, Mariella threw down her sketch-pad, chewing
on her bottom lip as she glowered at the images she
had drawn: babies...all of them possessing Xavier's
unmistakable features. She had hardly slept all night,

and when she had it had merely been to be tormented by such sensually erotic dreams of Xavier that they had made her cry out in longing for him. It was as though even her dreams, her own subconscious, were reinforcing her desire for Xavier's child.

In fact the only thing about her that was still trying to fight against that wanting was…was what? Fear… Timidity… Did she really want to look back in years to come and face the fact that she had simply not had the courage to reach out for what she wanted?

After all, it wasn't as though she would be doing anything illegal! She had no intention of ever making any kind of claim on Xavier—far from it! She actively wanted to be left to bring up her child completely on her own. All she wanted from him was a simple physical act. All she had to do…

All she had to do was to make it impossible for him to resist her! And whilst he was at the oasis he would be completely at her sensual mercy! It was even the right time of the month—she was fertile.

A wildly bold plan was beginning to take shape inside her head, and the first step towards it meant an immediate shopping trip, for certain…necessities! There was a specific shop she remembered from a previous trip to the busy souk in the centre of the city, which specialised in what she wanted!

Slightly pink-cheeked, Mariella studied the fine silk kaftan she was being shown by the salesgirl, so fine that it was completely sheer. Surely the only thing that stopped it from floating away was the weight of the intricate and delicate silver beading and embroidery around the neck and hem and decorating the edges of the long sleeves.

It was a soft shade of turquoise, and designed to be worn—the salesgirl had helpfully explained without so much as batting an elegantly kohled eyelid—over a matching pair of harem trousers. Their cuffs and waist-band had been embroidered to match the kaftan itself. It was quite plainly an outfit designed only to be worn in private and for the delectation of one man. The sheerness of the fabric would leave one's breasts totally revealed—and Mariella had not missed the strategically embroidered rosettes, which she doubted would do anything more than merely make a teasing pretence of covering the wearer's nipples—and as for the fact that the harem pants incorporated an embroidered and beaded v-shaped section at the front, which she had an unnerving suspicion would draw attention to rather than protect, any wearer's sex...

'And then, of course, there is this,' the salesgirl told her, showing Mariella a jewelled piece of fabric, which she helpfully explained was self-adhesive so that the wearer could easily fix it to her navel.

Mariella gulped. Her normal sleeping attire when she wore any tended to be sturdily sensible cotton pyjamas.

'Er... No...I don't think...it's quite me,' she heard herself croaking, her courage deserting her. Seducing Xavier was going to be hard enough without giving herself the kind of self-conscious hang-up wearing that kind of outfit would undoubtedly give her!

'I...I was thinking of something more...more European,' she explained ruefully to the salesgirl.

'Ah, yes, of course. There is a shop in the shopping centre run by my cousin which specialises in French underwear. I shall tell you how to find it.'

Mariella sensed that the girl was amused by her self-consciousness, but there was no way she intended to pay a sheikh's ransom for an outfit that would take more courage to wear than going completely naked!

The souk was busy, and she paused on her way back through it to admire the wares on some of the other stalls, especially the rugs.

There was far more to seduction than merely wearing a harem outfit, she tried to comfort herself as she headed for the modern shopping centre. Far, far more. Sight was just one of man's senses, after all.

By the time she finally returned to the villa Mariella felt totally exhausted. She was now the proud owner of a perfume blended especially for her, and a body lotion guaranteed to turn her skin into the softest silk; she had also given in to the temptation to buy herself some new underwear, from the harem outfit seller's cousin, in the shopping mall. French and delicately feminine without making her feel in any way uncomfortable. Low-cut French knickers might not be as openly provocative as beaded harem trousers but they did have the advantage of being perfect to wear underneath her jeans!

It didn't take her very long to pack. All she said to Hera when she summoned her was that she wanted her to hand the note she was giving her to Madame Flavel when she woke up from her afternoon nap.

By that time she should have safely reached the oasis, and her note was simply to calm the older lady's fears and told her only that Mariella had driven out to the oasis because there was something she wanted to discuss with Xavier.

She took a taxi to the four-wheel drive rental office, where the car she had organised earlier by telephone was waiting for her.

This time she made sure she had the radio tuned in to the local weather station, but thankfully no sandstorms were forecast.

Taking a deep breath, she started the car's engine.

With a small oath, Xavier pushed the laptop away and stood up. He had come to the oasis to put a safe distance between himself and Mariella but all his absence from her was doing was making him think about her all the more.

Think about her! He wasn't just thinking about her, was he?

The tribe were currently camped less than thirty miles away and on a sudden impulse he decided to drive over and see them. The solitude of his own company was not proving to be its usual solace. Everywhere he looked around the oasis he could see Mariella. There might be a cultural gap between them, but, like him, she had a very strong sense of responsibility, and like him she would not give either her heart or herself easily. Like him, too, once she was committed, that commitment would be for ever. And did she also ache for what they had so nearly had and lie away at night wanting...needing, afraid to admit that those feelings went way, way beyond the merely physical? And if she did, then... Could she love him enough to accept his duty to the tribe, and with it his commitment to his role in life...to accept it and to share it? Dared he lay before her the intensity of his feelings for her? His love? Could he live with himself if his secret fears proved to be correct and his love for her overwhelmed his sense of duty?

Switching off the laptop, he reached for his Jeep keys.

*   *   *

She couldn't ever remember a time when she had felt more nervous, Mariella acknowledged as she urged the four-wheel drive along the familiar boulder-strewn track. Up ahead of her she could see the pavilion and her heart lurched, slamming into her ribs. What if Xavier simply refused to be seduced and rejected her? What if…?

For a moment she was tempted to turn the four-wheel drive round and scuttle back to the city. Quickly she reminded herself of sexual tension stretching between them in the garden of the villa. He had wanted her then, and had admitted as much to her!

She had half expected to see him emerging from the pavilion as he heard her drive up, but there was no sign of him.

Well, at least he wouldn't be able to demand that she turn round and drive straight back, she comforted herself as she parked her vehicle and climbed out, going to the back to remove her things, and then standing nervously staring at the pavilion.

Perhaps if she had timed things so that she had arrived in the dark… Some seductress she was turning out to be, she derided herself as she took a deep breath and walked determinedly towards the chosen fate.

Five minutes later she was standing facing the oasis, unwilling to accept what was patently obvious. Xavier was not here! No Xavier, no four-wheel drive, no seduction, no baby!

A crushing sense of disappointment engulfed her. Where was he? Could he have changed his mind and returned to the city despite informing his great-aunt that he intended to stay on at the oasis? How ironic it would be if by rushing out here so impulsively she had

actually denied herself the opportunity of achieving
what she wanted!

But then she remembered that his laptop was still
inside the pavilion, and surely he would not have left
that behind if he had been returning home? So where
was he?

The sun was already a dying red ball lying on the
horizon. Soon it would be dark. There was no way she
was going to risk driving all the way back without the
benefit of daylight!

So what exactly was she going to do? Spend yet
another evening enduring her rebellious body's clamouring urgency for the fulfilment of its driving need?
It had simply never occurred to her that he wouldn't
be here!

The pavilion was so intimately a part of him.
Dreamily, she trailed her fingertips along the chair he
used when working at the laptop. The air actually
seemed to hold an echo of his scent, a haunting reso-
nance of his voice, and she felt that, if she closed her
eyes and concentrated hard enough, she could almost
imagine that he was there… She could certainly picture
him behind her tightly closed eyelids. But it wasn't his
mental image she wanted so desperately, was it?

She knew she ought to eat, but she simply wasn't
hungry. She was thirsty, though.

She went into the kitchen and opened a bottle of
water. Fine grains of sand clung to her skin, making it
feel gritty. Hardly appropriate for a would-be siren!
The long drive in the brilliant glare of the desert sun
had left her eyes feeling tired and heavy. Like her
body, which felt tired and heavy and empty. A sense
of dejection and failure percolated through her.

Slowly, she walked out of the kitchen intending to

return to the living area, but instead found herself being drawn to the 'bedroom.' Standing in the entrance, she looked achingly around it.

A fierce shudder that became an even fiercer primal ache gripped her as she looked at the bed and remembered what had happened there. It was just her biology that was making her feel like this, her fiercely strong maternal desire. That was all, and of course it was only natural that that urge should manifest itself in this hungry desire for the man whose genes it had decided it wanted, she reassured herself as she was confronted with the intensity of her longing for Xavier.

Just thinking about him made her go weak, made her want him there so that she could bury her lips in the warm male flesh of his throat and slide her hands over the hard, strong muscles of his arms and his back, and then down through the soft dark hair that covered his chest and arrowed over his belly to where...

She needed a shower, Mariella decided shakily. A very cool shower!

'Safe travelling, Ashar.' Xavier smiled ruefully as he embraced the senior tribesman whilst the others went about the business of breaking camp ready to begin the long slow journey across the desert.

'You could always come with us,' Ashar responded.

'Not this time.' Xavier shook his head.

All around him he could hear the familiar sounds of the camp, the faint music of the camel bells, the orderly preparations for departure. The tribe would travel through the night hours whilst it was cool, resting the herd during the heat of the day.

Ashar's shrewd brown eyes surveyed him.

Ashar remembered Xavier's grandfather as well as

his father. Alongside his respect for Xavier as his leader ran a very deep vein of paternal affection for him.

'Something troubles you—a woman, perhaps? The tribe would rejoice to see you take a wife to give you sons to follow in your footsteps as you have followed in those of your grandfather and your father.'

'If only matters were that simple, Ashar.' Xavier grimaced.

'Why should they not be? This woman, you are afraid perhaps that she will not respect our traditions, that she will seek to divide your loyalties? If that is so then she is not the one for you. But knowing you as I do, Xavier, I cannot believe that there could be a place in your heart for a woman such as that. You must learn to trust what is in here,' he told him, touching his own heart with his hand. 'Instead of believing only what is in here.' As he touched his hand to his head Xavier hid a wry smile. Ashar had no idea just how dangerously out of control his emotions were becoming!

He waited to see the tribe safely on their way before climbing in his vehicle to drive back to the oasis.

A sharply crescented sickle moon shared the night sky with the brilliance of the stars. Diamonds studded onto indigo velvet. For Xavier it was during the night hours that the desert was at its most awesome, and mystical, a time when he always felt most in touch with his heritage. His ancestors had travelled these sands for many, many generations before him, and it was his duty, his responsibility to ensure that they did so for many, many generations to come. And that was not something he could achieve from behind the walls of a high-rise air-conditioned office, and certainly not from the fleshpots of the world as Khalid would no doubt choose to do. No, he could only maintain and honour the tribe's traditional way of life by being a part of it, by sharing in it, and that was something he was totally committed to doing. He must not deviate from that purpose. But his feelings, his love for Mariella could not be denied, or ignored. The strength of them had initially shocked him, but he had now gone from shock to the grim recognition that it was beyond his power to change or control the way he felt.

He saw Mariella's vehicle as he drove up to the oasis. Parking next to it, he got out and studied it warily. He did not encourage anyone to visit him when he was at the oasis and he was certainly not in the mood for uninvited guests, right now! Where and who was its driver?

Frowning, he headed for the pavilion, not needing to waste any time lighting the lamps to illuminate the darkness, his familiarity with it enough to take him from the entrance to the opening to the bedroom without breaking his stride.

Mariella was lying fast asleep in the middle of the bed, where she had curled up in exhaustion like a small child. The white robe she was wearing was Xavier's and it drowned her slender body. She had lit one of the lamps, which illuminated her face, showing her bone structure and the thick darkness of her silky eyelashes. In the enclosed heat, Xavier could smell the scent of her, and of his own instant reciprocal desire for her.

Xavier's hand tightened convulsively on the cord that fastened the curtain to the bedroom's entrance, whilst his heart tolled in slow, heavy beats. If he had any sense he would pick her up and carry her straight out to the Jeep and then drive back to the city with her without stopping!

He let the heavy curtain drop behind him, enclosing them both in the sensual semi-darkness.

Standing next to the bed, he looked down at Mariella.

Something, some instinct and awareness, disturbed Mariella's sleep, making her frown and stir, her eyes opening.

'Xavier!'

Relief…and longing flooded through her. Automatically she struggled to sit up, her arms and legs becoming tangled in the thick folds of Xavier's robe as she did so.

'What are you doing here?' Xavier demanded harshly.

'Waiting for you,' Mariella told him. 'Waiting to tell you how much I want you, and how much I hope you want me.'

She watched as his eyes turned from steel to mercury and recognised that she had caught him off guard.

'You drove all the way out here to tell me that!'

His voice might be curt and unresponsive, but Mariella could see the way his jaw tightened as he turned his head away from her, as well as feel his betraying tension. Tiny body-language signs, that was all she knew, but instinctively she knew she had an advantage to pursue!

'Not to tell you, Xavier,' she corrected him boldly. 'To show you…like this…'

Standing up, she went to him, letting the robe slide from her body as she did so. She had never envisaged that she would ever feel such a pride in her nakedness, her femaleness, such a sense of power and certainty, an awareness of how much a man's still silence could betray how very, very tightly leashed he was keeping his desire.

She was standing in front of him and he hadn't moved. For a moment she almost lost her courage but then she saw it, the way he clenched his hand and tried to conceal his involuntary reaction.

Quickly she raised herself up on her tiptoes and cupped his face with her hands. Never in a thousand lifetimes could she have behaved like this simply for her own gratification, for the indulgence of her own sexual or emotional feelings, but she was not doing it for them, for herself, she was doing it for the child she so desperately wanted to give life! Silently she looked up into his eyes, her own openly reflecting her desire. Very deliberately she let her gaze drop to his mouth. There was no need for her to manufacture the sharp little quiver of physical reaction that pierced her, tightening her belly.

She brushed her lips against his—slowly, savouring the delicate sensual contact between them, refusing to be put off by his lack of response, drawing from her inner self to focus totally on the pleasure it was giving her to explore the shape and texture of his mouth. Very quickly her senses took over, so that it was desire that led her to stroking his bottom lip with her tongue tip rather than calculation, the same desire that drove her to trace tiny kisses along the shape of his mouth and then draw her tongue lightly along that shape.

Xavier couldn't endure what she was doing to him! Mentally he willed her to stop, but instead she opened her mouth over his and started to kiss him properly! Lost in what she was doing, what she was enjoying,

Mariella took her time, putting her whole self into showing him just how hungry for him she was.

And then sickeningly, she could feel the rejecting hostility of his body, and for a heart-rocking second when he raised his hands she thought he was going to push her away. She suspected that he had thought so too, because suddenly in his eyes she saw both his shock and his raw, burning hunger.

He could never be a man who would be a passive lover, Mariella recognised on a deep shudder of pleasure as his hands imprisoned her and his mouth fought hers for control.

How little he realised that her surrender was really her victory, she rejoiced as his tongue thrust urgently between the lips she had parted for him.

'I can't believe that you've done this,' she heard him saying thickly.

'I had to,' Mariella whispered back. After all, it was the truth. 'I had to be with you, Xavier...like this...as a woman.'

He had released her to look at her, and now he lifted his hand to her face. Instantly Mariella caught hold of his wrist and turned her head to run her tongue tip over his fingertips.

She saw the way his skin stretched over his cheekbones, running hot with colour, his chest lifting and falling as savagely as though he had been deprived of oxygen. His forefinger rubbed over her bottom lip, and when she sucked on it his whole body jerked fiercely.

'I want to see you, Xavier,' she told him softly. 'I want to touch you...taste you...I want. I want you to take me to bed and pleasure me, fill me.'

Taking his hand, she placed it against her naked breast.

'Please,' she whispered. 'Please now, Xavier. Please…'

'This is crazy. You know that, don't you?' she heard him mutter. 'You are not your sister, you do not… I have not… I am not prepared…' His voice had become thick and raw as he bent his head to kiss the exposed curve of her shoulder, her throat, his hands sliding down her back to pull her urgently against him.

'There is nothing for you to worry about,' she told him.

She felt light-headed with the intensity of her own longing—but she only felt like that because she wanted his child, she was quick to reassure herself. That, after all, was what was driving her, motivating her, even if that motivation was manifesting itself in an increasingly urgent need to touch him and be touched by him, to allow herself to luxuriate in the slow and delicious exploration of every bit of his skin, absorbing its heat, its feel, the essence of him through the sensitivity of her own pores. So that her child, their child could be impregnated through her with those memories of his father he would never otherwise be able to have?

Ruthlessly she stifled that thought. Her child would not need a father to be there. He or she only needed a father to provide that life.

What he was doing was reckless to the point of insanity, Xavier knew that, but he also knew that he couldn't resist her, that he had ached for her, yearned for her too long to deny himself the soft, sweet, wanton feel of her in his arms…his bed…

But once he had held her, loved her, he also knew that he would never be able to let her go. Could she accept his way of life…adapt to it? Would she?

She was kissing him with increasing passion, stringing tiny, delicately tormenting little kisses around his throat, her tongue tip carefully exploring the shape of his Adam's apple, her fingers kneading the flesh of his upper arm with unconscious sensuality. Xavier recognised his senses on overload from her deliberately erotic seduction.

Mariella gave a small startled gasp as Xavier suddenly lifted her bodily in his arms, so that her mouth was on a level with his own as he took it in a hotly demanding and intimate kiss.

Helplessly she succumbed to it, feeling the desire he was arousing inside her run through her veins as sweetly as melting honey. He lifted her higher, kissing her throat, his lips moving lower to the valley between her breasts, before trailing with heart-hammering slowness and delicacy to first one eagerly waiting, quivering crest and then the other, and then back again, this time to lap tormentingly at her nipple with his damp tongue tip; the leisurely languorous journey repeated again and again until her whole body was crying out in agonised frustration.

Unable to stand the sensual torment any more, when his lips teased delicately at her nipple she buried her hands in the thick darkness of his hair and held his mouth against her body.

Surely he must feel the fierce rhythms pulsing through her flesh; surely he must know how much she wanted him?

Her hands tugged at his clothes, her voice whispering a soft torrent of aroused female longing that swamped Xavier's defences.

His hands helped hers to quickly remove the layers of clothing that separated them.

When she finally saw the naked gleam of his flesh

in the lamp-lit room, Mariella sucked in her breath on a small sob of shocked pleasure.

In wonder she studied him as tiny but openly visible quivers betrayed her body's excited reaction to him. So compulsively absorbed in gazing at him, she was oblivious to the effect her sensual concentration was having on Xavier himself.

'If you are deliberately trying to torment me and test my self-control by looking at me like that, then I warn you that both it and I have just about reached my limit,' he told her thickly.

'Now! Are you going to come to me and put into action all those dangerously seductive promises your eyes are giving me, or do I have to come to you and make you make good those promises, because, I warn you, if I do have to then I shall be demanding payment with full interest penalties,' he added huskily.

For a moment Mariella couldn't do anything. Xavier was watching her as she had been watching him. Excitement exploded inside her. She took a step towards him and then another, measuring his reaction as best she could, but it wasn't easy given the extent of her own intense arousal.

She was only a breath away from him now, close enough to reach out her finger and draw the tip of it recklessly down his body, teasing the silky body hair.

'You don't know how much I've wanted to do this,' she breathed truthfully.

'No? Well, I certainly know how much I've wanted you to do it,' Xavier responded throatily, 'and how much I've wanted to…'

He gasped and shuddered as her fingertip stroked lower, and suddenly in the space of one single heart-

beat she was lying on the bed, with Xavier arching
over her.

'Play with fire like that and you'll make us both
burn,' he told her, his eyes darkening as he groaned.
'Do you know what seeing that look in your eyes does
to me? Do you know how much I've wanted to see
just what colour they turn when I touch you like this?'

Mariella hadn't realised just how ready she was for
his intimate caress until she felt his hand stroke softly
over her quivering belly, his fingers gently touching the
swollen mound of her sex, his gaze pinioning hers as
he parted the lips of her sex and began to caress her.

Mariella knew that she cried out, she knew too that
her body arched to his touch actively seeking it, eagerly
opening to it, but it was only a vague, distant knowledge, at the back of her awareness. Her self was concentrated on the mind-exploding battle to accept the
intensity of her own feelings.

Frantically she reached for Xavier. Touching him,
holding him, wrapping herself around him as she
pressed passionate kisses against his skin, willing, aching for him to complete what he had begun.

And when he did enter her, moving into her, filling
her moist sheathed muscles, filling her with such a
soaring degree of pleasure that they and she clung to
him, wanting to wring every infinitesimal sensation of
pleasure from him, it was like nothing she had ever
imagined feeling, a pleasure beyond any known pleasure, a sensation beyond any experienced sensation, a
driven need that shocked her in its wanton compulsion
as she urged him to drive deeper, harder, breaching
every last barrier of her body until she knew instinctively that he could not and would not withdraw from

her without giving her body the satisfaction it now craved.

They moved together, his thrusts carrying them both, delivering a pleasure so intense she could scarcely bear it, crying out against it at the same time as she abandoned herself to it.

She heard his guttural cry of warning and felt her body open up completely to him, the first tiny shudders of her orgasm sensitising her to the pulse of his, to the knowledge that she was receiving from him what she had so much wanted.

Was it that knowledge that made her orgasm so intense, so fierce that she felt almost as though she could not endure so much pleasure?

Long after it should have been over, the aftermath continued to send little shudders of sensation through her, shaking her whole body as she lay locked in Xavier's arms.

She had done it, instinctively she knew it. Her child, of the desert and of a man who was equally compelling, equally dangerous, had been given life.

Reluctantly, Mariella opened her eyes. She could hear a shower running, and her whole body ached with an unfamiliar heaviness.

'So you are awake!'

She stiffened as she saw Xavier coming towards her, his hair damp from his shower, a towel wrapped carelessly round his hips.

Leaning towards her, he bent his head to kiss her. He smelled of soap and clean, fresh skin and her body quivered helplessly in reaction to him.

'Mmm…'

He kissed her again, more lingeringly, his hand stroking down over her bare arm.

The quivers became open shudders of erotic pleasure as he pulled the bedclothes back.

She had got what she wanted, and so surely she shouldn't be feeling like this now that there wasn't any need for her to want him!

The towel was sliding from his hips, quite plainly revealing the fact that he most definitely wanted her.

A sharp and unmistakable thrill of female excitement gripped her muscles.

It was just nature's way of making doubly sure, Mariella told herself hazily as his hand cupped her breast, his thumb and forefinger teasing the already eagerly taut crest of her nipple. That was all, and, since nature wanted to be doubly sure, then obviously she must give in to her urgings. Urgings that were demanding that she experience the pleasure Xavier had given her the night before, and right now...

His hands were on her hips, holding her, lifting her. Already Mariella was anticipating the feel of him inside her, longing for it and for him. Needing him.

'There will be things we shall need to discuss once we return to the city.'

'Mmm...' Mariella agreed, too satiated to lift her head off the pillow as Xavier turned to brush a kiss across her mouth.

She looked so tempting lying there in his bed, her face soft with satisfaction and her eyes heavy with their lovemaking, he acknowledged, ruefully aware of the way in which his senses were still reacting to her.

It would be all too easy to let the desire between

them flare into life again, but there were practicalities that had to be considered.

'Mariella.' The abrupt note in his voice caught her attention. 'Because of my position as leader of our tribe, I have always believed that I do not have the…freedoms of other men. I could never commit myself to a relationship with a woman who might not be able to understand or accept my duties and responsibilities to my people. Nor could I change my way of life, or…'

'Xavier, there's no need for you to say any more,' Mariella checked him swiftly. Her heart was pounding heavily, a sharp, bitter little pain, piercing her even though she was fighting against admitting to it, stubbornly refusing to listen to the message it was trying to give her.

'I would never ask you or any other man to do any such thing! And I can assure you that you need have no fear that I might misconstrue what's happened. I shan't. I am most definitely not looking for any kind of commitment from you.'

Only the commitment of conceiving his child, she admitted inwardly.

'In fact, commitment is the last thing I want.' Assuming a casualness that defied everything she had always inwardly believed in, she gave a small shrug and told him, 'We are both adults. We wanted to have sex. To satisfy a…a physical need… And…now that we have done so, I don't think there is any purpose in us holding a post-mortem, and even less in getting involved in needless discussions about the wherefores of why neither of us want a committed relationship. Truthfully, Xavier, I don't want to marry you any more than you want to marry me! In fact, I shall never marry.' Mariella delivered the words in a strong voice underpinned with determination.

'What?'

Why was Xavier looking at her like that? Where was the relief she had expected—the cool acceptance of her claim that they had come together merely to slake their sexual appetite for one another? Xavier was looking at her with a mingling of barely controlled fury and bitterness.

'What are you saying?' she heard him demanding savagely. 'You are not your sister, Mariella! You are not one of those shallow, surface-living women who think only of themselves; who give in to their need to experience what they want when they want, who go from man to man, bed to bed without...whose whole way of life—' He paused and shook his head.

'You are not like her! You don't even know what you are talking about! Mere physical sex is not something...'

Mariella could see and feel the intensity of his growing anger, and she could also feel her own increasingly disturbing reaction of panic and pain to it, but she refused to allow herself to be intimidated by them.

'I am not going to argue with you, Xavier. I know how I feel, and what I do and don't want from life.'

Well, that was the truth, wasn't it? She did know what she wanted, and she had every hope that last night had given her...

'Do you really expect me to believe that you drove all the way out here just because you wanted sex?'

'Why not?' Mariella shrugged. 'After all, I could hardly have come to your room at the villa, could I?' she pointed out, trying to make herself react as though she were the woman she was trying to be—a woman who thought nothing of indulging her sexual appetite as and when she wanted to do so!

'This was the perfect opportunity!'

Xavier was looking at her as though he would dearly love to make her take back her words, Mariella recognised uneasily. It had to be his male pride that was making him react in such an unexpected manner, she decided. Men were quite happy to use women for sexual pleasure without being emotionally committed to them, but apparently they didn't like it very much when they thought that they were the ones being used.

Her legs began to tremble shakily as she mentally digested his reaction and tried to imagine what he might say—and do if he knew that she hadn't even actually wanted him out of sexual lust, and that the desire that had really driven her had been her own female need to conceive his child!

Somehow instinctively she knew that the reaction she was seeing now would be nothing when compared with what he was likely to do were he ever to discover the truth!

The unexpected shrill sound of his mobile ringing broke into the thick silence stretching tensely between them.

Out of good manners Mariella turned away whilst he answered the call, but she could tell from the sound of his curt replies that it involved some kind of crisis.

Her instincts were confirmed when he ended the call and told her abruptly, 'There is a problem with the tribe—a quarrel between two of the younger men, which needs to be dealt with. I shall have to drive out to do so immediately.'

'That's okay. I can find my own way back to the city,' Mariella assured him.

'This matter isn't closed yet, Mariella,' he told her grimly. 'When I do return to the villa, we shall discuss it further!'

Mariella didn't risk making any response. There wasn't any need, not unless she wanted to provoke a further quarrel. The frieze was finished; there was nothing now to keep her in Zuran, no reason or need for her to stay, and she had already decided that she was going to make immediate plans to return home!

CHAPTER ELEVEN

'ELLA, you have to go! The prince will be mortally offended if you don't and, besides, just think of the potential commissions you could be losing. I mean, I've done some discreet checking on the guest list for this do, and everyone who is everyone in the horse-racing world will be there, plus some of the classiest A-list celebs on the planet! This is going to be the most prestigious event on the racing calendar this year, and here you are announcing that you don't want to go! I mean, why? You already know just how impressed the prince is with your frieze, and this is going to be its big unveiling. If you'd been hired by the National Gallery itself you couldn't have got yourself more publicity for your work!'

Mariella could hear the exasperation in her agent's voice, and ruefully acknowledged inwardly that she could perfectly understand Kate's feelings.

However, Kate did not know that she had two very good reasons for her reluctance to return to Zuran.

Xavier…and… Instinctively she glanced down her own body. At three months, her pregnancy was not really showing as yet. She and the baby were both perfectly healthy, her doctor had assured her, it was just that being so slight she was not as yet showing very much baby bulge.

'Just wait another couple of months and you'll probably be complaining to me that you feel huge,' she had teased Mariella.

Even now sometimes when she woke up in the morning she had to reassure herself that she was not fantasising, and that she actually was pregnant.

Pregnant... With a baby she already desperately wanted and loved. Her baby! Her baby and Xavier's baby, she reminded herself warily.

But Xavier would never need to know! No one looking at her could possibly know!

And if she was not careful she could potentially be in danger of arousing more suspicions by not returning to Zuran for the extravaganza that was to be the opening of the new enclosure and the first public airing of her frieze than by doing so.

Tanya for one would certainly have something to say to her if she didn't go!

And of course it would be a perfect opportunity for her to see Fleur, whom she still missed achingly. Her niece would also always have a very, very special place in her heart!

But against all this, and weighing very heavily on the other side of the scales, was Xavier. Xavier whom disturbingly she had spent far too much time thinking about since her return home! Mystifyingly and totally contrary to her expectations, not even the official knowledge that she had conceived her much-wanted child had brought an end to the little ache of longing and loneliness that now seemed to haunt both her days and her nights. There was surely no logical reason why she should actually physically ache for Xavier now. And there was certainly no reason why increasingly she should feel such a deep and despairing emotional longing for him. Those kinds of feelings belonged to someone who was in love! And she knew far better than to allow herself to do anything as foolish as fall in love!

She had actually begun to question, in her most emotional and anguished moments, whether what she was feeling could in some way be generated by the baby—a longing on his or her part for the father that he or she was never going to know. She had promised herself that her child would never suffer the anguish of being rejected by his or her father, because she had made sure there would be no father there to reject it. She would make sure right from the start that her baby would know that she would provide all the love it could possibly need! She would bring him or her up to feel so loved, so secure, so wanted, that Xavier's absence would have no impact on their lives whatsoever. Unlike her, her child would never suffer the pain of hearing his or her mother talk with such longing and need about the man who had abandoned them both, as she had had to do. Her child would never feel as she had done that somehow he or she was the cause of that father's absence; that, given the real choice, her mother would have preferred not to have had her and kept the love of the man who had quite simply not wanted the responsibility of a child!

'You must go,' Kate was insisting.

'You must come,' Tanya was pleading.

'Okay, okay, I give in,' she told Kate, grinning as her agent paused in mid-argument to look at her in silence, before breaking into a flurry of relieved plans.

'You'll be staying with us, of course,' Tanya was chattering excitedly as she bustled Mariella outside to the waiting limousine. 'I didn't bring Fleur because she's been cutting another new tooth. It's through now, but we had a bit of a bad night with her. I can't wait for the opening. It's going to be the highlight of our social calendar. Khalid has bought me the most fabulous dress. What are you going to wear? If you haven't got anything yet, we could go shopping—'

'No, it's okay, I've already got an outfit,' Mariella stopped her quickly, mentally grateful for the fact that Kate had insisted on taking her on a whirlwind shopping trip, following her decision to attend the opening, so that she could vet the outfit Mariella would be wearing, to make sure it made enough of the right kind of statement! Her small bulge might not show yet when she was dressed, but someone as close to her as her half-sister had always been would be bound to spot the differences in her body in the intimacy of a changing room with her wearing nothing more than her underwear!

Of course she was going to tell Tanya about her baby—ultimately—once she was safely back in England, and all the questions her sister was bound to ask about just who had fathered her coming baby could be answered over the telephone rather than in person! The last thing Mariella wanted to do was to risk betraying herself by a give-away expression.

She knew exactly what she was going to tell Tanya. She had already decided to claim that her child was the result of artificial insemination, the father an unknown sperm donor.

They were speeding along the highway towards the familiar outskirts of the city.

'How far is it to your new villa, Tanya?' Mariella asked her.

She had been receiving a constant stream of emails from her sister full of excitement about the new villa she and Khalid were having built, and which they had recently been due to move into.

'Oh, it's several miles up the coast from Xavier's. I'm really looking forward to moving into it now, but I must admit I'm a bit worried about how Fleur is going to adapt. She adores Hera, and to her Xavier's villa is her home and so—'

'What do you mean you're looking forward to moving in?' Mariella checked her anxiously. 'I thought you already had!'

'Well, yes, we were supposed to, but then all the furniture hasn't arrived yet, and so we're still living with Xavier. His great-aunt is visiting at the moment as well. You made a real hit with her, Ella—not like me. She's always singing your praises and in fact... I...'

Mariella could feel her heart, not just sinking, but literally plunging to the bottom of her ribcage with an almighty thump before it began to bang against her ribs in frantic panic. She wasn't prepared for this, she admitted. She wasn't armed for it, or protected against it.

The villa was ahead of them. It was too late for her to announce that she had changed her mind, or to demand that she be taken to the centre of the city where she could book into a hotel! The car was sweeping in through the gates.

Hazily Mariella noticed that the red geraniums she remembered tumbling from the urns in the outer courtyard had been changed to a rich vibrant pink to match the colour of the flowers of the ornamental vine softening the walls of the courtyard.

'Leave your luggage for Ali,' Tanya instructed her.

Where was the trepidation she should be feeling? Mariella wondered as, completely contrary to any kind of logic, the moment she stepped into the villa she immediately experienced a sense of well being, a sense of welcome familiarity, as though…as though she had come home?

'We'd better go straight in to see Tante Cecille!' Tanya pulled a face. 'I'll never hear the end of it if we don't. She's even told them in the kitchen to bake some madeleines for you!'

Mariella had to bite down hard on her bottom lip to subdue the threatening weakness of her own emotional response. The last thing she wanted or needed right now was to be reminded in any way of the fact that she was so very much alone, so very bereft of family, unlike Xavier, who was not merely part of a large extended family group, but who also actively shared a large part of his life with them.

Treacherously Mariella found herself thinking about how a child might feel growing up in a household with so many caring adults, with aunts, uncles and cousins to play with…

'Ella, I'm so thrilled that you're here,' Tanya was telling her. 'I've really missed you! You're in the same room you had before. Xavier has given us our own suite of rooms whilst we're living here. Khalid says there's no way that he would agree to us living like they used to with separate men and women's quarters, which is just as well because there's no way I would agree to it either!

'I couldn't do what Xavier does and go into the desert with the tribe.' Tanya gave a small shudder. 'The very thought appalls me. All that sand…and heat! And as for the camels! Ugh!' She pulled a distasteful face. 'Luckily Khalid feels exactly the same way! He can't understand why Xavier lets his life be dominated by a few promises his grandfather made, and neither can I.

If Khalid was head of the family things would be very different…'

'Then perhaps it's as well that he isn't,' Mariella responded protectively, before she could stop herself.

She could see the way Tanya was looking at her, and she felt obliged to explain, 'Xavier is the guardian of some irreplaceable traditions, Tanya, and if he abandoned that responsibility a way of life that could never be resurrected could be totally lost…'

'A way of life? Spending weeks living in the desert, and having to do it every year! No, I can't think of anything worse. It might be traditional, but I still wouldn't do it! Well, there's no way it could ever be my way of life, anyway. I mean, can you imagine any woman wanting to live like that? Could you?'

Mariella didn't even have to pause to think about it.

'Not permanently, no, but in order to preserve something so important, and to support the man I loved, to be with him and share a very, very important part of his life, yes, I could and would.' Mariella hesitated, recognising that there was little point in trying to explain to her sister how much such a return to traditions, to the simplicity of such a lifestyle could do to rejuvenate a person in a very special and intensely personal, almost spiritual sense, to bring them back in touch with certain important realities of life. Tanya simply wouldn't understand.

'Yes?' Tanya stared at her. 'You're mad,' she told her, shaking her head. 'Just like Xavier. In fact…Tante Cecille is quite right. You and Xavier are two of a kind.'

Before Mariella could demand an explanation from Tanya of just how and when their similarities had been discussed, they were in the salon.

'Mariella, how lovely to see you again,' Madame Flavel exclaimed affectionately. Automatically as she embraced her Mariella held in her stomach, just as she had done when she and Tanya had hugged earlier. An automatic reflex, but one that wasn't going to conceal her growing bump for very much longer, Mariella acknowledged ruefully.

Half an hour later, holding Fleur whilst her niece beamed happily up at her, Mariella began to feel a little bit more relaxed. Xavier, after all, would be as keen to avoid spending time with her as she was with him— albeit for very different reasons! She might even not actually see him at all!

Totally involved in making delicious eye contact with Fleur, Mariella was oblivious to what was going on in the rest of the room until she heard Madame Flavel exclaiming happily, 'Ah, there you are, Xavier.'

Xavier! Automatically Mariella spun round, holding tightly onto Fleur more for her own protection than for the baby's, she recognised dizzily as she felt her whole body begin to tremble.

The sensation, the need slicing white-hot through her threw her into shocked panic. She couldn't be feeling like this. *Should* not be feeling like this. Should not be feeling this all-absorbing need to feed hungrily on the sight of every familiar feature, every slight nuance of expression, too greedy for them to savour them with luxurious slowness, aching for them; aching for him so intensely that the pain was sharply physical.

As the girl she had been before, she had fantasised naively about that wanting and about him, imagining, exploring in the privacy of her thoughts the potential of her secret yearnings for Xavier—she had never guessed where those feelings could lead.

But as she was now sharply aware she was not that girl any more. She was now a woman, a woman looking at the man who had been her lover, knowing just how his flesh lay against his bones, how it felt, how it tasted…how he touched and loved. And as that woman she was overwhelmed by the sheer force of her need to go to him, to be with him, to be part of him. Her knowledge of him, instead of slaking her desire, was actually increasing it, tormenting her with intensely intimate memories. She was no longer seeing him as a powerful distant figure, but as a man…*her* man!

But that wasn't possible. What did that mean about her feelings for Xavier?

'Xavier, I was just telling Ella how alike you and she are,' she heard Tanya commenting.

'Alike?'

Mariella could feel his gaze burning into her as he focused on her.

'In your attitudes to things,' Tanya explained. 'Ella, you really ought to have children of your own,' Tanya added ruefully. 'You are a natural mother.'

'I totally agree with you, Tanya.' Madame Flavel nodded.

Mariella could feel her face and then her whole body burning as they all turned to look at her, but it was Xavier's grim scrutiny that affected her the most as his glance skimmed her body, resting on the baby she was holding in her arms. The unbearable poignancy of knowing that in six months' time she would be holding his child as she was holding Fleur right now made her eyes burn with dangerous tears. What on earth was wrong with her? She was behaving as though…

reacting as though…as though she were a woman in love. Totally, hopelessly, helplessly in love. But she wasn't! She wasn't going to let herself be!

Bleakly Xavier watched as Mariella cuddled Fleur. He had told himself that the discovery that she did not return his feelings would be enough to destroy them. And it should have been! But right now, if they had been alone…

The sickening feeling that had accompanied her unwanted thoughts was refusing to go away, and Mariella began to panic. She had suffered some morning sickness in the early weeks of her pregnancy, but these last few weeks she had felt much better. This nausea, though, wasn't anything to do with what was happening inside her body. No, this nausea was caused by her emotions! And what emotions! They surged powerfully inside her, inducing fear and panic, making her want to turn and run.

Automatically she had turned away from Xavier, unable to trust herself to continue facing him. Tanya had run to greet her husband who had just arrived.

'Ella,' Khalid greeted her warmly. 'We are so pleased that you are here, and I warn you that now that you are we shall not allow you to go easily. Tanya is already making plans to persuade you to move permanently to Zuran. Has she told you?'

Move permanently to Zuran! The shock of his disclosure made Mariella sway visibly, her face paling.

Xavier frowned as he saw her reaction. She looked as though she was about to pass out!

'Khalid, get some water,' Xavier demanded sharply, going immediately to Mariella's side and taking Fleur from her.

Just the feel of his hand touching her bare arm made her shudder with longing, and it seemed to Mariella as though the baby in her womb ached with the same longing that she did, for his touch and for his love.

She was vaguely conscious of being steered towards a chair and instructed to sit down, and then of a glass of water being handed to her.

'There's nothing wrong. I'm perfectly all right,' she protested frantically. The last thing she needed right now was to arouse any kind of suspicions about her health!

'Ella, you do look pale,' Tanya was saying worriedly.

'I'm just a bit tired, that's all,' Mariella insisted.

'You will probably feel better once you have had something to eat. We are going to have an informal family dinner this evening.'

'No,' Mariella refused agitatedly. The last thing she felt able to cope with right now was any more time spent in Xavier's company.

'Tanya, I'm sorry, but I just don't feel up to it. I'm rather tired…the flight…'

'Of course, *petite,* we understand,' Madame Flavel was assuring her soothingly, unintentionally coming to her rescue. 'Don't we, Xavier?' she appealed.

'Perfectly,' Mariella heard Xavier agreeing harshly.

Abruptly Mariella opened her eyes. Her heart was thumping heavily. She had been dreaming about Xavier. She looked at her watch. It was only just gone ten o' clock. The others would probably just be sitting down for their evening meal. Her throat ached and felt raw, tight with the intensity of her emotions.

As she slid her feet out of the bed and padded to the

window to look out into the shadowy garden she shivered in the coolness of the air-conditioning. It was there by the pool that Xavier had massaged her aching shoulders, and she had realised how much she'd wanted him. Because she had wanted his child, not because she loved him.

Her eyes burned dryly with pain. What she was feeling, what she was having to confront now, went way, way beyond the relief of easy tears.

So she was her mother's daughter, after all! She was to suffer the same pain as her mother—a pain she had inflicted on herself! How could she have been so stupid? How could she have been so reckless as to challenge fate? How could she have ignored everything that she knew about herself? Surely somewhere she must have realised that it was impossible for her to give herself to a man with the passionate intensity she had given herself to Xavier and not love him?

All she had wanted was to have a child, she insisted stubbornly. A child? No, what she had wanted was Xavier's child. And that alone should have told her, warned her...

With appalling clarity Mariella suddenly realised what she had done. Not so much to herself but to her child!

One day her child was going to demand to know about its father. When that happened, what answers was she going to be able to give?

Now she could cry. Slow, acid tears of guilt and regret, but it was too late to change things now.

'I'm so sorry,' she whispered, her hands on her stomach. 'Please, please try to forgive me...I love you so much...'

She had stolen the right to choose fatherhood from

Xavier, and she had stolen from her child the right to be fathered...loved.

It was gone midnight when she finally stopped pacing the room and crawled into bed to fall into a shallow, exhausted sleep, riddled with guilt and anguished dreams.

'Well, what do you think? How do I look?' Tanya demanded excitedly as she twirled round in front of Mariella in her new outfit.

'You look fabulous,' Mariella assured her truthfully.

'And so do you,' Tanya told her. Mariella forced a smile.

Her own dress with its simple flowing lines did suit her, but she was far more concerned about how well it concealed her shape than how well she looked in it. In less than half an hour they would be on their way to the gala opening of the prince's new hospitality suite at the racecourse, and Mariella would have given anything not to have to be there!

Tanya, on the other hand, couldn't wait, her excitement more than making up for Mariella's lack of it.

The last three days had been total torture for her. It would have been bad enough simply discovering that she loved Xavier without the additional emotional anguish of having to endure his constant presence. Every time she looked at him the pain grew worse and so did her guilt.

She had hardly been able to eat because of her misery and anxiety, and she couldn't wait to get on the plane that would take her home!

Under different circumstances, although she would have been nervous about the thought of the coming event, it would have been a very different kind of nervousness, caused purely by her anxiety about people's reaction to her work. Right now, she recognised ruefully, she hardly cared what they thought!

'Come on,' Tanya urged her. 'It's time to go.'

Reluctantly, Mariella got up.

She could feel Xavier's gaze burning into her as she walked into the courtyard where he and Khalid were already standing beside the waiting car.

The hot desert wind tugged at the thin silk layers of her full-length dress and immediately Mariella reached anxiously to hold them away from her body.

To her relief Xavier got into the front of the car, but she was still acutely conscious of him as Ali drove them towards the racecourse. Unlike Xavier, Khalid favoured a strong modern male cologne, but she could still smell beneath it the scent of Xavier's skin, and deep down inside her a part of her cried out in anguished pain and longing, aching despairingly for him.

'Poor Ella, you must be so nervous.' Tanya tried to comfort her, sensing her distress, but to Mariella's relief not realising the real cause of it. 'You've hardly eaten a thing since you arrived, and you look so pale.'

'Tanya is right—you do look pale,' Xavier told Mariella grimly several minutes later when they had reached their destination and he had opened the car door for her, leaving her with no alternative but to get out. His hand was beneath her elbow, preventing her from moving away from him. Instinctively Mariella knew that he had been waiting for the opportunity to vent the anger he obviously felt towards her against her. She had seen it in his eyes every time he looked at her, felt it in the tension that crackled between them. 'What's wrong, Mariella? If it isn't food you want, then perhaps it's another appetite you want to have satisfied. Is that it? Are you hungry for sex?' he demanded harshly.

'No,' Mariella denied immediately, trying again to pull away from him. He was making sure that no one else could hear what he was saying to her, she recognised, and making sure too that she could not get away from him.

Had he deliberately waited until now? Chosen this particular time to launch his attack on her, when he knew she couldn't escape from him?

'No?' he taunted her. 'Then why are you trembling so much? Why do you look so hungrily at me when you think I am not aware of you doing so?'

'I am not…I do not,' Mariella replied. She could feel her face starting to burn and her heart beginning to pound.

'You're lying,' Xavier told her softly. 'And don't deny it. Unless you want to provoke me into proving to you that you are! Is that what you want, Mariella?'

'Stop it! Stop doing this to me,' Mariella demanded. She could hear her own voice shaking with emotion and was helplessly aware that it wouldn't be long before her body betrayed her by following suit.

'I spoke to your agent today. She told me that she was sure you'd be thrilled to learn that I want to commission you for a very special project. She certainly was especially when I told her how much I was prepared to pay to secure your exclusive…services.'

Mariella reeled from the shock of his taunting comment.

'Xavier, please,' she begged him fatally, her eyes widening as she saw the look of triumph leaping to life in his eyes.

'Please?' he repeated silkily.

'Xavier, Mariella, come on...' Tanya urged them.

'We're coming. I was just discussing a certain plan with Mariella,' Xavier said smoothly as he guided Mariella toward the throng of people making for the entrance to the suite.

'Well, sister-in-law, I think we can safely say that your frieze is an outstanding success,' Khalid commented, grinning at Mariella. 'Everyone is talking about it and it is very, very impressive!'

Mariella tried to respond enthusiastically, but she felt achingly tired from answering all the questions she had received about the frieze, and, besides, her whole nervous system was still on red alert just in case Xavier should suddenly reappear and continue his cynical verbal torment.

'Khalid and I are going to get something to eat, in a few minutes,' Tanya told her. 'Do you want to come with us?'

Nauseously Mariella shook her head. The last thing she wanted was food. She had been feeling sick all day and her stomach heaved at the very thought.

'Here comes the prince,' Tanya whispered as the royal party appeared.

'Mariella. My congratulations. Everyone is most impressed!'

As she acknowledged his praise Mariella suddenly realised that Xavier was with him. Her feeling of sickness increased, but grimly she refused to submit to it.

'Xavier has just been telling me that he has commissioned you to make a visual record of the everyday life of his people,' the prince was continuing. 'A truly excellent idea!' Smiling at her, he started to move on.

So that was what Xavier had meant! Already dropping her head in deference to the prince, Mariella suddenly raised it, intending to glare at Xavier, but instead she was overcome by a dizzying surge of weakness.

'Ella, what is it? What's wrong?' Tanya demanded anxiously. 'You look as though you're going to faint! Feeling sick…looking like you're going to faint—anyone would think you're pregnant!' Tanya laughed.

As her sister turned away Mariella realised that Xavier was looking straight at her, and she knew immediately from his expression that he had heard Tanya's teasing comment and that somehow he had guessed the truth!

The urge to turn and run was so strong that she suspected if the gallery had not been so crowded she would have done so. But once again Xavier seemed to be able to read her mind because suddenly he was standing beside her.

'Your sister isn't well,' she heard him telling Tanya curtly. 'I'm taking her back to the villa.'

'No,' Mariella protested, but it was too late. Khalid was urging Tanya to go with him to get something to eat, and Xavier was already propelling her towards the exit.

It was impossible for either of them to say anything in the car with Ali driving. 'This way,' Xavier told Mariella grimly once they were back at the villa, stopping her from seeking the sanctuary of her own room as his hand on the small of her back ushered her towards his own suite of rooms.

'You can't do this!' Mariella said shakily. 'I'm a single woman, remember, and—'

'A single woman who is carrying my child!' Xavier

stopped her savagely as he opened the suite door and almost pushed her inside.

Mariella could feel herself starting to tremble. She didn't have the strength for this kind of fight. Not now and probably not ever!

'Xavier, I'm tired. It's been a long day.'

'Why the hell didn't you say something? Or were you hoping that by not eating and by exhausting yourself you could provoke a natural end to it?' he accused, ignoring her plea.

'No,' Mariella denied immediately, horrified. 'No! How dare you say that? I would never...' Tears filled her eyes. 'I wanted this baby,' she told him passionately. 'I...'

Abruptly she stopped, her expression betraying her as she saw the way he was looking at her.

'Would you mind repeating that?' he demanded with dangerous softness.

Nervously Mariella licked her lips.

'Repeat what?' she asked him.

'Don't play games with me Mariella,' he warned her. 'You know perfectly well what I mean. You just said "I wanted this baby"..."wanted," rather than "want," which means...which means that it wasn't just sex you wanted from me, as you claimed, was it?

'What? Nothing to say?' he challenged her bitingly. 'Not even an "it was an accident"?'

Mariella bit down hard on her lower lip.

She wasn't going to demean herself by lying to him!

'You don't have to worry,' she tried to defend herself, her voice wobbling. 'I won't ever make any kind of claims on you, Xavier. I intend to take full responsibility for...for everything. I want to take full responsibility,' she stressed fiercely. 'There's no way I intend to let my baby suffer as I did through having a father who…'

'Your baby?' Xavier stopped her harshly. 'Your baby, Mariella, is my child! My child!'

'No!' Mariella denied immediately. 'This baby has nothing whatsoever to do with you, Xavier. He or she will be completely mine!'

'Nothing to do with me! I don't believe I'm hearing this,' Xavier breathed savagely. 'This baby…my baby has everything to do with me, Mariella. After all, without me he or she just could not exist! I'll make arrangements for us to be married as quickly and as quietly as possible, and then—'

'Married! No!' Mariella refused vehemently, her panic showing in her expression as she confronted him. 'I'm not going to get married, Xavier. Not ever. When my mother married my father, she believed that he loved her, that she could trust him, rely on him…but she couldn't. He left her… He left us both because he didn't want me.'

All the emotions she had been bottling up inside her whooshed out in a despairing stream of agonised denial, even whilst somewhere deep down inside her most guarded private self there was a deep burning pain at the thought of just how very, very much she wanted Xavier's total commitment for her baby and for herself. His total commitment and his enduring love! The pain of her own self-knowledge was virtually unbearable. She ached for him to simply take her in his arms and hold her safe, to keep her safe for ever, and yet at the same time her own self-conditioning was urging her to deny and deride those feelings to protect herself.

'I am not your father, Mariella, and where my child is concerned—' his mouth tightened '—in Zuran it is a father whose rights are paramount. I would be within my legal rights in ensuring that you are not permitted to leave the country with my child—either before or after his or her birth!'

Distraught, Mariella demanded passionately, 'Why are you doing this? Your own aunt told me that you had sworn never to marry or have children; that you didn't want a wife or children.'

'No,' Xavier stopped her curtly. 'It is true that I had decided not to marry, but not because I didn't want... The reason I had chosen not to marry was because I believed I could never find a woman who would love me as a man, with fire and passion and commitment, and that I wouldn't be able to find a woman also who would understand and accept my responsibilities to my people. I didn't think that such a woman could exist!'

'And because she doesn't...because I am carrying your child, you're prepared to marry me instead, is that it? I can't do it, Xavier. I won't, I won't be married, just because of the baby.' Her voice began to wobble betrayingly as her emotions overwhelmed her and to her own humiliation tears flooded her eyes and began to roll down her face. Helplessly Mariella lifted her hands to her face to shield herself, unable to bear Xavier's contemptuous response to her distress. It must be baby hormones that were making her cry like this, making her feel so weak and vulnerable!

'Mariella.'

Mariella froze with shock as she felt the warmth of Xavier's exhaled breath against her skin, as he crossed the space between them and took her in his arms.

'Don't!' His voice was rough with pain. 'I can't bear the thought of knowing that you and my child, the two people I love the most, will be lost to me, but I can't bear either knowing that I have forced you to stay with me against your will. When you came to me in the desert, gave yourself to me...it was as though you had read my mind. Shared my thoughts and my feelings, known how much I had wanted us to be together, and known too that I had been waiting for the right opportunity to approach you and tell you how I felt, but I was conscious of what had happened during your own childhood with your father. I wanted to win your belief in me, your trust of me...before I revealed to you how much I wanted to ask you to share my life! I knew how strong your sense of commitment was, your sense of responsibility, and I knew that the future of my people would rest safely in your hands. I thought that together you and I could...but I was wrong, as you made very clear to me... You didn't love me; you didn't even really want me. You merely wanted someone to father your child.

'I want and need both of you here with me more than I can find the words to tell you, but I cannot bear to see you so distressed. I shall make arrangements for you to return to England if that is what you want, but what I would ask you is that you allow me to play at least some part in my child's life, however small. I shall, of course, make financial provision for both of you...that is not just my duty, but my right! But at least once a year I should like your permission to see my child. To spend time with him or her. If necessary I shall come to your country to do so. And...'

Mariella fought to take in what he was saying. Xavier wanted her. Xavier loved her. In fact he loved her so much that he was prepared to put her needs and wishes above his own!

A new feeling began to whisper softly through her,

a soft warmth that permeated every cell of her body, melting away all the tiny frozen particles of mistrust and pain that had been with her from the very first moment she had known about her father. A feeling so unfamiliar, so heady and euphoric that it made her literally tremble with happiness, and excitement unfurled and grew inside.

Instinctively her hand touched her belly. Could her baby feel what she was feeling? Was he or she right now uncurling and basking in the same glow of happiness that was engulfing her?

Xavier's hand covered hers and that small gesture brought immediate emotional tears to her eyes as she turned to look at him without any attempt to hide her emotions from him.

'I didn't know you loved me,' she whispered.

'You know now,' Xavier responded.

She could see the bleakness in his eyes and the pain. Her body could feel the warmth of his hand even through her own. Gently she pulled her own hand away and leaned into him so that he could feel the growing swell of their child, her gaze monitoring his immediate and intense reaction.

Xavier would never do what her father had done, instinctively she knew that, just as she knew too how much time she had wasted, how much that was so infinitely precious to her she had risked and nearly lost because of her frightened refusal to allow herself to believe that not all men were like her father.

Alongside her bubbling happiness she could feel another emotion she had to struggle to identify. It was freedom, she recognised; freedom from the burden she had been carrying around with her for so long, and it was Xavier who had given her that freedom by giving her his love, by being man enough, strong enough to reveal his vulnerability to her!

She took a deep breath and then held tightly to her courage and even more tightly to Xavier's arm.

'It isn't true what I said,' she told him simply. 'It wasn't just sex. I tried to pretend it was to myself because I was too afraid to admit how I really felt, but I think I knew even before, and then afterwards when I still wanted you...' Her skin turned a warm rose as she saw the way he was looking at her.

'Don't look at me like that,' she protested. 'Not yet, not until I've finished telling you... Otherwise...'

'Still wanted, in the past tense or...' Xavier pressed her huskily.

'Still wanted then,' Mariella informed him primly. 'And still want now,' she added, her own voice suddenly as husky and liquid with emotion as his had been. 'I still want you, Xavier!' she repeated. 'And I don't just want you, I need you as well. Need you and love you,' she finally managed to say, her voice so low that he had to bend his head to catch her shaky admission.

'You love me? But do you trust me, Mariella? Do you believe me when I tell you that I shall never, ever let you down or give you cause to doubt me? Do you believe me when I tell you that you and our child...our children, will always have my love and my commitment?'

Mariella closed her eyes and then opened them again.

'Yes,' she replied firmly, and her melting look of love told him that she meant it!

'Xavier,' she protested unconvincingly as he started to kiss her. 'The others will be coming back.'

'Shall I stop, then?' he asked her, brushing his lips tormentingly against her own.

'Mmm… No…' Mariella responded helplessly, sighing in soft pleasure as his hand covered her breast, his thumb probing the aroused sensitivity of her nipple. Her whole body turned liquid with desire, making her cling eagerly to him.

'Every night I've thought about you like this,' Xavier told her rawly. 'Wanted you…ached for you in my arms. Every night, and every day, and if I'd known that there was the smallest chance that you felt the same I would never have let you go. I warn you, Ella, that now that I do know I will never let you go.'

'I will never want you to,' Mariella responded emotionally. 'Take me to bed, Xavier,' she begged him urgently. 'Take me to bed and show me that this isn't all just a dream…'

She was in his arms and being carried from the salon into his bedroom almost before the words had left her mouth. And even if she had wanted to retract them it would have been impossible for her to do so with Xavier kissing her the way that he was, with all the passion and love, all the commitment she now recognised that she had secretly ached for all along.

EPILOGUE

'WELL, what do you think of your anniversary present?' Mariella asked Xavier lightly, whilst she watched him with a secret anxiety she was trying hard to hide.

She had been working on this special gift for him on and off ever since their marriage, only breaking off for their six-month-old son's birth and the early weeks of his life.

Xavier shook his head, as though he found it hard to comprehend what he was seeing. 'I knew you were working on something, but this...'

The stern note in his voice broke through her self-control, forcing her to reveal how much his approval meant to her. 'You don't like it—?'

'Like it! Mariella.' Reaching for her, Xavier wrapped her tightly in his arms.

'There is nothing, excluding your sweet self and our noisy and demanding young son, that I would value more,' he told her emotionally as he swung her round in his arms so that they could both look at the series of drawings she had spent the early hours of the morning displaying around their private salon to surprise him when he woke up on this, their anniversary morning.

As a wedding present from her new husband Mariella had asked to be allowed to travel in the desert with the tribe. Conscious of her pregnancy, Xavier had initially been reluctant to agree, but Mariella had been insistent. It had been on that journey that she had made the secret preliminary sketches for what was now a visual documentation of the tribe's way of life, a visual documentation that betrayed, not only her fine eye for detail, but also her love for the man whose people she had drawn.

'I do have a gift for you, although I haven't followed Tanya's advice and booked a luxury holiday,' Xavier told her ruefully.

Following the direction of his amused glance, Mariella laughed.

Fleur, who was now walking was sitting on the floor next to her six-month-old cousin, the pair of them deep in some personal exchange, which involved lots of shared giggles and some noisy hand-clapping from Ben.

'Don't you dare do any such thing. There's no way I want to be parted from these two!'

With Tanya and Khalid living around the corner, both the families saw a lot of each other, and the two young cousins could grow up together.

'I may have another present for you,' Mariella announced semi-hesitantly, the way her glance lingered on their son informing Xavier of just what she meant.

'What? We said we'd wait.'

'I know…but this time it's your fault and not mine. Remember your birthday, when you didn't want to wait until…'

'Mmm.' He did a rapid mental calculation. 'So in another seven months, then…'

'I think so… Do you mind?'

'Mind? Me? No way. Do you?'

'I've got my fingers crossed that I'm right,' Mariella admitted. 'Although I'm pretty sure that I am, and if I'm not…' she gave him a flirtatious look '…then I'm sure we can find a way of ensuring that I soon am! Anyway, what about *my* anniversary present? You still haven't told me what it is.'

'Come with me,' Xavier instructed her, bending to pick up their son and hand him to Mariella before lifting Fleur up into his own arms.

'Close your eyes and hold onto me,' Xavier said as he led her out into their own private courtyard, and through it to the new courtyard that had been developed behind it.

Mariella could smell the roses before he allowed her to open her eyes, and once he did so she drew in her breath in delight as she saw the new garden he had been having designed for her as a special surprise.

A softer and far more modern planting plan had been adopted for the new garden than the one favoured by Xavier's grandmother. The design was reminiscent of an English country garden with the flower beds filled with a variety of traditional plants, but it was the wonderful scent of the roses that most caught her attention.

'They're called "Eternity",' Xavier told her softly as she bent her head to touch the velvet-soft petals of the rose closest to her. 'And I promise that I shall love you for eternity, Mariella, and beyond it. My love for you is...eternal!'

Warm tears bathed Mariella's eyes as she smiled at him.

'And mine for you!' she whispered lovingly to him.

Silently, they walked through the garden together, his arm around her drawing her close, her head resting against his shoulder, the children in their arms.

So you think you can write?

Mills & Boon® and Harlequin® have joined forces in a global search for new authors.

It's our biggest contest yet—with the prize of being published by the world's leader in romance fiction.

Look for more information on our website:
www.soyouthinkyoucanwrite.com

So you think you can write? Show us!